"This is why you should get more of the girls down at the laundry to join the League," Niko replied, slapping the table. "When it comes to the rights of the working class, it doesn't matter what kind of work, men's or women's!"

I raised a silent eyebrow. It didn't matter that a laborer was a woman—until it did. The limits that marriage and children would place on me were plain, and were plain to any woman.

The conversation shifted to finding work this winter, but the tone was tainted with the conversation that preceded it. They no longer spoke merely about job leads and which warehouses would have slower business over winter, but made implicit arguments for their discontent. I had nothing to add to their discussion and my coddle had gone cold, so I went home, but the echoes of the conversation followed me like a shifting shadow, deepening the cold dusk of the late autumn evening.

TORN

The Unraveled Kingdom: Book One

ROWENNA MILLER

www.orbitbooks.net

Copyright © 2018 by Rowenna Miller
Excerpt from *The Tethered Mage* copyright © 2017 by Melissa Caruso
Excerpt from *Thief's Magic* copyright © 2014 by Trudi Canavan

Author photograph by Heidi Hauck
Cover design by Lisa Marie Pompilio
Cover art by Peter Bollinger
Cover copyright © 2018 by Hachette Book Group, Inc.
Map by Tim Paul

Orbit
Hachette Book Group
1290 Avenue of the Americas
New York, NY 10104
orbitbooks.net

First Edition: March 2018

Orbit is an imprint of Hachette Book Group.
The Orbit name and logo are trademarks of Little, Brown Book Group Limited.

The Hachette Speakers Bureau provides a wide range of authors for speaking events. To find out more, go to www.hachettespeakersbureau.com or call (866) 376-6591.

Library of Congress Cataloging-in-Publication Data
Names: Miller, Rowenna, author.
Title: Torn / Rowenna Miller.
Description: First edition. | New York : Orbit, 2018. | Series: The unraveled kingdom ; 1
Identifiers: LCCN 2017046506| ISBN 9780316478625 (softcover) | ISBN 9780316478618 (ebook (open))
Subjects: LCSH: Dressmakers—Fiction. | Magic—Fiction. | BISAC: FICTION / Fantasy / Epic. | GSAFD: Fantasy fiction.
Classification: LCC PS3613.I55275 T67 2018 | DDC 813/.6—dc23
LC record available at https://lccn.loc.gov/2017046506

ISBNs: 978-0-316-47862-5 (trade paperback), 978-0-316-47861-8 (ebook)

*For my father, who taught me to sew, and my mother,
who read my first stories*

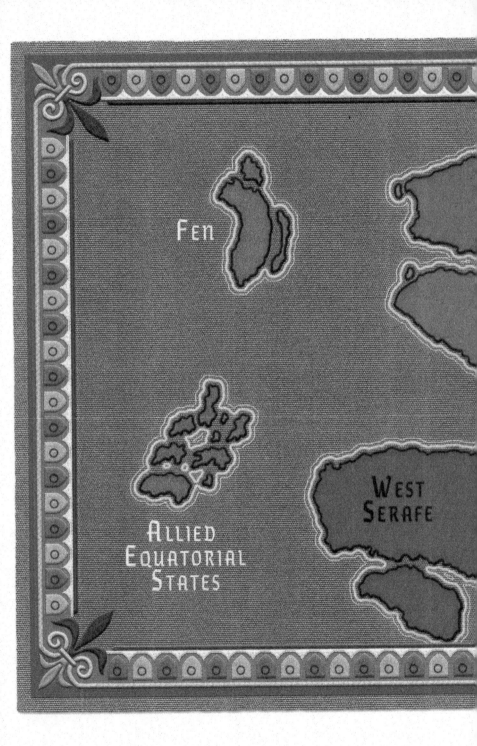

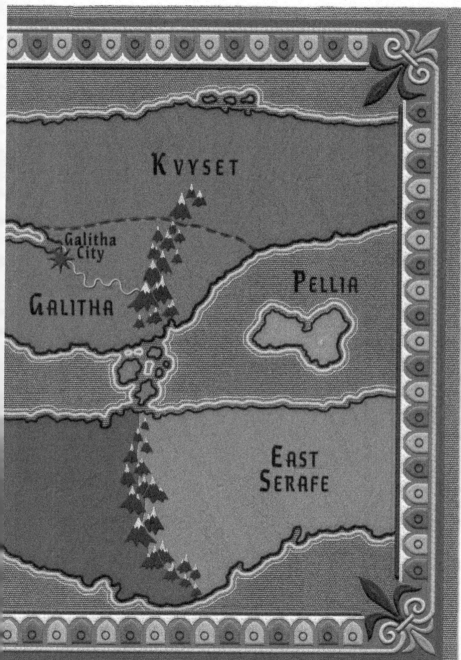

1

"Mr. Bursin," I said, my hands constricting around the fine linen ruffles I was hemming, "I do not do that."

"But, miss, I would not ask if it were—if it were not the most pressing of circumstances. If it would not be best. For all concerned."

I understood. Mr. Bursin's mother-in-law simply refused to die. She was old, infirm, and her mind was half-gone, but still she clung to life—and, as it turned out, bound the inheritance to her daughter and son-in-law in a legal tangle that would all go away once she was safely interred. Still.

"I do not wish ill on anyone. Ever. I sew charms, never curses." My words were final, but I thought of another avenue. "I could, of course, wish good fortune on you, Mr. Bursin. Or your wife."

He wavered. "Would...would a kerchief be sufficient?" He glanced at the rows of ruffled neckerchiefs lining my windows, modeled by stuffed linen busts.

"Oh, most certainly, Mr. Bursin. The ruffled style is very fashionable this season. Would you like to place the order now, or do you need to consult with your wife regarding style and fabric?"

He didn't need to consult with his wife. She would wear the commission he bought from me, whether she liked the ruffles or not. He chose the cheapest fabric I offered—a coarser linen than was fashionable—and no decorative embroidery.

My markup for the charm still ensured a hefty sum would be leaving Mr. Bursin's wallet and entering my cipher book.

"Add cutting another ruffled kerchief to your to-do list this morning, Penny," I called to one of my assistants. I didn't employ apprentices—apprentices learn one's trade. The art of charm casting wasn't one I could pass on to the women I hired. Several assistants had already come and gone from my shop, gaining practice draping, cutting, fitting—but never charm casting. Alice and Penny, both sixteen and as wide-eyed at the prospect of learning their trade as I had been at their age, were perhaps my most promising employees yet.

"Another?" Penny's voice was muffled. I poked my head around the corner. She was on her back under a mannequin, hidden inside the voluminous skirts of a court gown.

"And what, pray tell, are you doing?" I stifled a laugh. Penny was a good seamstress with the potential to be a great one, but only when she resisted the impulse to cut corners.

Penny scooted out from under the gown, her pleated jacket bunching around her armpits. "Marking the hem," she replied with a vivid crimson blush.

"Is that how I showed you to do it?" I asked, a stubborn smile forcing its way onto my face.

"No," she replied meekly, and continued with her work.

I returned to the front of the shop. Three packages, wrapped in brown paper, awaiting delivery. One was a new riding habit with a protective cast, the second a pelisse for an old woman with a good health charm, and the third a pleated caraco jacket.

A plain, simple caraco. No magic, no spells. Just my own beautiful draping and my assistant Alice's neat stitching.

Sometimes I wished I had earned my prominence as a dress-maker on that draping and stitching alone, but I knew my popularity had far more to do with my charms, the fact that they had a reputation for working, and my distinction as the only couture charm caster in Galitha City. Though there were other charm casters in the city, the way that I stitched charms into fashionable clothing made the foreign practice palatable to the city's elite. The other casters, all hailing from the far-off island nation of Pellia by either birth or, like me, ancestry, etched charms into clay tablets and infused sachets of herbs with good luck or health, but I was the only charm caster in the city—the only one I knew of at all—who translated charms into lines of functional stitching and decorative embroidery.

Even among charm casters I was different, selling to Galatines, and the Galatine elite, who didn't frequent the Pellian market or any other Pellian businesses. I had managed to infuse the practice with enough cachet and intrigue that the wealthy could forget it was a bumpkin superstition from a backwater nation. Long before I owned my shop, I had attempted charming and selling simple thread buttons on the street. Incredibly, Galatines bought them—maybe it was the lack of pungent herb scents and ugly clay pendants that marked Pellian charms, or maybe it was the appeal of wearing a charm no one could see. Maybe it was merely novelty. In either case, I had made the valuable discovery that, with some modifications, Galatines would buy charms. When I finally landed a permanent assistant's job in a small atelier with a clientele of merchants' wives and lesser nobility, I wheedled a few into trying a charm, and, when the charms worked, I swiftly gathered a cult following of women seeking my particular skill. After a couple of years, I had enough clients that I was able to prove myself and open my own shop. Galatines were neither particularly superstitious nor religious, but the novelty of a charm stitched into their finery captivated their interest, and I in turn had a market for my work.

"When you finish the hem, start the trim for Madame Pliny's court gown," I told Penny. The commission wasn't due until spring, but the elaborate court gowns required so much work that I was starting early. It was our first court gown commission—a sign, I hoped, that we were establishing a reputation for the quality of our work as well as for the charms. "And I'm late to go file for the license already—the Lord of Coin's offices have been open for an hour."

"The line is going to be awful," Alice said from the workroom. "Can't you go tomorrow?"

"I don't want to put it off," I answered. The process was never sure; if I didn't get through the line today, or if I was missing something the clerk demanded, I wanted several days to make it up.

"Fair enough," Alice answered. "Wait—two messages came while you were with Mr. Bursin. Did you want—"

"Yes, quickly." I tore open the two notes. One was an invoice for two bolts of linen I had bought. I set it aside. And the other—

"Damn," I muttered. A canceled order. Mrs. Penneray, a merchant's wife, had ordered an elaborate dinner gown that would, single-handedly, pay a week's wages for both of my assistants. We hadn't begun it yet, and so, per my own contract, I would have to agree to cancel it.

I glanced at our order board. We were still busy enough, but this was a major blow. Most of the orders on our slate were small charmed pieces—kerchiefs, caps. Even with my upcharge for charms, they didn't profit us nearly as much as a gown. Early winter usually meant a lull in business, but this year was going to be worse than usual.

"Anything amiss?" Penny's brow wrinkled in concern, and I realized that I was fretting the paper with my fingers.

"No, just a canceled order. Frankly, I didn't care for the orange shot silk Mrs. Penneray chose anyway, did you?" I asked, wiping her order from the board with the flat of my hand. "And I really do need to go now."

Alice's prediction was right; the line to submit papers to the Lord of Coin was interminable. It snaked from the offices of the bureau into the corridors of the drafty stone building and into the street, where a cold rain pelted the petitioners. Puddles congregated in the low-lying areas of the flagstone floor, making the whole shabby establishment even damper and less welcoming than usual.

I held my leather portfolio under my fine wool cloak, only slightly dampened from the rain. Inside were the year's records for my shop, invoices and payment dates, lists of inventory, dossiers on my assistants and my ability to pay them. Proof that I was a successful business and worthy of granting another year's license. I traced my name inscribed on the front, tooled delicately into the pale calfskin by the leatherworker whose shop was four doors down from mine. I had indulged in the pretty piece after years of juggling papers bound with linen tape and mashed between layers of pasteboard. I had a feeling the lady-like, costly presentation, combined with the fashionable silk gown I wore like an advertisement of my skills and merchandise, couldn't hurt my chances at a swift approval from the Lord of Coin's clerk.

I was among a rare set of young women, not widows, with their own shop fronts when I opened almost ten years ago, and remained so. My business survived and even grew, if slowly, and I loved my trade—and I couldn't complain about the profits that elevated my brother, Kristos, and me from common day laborers to a small but somewhat prosperous class of business owners.

"No pushing!" a stout voice behind me complained. I stiffened. We didn't need any disruptions in the queue—any rowdiness and the soldiers posted around the building were likely to send us all home.

"I didn't touch you!" another voice answered.

"Foot's not attached to you, eh? Because how else did I get this muddy shoeprint on my leg?"

"Probably there when you hiked in from the parsnip farm or wherever you came from!"

I hazarded a look behind me. Two bareheaded men wearing poorly fitted linsey-woolsey suits jostled one another. One had the sun-leathered skin of a fisherman or dockworker; the other had the pale shock of flaxen hair common in the mountains of northeastern Galitha. Neither had seemed to think that the occasion warranted a fresh shave or a bath.

I suppressed a disapproving sigh. New petitioners, no doubt, with little hope of getting approval to open their businesses, and much more chance of disrupting everyone else. I glanced again; neither seemed to carry anything like enough paperwork to prove themselves. And their appearance—I tried not to wrinkle my nose, but they looked more like field hands than business owners. Fair or not, that wouldn't help their cases.

Most of the line, of course, was made up of similar petitioners. Scattered among the new petitioners who were allowed, one week out of the year, to present their cases to open a business, were long-standing business owners filing their standard continuation requests. It grated me to have to wait in line, crawling at a snail's pace toward the single clerk who represented the Lord of Coin, when I owned an established business. Business was strictly regulated in the city; careful ratios of how many storefronts per district, per trade, per capita were maintained. The nobility judged the chance of failed business a greater risk than denying a petitioner a permit. Even indulgences such as confectioners and upscale seamstresses like me were regulated, not only necessities like butchers and bakers and smiths. If I didn't file for my annual permit this week, I could lose my shop.

As we moved forward down the corridor a few flagstones at a time, more and more dejected petitioners passed us after unsuccessful interviews with the clerk. I knew that disappointment well enough. My first proposal was rejected, and I had to wait a whole year to apply again. I took a different tack that second year, developing as much clientele as I could among minor nobility, hoping to reach the curious ears of nobles closer to the Lord of Coin and influence his decision. It worked—at least, I assumed it had, as one of the first customers when my shop opened a year later was the Lord of Coin's wife, inquiring after a charmed cap to relieve her headaches.

The scuffle behind me escalated, more voices turning the argument into a chorus.

"Not his fault you have to wait in this damn line!" A strong voice took control of the swelling discontent and put it to words.

"Damn right!" several voices agreed, and the murmuring assents grew louder. "You don't see no nobles queuing up to get their papers stamped."

"Lining us up like cattle on the killing floor!" The shouting grew louder, and I could feel the press of people behind me begin to move and pulse like waves in the harbor whipped by the wind.

"No right to restrict us!" the strong voice continued. "This is madness, and I say we stand up to it!"

"You and what army?" demanded the southern petitioner who had been in the original scuffle.

"We're an army, even if they don't realize it yet," he replied boldly. I edged as far away as I could. I couldn't afford to affiliate myself, even by mere proximity, with treasonous talk. "If we all marched right up to the Lord of Coin, what could he do? If we all opened our shops without his consent, could he jail all of us?"

"Shut up before you get us all thrown out," an older woman hissed.

I turned in time to see a punch thrown, two men finally coming to blows, but before I could see any more, the older woman jumped out of the way and the heavy reed basket swinging on her arm collided into me. I stumbled and fell into the silver-buttoned uniform of a city soldier.

I looked up as he gripped my wrist, terrified of being thrown out and barred from the building. He looked down at me.

"Miss?"

I swallowed. "I'm so sorry. I didn't—"

"I know." He glanced back at the rest of his company subduing what had turned into a minor riot. They had two men on the floor already; one was the towheaded man who had started the argument. "Come with me."

"Please, I didn't want to cause trouble. I just want to file—"

"Of course." He loosened his grip on my wrist. "Did you think I was going to throw you out?" He laughed. "No, I have a feeling that the Lord of Coin will close the doors after this, and you're clearly one of the only people in line who even ought to be here. I'm putting you to the front."

I breathed relief, but it was tinged with guilt. He was right; few others had any chance at all of being granted approval, but cutting the line wouldn't make me look good among the others waiting, as though I had bought favor. Still, I needed my license, and I wasn't going to get it today unless I let the soldier help me. I followed him, leaving behind the beginnings of a riot truncated before it could bloom. The soldiers were already sending the lines of petitioners behind me back into the streets.

2

—ᴍ—

BY THE TIME I HAD MY PAPERS STAMPED AND MY LICENSE APPROVED
for the following year, afternoon shadows were lengthening on
the cobblestones outside the Lord of Coin's offices. At least, I
thought as I gathered my cloak more snugly around me, the rain
had abated somewhat. The fine mist that replaced it still dampened my shoes, but it couldn't penetrate the fine wool of my
cloak. It was pointless to return to my shop now—I wouldn't
have time to get any work done, and Alice could lock up without me.

It wasn't my habit to stay out after work, but after waiting
in a line of strangers for hours, I had a hankering for a bowl of
sausage coddle and knew where I could find it—and likely some
company, too. Sure enough, my brother was already ensconced
at one of the long tables by the window of the Rose and Fir tavern, with several of his comrades from the docks.

"Sophie!" Kristos grinned, half standing and waving me
over. "What's the occasion? Full moon? Lost your way home?"

"Very funny." I tried not to smile. "You took the last of the
onion pie I was saving for supper, that's all."

"So you came down here for some fine company."

"I decided I could endure the company for the coddle." I

slid onto the bench next to him. Even a year ago I wouldn't have been willing to part with a few copper coins for supper at a tavern; I hoarded anything left after rent and shop expenses in case of a bad season or an emergency and, as a result, ate meals cooked poorly over a stove designed to warm a house instead of cook or, sometimes, went without hot food at all. Kristos and his friends, and most day laborers, bought food from street stalls and taverns whose cheap wares catered to their long days and short wages. They spent little more than I did, in the end, and Kristos made fun of the penny-pinching that resulted in eating the occasional raw onion for lunch instead of a proper meal.

I still worried that a dissatisfied customer could leave me out of work for weeks, or that the whims of those with money to spend would shift away from me. I needed more security than I had. With patience and the finest quality of work, I hoped I could gain steady clients who kept returning for my draping, not solely the charms that were often onetime indulgences, and connections to the city's elite who could give my shop more cachet. More income could mean another assistant, a larger storefront, perhaps moving closer to the square, where I could have more visibility.

"Saw the line for the licenses today," Kristos said after a long swig of ale. "You in it?"

"Of course," I said. Nice of him to notice—usually Kristos half forgot that I paid for our lodgings with my earnings, and all the work that my shop entailed.

"Damn long," he added. "Don't they grandfather you in it at some point? Make you stop performing their tricks and jumping through their hoops every year?"

I sighed—silly of me to think he might have just been interested in my day. I prepared myself for a repeat of the diatribes I'd heard in line. "No, they never do. The rules are very strict."

"Strict for whom?" he grumbled. "No one restricts trade or enterprise for the nobility."

"I'm well aware," I replied. "Arguing about it doesn't do any good, Kristos."

Fortunately, the serving girl arrived with my stew before he could fire back, and I turned my attention to it instead of the swiftly building political debate.

As Kristos lifted his mug of ale, I noticed a thick white wrapping under his shirt cuff. I grabbed his arm, making him slosh a little ale onto the table. "What's this?"

"Barely anything," he said, shaking me off. "Wheelbarrow got away from me down at the docks, wrenched my wrist a little."

"And?"

"And it will be fine in a day or two." He ran a hand through his disheveled dark hair, further mussing waves that were in need of a good combing, clearly annoyed with me, and clearly avoiding discussing what an injury meant—lost wages.

I suppressed a sigh, not wanting to make Kristos feel bad, but a day or two for his wrist to heal likely meant a day or two he wouldn't be working—at least. That, along with the canceled order and the start of the slow season, was not good news. I made more money than Kristos, of course, but we relied on both our incomes, especially as the additional burden of heating the house approached.

"Hey, Kristos!" My brother's friend Jack swung a leg over the bench across from me. "You hear about what happened at the Lord of Coin's this afternoon?"

I focused more intently on my stew.

"Porter the fishmonger—you know, he's been trying to open a proper storefront?" There were assents murmured around me. "Went down to apply for his license and there was a bit of a row—anyway, he turned the whole thing into a protest."

"Good on him!" A chorus of enthusiastic voices made me look up. My brother beamed. "That will show them!" he crowed. "He's one of the cornerstones of our Laborers' League—I'm not surprised he voiced his thoughts."

"Show them what?" I muttered, chasing a piece of sausage with my spoon. The Laborers' League—the ragtag coalition of day laborers Kristos met with to talk politics, as though it did any good. Kristos wasn't content, and he made it clear to me through his participation in the League. He never had been satisfied with working unskilled, manual jobs, and I could never find it in myself to blame him. Bright, quick with a pen, and conversationally competent in Fenian and Pellian as well as Galatine, he would have been a fine university scholar had he been born to the nobility—or been my younger sibling instead of older, able to wait until I had made enough money to pay tuition.

"They had to shut the whole place down to clear out the protesters," Jack bragged.

"You were there today, Sophie. Why didn't you say anything?" Kristos scooted closer to me. "Seems like it would have been something to see."

I bit my lip. "I was there for my papers. Not to cause a ruckus."

"So you were in ahead of them? Left before it happened?" He shrugged. "Must have, or you wouldn't have gotten your license today."

I found I couldn't admit I'd accepted help from the city soldier, help I earned with my silk gown and leather portfolio. "That's right."

Kristos sighed. "I just don't see how you can't care about how they treat us," he said. "After everything you went through to open your shop. How can you see it as fair?"

"It's not fair, exactly. It's just...it's how things are. And I did open my shop. Don't forget that, Kristos. You're railing as though it's impossible, and it clearly isn't."

"And you're forgetting the years where you barely scraped by working day-contract jobs and sweeping floors."

"I'm not forgetting anything." After our mother died of one of the consumptive fevers that swept the densely populated city every few years, I worked as a day laborer. As she had done and as my brother still did, I spent years finding a day's work at a time, sewing hems for a day's wages in one shop and sweeping floors in another the next day.

I wasn't forgetting our slim list of orders or the onset of winter's slow season, either. I wasn't forgetting the fear that I would have to fire one of my assistants, or that we wouldn't be able to afford enough coal to adequately heat our drafty workroom. Owning a shop came with responsibility that Kristos couldn't even fathom, and it was weighing on me tonight. "What, you think everyone in the city should own a shop? How would that work?"

"It wouldn't, and I never said—damn, Sophie. I just don't think you should have to wait in line every year to prove you have a decent shop, or that you should have had to fight so hard to build a dossier in the first place."

"The system isn't perfect, but it works," I argued lamely. "And it works for us."

"It works for *you*," Kristos replied, more bitter than I anticipated. "But—hey, Jack—there's some good news, too." He grabbed a thin Pellian by the elbow and dragged him toward us. "This is Niko Otni—he's one of the river sailors who's been coming to our meetings—"

"I remember," said Jack, shaking his hand with earnest fervor.

"He says the barge workers and the farmhands are ready to join with the Laborers' League," Kristos said with a grin.

Jack did some quick calculations, his thick fingers tapping his thumb. "That could double our numbers. And the barge sailors are already pretty organized; that helps."

Numbers—for what purpose? I didn't want to argue, so I feigned a smile. "That sounds promising," I said, even though the promise wasn't one I was fond of. More late nights yelling over drinks in the café. More days wasted earning signatures on petitions instead of wages. Though Kristos assured me again and again that the aims of the League were petitions and talks and education alone, plenty of people in it had ties to the violent riots that had consumed the city in the summer. I edged away from it like a horse shies from a snake—perhaps harmless, but perhaps capable of striking and killing.

"It is. Oh, Sophie, you have no idea. If we're going to topple the old system, we have to have the entire bottom rise up together." He leaned heavily on the table. It creaked under his weight. "Change requires these kinds of numbers."

I eyed him. He'd talked about change before, but never in words that sounded so much like sedition. I dreaded the wasted hours and tavern bills his League brought us, but this sounded more serious. "You're being careful, aren't you? You're not wrapped up in anything... anything illegal?" He and his friends talked about elected systems of government and economics based on free enterprise instead of noble control, but that was talk. Hypotheticals fueled by the lectures some of the professors at the university had begun offering, overviews of theory and philosophy, but hardly pragmatic. Talk over pints and bottles of cheap wine. At least, I hoped it was talk—not something that Kristos could get himself arrested over. After the near riot at the Lord of Coin's offices, I was less sure.

"Speech and press are still open in Galitha," Kristos retorted, "even if the minds of nobles aren't. So no, nothing illegal. Stop worrying like an old hen, Sophie." Jack laughed at my wrinkled brow, and Niko smirked at Kristos's joke.

I smacked his arm as though he were only teasing, but I didn't feel playful. As Kristos resumed speaking in low tones to the men sitting on the other side of the bench, I listened more attentively than usual, fearing that their talk had turned from theoretical to intentional, from conversations and lectures to more riots and arson like the summer's unrest.

"Porter had the right idea," one of the other men said. I didn't know his name, only that he was like the other day laborers, fresh from the docks or the warehouses. Perhaps he'd spent the day looking for work and coming home without a wage, as the bricklaying and building slowed in the winter.

Jack hedged his reply with a glance at me. "Maybe the right motive, but it didn't do much good except get a bunch of folks thrown out for the day."

"No, it sent a message," said Kristos. "We've been passive so long that the nobility can forget we even exist, let alone that we are at odds with their governance."

We? I pressed my lips together, biting back the retort that Kristos couldn't assume everyone without a noble title automatically agreed with him and his Laborers' League.

"They'll need a stronger message," Kristos continued. "What happened at the Lord of Coin today was small, spontaneous. Imagine the sentiment, but organized and bringing our numbers together." That sounded, to me, more like a dangerous riot than a message. I couldn't hide my dismay, and Kristos clammed up at my shocked face. "We've upset Mother Hen." He laughed, but I felt the jagged frustration in his voice.

I quietly stood and stepped outside. I had learned long ago that my brother's temper tended to flare and fade quickly, like sparks set to black powder. To my surprise, Jack followed me.

Jack wasn't poor company, I reasoned. He was kind, and gentle despite his broad shoulders earned hauling crates at the docks. More often than not, I had seen him brokering peace when Kristos's discussions grew too heated. "Sophie, you're acting kind of off. Is everything all right?"

I stared down the street, letting the cold wind cool my burning cheeks. "I'm fine."

"No, you're not. You're angry about Kristos riling everyone up."

Despite myself, I laughed. "You're right. I don't like all this talk—I'm not against discussing theories, if you think it's fun, or speculating on the best reforms, but this is all…it's getting a bit serious, don't you think?"

"It is serious, Sophie." Jack stepped into my line of vision, his face earnest. "Change is serious. The nobles—they have to start listening to reason. We're educated. At least, some of us—your brother is smarter than most of the lords, I'd wager. We're not mindless rubble." I resisted correcting him. "And things need to change."

"That's all I hear from Kristos, too," I dismissed him. "Change. He can barely remember to change his linens." Jack smiled at my joke, but I sensed that something had shifted, and the time for levity was over. My brother wasn't the lanky manchild I still imagined him to be, but a leader of a movement that was only gaining in numbers and momentum and, it seemed, aspirations.

"I guess I just don't understand, Sophie—why don't you want to help us? You're one of us."

I swallowed. I wasn't noble, certainly, and in the stark tiers of Galitha, that made me a common person alongside Jack. Yet, at the same time, I wasn't quite one of them—I owned a business. Even their revolutionary talk put me at risk. "You all are going to have to change without my help. I have a business, Jack. A business I built." No one—not my brother, not his friends— seemed to appreciate this. "My clients will stop buying charms from an active revolutionary. And for another"—I smiled at the impossibility—"if you succeed, what do I have left?"

"I know, if there's no more nobles or rich folk in the city, you don't have clients," Jack supplied. "You know, I've thought about that." He cleared his throat. "And, I mean, if you had— that is, if you wanted to—you could maybe not need the shop?" He reached for my hand.

I folded my hands under my cloak. "I don't know what you're getting at."

"I mean that you need the shop to support yourself. And Kristos. But if you—if Kristos had his own business or a job with tenure—that means a job with a contract that keeps you—"

"I know what it means."

"Then he could support himself. And if you had a husband who had a job like that, too…" Jack's ears reddened so deeply that I could see it in the dim candlelight seeping through the tavern's grimy windows.

I wanted to melt into the cobblestones. "I don't keep my shop only because I have to. I like working. Sewing and charm casting—those are my life. What I do well. How I—how I feel happiest." I swallowed. "I wouldn't want to give up the shop just because I was married."

I had never admitted so much to anyone before, even Kristos, and I hoped my honesty would end the conversation. Jack rolled his shoulders, as though trying to shrug off my rejection. I bit my lip, feeling guilty, but relieved he didn't press the issue.

"I'm going back inside," I said softly. Jack nodded, but paced down the street instead of following me.

I slumped on the bench next to Kristos. Of course I had considered marriage, but I loved my work. If I married, the laws of coverture would transfer my property to shared property—and shared property was controlled by the husband. I couldn't risk my shop for marriage. I hadn't entertained, seriously, the attentions of a man in... years, I realized as I stared into the froth that still swirled on top of my mug of ale. Coverture laws risked my business, but a dalliance that resulted in rumors or, worse, pregnancy could be devastating, too. Romance was a dangerous game, its stakes too high. So I didn't play. I had a responsibility not only for myself, but for Kristos as well. For my family, small as it might have been.

Plenty of women worked throughout Galitha City, as day and contract laborers in laundries, workshops, and stores all across the city, and certainly shared the concerns Kristos and the League discussed about their low pay and uncertain employment. They shared concerns with me, as well, I realized, that the League didn't seem to sympathize with. I felt the same intense responsibility to keep our family safe that my mother had; women with children no doubt felt it even more strongly. Stability meant work, work meant enough money, enough money meant no one would go hungry this winter. The young, unmarried men Kristos surrounded himself with had a luxury that most women didn't, even unmarried women, who, I knew from my assistants, saw their aging parents and younger siblings as their charges.

Perhaps this was why few women joined the long tables alongside the Laborers' League gathered in the Rose and Fir.

One ruddy blonde with thick arms like a dockworker's was deep in earnest conversation with Niko Otni; a tall girl with pockmarked, Pellian-bronze skin read a pamphlet.

The girl returned the pamphlet to Kristos with a shy smile. "It's even better than the last one," she said.

"This one focuses more closely on the economic instability that the nobility-controlled system creates," Kristos answered. She nodded, apparently more familiar with Kristos's technical jargon than I was.

While they pored over a passage together, I overheard the ruddy blonde arguing with Niko. "No, it's exactly like that in the laundry. Just because we don't haul crates at the dock don't mean we can't get hurt." I glanced as unobtrusively as possible at her as she flashed a bare arm, crisscrossed with sinewy dark scars. "These are from the irons—and you should see the girls who take a face full of steam. No compensation for it, just no work for days on end."

"This is why you should get more of the girls down at the laundry to join the League," Niko replied, slapping the table. "When it comes to the rights of the working class, it doesn't matter what kind of work, men's or women's!"

I raised a silent eyebrow. It didn't matter that a laborer was a woman—until it did. The limits that marriage and children would place on me were plain, and were plain to any woman.

The conversation shifted to finding work this winter, but the tone was tainted with the conversation that preceded it. They no longer spoke merely about job leads and which warehouses would have slower business over winter, but made implicit arguments for their discontent. I had nothing to add to their discussion and my coddle had gone cold, so I went home, but the echoes of the conversation followed me like a shifting shadow, deepening the cold dusk of the late autumn evening.

3

—ᴟ—

Kristos came home late, waking me as he tripped over a chair in our row house's tiny kitchen, and I woke early to get ahead at the shop, so we didn't talk about our argument at the tavern. I reworked our order schedule, pushed off an invoice I could avoid paying for a week, and managed to secure enough projected income in the coffers to be sure I could pay Alice and Penny for the next month. The door of the shop opened and closed as I finished my tabulations, and I left the book open in case of a new order.

Instead, a shy Pellian girl, her cloak a faded blue wool, stood nervously in the entry, just far enough inside to close the door against the draft.

"Emmi!" I had few friends in the Pellian quarter of the city—I lived in the working-class row houses near the commercial district where urban and provincial Galatines and recent immigrants washed together, driven by the necessity of proximity to businesses and trade at the center of town. Moreover, my business absorbed most of my time. I didn't have time to shop for Pellian spices in the Pellian market; I bought mainly Galatine produce and herbs from the nearby stands and street criers. I didn't socialize by the well like the Pellian housewives did; I barely socialized at all, only at predominately Galatine taverns with Kristos's predominately Galatine workmates when he prodded me.

In truth, both Kristos and I had followed Mother's example of working for Galatines, following more lucrative local work instead of maintaining strong ties to the Pellian community. She frequented the Pellian market, but dressed, spoke, and behaved in as Galatine a manner as she could to please her employers. If I were completely honest, I had taken her strategy a step further, distancing myself from the stereotypes of Pellian charm casting by making my shop as modish and Galatine as possible—and myself, as well, in the process.

"I'm sorry to bother you at work, but I—I had hoped to talk to you and wasn't sure where you lived, so..." Emmi's fingers worried the hem of her cloak.

"I'm at the shop more often than I'm at home anyway," I replied. "You can come in."

She edged further toward the counter. Over a year ago, two timid Pellian girls had approached me to ask how I managed to run a business selling charms. Emmi and Namira had both been trained by their mothers and sold charms out of their kitchens; they were shocked that a woman was running a successful business in the art. I was ashamed to admit that my first thought was protecting the uniqueness of my business, but remembered quickly that the Lord of Coin would not grant permits to too many identical businesses. It couldn't hurt me if a few backdoor charm casters could mend their linens with a bit of luck thrown in. We had a fluid clutch of around a half dozen women, from sixteen-year-old Emmi to octogenarian Lieta, meeting once a month to discuss the craft.

There was little I could teach anyone about basic charm casting that they hadn't already learned from their mothers, but the nuances of how to charm more than clay tablets and what to blend aside from herbal slurries soon took over our conversation. I found, as well, that I was curious about the Pellian quarter of the city, where I had never lived, and the Pellian customs that I had only a vague familiarity with. My parents may have been Pellian, but the way we had always lived, outside the Pellian quarter, working for Galatines, moved us farther away from the island our parents left. These women, however, kept Pellia far closer than my family had.

None of them had ever sought me out outside of our meetings, and I couldn't guess at what Emmi wanted now.

"Are you well?" she asked, a bit stiffly, mimicking proper Galatine greetings.

"I'm fine, Emmi, and you?" I'd cut her off before she began to inquire about my health and the health of my relations, as Galatine housewives were apt to do.

"All right." Of all the Pellian women I knew, Emmi was probably the most facile with Galatine culture—born here, attended Galatine school—and yet she still stood on the periphery of comfort in my shop. "I just—well, I was hoping to ask a favor."

I nodded, agreeable. "What do you need?"

"It's more than a little favor, I just—I wanted to know if you're hiring any assistants."

I was taken aback. Emmi had never expressed interest in learning my trade, only the transferable nature of charm casting. I wondered if she simply wanted a Galatine trade to advance beyond the barter-and-scrape marketplace of the Pellian district. She knew that the likelihood of replicating my business was very low, and hadn't had much luck charm casting in anything but the clay tablets she had learned on.

"I don't want to steal your business or anything!" she added in a rush. "I just—money's tight this year. I'm a quick learner," she said hopefully.

I sympathized—after all, my mother's tactic had always been integrating herself with the Galatine ateliers, not hiring out mending from the Pellian quarter. Still, I couldn't hire Emmi. Not now. I was unsure if I could even retain the assistants I already had—competent, able seamstresses who didn't require the extensive training that Emmi would.

"I'm sure you are," I replied slowly. "It's not a good time of year, Emmi. Everyone tightens the purse in winter—buy what they need for the winter in the autumn, and then my business drops off until spring. Maybe in the spring," I added, more for the benefit of reassuring myself that I would try than as any kind of promise.

She nodded. "It's only that—with the riots last summer, a lot of prices went up, and Papa hasn't had as much work because they canceled some of the building projects in our quarter, and the lady who hired Ma for laundry fired her. Not many Galatines are using the Pellian district markets—I mean, fewer than usual. I was hoping for—well, for any work right now."

I was surprised, and a little ashamed of my surprise, at realizing that things were difficult for Emmi and my Pellian acquaintances. "What's going on in the quarter?"

"People are nervous about the riots last summer and all the talk still going on." Emmi shrugged.

"But that—the riots were all over the city last summer." Many of Kristos's acquaintances from the Laborers' League had been involved, though he was quick to argue that the League didn't organize the riots. *Angry people throw things*, he'd said with a shrug when I pressed him. "The worst one was near Fountain Square, after all!"

"Plenty of people in the Laborers' League are Pellian. I guess people think the quarter isn't as safe as it used to be. One of the fires was in our market." I recalled this—a quick-moving blaze that was fortunately cut short by one of the summer cloudbursts that swept in from the coast.

"There are still more Galatines in the League." I sighed, frustrated. I filed this away as another grievance to raise with Kristos the next time he extolled the virtues of the movement. "Emmi, I'm sorry, but I don't have any work right now." Even if I did, I thought, I couldn't afford to train someone in fine stitching unless business picked up, which dug at my conscience more than anything. "If I do, I'll let you know, though. I promise. I'll think of you first." Maybe I could train her for some simple basting or hemming, or if we got very busy, sweeping and tidying the studio.

She chewed on her lip, disappointed. "I understand," she said quietly.

"I'm sorry. I really am, Emmi." I closed my tabulation book, still open, still not as full of orders as it needed to be, still precariously balanced between income and expenses.

"I'll see you at our next meeting. Usual time and place?" She managed a smile.

"Wouldn't miss it," I replied, reminding myself to come in early all week to free an afternoon to meet with my charm-casting friends.

I retreated to my private corner of the shop, blocked off with decorative screens, and picked up the kerchief I'd started for Mrs. Bursin. I needed to charm cast without distractions, but of course had to stay accessible to Penny and Alice, so my little fort built of fabric-screened frames worked well. Still, they both knew that when I disappeared inside, I wasn't to be disturbed except when they truly needed me. Both were so capable now that interruptions seldom happened. One or both would leave me soon enough for better jobs, I wagered with a sigh—and then I would have the expense of training a new assistant to grapple with.

I couldn't think about that now. Instead, I held the needle gently between my thumb and forefinger, and exhaled. When I inhaled, the seam I had sewn the previous day began to glow, faintly, to my eyes only. It looked like a single strand of golden sunlight woven through the plain fabric, softly lit from within.

My mother had taught me to charm cast and to sew. Years of derision from Galatines stopped her from trying to sell her traditional charms, though, and we never made more than her day wages, earned stitching yards and yards of hems at a small second-rate atelier. Despite her fatigue, she trained me to cast charms while evening stole the last of the light from our crumbling cellar-level flat.

Even with my mother's rigorous training, I didn't really know how it worked.

All I knew was that I thought about good fortune, or love, or health for the person the item was meant for, and my thread would begin to glow. If I maintained my concentration, every stitch I took with the glowing thread would be like one word in an incantation, one ingredient in a potion, the whole piece working as a completed charm when I was done.

There was a feeling, too, that welled within me when the process was working just right. A kind of deep-seated happiness, simple but complete, like the feeling that came with seeing a baby laugh or smelling fresh-baked apple pie or hearing soft rainfall on the roof. And though I was tired—and hungry—after working on a charm for a few hours, I was calmly content.

"We don't make house calls except to established clients," I heard Alice say as I set the finished kerchief aside. I whisked to the front room, where she stood behind the counter with a resolutely lifted chin, hands folded primly over her white apron.

The young woman waiting at the counter wore her hair piled fashionably high on her head, topped by one of the more ridiculous of the season's caps that I thought had an uncanny resemblance to diapers. Her gown was of a brilliant blue print, one that I would have loved to ply into a creation of my own, but had clearly been reworked. A smaller woman wore this gown before my visitor, I surmised from the way the front accommodated a new panel and the marks along the shoulders where the seams had been let out. The gown had been given to her. Probably by her mistress.

She was a lady's maid, I deduced before Alice could speak again. And ladies' maids often ran errands on behalf of their very wealthy and influential mistresses.

"May I help you?" I asked in my friendliest voice.

Of course Alice piped up first. "I was just explaining to Miss Vochant that we don't—"

I silenced Alice with a quick tap on her wrist and a tilt of my head that told her she was wanted in the back of the atelier. Immediately.

"Please continue," I said.

"I am sorry to intrude," Miss Vochant said. "But my mistress has heard...good things about your work."

"Indeed," I replied blandly. I never assumed patrons wanted charms until they asked for them. It maintained some of the mystery. Some of the intrigue. Some of the reason I could get away with charging so much.

"Yes, she...she has need of a few new items for her winter wardrobe, and would very much like them to have your unique touch."

Miss Vochant was coy. Most ladies' maids would have bumbled into openly asking for the love spell or money charm or whatever their mistresses wanted by now.

"And who, may I ask, is your mistress?"

"The Lady Viola Snowmont," she said.

My jaw threatened to drop. Lady Snowmont was a favorite of the queen's, one of her ladies-in-waiting, and even the court painter. Her father was the Lord of Keys, the justice magistrate, and head of the soldiers. I fought my composure back into line.

"And how might I best serve the Lady Snowmont?"

"She had hoped you could visit her salon next Thursday for a consultation. But of course if that is impossible—"

"I do apologize, but Alice was mistaken." I thought quickly. It didn't look good to make exceptions to policies for wealthy patrons—it could make me look as though my shop needed Lady Snowmont to survive. That I was grubbing for favor. No, another tack. "I do not allow my assistants to arrange house calls on my behalf. I must agree to them myself, and make the arrangements. We are so very busy," I added.

This seemed to work well enough. "All right. I shall tell Lady Snowmont to expect you at two o'clock." She dropped her voice and smiled. "And I wouldn't eat before coming if I were you. She always has quite the spread at the salon."

I returned the smile with a professional nod. "Thank you. Please leave your mistress's card with me."

I waited until the door had closed behind her before I did a happy jig around the store.

I half ran home at the end of the day, excited at the prospects my new client might open for my shop, but also because the wintry chill had deepened as evening fell and my thin silk mantelet, a fashionable new accessory I wore in a successful attempt to sell charmed versions to clients, wasn't enough to keep it at bay.

I trotted past Fountain Square, which separated the residential streets from the shops and tradesmen's ateliers where I worked. The imposing dark granite fountain at its center was covered in a dusting of snow, but it was the common green beyond that had changed the most with the turning of the seasons.

Squat white tents had mushroomed in the trampled pale grass of the park, populated by His Majesty's royal forces. Their pale blue uniforms, so brightly impressive on parade in the summer, looked wan and tired against the frosty backdrop of the winter city. I exhaled a white cloud as I passed them. Since they had encamped here, at the turning of the fall, the riots that had marked the summer ceased. The relief was palpable in the trade district, and my business had seen a comfortable resurgence after the threat of violence died away. Still, the unexpected summer lull had taken a toll on the year's expected profits.

"Kristos!" I yelled as I flew through the rattling back door on our low-rent row house. "Kristos, you won't believe the day I had!"

The quiet house absorbed my voice, and no one came to greet me.

Figures, I thought, prodding some fire into the stove and filling the kettle for tea. I have something happen—for once, something big—and Kristos was gone. I should have expected it, his days reaching far past sunset with the demands of the Laborers' League. It had been unusual for me to set the second plate at dinner for the last month. In fact, the dying riots of the summer had laid fertile ground for an autumn filled with more intensive activity in the Laborers' League.

I slumped in my chair, waiting for the water to boil. There was still some ham in the larder and half a loaf of bread. No reason to hurry to the market tonight. I traced the rough wood of the table. It was just the two of us, and had been for so many years that I forgot to think of our little family as missing anyone.

My parents had migrated from Pellia to Galitha before we were born, looking for work, so we had always been far from aunts and uncles and cousins. Pellia produced charm casters but little else; perhaps that was why Galatines didn't believe in the clay charms they saw Pellians peddling in the city. How could the most impoverished country in the hemisphere have any good luck at all? They didn't understand how Pellians measured luck—by days and by coins, not by lifelong health or wealth. They would buy a charm for a good day at the races or a kiss from a girl they liked and consider it well worth it.

Mother and Papa were like that—one day at a time, good luck for today and not fretting tomorrow. I fretted—Galitha City had taught me to worry. Papa, a fisherman, had drowned when I was still too young to truly remember a time before we lived on Mother's slim day wages alone, and Kristos and I had been fifteen and thirteen, respectively, when she died of a short but vile fever. It was fortunate we had keen noses for work and the survival instinct of stray cats. We lived like stray cats for a while—taking shelter in friends' kitchens when they could help us and unused sheds and alleyways when they couldn't, even swiping scraps from the bakers and butchers and things the street criers dropped. But we learned, and I had learned, more than Kristos, that Pellian ways didn't lend themselves to economic security in the city like Galatine scruples did.

Now Kristos turned to the Laborers' League, the workers' organization that he claimed was the wave of the future, and I honed my charm-making skills, which I considered a relic of the past. Both served us well, in their own way. I made enough money to keep us relatively comfortable, and Kristos's connections around the city led to jobs for him that funneled more money into our modest purse. If the run of luck with work he'd had through the autumn continued and my business didn't slow too much over the winter, I could harness more of my profits into growing my business. Well-worn fancies of a larger atelier positioned closer to Fountain Square, with large-paned windows showcasing my best work, quickly encroached on my more pragmatic thoughts. Winter meant, more than likely, slower business for my shop and fewer jobs for Kristos.

My kettle began to hum, steam pouring from the spout, and I poured the boiling water over some musty tea leaves in an old pot. There was a chip in the mouth and the beginnings of a crack along the handle.

The door creaked open and clattered closed again, and I was on my feet before Kristos stumbled into the room.

"Sister o'mine!" He grappled me into a bear hug that reeked of sweet wine. "Which for supper—the mutton hand pie or the chicken?"

"Why did you come home with two of them? They're huge!" I replied, taking the flimsily wrapped pastries from him and setting them on the table. One could feed both of us. And they smelled divine.

"Don't scold me," he said with a devilish smile. "They were a gift."

"Did I forget your birthday? Is there some celebration in order that I'm unaware of?" I asked, jabbing him in the ribs. "Your wrist better?"

"Yes—well, not enough to work today. Tomorrow. Jack's got me on a crew taking down some dead trees by the wharf."

"So what did you do today to earn a pair of hand pies?"

"I met with one of the university lecturers. He sends these with his compliments," he said. Hope flared—perhaps a lecturer could offer my brother some sort of work in the university itself, perhaps even allowing him to study. "He wants to help the Laborers' League."

My hopes fell. "What help is he offering? Mathematics tutelage?"

"Very funny. No, he's one of the faculty offering public lectures. It turns out he's like-minded," he said. "With the League. He's going to help us draft demands for the Council of Nobles."

"Demands?" I almost choked. "What position are you making demands from?"

"He suggested that it would be the only way to get their attention on what we want—and he's right. If they see us as a rabble of malcontents, they're not going to do anything but chase us off when we get too loud in the streets. If we have an actual platform—"

"A platform to hang you from," I retorted. "If you're not careful, you're going to be accused of treason instead of merely being a loudmouth."

"Of course I'm careful. I'm being very careful, for instance, not to gobble up this entire pasty by myself," he said, tearing some flaky crust from the pasty nearest him. The rich mutton filling seeped out onto the table. His meaning was clear—I was being a worrywart and he wasn't interested in arguing with me. My concerns about the Laborers' League weren't new, and I acknowledged that some of my fears were over-reactionary, but a word like *demands* carried enough weight to provoke a new brand of concern.

No point in cautioning him—he was going to make his decisions regardless of what I said. "Well, sit down and hand me a plate, then."

He forked over half the meat pie and tucked into the remaining half himself. "I wish," he said through a bite, "that you'd work up a little more enthusiasm. If for nothing else, for the pasty."

No matter how much Kristos extolled the virtues of

reforming the economic system so that the nobility had less control and instituting representation of the working classes in government, I couldn't get too attached to the idea. Our lives couldn't change much, I figured. I'd still make clothes; he would still labor at the warehouses and on building crews. The only change I could see was a mass exodus of wealthier patrons, like minor nobles, who were my best clients, if things got dicey in the city.

Nobles. I grinned. "You'll never guess who came into the shop today," I said.

"Probably not," he replied.

I ignored his disinterest. "The lady's maid of the Lady—"

"Again? Another rich noble? Sophie, I wish you would use the talents you have for more...I don't know, more worthy work."

I snapped my jaw shut. Of course Kristos wouldn't be excited about my latest lead. Even if the money I earned from whatever commission Lady Snowmont gave me could very likely heat our house all winter. The nobility's very existence offended him. Even if I understood his argument, it didn't change reality. Reality demanded money for food and fuel. I pointedly ignored Kristos and relished a bite of my pasty.

Kristos stared into his plate, remorseful. "I didn't mean to shout. I'm sorry."

"It's all right," I said crisply. "I should stop expecting my work to interest you."

"Actually, I...I kind of hoped you could help me."

I let a smile slip back into my tone. "What, a love charm? There's some girl who won't talk to you and you want to woo her? Tell me all about it, brother dear."

"Not that! As if I needed help," he said, flexing his shoulders. I rolled my eyes. "We're gathering a group on Fountain

Square next week," he said, his voice growing serious. "A demonstration, probably a hundred people. Maybe more."

"A hundred?" Kristos's meetings had always been small affairs, a few men in the café after work or a half dozen laborers gathered on Sunday morning outside the churches to hand out pamphlets. "But the soldiers—Kristos."

"What of the soldiers? We're lecturing, not rioting. People are listening, Sophie, listening enough to join with us. Consider it a celebration of our accomplishments, or a public lecture, not a demonstration, if it makes you more comfortable."

"You said you needed my help," I said with growing apprehension. I couldn't be seen with a laborer protest—not if I wanted to keep my noble and upper-class clientele. Which I did, because as much as Kristos didn't seem to care, I enjoyed eating and living under a roof that leaked sometimes.

"I don't expect any problems," he said quickly, a little too hurried. "But the soldiers might...interfere. And if they do, some of the lads might get sore about it."

"Maybe this isn't a good idea," I said.

"No, it's fine. Really. The chances of anything happening are so small, but I had hoped—maybe you could make us a few charmed caps," he asked in a loud rush, then shot me a hopeful grin before sopping the last of his meat pie's gravy off his plate with the remainder of the crust. "This is delicious—not quite like Ma's *pilla* and spinach, huh? How come you never cook like she did?"

I made a face thinking of the soggy spinach pie our mother said was a Pellian specialty—we hadn't eaten it in years. "Caps." I pursed my lips. "What kind of caps?"

"I left out the best part!" He smacked his head in mock self-punishment. "Of course, the caps. We're all going to wear red wool caps—ancient Pellian design. There was a lecture at the

university last week on ancient Pellian democracy—did you
know that the Pellians had a democratic form of governance?" I
shook my head, not really caring if our ancestral homeland was,
at one time, governed by parrots—the study of history and government didn't interest me as it did Kristos. "When they voted
or participated in public debates, they wore these special caps."

"Red wool caps."

"I have a sketch."

"Of course you do." I took the paper. "These look ridiculous. You do realize that everyone in Galitha City who missed
that particular lecture is going to think you're wearing a phallus
on your head, right?"

"Then they'll ask us and we'll explain what they mean."

"What do the Pellians in the League think about this?"
I asked, considering what Emmi had told me. Would using
ancient Pellian motifs draw more ire into the Pellian quarter?

"Sophie, we are Pellian," Kristos said with a laugh.

"I mean Pellians who live in the Pellian quarter. Who come
from Pellia, who speak Pellian."

"Niko came to that lecture and thought it was a good idea.
Everyone does." I glanced again at the ridiculous design, wondering if Kristos had a good handle on "everyone" and their
opinions. "The whole point of the League is that it's uniting all
the workers across the city—across Galitha, really. It shouldn't
matter if they're Pellian or provincial or born and raised in the
city."

"Shouldn't and doesn't are two different things." I shook my
head.

"It doesn't matter to us," Kristos said grandly. "The League
is egalitarian—no disparity between those born in the southern
provinces and those from the mountain province and those born
in the city and those who've adopted Galitha—those divisions

are artificial and encouraged by the nobility to keep us from uniting." How artificial, I wondered, when plenty of Pellians preferred to live in their own communities, and plenty of provincials still spoke different Galatine dialects? The customs of the southernmost provinces, hundreds of miles away, were nearly as foreign to city-born Galatines as Pellian norms. "All the workers in Galitha have common grievances," he stated as though it were a motto.

"It may not matter to *you*," I cautioned him. The League's intentions and others' perceptions were not necessarily the same thing.

Kristos just shrugged me off. "Well, no one in the League has any problems with the caps."

If nothing else, I'd make a cap with a protection charm for my brother. "How many caps do you need? There's no way I'm making a hundred of them."

"I know, that's asking far too much. Ten to start? That way we can spread them out among the group and have a protection charm on the whole gathering. Right? That's how it works, isn't it?"

I shook my head. "It's not quite so simple. Each charm bleeds over onto the people around the wearer. But it's not like there's a way to have them all connect together or anything." At least, not that I was aware of. "You'll wear one, won't you?" I caught his hand, growing more concerned by the moment about his plan.

"In the interest of fairness, we were going to throw the charmed ones in among the rest and let everyone pull one. Like drawing straws, you know?"

"I won't do it unless you wear one. You're my brother. I'm going to protect you first. Good heavens, I'm only even considering this so you'll be protected. I don't care about brawling dockworkers and farmhands."

Kristos shot me one of his best scolding looks. He'd inherited that look from Mother. "Yes, you do care. You don't want anyone to get hurt. I know you."

"Fine, you're right. But I'm serious, Kristos—I won't make a single cap unless you promise to wear one."

He hesitated.

"Promise!" I squeaked.

"All right, all right! I surrender." He smiled. "I've got a couple yards of wool in my pack."

"And you're going to clean up in here, right?"

"Sure," he replied with an easy smile that told me he would leave the dishes on the table and the floor unswept.

4

─ ⁓ ─

I stood outside the gate of the limestone town house, its address printed in swirling type on the card I held clutched in my hand, just underneath the name *Viola Snowmont*. I was grateful for my blush-pink leather gloves—they kept the sweat coating my palms from smudging the card I had kept in my pocket the past week, never losing the thrill of nerves and anticipation each time my fingers brushed the corners.

I lifted the latch with a steadying breath, and as the heavy wrought iron gate swung away from the fence, a trilling melody of chimes rang across the courtyard. I looked around for the source and found a set of bells, tucked in a viney tangle of roses and linked by a delicate golden chain to the gate.

I was still marveling at this clever design when the aqua-blue double doors at the top of an impressive flight of stairs flung wide and revealed a meticulously dressed housemaid in blue and white.

"Are you expected?" Her clear soprano voice floated down to me.

"Yes, I am Miss Sophie Balstrade, the seamstress she has engaged for a private consultation," I replied, forcing the shake out of my voice. I was speaking to a maid, for pity's sake—if I couldn't hold it together with the hired help, what chance did I have making a favorable impression on Lady Snowmont?

"Indeed, please come inside." She bowed her head, golden hair gleaming in the crisp sunlight, as I climbed the stairs and passed through the doorway. The warm blue paint made it feel as though I were walking into the sky, an illusion maintained by the long hallway I entered papered in diaphanous silver-and-blue florals.

The maid took my cloak and gloves, as the town house was warm enough without them. I was almost disappointed—the peacock-blue cloak with its caned hood, matched with the pink gloves, made a striking impression. Strawberry sellers and fishmongers hawked their wares in the streets with singsong rhymes; I wore brilliantly colored silks and fine cottons crafted into fashionably draped and painstakingly stitched gowns and jackets. For Lady Viola, I had worn the best example of my work that I owned—a jacket with wide pleats cascading from the shoulder to the hips, the forest-green silk laced tightly over an intricately embroidered stomacher. Glancing at the maid, however, I felt a twinge of envy for women who had someone else to dress their hair. Mine was neatly fixed and piled high, but it lacked the complicated curls and braids of a fashionable hairstyle.

I had never had a client of Lady Snowmont's prestige before. For the first time in years, my Pellian background concerned me. Would Lady Viola trust a Pellian seamstress to produce Galatine couture, clothing that was fit for her fashionable salon, for the social gatherings she frequented and hosted? The prospect of one of my pieces attending a royal event at the palace was exhilarating but reminded me of the seriousness of the commission. This could be my entry into a new level of clientele—or a quick rejection from it. Galatine nobility intermarried regularly with foreign nobility, and delegates from Kvyset, Serafan, and other foreign aristocracy were commonplace enough in Galitha City. Still, I wondered if a commoner, clearly Pellian by her golden complexion and tall, broad-shouldered frame, would receive the same kind of welcome.

The maid led me to Lady Snowmont's salon. I fussed with my skirts and checked to make sure that my jacket wasn't crooked. The room was bustling with ladies in exquisite silks and velvets. One played a harp while several others watched intently; another read aloud from a book. The Lady Snowmont's salon—known as the center of culture through all of Galitha. And here I was.

With, I realized, no clue at all as to which lady was the Lady Snowmont.

I pressed my lips together, ready to hover in the doorway until I was called for, but the maid shoved me forward with a light but persuasive hand. "This way," she whispered, and led me to the chaise where my prospective client reclined behind a screen.

I hadn't been sure what to expect. Lady Viola Snowmont was so well-known and rumored to be pretty that I had imagined she was a stunning beauty, but I speculated as I waited for the maid to present to me what she looked like. Would she be a golden-haired, fair-skinned lady, like a gilded angel in a church? Or a striking beauty with dark hair, and lips painted a fiery hue?

Neither, I saw as she leapt up from the couch and greeted me. Her face was pretty but not the perfect doll's face I had assumed. And her light brown hair, though thick and wavy, was quite ordinary.

It was her eyes, I saw quickly, that made the entire country say she was a beauty. Huge, fringed with thick lashes, and the rich color of liquid chocolate, their intelligence and expressiveness turned her from a plain woman into an extraordinary one. They seemed to see everything, everyone at once—and of course they did. After all, she was the court painter. In fact, she let several sheets of heavy linen paper covered with graphite sketches of a nearby bouquet flutter to the chaise as she came to greet me.

"Sophie!" she said, extending a hand. "I do hope we can dispense with formalities and use first names alone? It's my own rule, here in the salon—no one is a miss or a Mrs. or a lady or even a queen." She winked.

"Of course," I managed to stammer.

"Now, then." She swept the hem of her gown—a simple, loose-fitting sultana housedress, I saw, surprised—away from the clawed foot of her chaise. "I imagine my girl told you I have an interest in some new clothes?" She laughed. "Of course she did, otherwise why would you be here?"

"Yes, I—"

"Good. It's too loud in here to discuss anything." She caught my hand and pulled me toward a door, trimmed in ornate gilt, on the far side of the room. "My private sitting room, please."

Her merry smile faded as she pulled the door closed. I stood with my back to the silk-covered walls. This wasn't just a sitting room, I saw quickly—it was Lady Snowmont's boudoir, adjacent to her bedchamber. An open door revealed a heavily draped bed in the room next to it. The most private of public spaces, the most public of private spaces. There were complicated rules of etiquette of whom Galatines allowed in their boudoirs—certainly never someone whom one had known a mere five minutes.

"I'll dispense with any coy pussyfooting. You make charms. And I have need of such a service." She gestured to the pair of overstuffed lilac damask chairs nearest us.

I sank into one, not sure how to reply. "Yes, your ladyship, you are correct. I...make charmed clothing."

"Viola. Just call me Viola. Not to sound revolutionary, but if I am trusting you to make a charm for me, we ought to at least try to act like equals." My eyes widened, but I acquiesced with a nod.

"Good." Viola sat on the edge of her chair like a bird perching on a tenuous branch. "What kind of charms can you do? And how does it work? That is—is it the larger the item of clothing, the better the charm? Or is there something else to it?"

"What kind? Nearly anything—love, luck, money." I flushed. "Not that I assume you have need of any of those, they're just—"

"Your most frequently requested services?" She laughed. One of her front teeth was ever so slightly crooked.

"Yes. No surprise there, I imagine."

"None at all."

"And the strength of the charm is in direct correlation to how much work I put into it—how many stitches, to be exact. An embroidered kerchief could be as powerful as a gown."

"Even better," Viola mused.

"May I ask," I said, hesitating, "what exactly are you in need of?" Money and luck were certainly not lacking in Lady Snowmont's life.

She pressed her lips together. "Not a love charm, if that's what you're thinking." She fished a cheaply printed, shoddily bound stack of pages from a drawer in the deftly carved table beside her. She thumbed through a few pages and tossed it to me.

A People's Response to Monarchical Tyranny, read the off-center title. There was no printing house or address listed, just a stamped crest. Not surprising, given the inflammatory title. But the typeface was familiar—Kristos had pamphlets on economics and political systems that looked similar. Probably someone with a press in a shed, not a legitimate printer. No one with a business, I assumed, would risk his business printing inflammatory papers. Or maybe some business owners were more revolutionary and less risk averse than I was.

"The monarchy—it's not popular among the people right now, I gather." She watched me carefully. "No, you tell me. Is the monarchy popular with the people? Is the nobility?"

I opened my mouth, then closed it again. My brother and his angry friends didn't speak for the entire populace, but at the same time, I hadn't heard anything to contradict their views lately, either. I flipped through a few pages of the pamphlet, absorbing quickly that it wasn't a theoretical text—it called for action over talk. I caught words that made my breath catch in my throat—*protest, refusal to work, demands. Revolt.* "I wouldn't say it was unpopular with the majority of Galatines to the point of violence," I replied slowly. I handed the pamphlet back to her. The cheap ink left smudges on my fingers.

"Ever so politic!" She laughed. "Yes, perhaps so. But this?" She waved the pamphlet as though she could make the treasonous words fall out of it. "This is new. I fear a turn. The riots this summer were only the start, I believe. The anger of much of the populace seems to be...coalescing." I pressed my lips together. Kristos seemed optimistic that lectures and pamphlets were a shift away from the fragmented if motivated rioting, but what if they only represented unification and purpose that could end with violence? I thought again of the plan to craft "demands" for changes and feared, again, what force the League expected to leverage.

Viola continued. "I have always seen two forms of insurance for a noblewoman. Marrying well"—she made a face—"or making herself so well-liked among the nobility that she'll always have a place. The trouble with being among the most well-known and well-liked nobles is that I'm as well-known by the common people. That makes me a fine target if things turn sour."

In an almost perverse irony, she was like me, I realized with a start. We both balanced on a slim line between living off the nobility and hoping for some form of acceptance with the common people. Except she was nobility, and I was common—our realities could not have been more different. She likely had no idea what it meant to wonder where her next meal would come from, or even to think of how much it cost at all. Still, our securities were both threatened by the ideas in a few pages of bound paper. I had built a safe life for Kristos and me, a consistent livelihood; the ideas in that pamphlet put me at risk as well as the nobility.

I shook off that disconcerting thought. "If it's a protection charm you want, I can certainly oblige."

"Must I wear it all the time?"

"Only if you want it to work all the time," I replied. I had made charmed habits for riding and shawls for late nights out for some clients. I had a feeling Lady Snowmont wanted something more all-encompassing.

She thought for a moment, her eyes resting on a spot high above my head. I was going to suggest a white-work kerchief, something she could wear with any gown, when she surprised me.

"Linens," she said.

"What?"

"Underthings. Chemises and drawers. A nice utilitarian petticoat or two."

I almost burst out laughing at the absurdity of it, but found myself appreciating her ingenuity. Of course. She would wear them all the time—but no one would see that she wore the same thing day in and day out. For a woman in her position, silent protection was worth as much as continuous protection.

"That's positively ingenious."

"But will it be enough?" Viola watched me, searching my reaction.

"Against any normal sort of mischief or accident, yes." I hesitated. "No charm is perfect, my la—Viola." I paused, tracing a line of stitches along the hem of my jacket. "It will be as much as I can offer."

"Fairly stated. I assumed, of course, that there are limits to magic as there are to anything." She smiled, then glanced at my jacket. "Your designs are quite remarkable in and of themselves," she added. "I think I should like a gown, as well. Something for day, elegant but not ostentatious. Something I can entertain in here. No charm required."

"Of course," I said, trying very hard not to beam. "I can bring sketches and fabric swatches—next week, perhaps?"

"Fine. I like pink this year, if it can be arranged." She laughed. "As to payment."

"Have your maid arrange it with me," I replied automatically. That was the way every other noble handled business.

"That seems rather discourteous, doesn't it?" She pulled an elaborately embroidered wallet from a hidden drawer in the console table. "Consider this a deposit."

She dropped more coins into my hand than I had ever asked for any commission.

"I will pay the second half upon delivery."

"Yes, my lady," I breathed.

"Now, then. I had the kitchen make up a stone fruit tart, and I'm dying to see if they spiced it to my liking."

"I'll take my leave," I said, bowing my head.

"Of course you won't. You'll give me your opinion on this

tart." She stood and flung the door open into the salon. I followed her to a long table lined with food and porcelain plates and teacups so fine that they were translucent.

"Stay," she whispered, "and have a bite to eat. And chat with my friends." She smiled, conspiratorial. "I like collecting artists as friends. They tend to be interesting people, and interesting to one another. I'm sure you'll find their company as enjoyable as I do."

5

—ഝ—

I BALANCED MY TEACUP ON ITS TINY SAUCER, ACUTELY AWARE that any false move and I'd shatter the perfect porcelain. Lady Snowmont's salon buzzed around me. A different woman, with ruddy dark skin and a scarlet ribbon in her hair, now played the harp. Three ladies in elegant dishabille convened around a book bound in pink leather. I trained my ear toward them, expecting to hear a rehashing of a romantic novel. Instead, I caught snippets of a lively debate about labor economics.

"Don't be fooled by the cover," Lady Snowmont said, laughing at the surprise on my face. "I have a collection of political and economic classics bound in my favorite pink calfskin."

Of course she did.

I edged closer to the trio of ladies, craning my neck to read the title. *Alternative Arrangements of Economic Function* by Simon Melchoir. I started—my brother had borrowed a tattered copy from a friend and spent firelit evenings poring over it and quoting passages he particularly liked to me. The book, considered radical in its challenge of the established system of nobility and day laborers, proposed alternative ways an economy could work. Kristos ate it up. I listened as politely as I could.

"You must be the seamstress," a tall woman in yellow said.

The color was perfect with her deep skin and black hair—I admired her seamstress's taste. Clearly a local seamstress—she was certainly from the island nations in the equatorial seas, yet her gown was distinctly, fashionably Galatine. I found myself wondering if she liked it, or if she felt obligated to adopt her hostess's taste.

"Yes, I—I hope I'm not intruding."

"Not at all. Have you read Melchoir?"

"Yes—some—well, not all of it."

"We're not quite of one mind about the potential of the laboring class," another woman, this one wearing an aqua silk morning jacket, said.

"Pauline thinks the most efficient form of economic strata is a large laboring class," the third woman, a diminutive brunette in distracting pink, said. "But Nia and I tend to think that it leaves a disproportionate number of people in potential unemployment."

I had never expected to hear talk like this outside of Kristos's cadre of friends. I managed to close my gaping mouth and consider a reply. Before I could speak, Nia, in yellow, pressed me.

"Well, you're a sole proprietor of a business. Aren't you?" Her accent was faint but lent a serious, studious cadence to her voice.

"Yes, I own my business. I have two employees and I hire an errand boy."

"Wouldn't you say that your risk is greater than a day laborer's?" the woman in aqua, Pauline, said.

"Absolutely," I replied, thinking of my rent and the even greater expense of fabric. "But of course my potential for earning is greater, as well."

"That's precisely what I was saying!" crowed Nia. She smoothed her yellow gown with a triumphant flick of her wrist.

"It also," I continued, hesitant, "distributes wealth more

evenly. Rather than going to a shop owned by an already wealthy family, you can support your neighbor or your cousin." I felt myself beginning to ramble, and stopped talking.

"A fair point," Pauline conceded.

"But the current system doesn't permit the average common person to aspire to anything other than day wages," Nia pressed. "No, you tell me, Sophie."

I hiccuped over my words. She was so forthright—it was as though I were a witness being questioned by a barrister. "It's true," I stammered. "Anyone wishing to open a new venture must get permission from the office of the Lord of Coin. Most petitions are denied," I added, thinking of the half dozen people I knew personally who had tried and failed to open storefronts or even street carts.

Pauline considered this, then latched onto another argument. "For new businesses, yes. But taking over an existing business—"

"Requires the same paperwork," Nia interrupted. "So if the Lord of Coin wishes, he can deny all the apprentices for a certain business and watch it fold."

"It's not as though," Pauline retorted, smarting, "the Lord of Coin is in the business of denying petitions for sport."

"Surely, the point is that he can," Nia said. "Most of the people talking revolution aren't denied petitioners."

"No," I said cautiously. "But they know that they can do little to change their status, so they feel trapped. And their children after them, trapped."

"That's another thing," said Nia. "The generational disparity— the nobles grant or deny everything to the common class. Petitions for businesses, apprenticeship agreements, even university places. Yet your places are granted to you by birthright only."

I stopped—*your*? Was Nia not a noble, either? I had assumed she was the wife of a Galatine noble, one of the many miniature alliances forged in matrimony between powerful families across national borders.

"I suppose it is different in your country?" Pauline replied.

"No, it is not so different in most of the Allied Equatorial States." Nia glanced at me. "Yet we are smaller—the prince himself selected my father for university study and then for this diplomatic post. Perhaps its ethics are no different—the nobility determines the choices of the populace—but perhaps bureaucracy introduces its own set of complications."

I leaned forward, curious. The daughter of a diplomat from one of the Allied principalities—I wanted to know what other difference she saw between our nations, what other points we might be considering.

Pauline spoke instead. "Surely you can't suggest that everyone should be allowed to try their hand at university, or at owning a business. Most would fail."

"They'd fail of their own accord," I said without thinking.

Nia raised her chin, proud that her side had won me to its argument, but I clamped my mouth shut. I felt I'd shown my hand, said too much. If I wanted to keep my business, I reminded myself, I needed to avoid this kind of revolutionary talk. I wasn't even sure I agreed with the concept anyway—perhaps such oversight was better, after all, keeping more of the common people employed.

Pauline knotted her eyebrows, seeming to debate saying anything. Finally, she did. "I just hope talk like that doesn't turn the streets into riots."

"On that," Nia said, "I think we may all agree."

"The summer was terrible," Pauline said quietly. I detected a slight tremble to her voice. I had been frightened, certainly, when the shouting grew loudest, and when the fire set in the midst of Fountain Square leapt its bounds and licked the shingles off several buildings before it was controlled. This fear seemed deeper.

"My father says we'll leave if the riots break out again," Nia said. "And most of the diplomatic delegates agree with him."

The woman in pink finally spoke again. She was a pale blond, northern Galatine—though among the nobility and even the common people in the city, such regional differences began to blur as people intermarried. "It's all theoretical, isn't it? There may be angry people, but they can't really do anything against the soldiers." She waved a languid hand. Her nails were perfectly manicured.

"I have every confidence," the woman in pink continued, "that the reforms proposed to the Council of Nobles will appease some of their anger."

"Reforms?" I asked, biting my cheek as soon as I spoke. I sounded uneducated.

"Hardly common knowledge yet, don't concern yourself," she replied. "My husband is a Privy Councillor." I could have sworn I saw Pauline and Nia share a private smirk—the wife of the Privy Councillor must have flaunted this fact more often than was polite. "They involve increasing ratios of permits and, of course, the anti-conscription plans."

"They won't begin to address what we were just discussing," Nia countered. "I'm afraid the populace will remain disappointed."

"Certainly it's a start—and isn't some appeasement the most important thing right now? To prevent another outburst like last summer?" Pauline shrugged. "Governance doesn't mean everyone getting their way most of the time."

Nia laughed. "My father always said that if everyone left the chamber unhappy after a vote, a good compromise had been reached," she conceded. "But I imagine it's fair to say that the nobility is not unhappy with much in these reforms, and they will fall far short of what the populace wants."

Something else traced the edge of the conversation but remained unvoiced. The nobility was still prescribing for the populace what they would receive, not involving them in the process. Did they know how many hours the Laborers' League spent in the cafés, discussing their principles, their dissatisfaction, their plans? Kristos could write a set of reforms, I was sure, that would have made for a more robust debate in the Privy Councillors' chambers.

Though these ladies enjoyed having a conversation about the politics and machinations of reform, I doubted they would approve of much of what Kristos would have asked for. And what of my involvement, even by proximity? Gaining Lady Viola Snowmont as a client could be the entry I needed into the city's elite, to grow my clientele and my shop. What would they have said about the red wool caps I had spent half the night sewing? Though I placed my trust in the encampment of soldiers on the green, knowing that they could put down a riot, did I believe that their presence would deter violence from erupting to begin with? Kristos and his friends didn't intend to remain disappointed. Riots or even the threat of them could chase the nobility from the city and erase any advantage this commission from Viola might grant me.

I glanced at the gilt-and-porcelain clock on the wall. Kristos was expecting me after my meeting here, and I was later than I had anticipated already. The warm salon, its brightly dressed and intelligent guests, and the newly made commission didn't erase the cold uncertainty outside, and I wished we hadn't discussed the summer's unrest. I excused myself from the trio. Lady Snowmont was engrossed in sketching an arrangement of flowers.

Several women engaged in embroidery near her, but I noted that they discussed the merits of a collection of poetry they had all read rather than the vapid gossip I might have expected.

I gathered my things and turned to leave, nearly running into a man in a trim black suit at the door.

"My pardon!" He swept an apologetic bow. I stammered my own apology and he grinned, his hazel eyes warming like sunshine on an early spring day.

I backed directly into Lady Viola.

"Sophie!" She shook her head. "Leaving so soon? I was just going to get a game of blindman's bluff going—so much seriousness in here today."

"I did enjoy the discussion, my la—Viola, you were right. Your friends are fascinating people."

The man in the black suit slipped past me into the room, waving a greeting to Nia and Pauline. I found myself watching his honey-brown queue dip as he laughed.

Viola raised an eyebrow as she discerned my line of sight, but her expression was amused, not angry. "You'll come back to see me soon, I hope."

"With the sketches and swatches, of course."

"Very good. I shall look forward to it." Viola squeezed my hand and shot me an impish smile. Then she whirled back toward the salon. "Who thinks they can best me in blindman's bluff?"

6

THE AIR HAD GROWN WARMER OUTSIDE, THE SUN OBSCURED BY thick gray clouds rolling in from the north. We'd have rain before night, I guessed, and I hoped Penny had remembered to close the workshop window. I pulled my hood over my head, grateful for soft wool against my chilly ears.

Kristos had nagged me for three days to come to one of the cafés he and his friends frequented—ostensibly because they had just cracked the casks of winter ale and he insisted I try it, but I knew better. His tactics were so thin a child could have seen through them—immerse me in so much talk that I finally woke up one morning clutching one of those ridiculous red caps and crying for reforms.

As I walked toward the dumpy tavern Kristos had selected, the Hazel Dell, I steeled myself. I could enjoy a mug of ale, ask after everyone's families, and hope that someone started a round of songs before the talk grew too serious. A drink or two and then home to bed—or, if it wasn't too late, to make a few preliminary sketches for Lady Viola's gown. I smiled to myself. She wanted one of my pieces, for its own sake, for my skill in design and draping and sewing. That was the highest compliment I could be paid.

I passed through Fountain Square, moving quickly against the cold. The only soldiers out on the nearby green were sentries, looking cold and miserable as the wind rolled across the square. A few people were still out running their errands or hawking wares, peddlers hired by the owners of print shops and farms and butchers for a day at a time. One girl in a blue short cloak and a torn gown stood in the center of the square, singing. A ballad seller—the printer sent her out with broadsides of song lyrics, and she advertised them by singing the songs.

And charm casting.

I slowed and stopped. A faint glow bloomed around her as she sang, but very faint, and sporadic. Only a charm caster could see it, and only if she was trained, had learned to look for the light that slipped from the air and coalesced around a charm. The ballad singer had the same gift I did—but she didn't know, I guessed, how to sustain or control it, or how to funnel it into objects, either. My mother had trained me heavily as soon as she knew I had the ability, and it took years of strict practice to develop the ease with which I could pull a charm into a stitched object.

Mother never trained me in how to craft charms from anything but needle and thread, and only talked about the physical charms in clay and herbs that Pellian casters traditionally used. I hadn't realized until after she died that there might be other conduits for charms. I had seen a singer cast a charm once before, a fishwife on her family's boat, untangling a net. I had rushed to ask her how she had learned, and she backed away from me as though she thought me possessed. It was only then I realized that, without training, one didn't even recognize the ability. Galatines, so distrustful of charms, were rarely trained. The only other trained casters I knew in the city were Pellian, and all had been trained in the traditional clay-tablet and herb-sachet methods.

The ballad seller might have been Galatine or Pellian by birth, as her features were a clear intermarriage of the two. Her voice rose and swelled—she sang in a modern Galatine style, that was certain, not the folk song style of either Pellia or Galitha. She had a beautiful, clear tone, and the sad melody she sang floated and dipped like the undulations of a river. A dead soldier, his lover in search of him, vows never to rest or love again—the ballads from the print shops were full of such sentimental drivel. But for the first time hearing a song on the street like this, I felt moved, affected to the point that I stood rooted to the cobblestones and listened to the ballad seller. I couldn't be sure that it wasn't the wind, but tears formed in my eyes. All the while, the faint light glowed and wavered around her.

When she finished, the charm light faded away completely, and I shook myself. Had I been so affected because she had a beautiful voice, or because she was charming me? There was no way of knowing, and I was nearly sure she didn't even know she could cast. I dug a copper coin from my pocket and bought a song. She smiled, shy and missing teeth, and mumbled her thanks.

No, I ascertained as she began another song and the glow didn't reappear, she didn't know how to control the gift. Perhaps it benefited her a little, accidentally charming people into listening and opening their pocketbooks, but she wasn't intending it. All the same, I smiled for her as I hurried onward. Good for her, the shy ballad seller, finding a bit of an edge in this hard world.

The Hazel Dell stood on the corner of River and Cross Streets, a tall brick building whose façade was more refined than the clientele it served. Kristos waited inside at a long table already filled with his friends. I sighed. With so many people bound to talk politics, I was in for a long night of debates. Kristos made friends with everyone—everything, I amended, as I noticed a rangy-looking cat stropping his ankles. He waved, but didn't stop his conversation as I joined him.

I slipped onto the bench next to him, quickly shucking my cloak and regretting the choice of wearing the same ostentatious silk I had worn to Lady Viola's in a café like this. I stuck out like a bluebird among winter crows against all the linen and wool. Slowly, I inched my cloak back over my shoulders.

"Sophie! I already got you a pint of ale." Kristos's friend Jack shoved a large mug toward me, the froth sloshing over the sides. I moved back instinctively, covering my silk petticoat, then cringed. I looked like a snob, overdressed and fussy in a common tavern. *Make an effort*, I chided myself.

"Thank you, Jack." I forced a smile. "How is the winter ale this year?"

"Not bad at all, not bad at all." He sipped it, feigning a connoisseur's air. "Hoppy, just a little bit of—maybe pine?"

I tasted it. It tasted like ale. "Not bad," I said, though I wasn't sure what "good" would taste like.

"What do you think, Sophie?" Kristos said, interrupting Jack's next question.

"About what?" I set the ale down. "I couldn't hear—"

Kristos rolled his eyes. "You never pay attention to these conversations, do you?"

"Kristos, I just got here, and Jack—"

"Damn it, Jack, distracting Sophie from vital conversation with your flirting!" Kristos laughed, but I shot him a look. Flirting? Is that what Jack was trying to do? I thought I'd been perfectly clear with him the last time we spoke. "We were just discussing the finer points of a hypothetical Commerce Council replacing the Lord of Coin's sole control over economics in Galitha. You have personal experience running a shop."

"What about it?" I'd been here two minutes and already

Kristos was going to rope me into a political debate. He stared at me, prodding me silently to say more. To offer more evidence supporting his side, to prove yet again why the Laborers' League had the obligation to demand reform. To defend the protests the League organized. Thinking of the pamphlet Viola had shown me, I wondered—to justify violent action, too?

"Sophie." Kristos drummed the table with his fingers.

"Yes?" I lifted my eyebrows, innocent.

"What's that?" Jack interrupted, pointing to the ballad broadside I'd set on the table.

"It's just a song I bought," I answered.

Jack picked it up and started to read it, but Kristos wasn't done yet. "Sophie. I hoped you might actually enjoy, you know, talking about your shop," he cajoled. "Most people here don't have the experience you do."

I glanced around the table. All day laborers and League members, like Kristos. Most went to the university lectures with him. I could take a quick guess that they didn't much care about my unique experience beyond what they could glean for their own arguments.

"You'll be glad to know that the Council of Nobles is already entertaining a proposal for reform," I replied coolly.

Kristos snorted. "I already know. I read the published minutes of the council every week. It's too little, too late."

His scoffing stung—for once I thought I knew something about the workings of Galatine politics that he didn't.

"Perhaps you could consider accepting what the Council of Nobles is willing to give," I said.

"What they give us is only in their own interests." He dug into the interior pocket of his coat and produced a folded wad of paper. "Here—the minutes. Do you see this? They spent most of their meeting discussing appointing an overseer of curriculum for the public schools and expanding the schools' reach in the southern provinces."

"What's so terrible about that?" I almost laughed—the Galatine schools, available to any resident and providing education through age twelve, were generally regarded as a great advancement.

"You do realize why they even care about educating young Galatines, don't you?" Kristos snorted. "Their army—twenty years ago the provincial dialect was so different from the dialect the nobility speaks that the soldiers couldn't even understand their officers."

"So we've linguistically indoctrinated the populace." I recognized Niko Otni, the barge worker my brother had been so excited to pull into the fold of the Laborers' League. The academic vocabulary suited him awkwardly; he must have picked up the phrasing at one of the university lectures he attended with my brother.

I rolled my eyes. Even if they were right, the system had benefits beyond the martial. "Well, I know quite a few Pellian girls who are grateful to have had the opportunity to learn to speak—and write—standard Galatine."

Kristos ignored my argument. "You'll notice that these reforms—the ones the nobility has discussed—don't address conscription, which is one of our major complaints."

"Or the actual process of getting permits for new commerce," the man I recognized from the near riot in the queue at the Lord of Coin's office added. His name was Porter, I recalled.

"Not to mention representation," Niko said.

I scanned the minutes that Kristos had left on the table. Increased ratios of granted petitions—that wasn't a bad thing. Caps on marketplace taxes. Not the extreme measures of governmental reordering that the League wanted, but certainly beneficial to the common people they claimed to want to serve. "These all seem like decent concepts," I said, handing the paper back to Kristos.

Kristos wavered between pressing further, yelling, and ignoring me. He hadn't had too much to drink, I surmised, because he chose to ignore me and changed the subject. "Pyord Venko is confident that the demands will get the council's attention," he continued, speaking with the group gathered around him.

"And if it doesn't?" A heavyset man with an unusually red-blond beard replied. "I don't know that I've got much confidence in what some stuffy academic says about how the world works outside his library."

Niko raised an eyebrow. "Then we raise the stakes," he said. I clenched my jaw—Niko couldn't mean what he seemed to be saying.

Kristos glanced at him with a cool, steadying look. "We have our plans," he said. "Increased pamphlets and demonstrations. We'll get their attention."

Jack chimed in. "We're able to print far more now that Venko has secured us funding. Not everyone with money supports the nobility."

"And as we print more, it becomes harder to keep the people under the illusion that this is the only way to live," Kristos added. "We have money now for printing and for any other expenses, thanks to Venko."

"Who are you getting money from?" I whispered to Jack as my brother and Niko continued talking.

"This Venko—the professor?"

"He's not providing you much on a lecturer's salary."

"Not him—he's helped us learn how to raise our own money. Donations from merchants who aren't happy with the nobility. Plenty of the most successful trade vessels are owned by common people who have dug their way up—they want to see the common folks like them helped. Some foreign people, too—a Kvys banker, I think? And Fenian shipbuilders? Then—investing that money, too. Somewhere." It was clear Jack was on the periphery of this development, but what he told me was enough. I was shaken—this sounded more serious than the money needed to print on cheap pulp and buy red wool for caps.

"What is this money for?" I asked.

Jack shifted uncomfortably. "For now, just printing." I didn't press further, but the scheme didn't sit well with me. I thought of how money could purchase force in the form of weapons and even bribe soldiers.

The door slammed behind me, but the chill I felt wasn't from the cold draft that blew inside. This sounded like the groundwork for far more than pamphleteering and demonstrations. They couldn't be considering purchasing weapons, I chided myself. Could they? In the short months since summer, their focus had gone from talk to action, to organizing their numbers and securing funding. The inclusion of this Pyord Venko unsettled me—his influence seemed to provide a bridge between ideas and the potential for action.

"I'm stepping out for a moment," I said.

Jack followed me.

I sighed. "I'm all right, Jack. I don't need an escort."

"I know, Sophie. But look at this." He pressed a broadside into my hand. The print at the bottom was tight and almost difficult to read, as though they had condensed an entire pamphlet onto a single broadside sheet. But the top—the top was clear and printed in large letters. "We finished it. A formal copy sent to the council, and these distributed throughout the city."

"*Ten Demands of the Laborers' League.*" I traced the thick

black letters with my fingertip. The heavy printing press tiles had left indentations in the thick paper. *"Representation alongside the nobles. Abolition of the Lords of Coin, Keys, and Stones, to be replaced with Committees of Commerce, Safety, and Building, to be made up of common people."* I scanned further. *"No taxes levied without a vote in favor by the populace."* I laughed out loud. "These are impossible!"

Jack glowered. "It's not impossible if enough people fight for it."

I stopped, my face falling. "How are you going to force the nobility to grant these requests, Jack? Admit it—you can't."

"The nobility has had a stranglehold on the country long enough. We'll end the hold. We'll do what we have to do. Even...even if it comes to force."

I stared at Jack. "No, Jack. I know you all too well—you wouldn't. Too many people could be hurt, killed—"

"Too many people are living in enforced poverty not to act, even if it means bloodshed."

I looked back at the broadside—the words spooling out of Jack's mouth weren't his, I knew. He didn't speak that way. My brother did. The writers of these pamphlets did. Pretty words let people forget what bloodshed really looked like. I saw the printer's crest at the bottom of the broadside. It was the same as the seditious pamphlet Viola had shown me.

My hands shook as I handed the paper back. "I want nothing to do with that, Jack."

"I know you're worried about how you'd survive without the money from your shop. I—we'd be sure you were taken care of. You don't have to worry." His eyes widened, earnestly pleading without words.

Frustration boiled, catalyzed by fear. "I like my shop, Jack. I like my work, my life. It isn't only the money. I wouldn't want to lose what I've built." *I would lose who I am*, I thought, but I couldn't say it out loud.

"Well, I think that's—you're being selfish," Jack said, finally angry. "There are people who care about you, and you don't seem to care at all about them and what would make their lives better." I didn't know if he meant my brother and his thwarted goals, or if he meant himself and some half-baked idea of marriage. It didn't matter—he went back inside before I could reply, the door rattling behind him.

I slipped back inside and sat next to my brother, annoyed and angry with myself even though it was hardly my fault that Jack had continued to press me. Kristos chose that moment to glance at my face and the empty seat Jack had left. He raised an eyebrow to match mine. "You want another drink, Sophie?"

I considered telling him what I was thinking, that I had sacrificed any prospect of marriage or children in favor of my shop, that this decision supported our small family, that the actions of the League threatened my livelihood and could render that sacrifice for naught, that marrying one of his League friends would never change that. I didn't. "I don't care for ale," I said instead.

"Hey! Barkeep!" A blond barmaid hustled over. "Bring my sister a glass of red wine," he said.

"You remember I like it?"

"Of course. Hey." He hugged me around the shoulders. "Chin up. We're going to have a good night, all right?"

7

THE LATE NIGHT AT THE TAVERN AND THE CONVERSATION WITH
Jack didn't make for a good mood the following morning. Neither did the mess at home, which Kristos had added to when he
left for work. I nudged dirty stockings off the bread trencher with
an exaggerated gag no one was there to see. Kristos had also left
another pamphlet on the table. I brushed it aside, annoyed. He
was as close to an adult as I expected him to get; couldn't he clean
up after himself? Unless, of course, he left the little book there
hoping I would see it. Not unlikely, I admitted, as I picked up
the thread-bound paper. Freshly printed, freshly bound. It still
smelled of ink, the now-familiar printing house crest decorating
the title page. I turned the pamphlet over in my hands.

"*Vindication of the Laboring Class: A Primer of Rights*," I read.
I rolled my eyes—adding fancy words to Kristos's rants didn't
make them any more appealing, especially after listening to a
solid two hours of them the night before. I glanced at the rest of
the cover. *In which we attempt to explain the artificial divisions between
classes and illustrate the benefits of removing legal division, creating a
democratic government, and providing for laborers' rights. By K. B.*

Those were Kristos's initials. I set the booklet down with
a trembling hand. The ink had stained my fingers. I knew he

was reading the pieces, that the League was producing them, but Kristos was writing them? I didn't dare read the rest of what the booklet said—the cover was damning enough. This wasn't an educational primer. Vindication—this was potential treason. Kristos was not only promoting active anti-monarchism; his name was on a treasonous paper. This was worse than any of the activities he'd undertaken already—organizing meetings, contacting different groups of workers, dragging hordes of League members to lectures, selecting motifs like the caps. Those had all been ephemeral, talk in moments passing quickly. This was permanent, and he could be held accountable.

I couldn't stay at home, waiting for Kristos to roll out of bed to talk to him, and I wasn't sure I wanted to. He hadn't told me he was putting his name on treason, probably with good intentions. Not only did he know exactly how I would react, he must have understood that affiliating with his dangerous thoughts wasn't exactly safe for me. The less I knew, the better.

I almost appreciated his thoughtful protectiveness.

Still, my mood hadn't improved by the time I got to work.

"Penny, these ruffles are a mess," I said without meaning to sound as harsh as I did.

Penny flushed and took the sleeve ruffles she had made back from me. The hems were too wide and the gathers were uneven—work I knew she could do well.

"What happened?" I asked, more gently this time.

"I don't know," Penny snapped, cross. She softened. "I'm sorry. I think I was distracted."

"Well, we can't have you distracted this week. We have a full slate of orders, plus we need to work on that court gown." I watched Penny. After the scolding I'd given her, she could use some confidence. "I had wanted you to take the lead on beading the court gown. Can you do that?"

She brightened. "Of course!" And I knew she could—when Penny focused, her work was not only meticulous but had a creative flair.

She bustled off to rework the ruffles while Alice fiddled with the sheer layers of an ornate cap. I pulled a bolt of midweight linen from a high shelf and, with only my measuring stick and my memory, cut three sets of underthings for Lady Viola.

"We don't use that weight of linen very much," Alice said, gesturing to the bolt of nearly sheer fabric. She was right—though most of us wore simple linen shifts under our corsets and clothes, our shop didn't have a habit of making very many of them. We made the complicated clothing people couldn't sew by themselves; any idiot with a needle and thread and some practice could make a shift.

"Lady Snowmont had a clever idea," I answered. "Charmed underthings."

"That was all she wanted?" Alice replied, clearly disappointed.

"She also wanted a gown." I folded the linen carefully. I knew that the simple shifts should take priority, but a gown for a noble like Viola Snowmont would infuse the atelier with a bit of liveliness to combat the dreary rain and slowing orders that late autumn brought us. "I'll start on sketches this afternoon. She wants pink—get me a swatch of every pink silk we have with enough on the bolt left for a gown."

Alice complied, and Penny was still busy with her ruffles.

I stitched for most of the morning in my screened corner, then emerged, prodded by the list of receipts and invoices I'd remembered I had to tally. Alice was adding a finishing ribbon to the cap she'd been working on, but Penny was gone.

"Where's Penny?" I asked.

Alice looked up. "She must have gone outside for lunch—she

said she was going to step out for a midday break, since it's warm again."

It was unseasonably warm. But it wasn't lunchtime yet, and the stack of invoices I'd asked Penny to sort sat untouched on the counter. I sighed. Distracted, indeed.

I stepped out onto the little stone landing and glanced around. No Penny.

But I heard a distinctive giggle coming from the alley between my shop and the next.

I pursed my lips. Was there any way to avoid barging in on Penny and her apparent tryst mate without sounding like a scolding fishwife? Probably not, I acknowledged. But I couldn't tolerate inattention to work.

"Penny!" I called in my most authoritative voice, striding into the alley. "You are absent from work without permission." As I spoke, I saw her face clearly, snuggled on the shoulder of a tall man with clubbed dark hair. "And I absolutely cannot tolerate canoodling on company time—oooh!"

Penny's gentleman friend had turned around.

"Kristos! You rake!"

"Canoodling? Are you eighty, Sophie?" Kristos laughed, and I was seeing red. "Canoodling! That's rich!"

"Penny," I said through clenched teeth, "get inside and begin sorting the invoices that you were supposed to complete this morning."

She probably muttered something like "Yes, mistress," but I was too focused to hear. As soon as I heard the door click on its latch, I turned on Kristos.

"What in the world are you thinking?"

Kristos shrugged. "It's not really any of your business whom your employees 'canoodle' with."

"It is when they are shirking work to do so," I replied.

"Besides. One of the best employees I've had. You know I have a hard time keeping good help—they find other work. Ellie, Greta, Florence—all in the past two years."

Kristos's ears were growing red, and he had a markedly awkward expression spreading over his face.

"You! You didn't! You—you fooled around with my employees! That's why they...oh, I am going to skin you alive in your sleep!"

"I think I'll wake up for that," Kristos said. "Yes, I may have...dabbled with Ellie and Greta. Not Florence. She was too short for my taste."

"Is that why they left my shop? Because you broke their little hearts? You cad!"

"Hey! Hey, now. No, I didn't do any heartbreaking. Maybe Ellie took things a little too seriously at first, but no—it was all in fun and they had fun, too. They left because it was time to add another shop to their reference list."

"Fine." I huffed. "But Penny—she's so young!"

"She's sixteen. Old enough to make her own choices." He raised an eyebrow at me. "Old enough to get married if she wanted, legally speaking."

"Oh, lovely. You must have talked to Jack."

"It's to your credit that he said it was the kindest outright rejection he's ever gotten." Kristos ran a hand through his disheveled hair. "Sophie, why? How many options do you really have left?"

"Options—who said I was looking for options?"

"Anyone with any sense. I'm worried about you. You're twenty-seven—"

"I'm twenty-six."

"Twenty-six. Who are you waiting for, anyway? Are you going to put off getting married forever?"

"That's the plan," I retorted, but his words stung. I wasn't waiting for anyone. I didn't think that highly of myself. "I won't lose my shop to a husband. Or his family. Or anything at all." Did any of his pamphlets, with their academic language and fancy typesetting, consider the rights of women? I doubted it, a fresh ember of anger glowing in my chest.

"It's just—if anything happened to me, I wouldn't want you to be all alone."

"If you like marriage so much, quit fooling around with the pretty girls I employ and get married yourself."

"I'm not just fooling around." Kristos's face had softened into something honest, approachable. His usual smirk and swagger gone.

"You're not?"

"I really like this one." He cleared his throat. "Penny's a fine girl."

"She is." I wavered, feeling lost. She was so young—but no younger than plenty of Galatine girls when they married. After all, she could legally sign my annual employment tenure. And, I recalled with a smile, I had been convinced of my own maturity at sixteen. Penny was certainly convinced of hers. "Just don't come around when she's not on break. She gets distracted easily, and we have too much work for that. Fair enough?"

"Fair," Kristos said with a grin. "I'm getting too busy for dropping by on her during the day anyway."

"With work?" I asked pointedly. Clearly he hadn't made an effort to get work today.

"Don't start in. There's a big construction job starting tomorrow, and I've got it on good authority from the masons that they'll hire me to tote bricks. No, I've been busy with the League. I've got that big demonstration planned tomorrow." He looked at me hopefully.

"You planned a demonstration?" Kristos could barely plan breakfast.

"Not by myself, no," he said. "Niko got the word out and Jack helped. And Venko—he can see the whole picture of a thing, like he's looking at it from the top down. He says I've got a gift for motivating everyone to follow it."

"Kristos, I can't protest with you all. My reputation—"

"Is important, I know. I won't ask you to march around holding a sign. No, just come see us. See how serious we are. How many people we have on our side."

I couldn't deny him that. "Wear your cap," I told him.

He grinned. "You got it. And that's another thing—that professor, Venko, he wants to meet you. I told him about the caps."

"What does he care about a charm-casting seamstress?" I laughed.

"He studies it, Sophie. Studies magic."

"No one studies magic," I scoffed. "It's—it's like saying someone studies brickmaking or does research in the nuances of mud puddles."

"He does. He's—really, Sophie. A genius. And I kind of told him I'd bring you by this afternoon."

"Kristos! First you distract Penny half the morning, and we have a full slate of orders, and I'm behind on drafting the pattern for the caraco jacket Mrs. Norris ordered, and she'll be in tomorrow for a fitting, and—"

"And I'm sure you'll finish all those things in plenty of time, like you always do. I know as well as you do that you build in about a week of extra time on every order you take." I flushed—he was right, but it was smart practice to count on delays. "Professor Venko really wanted to meet you, and I don't want to disappoint him. Now, how about a sausage on a stick for lunch? I'll buy. There's this vendor who grills them up with onions—it's perfect."

I sighed, but I let Kristos drag me down the street.

8

—ᴍ—

I HAD LIVED IN THE CITY FOR OVER A DECADE, BUT I HAD NEVER been inside the university grounds. I had no reason to go there. Nothing taught at the university—philosophy, science, theology—interested me, and none of those disciplines took any interest in people like me. Seamstresses apprenticed or took a string of assistant jobs to learn the skills they needed, and charm casters learned from their family—usually their mothers. The former was a respected trade that could bump one into the middle-class ranks of shop owners, the latter an archaic cottage industry typically shunned by all but the Pellian immigrants who bargained for charms alongside the sesame oil, bright spicy peppers, and poppy seeds that flavored their favorite dishes. Universities were for another kind of learning, theories and mathematics and sciences with little practical application that I could imagine.

Kristos should have been a scholar, I admitted, and a more open system might have allowed him. The same eloquence and investment that fed his fiery arguments in the taverns could have made him an excellent lecturer; the single-minded dedication that made him a leader in the League would have served him well in research and scholarship. He would never have made a good business owner, I guessed; he didn't have the right kind of plodding steadiness.

Kristos tugged my arm, impatient for me to finish my sausage on a stick. It was good, as he had promised, the onion flavors lingering on the sausage's blistered skin. "I'm trying to enjoy my meal, not wolf it down like a mongrel dog. We don't have to eat like street urchins, ready to run away from the trash bin when they're caught." *Anymore*, I added silently, thinking of the particularly difficult winter after Mother had died.

"We'll be late," he said, glancing at the clock tower in the Stone Castle, just visible over a row of tiled rooftops.

"I wasn't aware we were on a strict schedule," I replied, nudging the last of my sausage off the stick.

"He's lecturing later."

"Then why—" I let it drop. No matter. At least I would make it back to the shop in time to get some work done if this Professor Venko didn't intend to keep me all afternoon. "Venko—is he Kvys? That name sounds Kvys." I didn't know many people from the country across our northern border—by all accounts their isolated location behind stoic mountain ranges had made for a closed, heavily religious culture. Few Kvys, aside from diplomats from their patrician families and delegates from their country's complicated trade guilds, lived in Galitha. Common Kvys people didn't tend to uproot and move to Galitha; there was no Kvys neighborhood in the city like the Pellian quarter. And they were distrustful of, and often outright hostile to, charms.

"I think by parentage, yes. But he's lived in Galitha City most of his life. He's not some stodgy Kvys monk. He doesn't even have an accent," Kristos added, as though that explained everything. "Are you done? Finally."

I let him take the lead as we walked through the tall limestone gates of the university. The first university had burned down a century ago, and the new buildings had all been in creamy white limestone. Half the books in the collection were now housed in the archive near Fountain Square at the city's center, so that a fire couldn't destroy all of the university's books ever again.

It may have been born out of disaster, but the university looked like a beautiful white city. The buildings were in a mock-antiquated style in homage to the ancient universities of Serafe, but undersize and planted in neat arrangements by subject area, interspersed with garden beds and manicured trees. Reliefs on the buildings indicated their purpose—a tree of life sprouting with animals of all forms must have been for biology, and I smiled at the beautiful scrollwork at the top of one building with what I recognized were the names of famous philosophers.

"This is us," Kristos said, steering me away from the broad main avenue into a path of crushed shells leading to another set of buildings. "Humanities," Kristos explained.

"Well, I didn't expect the magicians to study at the physics building, I suppose."

"He's not a magician," Kristos sighed. "And he doesn't study only magic. Officially, he's an antiquarian."

"A what?"

"Antiquity. Ancient languages and cultures. Including," Kristos said, pushing open the gate of a boxwood-ringed garden, "ancient Pellia."

If I was supposed to be impressed that people studied the storied history of our homeland, I wasn't. I wasn't truly Pellian, even if my dark golden skin and tall build marked me as such to Galatines. I had never seen Pellia; I didn't speak the language. The only thing Pellian about me was charm casting. Which, I figured, explained this professor's interest in charms—if he studied ancient Pellia, maybe they cropped up as far back as ancient times. In that case, he'd be better off asking an actual Pellian person about them, not me.

"Kristos!" A tall man dressed in an unobtrusive but pristinely tailored black suit rose to greet us. He looked like I'd imagined nobility would when I was a child, distant and imperious, with serious blue eyes and a long, straight nose, and a way of regarding me that made me feel instantly smaller. "This must be your sister. I am Pyord Venko, professor of antiquities. And I have quite an interest in your abilities."

Kristos was right—no accent, and he looked more Galatine than Kristos or I did, but still had the broad cheekbones and icy pale eyes that Kvyset's people were known for. Perhaps it was the coldness of his eyes, or the chilly near-winter breeze through the garden, but I shivered in my cloak.

"I'm terribly sorry," he said, apparently noticing the tremor of my shoulders, "but I'm only a lowly lecturer, and we must share offices. This is the sort of conversation I prefer to keep quiet."

I pursed my lips. Kristos made it sound as though this man's interest was professional, but was he about to rope me into a conversation about protests or revolution? Or worse, rope me into doing more than sew a few charmed caps for the cause?

I considered making my excuses then and leaving, but Kristos nudged me forward. "We understand completely. Don't we, Sophie? You always keep mum about what your clients use your, you know, *services* for."

I flushed red and swallowed, now grateful for the privacy of the garden. I glared at him, hoping my message—*I'm not a prostitute, idiot*—translated.

"And for similar reasons, I don't discuss this with or in front of my colleagues. At least, not anymore." He sighed. "I'm sure I don't need to tell you that charm casting is not a respected art, Miss Balstrade. No offense meant, of course."

"None taken." I sat down at his invitation on a bench facing him. "I've managed to infuse the practice with a bit more cachet. It's how I make my living. But I certainly didn't expect anyone at the university to show an interest."

"Nor should you. They're all—they don't recognize what I've discovered. Well, I should rephrase—what I've realized Pellian charm casters like you discovered centuries ago."

"There's not much to it," I demurred. He seemed so eager, icy excitement glinting in his eyes. I didn't want to disappoint him. "It's just good luck charms, not fairy-tale magic where you can conjure something out of thin air or turn things into gold."

"Yes, good luck charms. And curses," he added. He must have seen the look on my face, because he left that subject alone. "I believe there may be more. I believe the ancient Pellians found the beginnings of much more than simple charms."

"Then why didn't they develop it?" I asked. Despite myself, I was a little intrigued. "Pellia is—well, you know as well as I do what everyone sees Pellia as. A backwater. If they were hiding some great magical knowledge, it seems they'd be wise to deploy that at some point."

"Not loyal to the mother country, I see." He chuckled, and I bristled. "It's all right—I'm not a loyal Kvys citizen, either. I said they began to develop the study of magic. The cycle of seven-year droughts, followed by the invasion by the Equatorial States—they were one united archipelago then, and they had just discovered black powder—the writings on magic stop after that. They stopped studying it because they were starving. And it hasn't been developed since."

"Very interesting," I said. I wasn't sure what to make of him.

"I presume you learned from your mother?" he asked abruptly.

"Yes," I replied. "Most of us do."

"The sewing, as well? That is, did she teach you to embed charms in sewing?"

"Yes, but I combined it with actual clothing construction on my own. I used to make thread buttons to sell, and I practiced charm casting on them, and one thing led to another. By the time I was apprenticed with a seamstress, I realized I could put a charm into anything I sewed and started making some extra money on the novelty of it."

"Fascinating," Professor Venko said, and I knew he didn't mean my business model. "That indicates a plasticity in the charm-casting skill that I haven't yet seen in practice. Fascinating. Would you—that is, could you—demonstrate?"

I blushed. Charm casting was something I did in private, not a performance art. I had my housewife in my pocket, stuffed with thread and needles and scissors and my favorite sweet-scented beeswax for waxing the thread. Reluctantly, I pulled it out.

"I don't have any fabric," I said, hoping for an out.

"Take this," he said, pulling a handkerchief from his coat pocket. I hesitated. Kristos nodded, encouraging.

I threaded my needle, hands shaking a little bit. I hated being watched when I sewed; occupying the center of attention was uncomfortable anytime, but especially when I was plying my trade. I tacked the thread with a few anchoring stiches, then began to charm cast, as discreetly as possible, drawing in the subtle glimmer of light from around my hands into a few inches of backstitched good luck. I snipped the end of the thread and handed it back to Professor Venko.

"That's it?"

"Well, if it were a commission, I'd stitch the whole thing in charmed stitches."

"No, I meant the process. No chanting, no incantations, just the sewing."

"Yes. Mother said the chanting can help some casters

concentrate, but she thought it was better to learn to work without it. I agree."

"Fascinating. Just fascinating."

"If you don't mind me asking—Kvyset isn't known for charm casters," I said, hoping the question wasn't as rude as it sounded.

He shook his head. "Indeed not. It's illegal, of course, in Kvyset. The Church forbids its use, and the Church is, quite nearly, the state." Kristos nodded, more attuned to differences in political systems than I was. I knew that religion in Kvyset was far more influential than in Galitha, where the local parishes, even the great cathedral in Fountain Square, devoted to the vague concept of the Galatine Divine, were more civic centers than powerful seats of religion.

"I came to Galitha City as a youth, with my family. I had never encountered charms before, but one day wandered through the Pellian district and saw the women hawking their wares. As luck would have it, I'd just started studying ancient Pellian and found theoretical treatises on the subject in the ancient works. The theory—it was incredible, truly, that it had not been more fully explored. I believe a more complete understanding of Pellian magical theory would in fact change our conception of their religious and political views."

"Professor Venko is working on a full translation of Pellian theoretical texts," Kristos interjected.

"A luxury I am granted here." He turned to me. "When my family returned to Kvyset, I tried to continue my studies of Pellian, but Kvys universities are truly nothing more than theological seminaries. I was entirely unable to continue and, it might be noted, blacklisted among my peers for my interests." A shadow crossed his eyes, making him seem suddenly volatile. "Kvyset is academically stagnant," he added, "so I came here, even if the university system favors the nobility so that I cannot advance beyond my position now. I can't even petition for entrance for very promising students," he said with a glance at Kristos.

"Well, even those of us who can't attend the university are grateful for the open lectures," Kristos said, ears reddening. "He started them and even got some of his colleagues to give guest lectures, too. Sophie, you should come sometime. Maybe Professor Venko will lecture on charm casting," he joked.

"A topic which even my most indulgent colleagues would likely find undignified to provide in open lecture to the public." Venko laughed. "I'm afraid, given our increased investment in the League's activities, that the open lectures will have to cease for now."

Kristos nodded. "You've done so much already," he said in a tone that expressed what I gauged as disproportionate gratitude for a few free lectures. He wasn't, I realized, discussing the lectures any longer, but Venko's participation in the League.

Venko leaned toward Kristos, adopting a confidential tone. "Many of my colleagues are unduly loyal to the nobility, even those who are not of noble lines themselves. They've become... uncomfortable with the number of red caps they see in the audiences. They've refused to continue participation, and it's best if I don't set myself apart by doing so alone."

A heavy bell tolled across the university grounds. "I have to be in my lecture hall in fifteen minutes," he said. "Tell me, Miss Balstrade. You stitched caps for your brother and his comrades, didn't you?"

"I did," I replied. I wasn't sure where he was going. There was an eagerness to his eyes that I didn't like.

"For which they and I and everyone in this movement are already grateful." He was pouring it on thick. "Would you ever consider doing a bit more work for us?"

I hesitated. "I told Kristos I would stitch more caps," I said, noncommittal.

"Very good, yes, and we thank you. I was thinking of something a bit more—direct. And potentially intricate. It would test some of the theories in the ancient Pellian texts."

"I'm afraid I can't accommodate any more work at the present," I replied crisply. I would make charms to protect my brother and his friends. I didn't want to see them hurt. But I wouldn't involve myself any further. "I'm sure you can appreciate my position, managing a business that is our family's primary income."

Pyord Venko's eyes narrowed briefly, like a cloud skidding across the sun, but he recovered. "Of course. I understand." He rose, and bowed in formal farewell. "Kristos, thank you ever so much for allowing me to meet your lovely sister."

We said our farewells, and Kristos looked faintly conflicted as we passed between the tall white gates. "Is something the matter?" I asked.

"I just—I know you're busy. And I know this movement doesn't inspire you the way it does me, though I don't know why." He ran his fingers through his thick, dark hair. Pellian hair, black and glossy and full of waves, like mine. "But damn, Sophie. You have a gift. I wish—I just wish you'd use it for the greater good, you know?"

My first impulse was to argue with him, but it wouldn't help. In the thin golden light of the wintry afternoon, he looked so desperate and earnest, strange and foreign to me, valiant and brave like a hero in a fairy tale. I couldn't take that away from him. Instead, I slipped my arm through his and leaned my head on his shoulder. "I know, Kristos. I know."

9

———

"WE HAD TWO NEW ORDERS WHILE YOU WERE GONE YESTERDAY," Alice said as I scanned the slate with our schedule. "Recognize any names?"

"A charmed mantelet for Sanna...Eastlake? As in, the Lady Eastlake?"

"The very same," Alice said with a smile. The Eastlakes were not a major house of nobility, but rumor had it that Lord Eastlake and his wife, a Serafan minor princess, were rising in status, the lord favored by the king for appointment to the office of the Lord of Stone when old Lord Suthermount retired from the position. "And a merchant's daughter with a love-charmed ball gown."

"A ball gown—that will be quite a bit of work. Is she returning for a consultation?"

"Of course," Alice said. "She already said she wanted green, so I made a swatch set for you." She paused. "I hope that's all right."

I was impressed with Alice's forethought and initiative. "Yes, thank you—that is, if she can wear green. Not everyone can." I laughed, giddy at the nearly full slate of orders.

"She can," Alice replied, confident. "And Penny will be late."

I raised an eyebrow. "I hope she had a good reason," I said

before I could stop myself, hoping Kristos didn't have anything
to do with her tardiness.

Alice shrugged her rounded shoulders. "She said her mother
needed something," she replied, evasive.

"But you don't think so?" I pressed.

Alice pursed her lips. "I don't want to gossip. But she and her
mother had a falling-out." She cleared her throat. "Over Kristos."

To my credit as a sister, I felt immediately defensive for my
brother. "Well," I said, keeping my voice level, "plenty of Galatines don't prefer their children getting involved with Pellians."

Alice cocked her head. "I don't think it's that," she said. "I
mean, yes, plenty avoid the Pellian quarter, but you're not—"
She flushed and moved to the other side of the counter, tidying
stacks of papers. "No, it's the Laborers' League. She doesn't want
Penny tied up with that."

"Of course," I said. For the same reasons, I imagined, that I
didn't want to be tied up in it.

"I'm sorry; I didn't mean anything by it." The red in her
broad face intensified. "It's not that there's anything wrong with
the Pellian quarter," she added.

"Nothing to apologize for, Alice." My hands hesitated over
an order to be wrapped. "You said I'm not—I'm not what?"

She bit her lip. "I don't suppose I think of you as Pellian. In
the same way as the Pellian quarter."

I nodded. This was not exactly surprising and, if anything,
was the image I had curated of myself. A high-end Galatine
seamstress, not a Pellian market woman. Still, it made me a little uncomfortable. "What do you think of as Pellian?" I asked,
curious.

"I suppose I think they keep to themselves, dress a little
differently, wear kerchiefs instead of caps." She shrugged. "I
don't need anything from the Pellian quarter and they don't

need anything from me, so I don't see much of them." Alice's pragmatism was one of her strongest and best traits, I reminded myself with a small smile, but her outlook seemed to be common enough—Pellians were the people who kept to themselves, spoke a different language, and thought spinach pie was a perfectly good dinner. Kristos and I seemed to be part of a different group, more like the children of provincial Galatines who moved to the city—perhaps not native, but acclimated.

I left Alice with a list of tasks and set off to see Kristos's demonstration, as I had promised. Fountain Square was quiet, but I wasn't surprised as I walked across the wide plaza. Fridays were market days, many mornings and evenings saw services honoring the Galatine Natures at the cathedral, and plenty of days in between saw the square play host to entertainment, small fairs, and specialty markets. I always came for the Silk Fair, when merchants from around Galitha and beyond brought the finest silks and specialty cottons and wools—fabrics I couldn't buy even at Galitha City's best drapers most of the year.

I always managed to buy a few bolts of silk that no one else did, too. By my second year perusing the stalls, word had circulated that I was not just any seamstress. The Serafan silk merchants thought I was a sorceress like those of their royal court, and treated me with deference and respect. A family of Kvys wool weavers called me a witch behind their hands and prayed to their preferred saints when I passed. One wisp-thin woman from the mountains who ran a workshop stamping the finest-quality cottons was convinced I was a fairy. Accordingly, some merchants refused to do business with me, but others offered me, in tentative, hushed tones, enticing deals. Their best fabrics, usually reserved for direct sale to the queen's house. A full bolt for the cost of half. First pick of their private stock.

I quickly selected the merchants whose stock was unique,

beautiful, and of the highest quality, and struck deals with them. One wanted a health charm for her rheumatism, another a love charm for his shy daughter. For many, trade throughout Galitha was the only access to charms they had, and many had not encountered the Pellians, who had little use for fine silks and expensive cottons, in other Galatine cities who could have cast for them. Plenty of countries did not allow casting, whether they believed in charms or not—the concept went against religious or moral codes. On the hard-bitten, cold island of Fen, magic, even illusion and card tricks, was illegal, and I'd never even heard of a caster from Kvyset, where they said the only thing deeper than the nation's faith in their saints was the snowdrifts in winter. I was happy to fulfill merchants' requests, working through the night to have kerchiefs and caps and shawls complete before they packed their stalls and departed.

When the charms worked, I had permanent allies at the fair.

It was still months until the next Silk Fair, I was reminded by the cold expanse of cobblestones. A few people bustled through, hurrying from the docks to the shops, from the mills on the west side of the city and the docks by the river to their homes on the east. Hardly anyone loitered in the square today.

Hardly anyone, save a knot of people in front of the church, waving banners. And wearing red hats.

Kristos's protest. I hovered beside the huge bronze fountain in the center of the square, debating whether to acknowledge Kristos with a tacit hello or to simply go home. He had insisted I see his demonstration, and I had obliged. Even if I wasn't participating, I didn't want to be seen. Yet I knew that ignoring him would upset him—he wanted to make me a true participant in his crusade. Didn't he realize that our livelihood depended very much on my staying in the good graces of nobles—the very nobles he was probably shouting about at passersby right now?

With a rueful laugh I thought of Lady Viola's friends dis-cussing Melchoir in the salon. Kristos would never believe that noble ladies could give a second thought to the same issues he was arguing.

I watched a few moments longer, inspecting the scene as though it were a garment I could mentally deconstruct and draft a pattern from. A woman in a brown cloak distributed broad-sides to passersby, whether they wanted them or not. I recog-nized her from the Hazel Dell—the laundress with the ruddy face, her scarred hands pressing broadsides into the small crowd that began to coalesce around the members of the League.

The laundress had clearly not convinced many of her com-patriots to join her. A half dozen women joined the dozens of men present. Two, the tall Pellian girl included, carried home-made banners and waved them at the people passing through the square. The rest of the group was, I admitted, larger than I had anticipated. They were all clearly laborers: young, barrel-chested men and older men carrying years of work on bent backs; natives to the city; northern Galatine provincials with straw-blond hair; southern provincials with nut-brown eyes and hair; Pellians; and one man who might have been Kvys. It was as though a cyclone had whipped through the warehouses and docks of Galitha City, picked up whatever workers it could snatch, and dumped them here. Nearly half wore the red caps like the ones I had made at Kristos's request; a flash of golden glimmer in the seam of one cap, worn by a man I didn't know, confirmed that, as Kristos had said, they would be distributed randomly among the dem-onstrators. Even without the caps, they looked as though they had a uniform: patched and roughspun clothing, eschewing any attempt to wear "market best" clothing and sticking to the can-vas trousers and woolen jackets meant for work.

The only exception was a man in pristine black, standing at

the back of the crowd, speaking quietly to Niko. Pyord Venko, I realized with a start, looking almost comically out of place next to so much roughspun. His conversation with Niko seemed almost like a shop owner directing assistants. The only thing that looked like a podium, a rickety stack of crates meant to imitate a stage, was already occupied.

By my brother.

"For pity's sake," I muttered. He was standing on a crate, gesturing exuberantly and speaking words that were whipped away by the wind before they reached me. I rolled my eyes. He looked like one of the preachers who sometimes set up a box at the edge of the square on market days—vehement, passionate, and, I thought, absurd.

Then I saw the soldiers.

They entered the square from the little side street that ran beside the church. A mousy woman in faded green pointed from the corner, and even though I thought my brother and his friends were behaving like idiots, I hated her more than I'd hated anyone in my life at that moment. She'd complained. She'd brought the soldiers into this—and like as not they'd end up making arrests. I imagined my brother spending the night in a cell in the gaol block of the Stone Castle, and I shivered.

Despite the fact that I had no idea what to do or say, I took off across the square.

Kristos saw me before he saw the soldiers, probably because their ranks of pale blue coats hadn't yet emerged from the shadows between the tall buildings, and I was as brightly colored as a parrot in my cloak and gloves. He waved and, to my relief, stepped down from the box.

"Sophie!" He gestured with wide, excited arms. "Isn't this grand? We've handed out over a hundred pamphlets and—"

He stopped speaking as soon as he saw the soldiers. Their

captain spoke to a squirrely-looking protester who had been waving a large misspelled sign.

I heard his voice rise, an argument brewing over a necessary assembly permit. Of course—the office of the Lord of Stones would have to approve any assembly in the city. I was fairly sure Kristos and his subalterns hadn't applied for one. In fact, I was fairly sure that they had deliberately avoided doing so, knowing full well that their coalition of Red Caps speaking against the nobility would be denied.

"Without the permit," the soldier captain intoned, "you will have to disband immediately." With that, he grabbed the sign nearest him and cracked the wooden stake it was mounted on across his knee. I flushed—there was no need for anger, not now. Kristos and his comrades would leave, I was sure of it.

The soldiers held their ranks, and then, as though moving slowly, against an ocean wave, they formed a line, muskets at the ready. Their faces were resolute, impassive. The crowd behind me hadn't wavered, I realized, and even now pushed forward slightly. I was caught in the swell like a fish in the ocean foam, unable to swim opposite the current.

"What's the idea?" someone with a gravelly voice shouted. I was forced forward as the crowd of protesters surged toward the soldiers. Any objection I voiced came out as a mere squeak, and I realized that the burly man and the stocky woman next to me had picked up loose bricks. I saw Jack trying to convince those nearest him to put down their bricks and signs, while Niko shouted back at the captain. Pyord Venko was nowhere to be seen.

I pressed against the throng around me, trying to disentangle myself from them. I had to find Kristos. With him, I was safe—and with me, so was he.

He had already scrambled up on the box platform again. My

throat tightened—no. He was making a spectacle of himself, a target.

"Please," he called, his voice incredibly steady, "do not answer this challenge with violence! We must practice peaceful methods if we're to convince anyone—"

A brick flew from the crowd pressing against me and struck one of the soldiers in the head. He dropped to the ground like a sack of flour. I heard screaming, and realized it was me.

"Stop!" I yelled, begging now, begging for anyone to hear.

"Stop." The same word I had cried, but echoed in icy control by the captain.

The throng around me only yelled louder.

And then the captain had the soldier nearest him raise his musket and aim.

Right at Kristos.

My breath stalled. My mind stopped processing anything but that musket and Kristos's exposed body; I would have sworn that even my heart stopped. The crowd around me was silenced.

Kristos didn't move, but it was determination, not fear, that spread over his face. He squared his shoulders.

The soldier squeezed the trigger.

Nothing.

The crowd ran, dispersing in all directions as the soldier picked at the lock of his musket, which, in the cool damp, had misfired. I dropped to my knees, strangled noises like a kitten's sobs escaping my lips.

The captain gestured, once, and the soldiers marched out of the square. Someone helped the soldier who had been struck with the brick to his feet, and they staggered after the crisply uniform line. Kristos jumped from the platform and gathered me in his arms.

"Let me take you home" was all he said.

10

"You were wearing the cap, weren't you?" The firelight
played on the wall, and a bird outside the window sang a merry
tune, but I wasn't in a laughing mood. My brother almost died—
I almost watched someone shoot him. My hands felt like lead in
my lap, and I couldn't quite erase the image that wormed its way
into my thoughts, of Kristos with a bullet wound in his chest,
pouring blood onto his white shirt.

"Yes," he said.

"At least—thank you," I whispered.

"It was supposed to be by lottery," he added, and I snapped
to attention.

"I told you to wear it," I said, an edge in my voice. "You.
Because I made it for you."

"It didn't seem fair. We had enough for only a few of us. It
didn't seem fair," he said again.

"I don't care about fair!" I shouted, suddenly enraged. He
would put himself in danger and not even show me the courtesy
of doing the one thing, the one simple thing, that could help
him avoid harm? "I made the caps so you could stay safe, not
because I give a whit about your cause or that rabble out there."
While he envisioned grandiose schemes and waves of change, all

I could picture was his unprotected figure on the square. He was the only family I had left, and if he died...I shuddered. I didn't know what I would do.

Kristos had already latched onto a new argument, however. "Rabble. They're rabble to you."

"They were willing to let you get shot," I said, voice low but simmering. "They weren't going to help you. And they weren't behaving in a very dignified manner, shouting in the streets. So yes. I would call them rabble."

Kristos pushed his arms close against his chest, folded as though pressing whatever he wanted to say back in. I breathed slowly. I'd always known that my charms worked—I'd seen them work. I'd seen people struggling to pay their bills come into small fortunes. I'd seen people ignored by their sweethearts married within the year. I'd seen people who couldn't get work to save their lives employed after a luck charm.

I had never watched a musket misfire, watched one of my charms cripple a weapon intended to kill the person wearing it.

"Please stay out of trouble," I whispered. Dusk had gathered in the corners of our little kitchen, darkness a welcome mask to a pair of faces that didn't want to fight but didn't want to let this go, either. "The soldiers aren't going anywhere. You can't stand up against that with words—or bricks," I half spat.

"I can't abandon this, Sophie. Not now."

"You could go about it differently. Am I the only one who thinks this is getting out of hand? That it's getting dangerous?"

"It's getting serious," Kristos countered. "We have real plans now, real organization. Venko says—"

"Oh yes, Venko. What was he doing for your glorious cause today, anyway? He could have spoken to the officer, I'm sure. They would listen to a university professor, wouldn't they? But he just...disappeared."

Kristos flared again. "He has to protect himself, too. He's able to help us from his position. Because of it. If he loses his position at the university, he couldn't do as much for us."

"What exactly is he doing for you? He seems to—I don't know, direct you all somehow. I thought the League was for workers."

"He doesn't direct us," Kristos shot back, and I knew I'd scraped against a sore point. Venko was asserting himself as a leader, in ways Kristos didn't necessarily appreciate. "He's a good planner, good at seeing the flaws and the benefits in any plan. And he's funded us."

"He taught you how to ask for money. You could have learned on your own."

"None of us knew how to invest money. How to invest it so that we're not at risk ourselves, not tied to it personally."

"Well, that just sounds illegal."

"It's not illegal," he snapped. "It's just using opportunity, the way entrepreneurs and speculators do. And he has connections. With merchants. With Kvys patrician families."

I pounced on this, ready to demand answers. "Kvys are funneling you money? Why?" For some reason this disquieted me more than Galatine merchants casting a lot in with the Red Caps. What interest could foreigners have in the Red Caps' aims?

"And some Fenians. They're funding the printing of new ideas, of applied political theory, of—"

"That's what you're calling your writing? Applied political theory?"

Kristos simmered with anger but kept his voice controlled. "Pyord Venko is an invaluable asset to our cause."

"What does he get out of this?" I asked. "I mean, really. Why throw in his lot with the Laborers' League?"

"The university system is as unbalanced as the rest of the

economic system," Kristos said. "He should be running the College of Antiquities, not stuck in a lecturer position."

"According to whom?"

Kristos didn't answer, but I knew—according to Venko's clearly elevated opinion of himself. "But he really believes in what we're doing. His heart is Galatine, Sophie, a Galatine who's educated himself in all the ways in which we're failing as a nation. He believes it can be better, that we can emerge from this dark age of noble stranglehold stronger."

"I don't trust him." I hadn't meant to say it so bluntly, but his calculating manner and self-preservation both unnerved me.

"Because he's Kvys? Because he's an academic? Why?"

"Because he's..." I searched for the right word, the term that could capture the unnerving superiority I had felt from him. "He's very distant," I finally said. "Let me ask you this—does he trust you?"

"Of course," Kristos snapped, but he looked away.

I could have pressed, seeing in my brother's narrowed eyes that there was some weak point in the leadership of the League. I didn't. I envied him, a little, for really believing in something. I didn't believe for a minute that their protests and talking and pamphlets would change the regime. A strong monarchy and an oligarchy of nobles who ran everything? How could a few printed fliers make a difference against that?

"Where do you go from here?" I asked. "You had your assembly in the square. You're printing your pamphlets. What else can you do? What else does Pyord say you ought to do?"

Kristos shifted, positioning his face, already half in shadow, farther from me. "You know enough," he said.

"Kristos..." I didn't have the words to argue everything I wanted to say. "I just—I don't know what I would do if something happened to you."

He paused. He had been ready to deliver one of his fiery speeches, as though he were debating a pro-monarchist on the street. Instead, he slumped in his chair.

"You know how to win me over." He sighed. "This is what I care about, Sophie. I'll never have work I care about—at least, not in the world we live in now. You care about your work, I know."

"There just...there must be a better way," I offered weakly.

He leaned into his hands. His profile was outlined by the flickering candlelight, and he looked strangely stoic and gallant for the long moment he sat thinking. "Maybe there is another way. Maybe in the end, it would be better. If only because it's necessary." He gazed into the candle flame without seeing it, suddenly looking much older, lines furrowed into his brow where I had never noticed them before.

A light rap on the door forced us both to our feet. I immediately feared the worst—the City Guard had come with a warrant to arrest Kristos. But he crossed our kitchen in three easy strides and swung the door open, unconcerned.

It was just Jack, not an armed soldier ready to drag my brother to prison. What kind of life had Kristos brought us into where it wasn't complete hysteria to consider that it could have been?

Jack wrung his red wool cap between his hands. "I just wanted to make sure you two were both all right."

"Of course we are," Kristos said with more swagger than he needed to.

"Figured you were. But I worried Sophie might have been a little shaken up, so..." Jack didn't carry a grudge—I could grant him that. Despite our last parting, he bore no residual anger.

"I'm fine, Jack." I slumped back into my chair by the fire. The cane seat creaked. "Thank you for coming by," I added in rote courtesy.

"I'm going to get some water," Kristos announced, grabbing our mottled ceramic pitcher. He was out the door before I could protest.

Jack and I stared at the fire's low coals. I scanned my thoughts as though inventorying the bolts of fabric on my shelf at the shop—what could I possibly talk about with Jack? Something polite, something that wouldn't encourage him in any half-baked romantic notions.

"It's getting cold early this year" was the best I could muster.

"Hmm? Sure is. It was a short autumn." He turned back toward the fire. Maybe he preferred the quiet. I was almost getting used to a nearly amicable silence when he cleared his throat. He began to speak again, stopped himself, and then exclaimed, "Don't you worry what people will think?"

"What?"

"About—everything. Not helping out more with the League, not getting married. Doesn't it bother you?"

"People already think of me as—as different." It was true—a charm caster, a woman who owned her business, a commoner who tied her fortunes to the nobility, a Pellian by birth who lived like a Galatine. "I am different."

"I don't—I'm not a gossip, but people are saying things."

"Things."

He shifted. "Just that you seem more invested in the nobility than in your neighbors."

"The nobility pays my bills," I answered. "My neighbors don't." I sounded more distant than I meant, and more callous.

Kristos banged through the door, water pitcher in hand. "It's so cold I think this froze halfway between here and the well!" He laughed. Then he saw Jack's pinched face and my blanched one.

He cleared his throat and changed the topic. "Jack, you

did well getting so many of the field hands into the city for the demonstration."

"Wasn't too big a trick—they're all out of work except the few hired to tend winter wheat. You were right—this is the right time."

I took the water jug from Kristos and absently traced the stoneware handle. It held the cold of the winter night outside and chilled my fingertips. The right time—for what, exactly? Jack's tone implied that the League's plans depended on more complicated clockwork than simply gathering a few dozen demonstrators or printing pamphlets at a haphazard pace.

"Of course I was right," Kristos said with a grin. "We had good advice—Professor Venko said the same about exploiting the slow season for workers."

"He's an odd one, but he's yet to steer us wrong once," Jack agreed.

Kristos nodded. "And he understands politics. He sees a revolution, not just a loose organization. We have to press any advantage, convince the nobility that they're better off coming to a parley."

Those were military terms, I realized as I set the kettle on the stove, the lid rattling under my shaking hand.

"I should be going," Jack finally said. Kristos stood to walk him out, but I stopped him.

"Jack," I said as we stepped outside. "I'm sorry. I really am. I—I wouldn't make you happy."

He nodded, still dejected. I wished there was something I could say to assuage the hurt in his face, but I just let him wish me a good night instead.

I returned to my chair, watching the heat rise off the coals in our pathetic little stove.

"I don't blame you, you know." Kristos settled into the chair beside mine.

"What, *you* don't want to marry Jack and curate an impressive collection of small towheads like him, either?"

Kristos smiled ruefully. "No, not particularly. But—well, if I don't understand you, I'm guessing poor Jack Parry never will."

I picked up Kristos's red cap, his initials embroidered into the edge. "You come closest to understanding. So don't get yourself shot. Fair?"

"I can be careful. And you," he said, his teasing grin returning, "can make more of those caps. Since they work so well."

I smacked his arm, but I unearthed the red wool from its pile on a high shelf and cut out another dozen caps that night.

11

THE WEEK FOLLOWING KRISTOS'S NEAR MISS WAS BUSY, AND OUR shop worked to complete orders and schedule new ones, relieving some, if not all, of my worries about a difficult winter. It took most of the week to ready Lady Snowmont's sketches, and I left the shop early to meet with her, fretting quietly about whether Alice would set the sleeves on the ball gown correctly.

"Lady Snowmont is conversing privately with a friend," Miss Vochant said when she answered the door, her starched cap bobbing along with her lilting voice. "She will see you in a moment, and said to please make yourself at home in the salon."

I smiled and handed the maid my cloak and gloves, but my cheer was forced. Though I was now familiar with Lady Snowmont's beautiful salon, I was still uncomfortable here. My clothing rivaled the other ladies' ensembles, but I felt like a fraud, treated like a guest when I was a tradesman here for work. And such a strange contrast—mere days before, chased from the square with a band of protesters, today surrounded by the elite of Galitha.

I hovered at the edges of the room, watching a dark-haired woman pluck the strings of a harp. Her pale green, upturned eyes focused intently on the strings, as though she could see right through them to the notes they were producing, and her hands seemed to move faster than the melody she created. Though I tried to anticipate her next sequence of notes, I couldn't.

"Marguerite is a wonder." I jumped—the speaker was right next to me. Nia, one of the women I'd spoken to before. She had mastered the art of walking quietly in her fashionable pointed-toe shoes.

"Her music is lovely," I agreed, unsure what else to say.

"Lovely, and yes—hers." Nia smiled. "She's a composer, not just a harpist. That's one of her own pieces."

I gawked. I had to admit to myself that I had held a bit of superiority over most of the rich women who congregated here, assuming that they were perhaps talented in their niches, but not artists themselves, despite the cultured tenor of Viola's salon. That I was something special here, even that nobles could not also, save rare exceptions like Viola, be artists, too.

Clearly, I was not.

"Do you—that is, are you an artist of some kind, too?" I asked Nia.

She laughed, her white teeth bright against her walnut-stain-hued lips. "No, I am no artist." I felt moderately relieved until she added, "I study ancient history and languages. I'm in the middle of translating a set of ancient Pellian scrolls at the moment."

I realized my mouth was open again. "Ancient Pellian? Aren't there—what? Five people in the world who can read that?"

Nia laughed. "Yes, just about right. But I find the study of ancient practice and language fascinating."

She was lucky, I reasoned, to be able to study it. Her father must have indulged her interests. Or perhaps female scholars were more common in the Allied Equatorial States.

"You are of Pellian descent, no? I am sorry—that was perhaps a rude question."

"Not at all," I replied, though most Galatines did not make

so bold as to discuss lineage aside from family ties and noble houses. "I certainly don't know much about ancient Pellia." I laughed. *Or*, I didn't add, *contemporary Pellia*.

"I visited the Pellian quarter—it is difficult to find remnants of the ancient culture among its modern descendants. Not that this is unusual—Galatines no longer sacrifice birds to the sky god," she said as though this were a joke anyone but an antiquarian would understand.

"The seamstress!" Another woman I remembered from before, Pauline, the petite brunette, joined us. "She's back. Is she talking economic theory again?" I started to bristle, but Pauline was earnest. Had she actually been interested in what I had to say?

"Not yet," Nia replied. "We were discussing the Pellian quarter and its ties to my studies. Do you know, the most common Pellian thing I saw was a rather unusual cap."

"Yes," I said, hedging my reply. "A symbol of the workers' group."

Nia nodded. "The Laborers' League." I shouldn't have been surprised that a member of Viola's clearly well-read salon knew their proper name. "I admit to confusion—I had not believed them to be a Pellian organization."

"The Pellians are discontent with the work they get," Pauline answered quickly, then flushed, glancing at me. "I mean, the most recent immigrants. They suppose Galitha to be a cornucopia compared to Pellia—maybe it is, but the work is still scarce in the winter."

"It isn't only the Pellians," I replied carefully.

"Of course not," Pauline replied. "If Nia extricated her nose from her books more often, she'd have seen those caps on Galatines already."

"Is that so? What an unusual choice." Nia looked amused.

"The shape is hardly flattering. So is the unrest due to the Pellians, or no?"

I deferred to Pauline, curious what her perspective would be. "It isn't only the Pellians," she agreed with me. "Not by far. They're simply one group that this League has convinced to join." She shrugged. "I don't even know that they've joined in larger proportion to the Galatines. Sophie?"

"No, I don't think so. Of course, they don't have a census," I joked. "I admit, I was worried the Pellians would be blamed."

"That would be foolish," Pauline replied.

"Frightened people often are," I said evenly.

"Well, among my circle no one seems to blame them," she said, as though her circle's opinion settled the matter. In some ways, it did—if the nobility was not singling out the Pellians, official reactions to the League wouldn't focus on the quarter. "The Pellians are discontent. The Galatines are upset. The provincials are dissatisfied. It seems there is no one place to foist blame except this League, and this League seems to be truly that—an alliance of all sorts of moderately disgruntled people."

I was grateful no one asked my opinion about the League itself before Pauline changed the subject. "But did you hear about the riot in Fountain Square? They said there were hundreds of protesters, and that the soldiers had to threaten them with their rifles."

I didn't like that Kristos's protest was taking on near-myth status. "Not hundreds. And it was the regulars who deployed, not the riflemen."

"You saw?" Pauline asked, breathless. I started to brush her off, but Nia was also listening, rapt.

"Yes. I—I ran into the whole mess walking home," I lied. "The soldiers were only called because a local shop owner complained. It wasn't very exciting before they showed up."

"Well? What were they doing?" Nia asked.

"Just handing out pamphlets. They had signs. One man was talking, giving a speech," I added, remembering Kristos's impassioned voice.

"Not as exciting as the gossip mill made it out to be. Fiona said they shot someone!"

My stomach wrenched. "No. They didn't shoot anyone." I paused, letting the nausea settle. "The captain ordered one man to ready his gun but...no one was shot," I reiterated.

"Good heavens, you were right there," Nia said, her eyes narrowing. The harp music had stopped. I wished it would start again. Anything to fill the silence. But Marguerite rose from her chair by the harp and joined us, instead. "Some of the men in the diplomatic corps say that they should start searching homes for caches of weapons," Nia added.

"You don't think—really?" Pauline gasped. "That they're considering—revolt?"

I blanched. I had suspected the same for weeks, but hearing others express the same concern made the threat suddenly real, coalescing like threads of a dream into a cohesive image. Could there already be weapons stashed in League houses throughout the city?

Nia shrugged. "You know your countrymen better than I do. But the Allied States are watching this with concern, I will tell you."

It hadn't occurred to me that the Red Caps' squalling could be heard as far away as the Allied Equatorial States. "And what do they think?" I asked.

Nia shrugged. "They don't care what kind of government your nation has, so long as you buy our sugar and cotton. But political unrest means economic unrest. They aren't happy at the prospect of our biggest trade partner being embroiled in civil war."

"Civil war!" Another woman, in a brilliant cotton chintz

probably produced in the Equatorial States, shook her head. "It's pamphlets and occasional riots—surely that's all. Surely."

"That is how the Serafan Civil War started," Marguerite, the harpist, said. Her slight build and intense eyes were inherited, perhaps, from a Serafan parent or grandparent, a noble intermarriage. "Less pamphleteering and more secret meetings and speeches, but it ended with pikes in the streets and hangings before the summit finally split East Serafe from West."

I was curious—history had never been a keen interest of mine, and I was woefully behind these women in studying international politics. The Serafan Civil War was over a hundred years past, but I knew little else about it. I debated if I should ask for clarification of this particular historical turn, or if that would make me look a complete bumpkin.

Before I could decide, the door to Lady Snowmont's private chambers opened, and she emerged, a young man holding the door for her. The young man from the last time I was here, with the hazel eyes. I took a better look—I could tell by his fine silk suit and the delicate filigree gold medal looped over his left breast that he was nobility. I squinted, but I couldn't make out the device on the medal that would tell me what house he belonged to. He shared a private smile with Lady Snowmont before stepping toward the harpist with a greeting.

I blushed. There were always rumors, of course, of Lady Snowmont's salon being a gathering place for lovers and a den of romance for secret rendezvous, but I had never paid them any more heed than any other fanciful story about the aristocracy. But the young man—handsome with his rakishly unkempt honey-brown hair—had clearly been in Lady Viola's private company.

Nia must have seen my flushed cheeks, because she laughed. "What are you thinking, little Thimble Thumb?"

I felt my ears growing even hotter. "Nothing, I—he's—who is he?"

Nia laughed harder. "Theodor, First Duke of Westland. Son of the Prince of Westland, first heir to the throne. And he's not Lady Snowmont's lover, in case you were wondering."

"I—no." I clamped my mouth shut.

Nia was not fooled, but she politely didn't say anything further on the subject. "I believe the First Duke is going to be showing us the sketches of the plantings in his greenhouse," she explained. Theodor of Westland looked up from his conversation with Viola and glanced at me. I flushed as he dipped a polite bow and broke into a broad grin. He recognized me.

"A greenhouse? That's fascinating," I said, biting back my embarrassment as Lady Viola Snowmont joined us.

"It certainly is." Lady Snowmont caught my arm. "But for now I think you have plans of an entirely different sort to show me."

She led me to her private sitting room, and I hesitated before sitting down beside her. I had a fistful of swatches, and I had been confident in the design I had sketched. Plunging back into the elegant salon, however, had drained my confidence, and now I was second-guessing the work I had done.

"You—you said you wanted pink," I began, fishing the swatches from my satchel. Alice had done what I'd instructed, cutting a slip from each of our pink fabrics, and I had a dozen different silks and several cotton prints on hand.

"Yes, pink sounds perfect for this winter. It's already feeling so...dull, isn't it?" She took the fabrics from me, her small fingers appreciating the weave and weight of each. "Pink seems just the thing to counteract January."

I smiled—already I liked Viola's style. While most women chose dour colors for winter clothes, or pristine white like the snow, I grew tired of seeing washed-out clothes on a washed-out landscape. Still, my fingers grew twitchy as I pulled the sketches from the bag.

She was silent as she scanned each image carefully. My confidence sank further. The gown I had designed was simple pink with white undersleeves and a white underbodice, unencumbered by excessive trim and cut slim through the skirts, fuller at the back with a gentle, curved train. This was the next wave of fashion, I was certain—gowns that were festooned like wedding cakes and so broad in the skirts that the wearer had to slip sideways through doors were looking like tired affectations; the most fashionable women in the city had eschewed the fussiest styles already.

But I had the chance to design a gown for the most renowned noblewoman of our day, and I had undershot, horribly.

"It's perfect," she finally said.

My eyes darted from their disappointed gaze, locked on my lap, to Lady Viola. "Really?" I exclaimed without thinking.

To her credit, Viola laughed kindly. "Of course! You're a genius—so simple, but properly fitted and in a rich fabric—like this satin," she said as she swiped a piece of blush-pink duchesse, "and it will look positively sumptuous."

"Thank you," I stammered. My doubts melted—I had deciphered Viola's style, and perfectly.

"I may have to make you my personal dressmaker," Viola said. "So many of them are still...well. They can charge more for three layers of trim and silk ribbon rosettes, I suppose."

"I wouldn't worry about them," I said. "Fashion for gowns and jackets is getting a bit more streamlined, but I foresee elaborate hats being the next big thing. Literally big. They'll go into millinery."

Viola laughed and handed me the papers and her chosen swatch. "Perfect. Take the measurements you need."

I had my favorite tape and notebook, and quickly jotted down Viola's enviably petite measurements. I had Pellian height, but also Pellian broad shoulders. Delicate Galatine gowns looked perfect on women like Viola with little finagling; I had to adjust proportions widely to get a flattering fit for my larger frame.

"You'll stay for luncheon, of course," Viola said as I checked the length of her hemline. "You'll ruin the seating arrangement if you refuse," she added. Even though her back was to me, she must have sensed that I was ready to argue.

"I suppose I can stay," I replied carefully, trying to tread between sounding as cowed by the prospect of a formal lunch with nobles as I was and rudely refusing.

"And—how are my special pieces coming?"

I folded my tape and slipped it into my satchel. "Very well. I'll have them finished in less than a fortnight."

"Can you have them finished any faster?" Viola's voice was rushed. "This unrest is growing, I fear, and there seems little consensus on what to do about it. If I could ask you to expedite my order, I'd be happy to pay an additional fee."

"No need," I demurred. "I can have the first set to you tomorrow if you like, and the others—" I did some quick math. "Less than a fortnight." It meant rearranging my scheduled projects, but it was doable. "May I ask—that is—is there a particular threat to you, my lady?"

"There was an anti-monarchist riot in Fountain Square last week." Yes, my brother's demonstration might be considered a riot. Viola's huge doe-like eyes were suddenly sharply focused, intensely intelligent. "There are hundreds, perhaps thousands, of anti-monarchist pamphlets circulating throughout the city—and beyond. Any effort to dissuade the riots only encourages them. This could be a flash in the pan, or a true explosion."

I nodded, confirming what I knew. I wanted to argue that

men like my brother wouldn't hurt anyone, but I wasn't so sure anymore. I recalled the violent pamphlet I'd read in this very room. I remember the brick sailing through the air at Kristos's demonstration, aimed to hurt a soldier. And now, open talk of revolt.

"Yes, you're right," I whispered. "I'll have the first set of underthings to you tomorrow," I repeated.

12

I had expected the lunch to be held in the formal dining room of Lady Viola's home, but instead we were trooped all the way upstairs to an expansive space, surrounded on all sides by windows and topped with a glass dome. A ballroom, albeit a small one, I appreciated with wide eyes as we crested the top of the staircase. Scattered about the room were low tables with cushions and, by the windows, tall tables with no chairs at all.

"One of Lady Viola's clever surprises," a male voice spoke beside me. I turned—Duke Theodor.

"It's—impressive," I said, unsure how to respond.

"Indeed. Lady Viola never hosts quite the same event twice," Theodor said.

I remembered what Viola had said about seating arrangements—there was no way a formal arrangement was required here. Her insistence I stay had been a fairly obvious ruse, but I wasn't upset.

Or perhaps not a ruse, I realized—Miss Vochant handed each guest a scarf at the top of the stairs. Red, yellow, pale blue, lilac, azure, pink—the rainbow of chiffon fluttered like a bright fog around the guests.

"Gather with the others who have the same color scarf as you." Lady Viola's bright voice rang out over the questions and chatter. "You'll find a table with that color somewhere in the room; you'll be asked to rotate to keep things fresh." She grinned and tied her scarf—an orange the color of a summer butterfly—around her arm.

Most of the guests followed suit. I tied mine like a sash over my gown and, glancing at Theodor, realized that we sported matching spring-green scarves. The brilliant shade complemented his eyes; he should have had a whole suit made of it.

"Shall we?" he asked as he offered his arm. I hesitated only briefly—he was offering to be my escort to the first course, not suggesting a romantic affair. And after all, I thought with a forced cavalier swagger, what was wrong with enjoying the company of a duke with my luncheon? Duke Theodor led me to a low table surrounded by crimson cushions under a windowed alcove, festooned with more spring-green scarves matching ours. I dropped as gracefully as I could onto the lush cushions— the fabric was like something I'd make a gown out of, and here I was, sitting on it.

Two others joined us, but the young man had scarcely introduced himself when he resumed flirting with the wasp-waisted blond woman next to him. Seating arrangements, indeed.

"I'm to understand you're a seamstress and economic theorist," Theodor said, taking two crystal glasses of sparkling wine from a servant.

I accepted his offered glass, but shook my head. "They shouldn't make fun of me," I replied. "We talked economics a little, but I'm no expert." I almost added that my brother knew more than I, but stopped myself. It wouldn't be wise to announce to a roomful of nobles that my brother associated with anti-monarchists, especially the First Duke, son of the heir to the throne.

"They were most impressed with your ideas," Theodor said.

"Not making fun at all." He shifted his sword, a delicate, decorative piece, so he could lean more comfortably on the cushions.

"If I'm a seamstress and economic theorist, what would you say you are?" I asked, sipping my wine. It accosted my nose with bright bubbles. "Aside from being a duke, of course."

"Aside from being a duke?" He laughed. "Now, according to my father, there is nothing aside from that. King's brother, first heir to the throne, making me second in line, and, as he says, that is all I need worry about." There was wistfulness, almost childlike, in his speech. I softened a little—First Duke of Westland, second heir to the throne unless the king's daughter produced a son, but perhaps he was more interesting than his titles alone.

"And according to you?" I asked.

"According to me, I'm a horticulturalist and explorer."

"Those hardly seem to go together." I smiled as I took another sip of wine. Once one got used to the bubbles, it was quite good.

"On the contrary." Theodor took two plates from the servant who waited by the table. They held dates stuffed with cheese and pistachios. "I have an interest in plants; there are thousands upon thousands of plants in the world; only a tiny minority grow in our corner of it."

"And so you want to sail off and discover...plants." I popped a date into my mouth; it practically melted. The food, the wine—this might have been heaven.

"Precisely. Who knows what medicinal properties, what culinary spices, what beautiful blooms might be discovered if we explore further. The Allied Equatorial States, for instance—the climate produces a range of flowering shrubs like nothing we have here. And the northern lichen distribution of the steppes of Kvyset—" He stopped.

"You're really going to do it?" I asked, incredulous. "Sail to Serafe with a pair of shears and a sketchbook? Catalog the botany of the Great Taiga of Kvyset?"

"Someday. Yes. Now don't laugh."

I promptly began laughing.

"Hey now!" But he was laughing, too. "My father is sending me on an envoy to the Equatorial States after Midwinter. A grand tour of principalities, and I intend to find time for study." He speared an olive and examined it before popping it in his mouth. "I fear the trip will be focused more generally on broaching a military alliance and reaffirming trade agreements, but I'm sure I can finagle some time for flowers."

I was growing impressed, I had to admit. Even Kristos would have appreciated the First Duke's dedication to his scholarship. "Make sure," I joked, "that those trade agreements include continued imports of that wonderful equatorial cotton."

"I shall keep that in mind." Theodor hailed the servant, who brought me a fresh glass of wine. "But only," he said, "if you promise not to go too fast. This sparkling stuff catches up to you."

He was right—my laugh was coming more easily and I was actually enjoying myself. "Are you speaking from experience?"

Theodor inclined his head toward me, as though sharing a great secret. His eyes widened. "I once had to be uncoupled from a potted palm tree at the Grand Duchess Pristina's birthday ball."

I erupted in laughter, and even the blonde and her enamored suitor stopped whispering in one another's ears long enough to stare.

"Up, you four!" Viola stood over us like an imposing statue despite her petite frame. She waved her arms like a conductor. "Move to the tall table by the north window for your next course."

Somewhere between our first table and the tall table spread with cheeses, paper-thin sliced meats, and exotic fruits oozing

ruby juices, we lost our companions. Theodor didn't say anything, but I thought they disappeared into one of the adjacent
rooms. I tried not to stare after them even though Theodor
didn't seem surprised—were such obvious trysts common with
the nobility? Or only at Viola's salon?

"How does Lady Viola decide who to invite here?" I mused
out loud, wondering partially about the rude behavior of our
companions.

"People who please her in one way or another," Theodor
answered. "Some she finds entertaining. Some who connect her
to the people she actually wants to invite. Some she is impressed
by or enjoys their pursuit of their art." He speared a cube of
cheese with one of the tiny forks provided to us. "I like to believe
I'm in that category," he added. "You most certainly are."

"I—thank you," I replied instead of arguing.

"And some she wants to sleep with."

I stared at Theodor, mouth agape.

"I'm joking! Mostly," he amended. "Come now, you've
heard the rumors."

"I—I confess that I haven't heard any specifics."

"I forgot you don't move in these upper-crust circles so
bored by their own useless opulence that they have to invent
stories and embellish the few real ones that float about." Theodor took a larger-than-necessary draught of wine. "The old bats
like to say that the only reason Viola invites any of the young
gentlemen or ladies here is that she has some sort of insatiable
nymphomania. I tend to think they're all a mite jealous that they
aren't invited."

"I can't imagine rumormongers like that would have any
real reason to be here," I replied.

"See? You understand the salon better than most already. It's
supposed to be a place for conversation, learning, advancement.

That was Viola's concept, her plan. How she wanted to influence the world for good."

"You have had quite a bit of that wine, haven't you?"

Theodor grinned. "Yes, I have. Hide the palm trees lest I get any ideas." His smile softened. "It is a noble venture, Viola's salon."

"You said 'mostly.'" The wine had taken its effect on me, as well, loosening my tongue on subjects I would never have discussed otherwise.

"What?"

"You said you were mostly joking. About this den of iniquity."

The duke laughed. "Not just here—" He stopped when he saw my face. "I forget that you're, well..."

"Common?" I supplied.

"Hardly," he replied with a grin. "Not of the nobility. This kind of thing"—he waved toward the closed door of the anteroom where our companions had retired—"it's hardly unusual."

"But she—if there were a child—she'd be—"

"Ruined? Not at all. Many a lady's marriageable reputation has been made by her ability to conceive. The bastards haven't the rights of inheritance, of course, but no nobleman would think of not supporting them."

I stared at him. "I'm sorry. I shouldn't have even thought to discuss something like this."

"No, I brought it up." He scrutinized a sliver of fruit. "Tactical error on my part. We grow so used to it—to marriage being a political strategy, to children being heirs." He sighed, and I wondered if he regretted that reality that made affairs the temporary escape from arranged marriages.

Of course, I didn't even have escapism when it came to romance. Without the insurance of copious amounts of money, a bastard was a liability and nothing more. And though I had, rather unwisely, engaged in a few flirtations with shopkeepers' apprentices and tradesmen over the years, the care I had to take made the whole enterprise feel hardly worthwhile. A bastard for a noble meant assurance of marriageability, but for me it meant a sudden loss of income with an extra person to provide for. I had long since decided that the risks were too great for a woman in my position. I hadn't even allowed myself the pleasure of talking—flirting, I admitted—like this in years.

I stabbed a hunk of cheese, frustrated. The duke watched me with concern blooming behind his hazel eyes.

"We are speaking of such foolishly serious things when there is sparkling wine and delicious food at hand."

"And hardly know one another," I added, by way of apology. It wasn't his fault that I had chosen a detestably difficult personal life for myself.

"You're right! We ought to know one another better," he said, eyes brightening. "Have you any sisters? Brothers?"

"One brother," I replied simply. "You?"

"Five brothers and one sister, smack in the middle of us."

"Five!"

"Yes. The Dukes Second through Sixth." He paused. "Parents?"

"Both dead. You?"

"Sweet mother, very alive and very meddlesome father." He arrested himself and burst out laughing. "Now that was just awful—this is the worst conversation I've ever engaged in!"

"Truly?"

"The worst because it's one of the best. Very honest." He leaned closer and rested his hand on the small of my back.

I began to protest, but stopped myself. He was a noble—a high-ranking one. There was no chance he was about to suggest marriage to me, like Jack Parry outside a tavern. It was absurdly perfect. And though I had no plans to slip off to an anteroom with the duke, I admitted that I was less inclined to turn it down immediately than I would have believed. I enjoyed talking to him, and his deep melodic voice, and his smile.

"What's your favorite plant?" I asked softly.

Theodor looked surprised. "Rose balsam—garden jewelweed. Grows nearly anywhere. It can be cultivated in a wide range of colors, and the stems are a dermal medicinal."

"But why is it your favorite?"

"All of that wasn't enough?" He smiled, and I was acutely aware of his fingers on my waist. "I like that it's beautiful but hardy. I don't care for fussy flowers. I like that it's a common garden plant with a useful function. And I can remember planting them and then promptly ripping them out of the garden as a child. So there. Satisfactory answer?"

"Very much so." I rolled a thin slice of meat around a sliver of fruit.

A servant appeared, quietly directing us to another low table, this one with a view of the wide river and the public gardens beyond. A tray with miniature cakes and dark chocolate wedges was laid out.

Theodor dropped onto a cushion. I wanted to sit beside him, but that seemed too presumptuous, too close. I sat opposite him instead. I thought he looked faintly disappointed, but he swiftly handed me a piece of chocolate.

"Cacao may be one of my other favorite plants," he said with a wink. "Something else to make sure remains on the trade agreements with the Allied States."

Our hostess reappeared and settled herself beside me on a cushion. "I am so very glad you stayed," Viola said.

"As am I," Theodor said softly.

"She must come again," Viola said to him with a conspiratorial smile. "Perhaps you could help me convince her of that."

I began to demur as I always did, but I stopped myself. Why argue? I liked visiting the salon—I liked the ladies here with their varied talents. I liked Theodor's company. I liked Lady Viola and her high ideals that pushed her to create this small community.

"I will certainly make my case," Theodor said with a smile.

13

"WHERE WERE YOU ALL AFTERNOON?" PENNY SWEPT A PILE OF threads from the table in front of her. "We had three new orders—three!"

"Three?" I did a quick tabulation. This made seven new orders in a week and would certainly increase our wait time for any more orders. Perhaps I would be able to bring Emmi on, at least for a few hours a week. I didn't even begin to complete the math on cost for another hire, especially a hire I would have to train, before Penny continued.

"Yes, three—and Alice and I were up to our ears in work!"

"I'm so sorry," I replied. The afternoon in Viola's ballroom had felt like a dream, a fairy tale, but now the bubbles from the sparkling wine faded and paled, and I was back to what I knew was my real life. I looked over Alice's head, dutifully bent over a length of fabric, marking it with chalk, and saw the piles of unfinished work scattered about the studio. Already the light was fading outside.

Guilt sank into my stomach, a hard, bitter feeling. I had whiled away my afternoon on a frivolous party while Penny and Alice had worked.

"I—it took longer at Lady Snowmont's than I had antici-pated" was all I could muster in response.

"I bet it was gorgeous," Alice said, depositing the pile of scrap into a dustbin. "What were all the ladies wearing?"

"You're not angry?" I asked, incredulous.

"Of course not," Alice replied, brushing her hands on her apron. "Most exciting new client we've had since I've been here. Aren't you expected to—what do the merchants call it? Network?"

"I suppose I did that to some extent," I said. In truth, while the other ladies knew me by sight and by name now, I'd spent the afternoon talking with one particular handsome duke. I sighed at myself—what a waste. I should have been handing out trade cards and consulting over silk colors, not simpering over a nobleman.

Penny eyed me suspiciously, as though she could read the reticence in my face. She probably could. "And the food? I'm guessing it was more than I see in a week."

I bit my lip. "Yes, Penny, it was obscene. And I won't lie, it was delicious."

Penny shook her head so that her cap ruffles fluttered like the wings of an agitated bird. "My neighbor hasn't worked this week—his family had to rifle through the leavings behind the baker's shop and beg soup bones off the butcher. All the while, the nobility nibbles on delicacies."

"You eat because they pay us for gowns," I snapped, instantly regretting the harsh words.

Alice glanced from one of us to the other. "Did Lady Snow-mont like the gown sketch?" Her voice was muffled by the tape measure in her mouth.

"Yes, very much. Set up a mannequin; we'll start drap-ing tomorrow," I said, handing Penny the paper with the measurements.

"Lady Viola Snowmont, in a gown I helped to sew," sighed Alice.

"Lady who now?" I nearly jumped through the counter at the sound of my brother's voice.

"Kristos, don't sneak in like that!" I shouted, throwing a wad of scrap linen at him.

"Hey now, put a bell on the door if you want to know when people come in," he said. "But like I said—Lady who?"

"Sophie got a commission for Lady Viola Snowmont!" Penny called from the workroom, bustling out to see Kristos.

"It's the most lovely thing, a gown with a geometric bodice inset, in pink duchesse," Alice added.

"Great, a something out of pink something," Kristos said as Penny plowed into him. I rolled my eyes. They weren't even going to bother with the pretense of hiding this from me any longer?

"Yes, a pink something." The bells from the cathedral echoed down the cobblestone streets—nearly the end of the workday already. "Alice, finish that hem, and Penny, sweep up." I quickly stacked orders for delivery, glancing at the order board, chiding myself for the lost hours of work. I would stay late tonight. I needed to finish Lady Snowmont's chemise and drawers, and preferred the quiet of the atelier to the row house. "It will be time to leave when you're done, I'm sure."

"Lady Snowmont," Kristos said as the girls disappeared into the workroom in a flurry of excited chatter.

"Yes. Viola Snowmont."

"You didn't think this was big enough news to tell me?"

"I tried!" I punched his arm playfully, but Kristos wasn't in a laughing mood. "I tried telling you when her lady's maid came, and you had no interest."

He screwed his lips together and shrugged. "I guess I wasn't thinking."

"Thinking about what?"

"Well, Lady Snowmont, Sophie. She runs the most influential gatherings in the whole city. It's practically the cabinet in there."

"Not quite," I replied.

"And all you did was show up and take measurements. But you could have talked to them, influenced them. If you had one of my pamphlets."

I bristled. I had spoken with Lady Snowmont's guests—they had been impressed with me. A duke—the First Duke of Westland—had chosen to spend a luncheon talking to me. I wanted to throw that in Kristos's face, but I was too flustered—one of his pamphlets? I was supposed to tote one of his pamphlets to a lady's salon with me, as though she wasn't already aware of the pamphlets swirling through the city and the sentiments published in them?

"That would have been most indecent," I replied through clenched teeth. "Kristos, I won't argue you pursuing your political interests. But they are not mine. Even if I did agree with you, I wouldn't bring political propaganda to a client meeting."

"Fine." He tugged his red cap down over his eyes. He wore that thing nearly every day now—were they protesting that often? Or had their lives begun to morph into a constant protest? "I can't imagine it would make for pleasant conversation over tea."

"You would be surprised," I countered. "If you could hear what they have to say, too—maybe you would be willing to see what the reforms they're working on could do."

"They have no interests but their own," he spat. "Nothing they are willing to do without pressure from the populace will amount to anything. And I can't hear what they have to say, because I'm not invited to their parties like you are."

"Don't be angry," I said quickly. "Please?"

He didn't reply. "You're staying late here, aren't you?"

"Yes. I have a commission to finish. For—" I stopped myself.

"For Lady Snowmont. It's not just a pretty gown, is it? You're making her one of your specialties."

I stood straighter. "Of course."

Kristos looked like he was ready to crack, his face hardened so much. "I can understand taking a client and plying your trade, but when you use your gift to help the nobility—I can't help but wonder whose side you're on."

I wanted to argue, but he swept out of the shop before I could. I wouldn't have heard the bell he suggested over the slamming door.

14

—ɱ—

THE COFFEEHOUSE WAS ALMOST DESERTED IN THE WANING LIGHT
of the afternoon, with the morning rush over, the crowd
descending for chatter and hot drinks after lunch gone, and the
evening's social circles still hours away. That was why, the day
after the second market day of every month, anyone frequenting
the Aromatic Flower coffeehouse mid- to late afternoon could
find a knot of Pellian Galatines talking charms over carafes of
hot, black coffee.

Today it was just Emmi, Namira, Lieta, and a flustered
Venia, whose sister was getting married in a week and had the
whole family busy with plans. "She wants a huge cake like the
Galatines have, instead of *baka*," Venia complained, referring to
the sweet pastry Pellians defaulted to for dessert. "But none of us
know how to make a cake like that."

"I'll help," Emmi said. Unlike the others, but much like me,
she had been born in Galitha. "I know how to do it. It's not
hard."

"Everything Galatine," Venia continued. "Even the gown.
She won't wear my mother's veils and *sulta*." I had seen the elaborately draped robes and veils of a Pellian bride only at a distance, when a wedding procession clipped Fountain Square. I

didn't blame Venia's sister—the getup was hardly flattering and could never be worn again, unlike a Galatine-style gown.

"I made her this," I said, handing her a lace-edged kerchief. "She can wear it with the gown if she wants, or carry it, or wrap the bouquet—"

"Bouquet?" Venia wrinkled her nose.

"Most Galatine brides carry a little nosegay with flowers—for luck," I faltered, trying to explain a tradition that seemed so normal to me. "The kerchief is a good luck charm," I added.

"Thanks," Venia said. "I wish I could have made her something."

I had quickly realized in working with the women that charm-casting skill varied. I hadn't known that some casters were naturally better than others, though it made sense, the same way some people are better than others at music or math or footraces. Venia was not terribly talented, but moreover, her skill was less fluid. If she was careful to focus her energies, she could etch a decent, generic good luck charm into a clay tablet. She couldn't direct specific kinds of luck—health, love, wealth—and she couldn't transfer the skill into anything else.

Lieta and Emmi could both quickly inscribe a tablet, and Lieta had taken to attempting traditional beadwork as a form of good luck charm with moderate success while Emmi had, under my direction, practiced more specific charms in the herbs she blended into sachets. I toyed with the idea of stitching pouches with embedded charms for Emmi's blends. It was an interesting idea, but there was no process to test the efficacy of layered charms, any more than one could scientifically isolate whether a charm worked or not.

"I hope it doesn't rain for the wedding," Venia continued, interrupting my hypothetical attempts to devise a blind test to figure out if layered double charms would be more effective than a single one. "She wants to have the dancing outdoors, of course, and it's cold enough already that I think it's a bad idea."

"For an hour or so, I don't think anyone will get frostbite." Emmi laughed. "A cold, clear night would be beautiful—the stars will be brighter than when it's all hazy in the summer."

"You're used to these winters." Lieta shrugged. "My bones are still Pellian, and they ache when the weather goes cold."

"Mine too," Namira said, though I knew she hadn't seen Pellia's shores since she was a child of ten. Yet she still wore her hair braided and bound like a Pellian matron, and I knew she carried *lya*, religious totems representing her ancestors and the particular spirit of her family, in her pocket. My mother didn't even carry *lya*, and we had never put up the larger *ab-lyret* shrines in our house like most of the Pellians I knew did. "Still, I'd be more concerned about...interruptions."

The others shared a knowing look, and Emmi rolled her eyes. "What kind of interruptions?" I asked.

"The Red Caps," Emmi said. "They're in the market every day with their broadsides. They don't cause trouble, really, but they have this song they sing and they get loud."

"They don't cause trouble until they get into shouting matches with the *dhamas*," Namira joked, using the diminutive Pellian word that translated, roughly, as "little old ladies." I could imagine the bow-backed, white-haired Pellian market women, half-shrouded in shawls, shaking their fingers at any Red Cap who dared block their cart or stall.

"So they're active in the quarter," I said.

"Very," Lieta said. "And it's our own boys, not Galatine rabble-rousers." I wasn't sure if this worried or relieved her. "But they don't stick around much at night, Venia. I'm sure they won't interrupt the wedding party."

"Do you think you could eat charms?" Namira mused suddenly.

"Eat them?" Venia said.

"You know, bake charmed *baka* or something."

"What would happen?" Lieta wondered. "Would the charm last as long as the food was in your stomach? Would it work at all?"

"Maybe it would stick around," Namira said. "Like when you eat garlic and smell like garlic for a few days."

"Or maybe it would kill you." All of them looked at me, aghast. "Well, who's to say? I don't know that it's ever been tried—did any of your mothers suggest you do it?"

They all shook their heads.

"Maybe there's a reason. Maybe it would make you sick."

Namira stood up and went to the counter. The only difference between the design of a coffeehouse and most of our taverns was the product offered; a barkeep served customers from behind a long counter, and the day's offerings were written in sloppy chalk on a slate over the bar.

The door opened, letting a gust of chill sneak in. I glanced at the trio of greatcoats entering the coffeehouse. Fine wool, deep black dye, modest design. I looked at the faces.

One was Pyord Venko. It had been nearly two weeks since I'd glimpsed him at the demonstration, but I easily recognized his imposing features. The two men with him were young, younger than my brother. Probably students, I surmised, and both Galatine. If they were students, they were likely noble, though very likely of lesser houses if they weren't already at court or managing their own estates. I thought I glanced the metalwork device indicating a noble house, pinned to the coat one of the men wore.

They sat at the next table, even though there were plenty of open seats. I considered greeting Pyord, but we were far from friends, barely even acquaintances. Besides, I didn't feel like explaining my little coven of charm casters to an outsider right now, even—especially—an outsider with an overactive interest in charms. Namira returned before I had to decide.

"All right. This," she said with a flourish of her hand, "is a coffee with steamed milk. Observe the foam piled on the top," she added. We laughed—she mimicked the mannerisms of a street magician perfectly. She picked up the tiny demitasse spoon resting on the saucer and dipped the handle end into the foam. She swirled it slowly, pulling just enough of the coffee to the surface to form a design. I watched the golden light form around her makeshift stylus, depositing a trail of light into the foam itself, mimicking the method traditional charm casters used to inscribe tablets. When she finished, an intermingled web of marbled milk and coffee and charmed light rested on top of the cup.

"Now what?" Venia asked.

"You're not going to drink that," I cautioned.

"I thought we could see how long the charm rests in the coffee," Namira said. "Can't hurt."

I nodded, watching the design begin to lose form and coalesce at the top of the cup.

"It wouldn't likely hurt you." Pyord. I turned to face him, curious and annoyed at the same time.

"Yes?" I said. The other women watched me, unsure of why this stranger was speaking to us, or how he even knew what we were doing.

"I apologize," he said coolly. "Your brother told me that you meet with several fellow practitioners, and I thought my students and I might observe."

"It's customary to ask," I replied evenly. "We aren't the surgical theater. You can't just toss a coin in the box and watch." A nearly maternal protectiveness flared in me; I was responsible, in a way, for these women. Having someone observing them like a sideshow was never my intention, but my suggestion to meet publicly had led to it. Pellians were shy enough about their customs, having them degraded so often by Galatines, but this bordered on something more aggressive. Pyord and his students wanted something from these Pellian charm casters, and the discrepancy in their social position was making my friends visibly uncomfortable. Their disquiet was palpable—how could you refuse a university professor, or a minor noble like his student?

I trapped my tongue between my teeth in frustration. Why would Kristos tell a near stranger where to find us, and when? It was almost refreshing—I'd have something besides the Red Caps and my reticence to join them to argue with Kristos about tonight.

"Again, my apologies. But ancient texts indicate no ill effects from ingesting charms. Well, they indicate no ill effects from curses," he said with a slight smile. The two students with him realized a second too late that this was intended to be funny, and guffawed too loudly. "Early experiments with curses found that the worst they did was give someone a little indigestion—though that was just as likely from the ingredients of the potion as the curse itself."

The students waited for my response. Annoyed when it wasn't immediate, one spoke up. "And if a curse wouldn't harm someone, it's doubtful a charm would."

"Yes, I figured." I glanced at the three of them, still wearing their identical greatcoats. "Well, which of you cares to sample Namira's drink?"

The two students faltered. Venko smiled the joyless smile

of someone who is in the midst of a very competitive card game and has just been outbid. "I couldn't dream of allowing a lady to buy a drink for me," he replied.

"Very well," I said. I looked back at Namira's coffee. The golden light was fading, the design she had created nearly gone. It seemed the charm only lasted as long as the drawing in the foam did.

"Sophie..." Emmi shrank into her chair, clearly intimidated by the men staring at her and the others. My anger flashed again, at the objectification these supposed scholars felt was acceptable. "I think maybe I need to leave."

"Me too," Venia said, fastening her short cloak and wrapping her shawl over her head, in a hybrid style more Pellian than Galatine. "I need to figure out how to bake a cake, remember?"

Lieta and Namira hesitated, and I could tell neither was going to discuss the progress they'd made in charm casting since the last time we had met, nor the best gossip from their quarter of the city, nor anything at all, as long as Venko and his students watched them. They gathered their things and said quiet goodbyes, leaving half-finished coffees on the table.

I suppressed an annoyed sigh. I had hoped to talk to Emmi about coming to work for me, to discuss whether her interest was primarily focused on income, or if she hoped to learn the trade, or if, perhaps, she even wanted to apply charm casting as I did. She was right that the unrest in the city was not making finding work any easier for anyone, and the Pellians and others who were not well integrated into common Galatine culture, like provincials, were likely to suffer more than others.

I pushed my chair back and faced Venko. "I should probably leave, too. I have work waiting at the shop." Not quite a lie. There was always work waiting at the shop.

Venko's students slouched a little bit, disappointed. What

had he promised them, a full magic show complete with disappearing doves and sword eating? That kind of magic was all illusion. The magicians of the Serafan court were masters at the art, according to some of the nobles who liked to talk too much while I took measurements and completed fittings, and some asked if it was possible that they augmented their tricks with real charm casting. How, I couldn't imagine. Visible magic, I liked to remind anyone who would listen, was entertainment or fraud. Real magic—charms that worked—was invisible to all save practitioners.

"You really should listen to him," one of the students finally said. He had a pockmarked face; nobility didn't excuse anyone from acne or the pox. "He's a genius," he nearly whined.

"Frederick, leave her be." Venko watched me quietly. "We should not have barged in on her and her friends. We surprised them, you see. Caught them off guard. I'm sure they'd be more willing to speak in a better setting."

"I can't speak for them," I answered crisply, but I knew that they would be reticent if not outright unwilling—Galatines made fun of charm casters and backwater Pellians far more often than they wanted to talk to them.

"Then speak for you." Venko leaned forward. "I've been studying the theory of magic for years. But the practice—it is not a theoretical art, is it, Miss Balstrade?"

"I suppose not," I said. "Why study it, anyway? No one can possibly take you seriously. Ever," I added.

His students sat bolt upright, ready to defend him, but he waved them off. "I don't care if I am ever recognized for my contributions," he said, with the flint of pride edging his voice that told me he full well did want recognition. "But if we can combine theoretical magic study with practical application, the gains could be as great as many being made in the other sciences.

Imagine if the same rigor could be applied to magic as to physics, or chemistry. It wasn't until we studied the chemical compositions of minerals that we could create gunpowder," he said.

"Gunpowder—what a pleasant example," I said instead. "You'll notice that none of us practice black charms."

"None of you do," Venko agreed, but there was an unnerving emphasis on *you*. "Your art could work for good, more effectively than it does now," he continued. I thought of my untestable hypothesis that layered charms could work more effectively than single ones. Though it irritated me to admit it, it was possible that Venko understood more than I did about how charm casting actually worked. If there was science to it, some understanding of the order of the natural world that explained how my charms worked, I certainly didn't comprehend it. With an uncomfortable thought, I had to admit that I didn't know for certain that Serafan court magicians weren't true practitioners or that magic could never be visible—I only knew what I had experienced.

"Perhaps so," I conceded. Pyord smiled, but cool victory bled into an otherwise friendly expression. He liked winning too much, I thought with distaste. The sycophants accompanying him only intensified my mistrust. The students stared at him as though he were a priceless artifact on display at the Public Archive, an illuminated manuscript behind ropes that they could hardly hope to understand.

Pyord glanced at his students. "Do please excuse us a moment," he said. "I will walk back to the university alone." Clearly disappointed, the students shuffled to the door. Pyord smiled at me, as though suggesting privacy could allow us to start afresh. It didn't change anything. "I could happily elucidate you further on the theories. You, and any of your Pellian friends who have interest."

Curiosity couldn't overcome distrust. Though I may have lived, spoken, and managed a business like a Galatine, there remained some latent Pellian part of me, a protectiveness of my craft against an outsider, a suspicion why any non-Pellian would have such intense interest. I shook my head. "I am quite content with what my charms can do now."

"Yes, I am sure. And to be frank, from what little I have observed, I am unsure that tutelage in theory could improve your friends' abilities overmuch. You, however—your application is already more nuanced."

Though I was sure he intended the commentary on my skills as a compliment, it snagged on my loyalty to my friends. "I'm no better than them."

Pyord's amused smile told me he didn't agree. "With a better understanding of the theories, a charm caster could be a great asset to a cause she chose to support. The two of us together—we could greatly assist the aims of the League. Imagine if you could influence the outcomes of this enterprise."

This again. "I have no interest or ability to assist. And there is a full roster of charms waiting for me at my shop."

Venko watched me leave, but I couldn't help but feel that I had far from satisfied Venko's scholarly interests. He would be back.

15

—⁓—

"I HOPE YOU'LL FORGIVE THAT I HAVEN'T TIME TO VISIT." VIOLA took the packet of clothes, neatly folded in brown paper and tied with a peach-pink silk ribbon, and laid it on the table. "I am expected at my father's for some formal luncheon with the city Lords and am already running late."

I edged toward the door, embarrassed to have asked to see Lady Viola in the first place instead of merely delivering the package of charmed linens. I had debated before setting off this morning—was it too familiar to call on her with the delivery myself? "I'm so sorry; I'd have been here sooner if—"

"It's not your fault at all." Viola laughed. "Your habit of apologizing for everything is quite sweet, but it will get you into trouble someday." She gestured to Miss Vochant, who held out a large silk-covered hat festooned with ostrich plumes in one hand and an emerald-green caned bonnet in the other. "I'm the one who agreed to go in the first place, sentencing myself to three hours of talking rubbish about Fountain Square fair permits and animal refuse regulations."

I smiled, but there was a placid acceptance to Viola's jokes, as though she might like her father very much despite not wanting to admit it. Viola chose the silk hat, and I nodded in approval.

She laughed as she stabbed a pin through the silk into her hair. "Permits and regulations—do you know the palace had to get a permit to have repairs done on the dome in the ballroom?"

I imagined the king standing in line at a clerk's desk, and stifled a smile. "What's fair for one is fair for all, is that it?"

"I suppose so," she said, checking her reflection in the mirror. "Of course, the talk will probably turn to the riots. You're quite safe, aren't you, Sophie?"

I was taken aback. "Certainly," I said, stopping myself before revealing that my brother the ringleader wouldn't let me get hurt. "Mere protests don't worry me, and they're mostly sticking to Fountain Square. Far enough from my shop."

"Crowding up Fountain Square and lacking permits," Viola said with a sigh. "And the Lord of Stones loves his permits." She pulled a face. "I'm sure I'll get to talk all about permits."

"The seamstress returns!" Theodor turned a corner and flashed his impish smile.

"Delivery girl this morning," I replied, but I blushed. He was here awfully early—unless he had spent the night.

"Either way, a lovely surprise for me. Viola, I'll make my excuses and leave now, if you don't object."

She waved a hand. "Fine, fine. You know where I'll be if you decide you want to talk permits over roast beef."

"I'd call it a kind offer, but I know it isn't," Theodor said with a laugh.

The servant showed us out, and Theodor held my cloak for me. I accepted the offer of his hand on the steps, even though I was unused to this kind of courtesy. I was lucky if Kristos didn't shove me on our steps at home, trying to get out the door before me.

And what had he been doing at Viola's so early in the morning, anyway? My ears burned with embarrassment—had

I caught one of Viola's lovers' trysts that Theodor claimed the court gossiped about?

I was vaguely disappointed and yet relieved when Theodor let my hand drop at the base of the stairs.

"May I walk you home?"

"What?" I gaped at him, the brim of my silk hat obscuring part of my view.

"I'm finding myself delightfully free of obligation this morning. May I use my newfound time to walk you home?"

"Yes—I suppose—that is—I'm not interrupting anything?" I stammered.

Theodor stopped, forcing me to arrest my steps and turn to face him. "I said I was free. So no, you're not interrupting anything." He raised an eyebrow.

"Fair enough," I said, turning my steps back toward the atelier. Why did a duke want to walk with a seamstress anywhere, especially after spending the breakfast hour with a noblewoman?

"We were just playing backgammon."

"What?" I found myself inarticulate once again.

"This morning. Lady Viola and I. I was only there because we stayed up late playing backgammon, and I fell asleep on her sofa and spent the night drooling on her cushions."

Despite myself, I laughed. "I wasn't going to ask."

"I know you weren't," Theodor replied. We came to a street corner, and he checked for carriages before ushering me across the street. "But I knew you were curious, maybe even concerned about it, so I thought I'd just tell you."

"How could you tell? That is, if I was? Which I wasn't."

"If anyone ever suggests that you become a spy, or a professional gambler, or anything else that requires you to mitigate your facial expressions, don't."

"That's hardly true, I can be quite professional if I—"

"You're blushing as red as the inside of a pomegranate."

"Fine." I gave in and laughed.

"I've a confession. This morning was a pleasant surprise, but the luncheon last week—it was no mere coincidence."

"No?"

"No, I—I admit that I asked Viola to pair us together. There, I said it. And worse, I asked that the two of us be seated with the Duchess of Lyvel."

"Why?"

"Because I know she takes any opportunity to tryst with that sculptor she's infatuated with but can't marry." He gauged my reaction. "I figured the two of them would slip off somewhere within the first ten minutes of the meal."

"You did have everything planned," I answered carefully. No boy from our quarter who had tried for my attention ever went to such lengths. Of course, none had such means.

"I—I saw you at Viola's salon, and heard the ladies talking about the seamstress who could talk politics and, well, wanted to get to know you. Viola said it might be a challenge."

I started, breaking my stride from the easy match I had fallen into with Theodor. "How so?"

"Nothing improper! No, she simply said you were a bit guarded. That you were a superb artist and a fine guest at the salon but unused to our set and how—well, we can be a bit forward."

I hesitated.

"You can agree."

"Fine, you're a bit forward. But it's not really that." I struggled to explain. The boys I'd grown up around were just as forward, but they were less genteel. There was no question about their motives. "The dance is essentially the same everywhere, but the steps you use are different."

"The music dictates the dance," Theodor said, quoting an old proverb. It was true—the finely furnished, sweetly scented rooms of Viola's house crafted a music far different from the smoky taverns and riverside boulevards where a few boys had tried to court me when I was younger. I didn't mind this dance, for a while, but I wasn't sure what the expectations of its duration were. Surely this was a short reel, not a lengthy mazurka or promenade.

People glanced at us as we passed; I was a well-dressed commoner, certainly, but Theodor was wearing his family device and carrying a ceremonial sword and clearly noble by birth. I saw whispers behind hands—what is she doing with him? I'd been gossiped about most of my life for my idiosyncrasies—learning I could stitch charms into cloth had that effect on many people. The whispers didn't bother me, and I could think of far less flattering things to be affiliated with than the attention of a duke.

"I might be pressing my luck," Theodor said as a woman herding a trio of geese scurried out of the way, "but I wonder if you might be persuaded to visit the public gardens with me. I have a few projects there that I'd like an artistic criticism of."

"I'm not sure my eye for gardening is quite what you think it is."

"You can fashion works of art out of silk and velvet and wool; why wouldn't I think you could appreciate the same out of moss and foliage?"

"It's your design?" I asked, lowering my voice. I knew how protective I was of my first trials at any project, how I guarded the sketches until I was sure the design was workable, how I slowly tested the response with a few trusted people first.

"It is, to the best of my ability. It's a new garden, a sort of horticultural artwork." He cleared his throat. "It's in a closed section of the gardens, so you needn't worry about being seen with me, if that's your concern," he added. I wasn't quite sure he was joking.

"I'd be honored," I said. "And I'm not worried about your affiliation," I added.

He chatted amiably as we walked, about the plant seeds he'd ordered from overseas and the difficulties of calibrating soil acidity. Meanwhile, I forced myself to think of the practicalities of even a friendship with Theodor. He was very handsome. And charming. The duke as a friend would be a great boon to me professionally. Perhaps even personally, as a fellow artistically minded friend.

"What's this?" Theodor slowed his step slightly. I glanced up the street. A cabal of red-capped, broad-shouldered dockworkers gathered in the intersection of River and Wells Streets, shouting down passersby.

"The usual rabble," I replied with more gall than I intended. River Street bordered the main commercial district filled with shops and small markets, separating it from the warehouses and docks and, further afield, tanneries and slaughterhouses and other less savory installations. I considered those rougher sections of town fair game for the Red Caps, their territory. This presence, coupled with the large demonstration in Fountain Square and the increasing presence in the Pellian quarter, concerned me. The Red Caps made my customers nervous. My shop was only a few blocks away—if this kind of display filtered over to our commercial street, I might lose business.

Theodor rested his hand on his sword and took my arm, drawing me a bit closer. Protective. The effect was strange—he couldn't have done much with the flimsy ceremonial rapier he carried, and a word from me claiming affiliation to my brother would be more beneficial. But there was a queer tumult in my stomach, an excitement I hadn't felt about a man for years, produced solely by his closeness.

"They're nothing," I whispered. "They won't hurt anyone—just handing out pamphlets, see?" I sounded frightened, but it wasn't because of the Red Caps in the street. It was of my reaction to the noble hand on my arm.

Theodor nodded, but didn't release my arm. "My father said I should stick to the carriage instead of walking. I disregard a fair bit of his advice, but that may have been sound." We skirted the intersection and continued toward the gardens with less chatter than before.

I felt calmer, more accustomed to Theodor's arm on mine, by the time we walked through the elaborate wrought iron gate of the public gardens, the scrollwork metal vines curving away from us and the crushed shell path widening before us. Tall boxwood hedges obscured the view from the road, but I knew that beyond them, there were exhibition gardens and rose gardens and fountain gardens and maze gardens. All slumbering for the winter. What could Theodor possibly be showing me now?

We turned toward the mouth of the river, which ran alongside the gardens, and stopped beside a massive structure.

"What is this place?" I whispered. I hadn't seen it before—it had been well over a year since I'd visited the gardens.

"Nothing important," Theodor answered with a smile, opening the door of the greenhouse for me. "Only my masterpiece."

The building looked like an overturned shipwreck of metal and glass. A few workers puttering around the entrance stopped to watch us enter. They seemed to know Theodor, giving him friendly waves along with polite bows as we passed. Inside, I gazed upward. Metal arches rose above me like an iron rib cage. Suspended in the space between each was murky, opalescent glass.

And spreading out before me was a garden.

In the face of winter, a garden. I pulled my hood down and pressed further inside, letting the surprising warmth and mugginess surround me. I gasped, taking in rows of begonias and petunias at one turn, a tangle of ferns at another, and, best of all, long lines of tea roses and climbing roses surrounding a small but elaborate fountain covered with marble merpeople playing marble instruments.

"You made this?" I said, finally turning to face a beaming Theodor.

"In a manner of speaking," he said. "The workmen did most of the actual building. And gardeners planted most of it. I planted those, though," he added, nodding toward a tidy row of blush-colored impatiens.

"Rose balsam," I said. He smiled.

I wandered to a hedge of blooming flowers, brushing their soft petals with my fingertips. Like touching living silk. "It's like it's always summer here," I said.

"Like living in the countries nearest the equator," Theodor confirmed.

"Where you could study botany all year round?"

Theodor laughed, but he didn't sound happy. "My father thinks there are better uses for me here. Where winter comes and puts a right quick stop to botany."

"But not in here," I said, gesturing around me. "Is that why you built it?"

"Partially, yes. And partially in hopes that it will be a great success and convince my father that this sort of study is worthwhile. It doesn't matter how old an heir is," Theodor explained. "My endeavors are always tied to my father's indulgence. Even so, I hope the whole city comes and spends summer afternoons here in the middle of winter."

"I know I will," I said. "Though I love winter, too."

"Snow and gray and freezing rain. Piles of dirty slush in the streets. Yes, there's so much to love."

"Now, you can't disagree that Fountain Square looks like a fairy kingdom after a heavy snow. And besides," I said with a shrug, "it's excellent for business. All those cloaks and capuchins and muffs and mitts and mantelets. I pull in quite a bit of extra business each fall."

"Just as mercenary as I am," Theodor said, sidling closer to me. He slipped a hand behind my back and guided me toward a bank of climbing vines. Even in the heat of the greenhouse, his fingers were warm against my waist.

"What are these?" I asked, tracing the slender branch of brilliant green vine.

"Trumpet vine," he said. "See? It's budding. Blooming for the third time this year. I'm fascinated by the effects of climate on blooming seasons."

He took my hand and escorted me on a tour of the rest of the greenhouse, naming plants and explaining their significance to his research interests.

"And that's where my abilities, sadly, end," Theodor said. "I know what they all are and how they grow and that's it. If I want the public to gravitate toward this place, it needs to be aesthetically pleasing, as well."

"You think it's not?"

"I have no idea. You're the artist, not me."

"Hardly an artist," I murmured. I looked around. "It's beautiful as it is. But you could consider mixing the textures a bit more."

"How so?"

"If I have a shimmering silk, I might put fur next to it. If I have a rich brocade, I trim it with sheer organza."

Theodor stared at me blankly.

"You could try, say, putting mosses in among the ivies or something with rough bark next to those fuzzy-leaved plants."

"I think I see," Theodor said, examining a long bed of sweet white blossoms. "Contrast, is that it?"

"Precisely."

"What about colors? Do these all go together?"

I gazed around me. There had been no thought given to coordinating shades of color; purples bloomed next to oranges, and pinks cropped up among reds. In a gown they would have been disastrous.

Here, they were perfect.

"It's incredible how nature's colors behave so beautifully together," I said. "I don't think you can go wrong. In fact, carefully curating the colors would make this feel like a garden. As it is, it feels more like a summer wood."

"Or, perhaps, a jungle?" He grinned. "If so, I've succeeded." He placed my arm over his and led me slowly down the rows.

I wanted to see everything, touch everything, smell each sweetly scented blossom. And to spend more time with the handsome duke escorting me from plant to plant.

I forced myself to stop next to a sweetly scented trumpet vine. I needed to get back to work. Penny and Alice had been without me all morning, and we had orders that needed my charmed stitches before they could finish them.

"I—I really ought to leave." I felt a pang of jealousy toward nobles without schedules who could loiter in greenhouses all day.

"And here I had hoped to talk you into a summer picnic in my garden. I brought cheese and bread, and there is at least one pitiful little orange on one of those trees in the back," he said.

"Very tempting," I said, "but my assistants have been without me long enough."

"I suppose I can't expect to drag you away from your shop for so long," he said. "Perhaps another day? I'll want you to see the changes we discussed in action."

"I very much hope so," I answered honestly.

"Then I'll walk you back to your shop," he said with a smile.

16

—⁓—

WHEN WE REACHED MY SHOP, I LOITERED IN FRONT OF THE STOOP as Theodor glanced up and saw the sign hanging above the door.

"Quite a nice place you have," he said. I had the feeling he was fishing for something kind to say—my shop was nice enough, but it wasn't Lady Viola's luxurious salon.

"It serves me well," I replied modestly.

Theodor hesitated. "You wouldn't be interested in—"

The door flew open and Penny lunged outside. "Kristos is missing!"

"What?" I scrambled up the stairs and caught Penny's flapping hand. "What do you mean, my brother is missing? He was here yesterday."

"Yes, but he was supposed to be here first thing this morning and I've been waiting for hours—"

"First thing this morning? Here? Penny, I will not stand for these kinds of meetings happening in my shop, during hours that clients could come by."

"No, no, nothing like that. We've been meeting before work to have a bit of tea and a biscuit and talk..." She stared at me, imploring me to trust her.

"Fine, fine, he didn't come this morning. It's not unlike my brother to get caught up in something else and forget, you know." I flushed red—the last thing I wanted was for Theodor to witness some kind of melodramatic scene from Penny, and about my anti-monarchist brother, to boot.

"Did you see him this morning? At home?"

My hands turned cold. I hadn't—in fact, I had been surprised, as I washed my mug and cut a thick slice of brown bread for breakfast, that he hadn't come down to eat anything yet. When I had fetched a roll of brown paper from the closet between our rooms, I noticed through his door, left ajar, that his bed did not look slept in.

But none of this was terribly unusual for Kristos—like Theodor playing backgammon all night and falling asleep on Viola's sofa, Kristos had a habit of staying in the cafés until they closed and then making use of a nearby friend's floor.

Still, he hadn't failed to come home all night and then not stopped in the next morning for a very long time. My confidence faltered.

"Is there anything I could do to assist?" Theodor waited at the base of my steps.

"I'm sorry, but no," I answered, vague. My anti-monarchist brother meeting the duke who walked me home—that would go over like a tavern song in the cathedral. Better that he was missing than if he were here. I should have, I chided myself, thought of that. "Thank you for the walk."

"I'll drop a note about the gardens," he promised as he turned to walk away.

"What are we going to do?" Penny whimpered.

"We're going to wait," I answered. "I'm sure he's just caught up writing a pamphlet or organizing a protest," I added, though I wasn't nearly as sure as I tried to sound. "You must be very upset."

"Of course I am! Why would you say that?" Penny cried, rubbing her running nose on her apron.

"Because that was Theodor, First Duke of Westland."

I let her stare after him as I went inside.

Though I had thought that Penny was overreacting when she panicked over Kristos not showing up on time for tea and a biscuit, I grew concerned as I sat in our silent house that evening, the shadows growing long around me. It was entirely possible that he had neglected to tell me he was going to stay with a friend—sometimes, when he had a job on the outskirts of the city, he didn't come home but stayed with a workmate closer to the job site. The increased activity of the League nagged me, however. What if he had dug himself deeper into something? He might not tell me if he were involved in something truly illegal—smuggling weapons or the like. I shook this fear off. Even Kristos, even at his most grandiose, couldn't push for open revolt, for violence, for killing even the elite he despised.

Yet the elite were afraid, I knew from the women in Lady Viola's salon. Afraid enough, I was sure, to arrest Red Caps if they became disruptive, and Kristos was certainly capable of disruption. That Kristos was spending the night in a cell in the Stone Castle, and that he might be there for days, awaiting audience—this was a cold but very real possibility. It soured my stomach with fear, and I found I couldn't eat, or sleep, either. I stayed up later than I should have, eking an extra hour out of a candle stub, sewing to justify not going to bed. My seams were distracted and crooked. I eventually stabbed myself under my nail with my needle and decided I'd had enough.

I went to bed so late that I slept far later than usual, and wide swaths of sunlight streamed through my unshuttered window by the time I awoke. I dashed to Kristos's bedroom.

He hadn't returned.

I went inside, tentatively prodding the door open and tiptoeing in, acutely aware that I was trespassing. When one lives with an adult sibling, there are certain holy lines one does not cross. We didn't go into each other's rooms without express invitation.

I thought that this constituted a worthy enough emergency to break the law of the house.

Kristos lived a fairly spartan if unkempt life in his room under the eaves—two spare shirts were thrown haphazardly on a stool, his stockings were scattered, mateless, around the room, and a single pamphlet lay open on the floor beside the bed. I knelt to look at it. *Indentured to Nobility, or, the Rights of Free Men* was the incendiary title scrawled across the cover. I glanced at the author; Kristos hadn't written this one.

He had, however, left a stack of papers on his desk filled with his cramped, thin-stroked handwriting. The pen and ink were neatly put away—there was one thing in his possession Kristos apparently cared about. I squinted at the pen scratches, trying to read the first lines of the top page.

"*For when merchants and tradesmen must be licensed and vetted by the nobility to operate, there is a . . .*" I struggled to make out Kristos's cramped writing. "*. . . a monopoly perpetuated by the nobility. Likewise, when a government is ruled by a sole king, a monopoly on justice and liberty exists, doled out only to those he favors.*"

More of the same. I sighed. I almost wished I'd stumbled across a love note to Penny. I blushed—there might be one of those in this stack of papers. I backed out of the room, sweeping it once more for anything unusual. Was there anything here that shouldn't be? Anything missing?

The red cap. I scrutinized the room once more, realizing it was gone. That wasn't terribly unusual, but it did tell me where Kristos had been before he failed to come home—some gathering or protest with his anti-monarchist cronies.

Which made the possibility of arrest, I thought, all the more likely. Still, I reminded myself, two nights away from home was hardly something worth panicking over, and certainly something Kristos had done before. If he wasn't home by tonight, I promised myself, I would shore up my courage and go to the Stone Castle myself. I went to work, just as I usually did, stitched charms until Alice and Penny arrived, and we worked together on Madame Pliny's court gown. Alice did well, the fine stitching on her trimming improving, but Penny could barely sew a straight line. I tasked her with putting bolts of fabric back on the shelf; she was far too distracted to do anything else, even though it would have been helpful for her to heat irons to press Alice's seams. I imagined overheated irons burning a large hole through Alice's work and decided this wouldn't be a wise idea. The most complex job I could trust her with was wrapping orders in paper and twine.

"Something came for you," Alice said, calling from the counter where she was sorting receipts.

"Who brought it?" I asked, hurrying over to see if it was from Kristos.

"I don't know, some delivery boy. No one we've used before," she said. "I'm going to take my lunch break now, unless you need something else?"

"Of course, take extra time if you want." Alice pursed her lips—I knew she'd be back early. While Penny was drowning in worry and I spent time with nobles instead of sewing, Alice was the shop's anchor.

The parcel on the counter turned out to be a bouquet of flowers, wrapped in patterned paper. A note accompanied them; I tore it open.

Thinking of you, in hopes you've found your brother safe and well, it read. Signed, *Theodor.*

My stomach flipped. I'd hoped this was a message from

Kristos, but the kindness of Theodor's gesture touched me despite my disappointment. I folded back the paper and held up the flowers—rose balsam, I realized with a start. Theodor's favorite.

The door banged open and closed again, and I heaved an agitated sigh. Some clients galloped about like wild boars.

But it was Alice, not a rude client. I had never heard her so much as roughly shove the door, let alone slam it.

"Alice, what in the world—"

"There's a fight in Fountain Square," she breathed.

Penny darted out from the back room, but I stayed rooted by the counter. "A fight?" I asked. "There are fights in this city every day."

"No, not like that." Alice panted, trying to catch her breath. "Not a tavern brawl or two fellows going fisticuffs. The Red Caps and the City Guard."

"What kind of fight?" I gripped the counter.

"I'm sure the Red Caps were provoked," Penny asserted quickly. "They aren't idiots, you know." I glanced at her—had Kristos's fiery speeches kindled embers of discontent in her, as well?

"What kind of fight?" I repeated. "Alice, were they just arresting them or did they fire on them?"

"I don't know how it started. They were yelling before I got there. The Red Caps were lined up—almost like the army or something." My stomach dropped—adopting military posturing was beyond the pamphleteering and grandstanding they'd restricted themselves to thus far.

Alice continued. "There were a few City Guards telling them to leave and—someone shoved them."

"Who shoved whom?" I asked, voice cool and clear as ice.

"The Red Caps. They pushed the guards. But I couldn't be sure if they really meant to start anything serious, or if a few of them got out of line. Then there were reinforcements from the Stone Castle, with rifles, they were wearing rose-colored uniforms, so I know they were riflemen, and they—" Her voice caught.

"They shot them?" Penny screeched. "For just—for just pushing the guards?"

"They wouldn't disperse and—someone fired. I don't know if he was supposed to. But then it was turning to chaos, so I ran." Penny glowered, and Alice started crying.

I hesitated, then asked the question that had been needling me since Alice began the story. "Did you . . . recognize any of the rebels?"

"You mean did I see your brother?"

I flushed hot, but Alice's tone wasn't judgment. It was mere clarification, pointing out a fact we all knew already. "Yes, that's what I meant."

She softened slightly. "No, I didn't. But I can't help but wonder—maybe that is why he's gone."

Penny started. "What does that mean?"

Alice folded her hands, patient like a schoolmistress. "If they're attacking soldiers, they must have some sort of plan, yes? And if Kristos is as heavily invested as he's always seemed, it makes sense he might be underground somewhere, waiting to act."

"They weren't attacking the guard," Penny bristled. "They were fired upon." Alice just shook her head, still too upset to argue.

"Kristos wouldn't," I said. "He wouldn't be involved in violence. He always said we had to change people's minds . . ."

"For what?" Penny's voice startled me. "Change whose minds? The nobility isn't changing." I swallowed—this was the kind of extremism Kristos resorted to after long nights debating in the tavern. I had never taken him seriously, but if Penny was parroting him? Or, I admitted, not parroting him at all, but voicing the common thoughts of a movement I had underestimated?

"There will be no talk of sedition in this shop," I said. "Let's keep in mind, ladies, that we can't afford sedition," I added with a pointed nod toward the work board, populated with names of noble families. No one as high ranking as Lady Viola, but lesser nobles paid good money, too, as did successful tradesmen's wives and daughters who no doubt didn't wish to risk their success on revolt.

"I won't talk of it," Penny said. "But can you honestly say you don't sympathize, at least a little?"

I hesitated. "It doesn't matter if I—"

"Of course it does! My brother trained as an apprentice to a butcher in our neighborhood for four years—no pay, just training, all in hopes that the Lord of Coin would sign off on the transfer of ownership of the shop someday. He didn't."

"I know, it isn't fair, and I don't like the rules governing business, either."

"If you don't like them, why not fight them?" It was the sort of argument Kristos made, over and over. "My cousin's family had to beg last winter when he couldn't get any work. When the nobles decide who works and who doesn't, maybe they're forgetting that means some eat and some don't."

"Penny..." Alice wiped her damp cheeks with the back of her hand.

"No!" Penny yelled, and I had the feeling they had discussed this, many times, out of my hearing. "I'm tired of being told to wait and see, that what we have now is better than what revolution could bring." She pressed her lips together, and I saw tears pinpointed in the corners of her eyes. "Even without Kristos here, Jack and Niko have plenty of ideas, and the League listens."

Alice opened her mouth to argue, but I shook my head, even though I had never been more unnerved, even listening to Kristos's most fiery arguments, even reading the most incendiary of the League's pamphlets. If even Penny could be a revolutionary, open and arguing for an uprising, anything could happen. "I understand their frustration, but I will not sympathize with violence. No one here will, at least not in my hearing or where our—your—clients can hear you. Is that clear?"

Penny nodded grudgingly, and though I had to hold a firm line in the shop, the creeping realization that I did understand the frustration that led to sedition unnerved me. I could no longer pretend that the League was working in words only. Whether they had intended it or not, I knew that the events in Fountain Square meant that some invisible line had been crossed, erased, even. The Red Caps would risk their lives for their cause; if they would stand against the king's riflemen, open revolt seemed far less impossible than it had before. And if it came to full revolt, whose side was I on?

17

FOUNTAIN SQUARE FELT DIFFERENT THE NEXT DAY. THOSE WHO sympathized with the Red Caps called it The Massacre, for the twelve comrades who had been shot and the five who died. Those who sympathized with the soldiers called it The Riot for the mass gathering of Red Caps, who had clogged the square with their shouting. I wasn't sure what to call it. In the aftermath, the Lord of Keys added an armed patrol to the square and the surrounding streets. No one felt any safer.

Though a couple of businesses shuttered temporarily, Alice and Penny still came to work the next day, stoic or stubborn or simply reliant on income. We kept sewing with a quiet determination, as though the certainty of our needles and the persistence of our threads would make some sort of difference in the growing unrest just outside the doors of the shop.

After the violence in the square, I had decided not to ask after Kristos at the Stone Castle, concerned that I could be caught in another spate of fighting. I worried more than before that he had been arrested, that the Lord of Keys had sniffed out potential insurrection and its ringleaders. I was beginning to consider Theodor's offer of help with my brother—after all, he had connections within the city, especially with the Lord of Keys, who commanded the city's soldiers. So when a note came from him inviting me to come see the changes at the greenhouse, written in thick calligraphy on paper redolent with rose scent, I was relieved but still unsure if I could even ask for assistance. In truth, Kristos often had the bad habit of thinking of himself and his whims first and other people second. He jumped so wholeheartedly into every new endeavor that he more than once had forgotten to tell me that he was going down the river for a job for the week or that he would be at a friend's near the university for a few days to attend more lectures in the evenings.

Still, with the unrest in the city, the jail in the Stone Castle reportedly full of Red Caps arrested for rioting, and the mounting distrust between the soldiers and the Red Caps, I was afraid, and worried enough to ask for help.

I met Theodor at the greenhouse. His sleeves were rolled past the elbow, and he wore the coarse linen apron of a tradesman. It was smudged with dirt, which made me smile without meaning to. He caught my hands and gave me the kiss on the cheek that I knew was quite normal for nobles—though from him it made my cheeks flush a little.

"Thank you for asking me," I said, not sure how to broach my question.

I didn't have to. "Now that we're in relative privacy," he said, "have you heard from your brother?"

I swallowed, surprised and a bit overcome by his immediate concern. "No. Nothing at all."

"Care to tell me how I might help?"

"I'm not sure what you could do," I answered honestly.

"Well," Theodor said with a maddening smile, "I have a dizzying network of friends, a very powerful family, and plenty of money. Those things aren't worth much in the long run, but in the short run they can make quite a difference. I'll make inquiries with the Lord of Keys if you wish."

"Very well," I said. That was more than I could have done by myself. Kristos would never forgive me. "I...don't think he would want your help," I added.

"K. B., the infamous anti-monarchist? Probably not."

"You know?" My mouth dropped open.

"He's actually a rather good writer."

"You've read it?"

"It? I've read them—all three of the long pamphlets he's put out, as well as the condensed broadside versions. We discussed them at Viola's a week ago."

"So everyone there knows that..." I let my voice trail away in disappointment. My brother was missing, and now I'd lost what was shaping up to be my best shot at expanding my studio. My entire clientele would abandon me. I wouldn't even be able to afford to eat in a few weeks.

"Of course not. I'm cleverer than most; I figured it out." He shrugged. "That, or one of the gardeners here is an acquaintance of his, recognized you, and said something to me. I'm sticking to the 'clever' story myself."

I laughed, but I was embarrassed. "And you're still associating with me?"

"You're not your brother," he said. "Some of his ideas are actually quite good. Not the ones involving toppling the nobility, of course. But he has some excellent points regarding the benefits of committees over individuals for building code decisions, and the impacts of deregulation of business permits." I raised an eyebrow—Kristos had studied his Melchoir and other economists more carefully than I had realized, if he could impress an educated noble. "In any case, I'm helping you, not him or the Grand Revolution. If ransom money comes into play—"

"Ransom money!" I blanched.

"Not that I expect that," he said. "Please, let me do what I can. I'll make some inquiries, ensure he hasn't been arrested." He paused, suddenly aware of what he had said. "I suppose you must have known that was a possibility," he added more gently.

I nodded. "I don't know what I'll do if—" Suddenly, I was almost crying. I bit back hot tears as Theodor caught my hand.

"A bit of distraction, then," he said, confident. "You know, you're the only person I've shown around in here. I mean, besides the architects and the workers and all."

"Me?" A smile threatened to break through my melancholy. "Not your parents? Your noble friends?"

"My parents don't care," he said swiftly. "To them, gardening is a diversion, and a noble is allowed diversions, but not passions outside of their duties to the Crown."

"I confess, I suppose I see only the diversions—the gowns and parties and fine houses." I hesitated, not sure if I'd said something offensive.

Theodor tilted his head with a dim smile, as though finally comprehending some problem that had eluded him. "That does explain a certain level of animosity I've never quite understood among the more vocal Red Caps. As though we do nothing for the country, as though all we do is skim the cream for ourselves and then leave the milk to sour. We—nobles—take our duties exceptionally seriously. Even the most minor among us see ourselves as pledged first to Galitha, then our own interests. There is precious little freedom in that."

"But not everyone is a Lord of Coin or Keys or a council member," I argued. "You can understand why—say, Viola for example—why a common worker would see her life as one of diversion alone."

"Then they don't know what responsibility is requisite of

even the most underling noble. Direct service to the Crown, either civic or military, whenever it's called upon. Management of lands to produce enough grain to feed his own people and export. We don't go to our country estates every summer just to enjoy the air—we have to split our time between the capital and the lands we manage."

I had known this, but only vaguely—that the farms and orchards and vineyards that ran the breadth of Galitha's rich heartland were noble estates, often hundreds of miles from the capital. Theodor continued. "Imagine running your shop but instead of two employees, you've dozens or hundreds of families in the village under your employ. Imagine a failed crop spelling their starvation." He exhaled, cheeks red with frustration. "Yes, we have our diversions and our wealth—but it comes at some cost."

The duties of a noble—of course Theodor had no more choice in this than my brother did in being a day laborer. I felt, all the more keenly, the prize I had fought for and attained— the choice in my work, the ability to drape fabric into a life for myself.

"I had no idea—I hadn't considered that. Truly."

He nodded, but he hadn't finished. "Even Viola—when she's not hosting her salon or painting, she's writing letters and reading invoices and paying bills. The Snowmont estate's vineyards have done exceptionally well under her management while her father's attention has been on his duty as Lord of Keys. And yes, it means fine silks and money for parties." His cheeks reddened further, as though this were something he felt he must apologize for. "But it also means increased revenue to the Crown and, through that, benefits to the entire nation.

"A noble who thinks only of his own interests, of her own enjoyment, is a disgrace to both family and Crown," Theodor concluded. I sat in silence a moment. "I didn't mean to raise my voice," he added, quieter. "And certainly not at you. I just—I hadn't realized what you must think of all of us."

"I think I understand a bit better now," I whispered. "But you must be able to see—you didn't choose your duties, but the ordinary people—my brother, for example—didn't choose not to take on the responsibility you describe. I rather think some would take it upon themselves, and gladly."

"I suppose you're right. It's in all their writings, swimming just under the surface. The council is behaving as though we're quelling riots, not dealing with a deeper discontent. I've proposed several small concessions—an elected council of common people, a trade committee to share authority with the Lord of Coin. I've been roundly ignored and told in no uncertain terms by my father that I'm treading shaky ground."

"Do they not believe the common people want responsibility of governance, or that they're not capable of handling it?"

"I don't know. Both, most likely. Not to mention, they all accept the old theory that concession—especially of the variety that gives some of our authority to the populace—is the mark of weak governance. Half the council thinks they should all be arrested and tried for anti-monarchical treason; the other half thinks we should just ignore them and wait for them to get hungry enough to decide to get back to earning a wage instead of shouting in the street. Both ideas are, of course, rubbish, unless we really do want a revolution." He sounded quietly frustrated yet unsurprised.

"But you're right," I blurted out before I could think. "I don't mean that I agree with armed revolt, but you're right."

He raised an eyebrow. "Your read on the populace is similar to mine, then?"

"I don't know if I'm anything like an expert," I cautioned him. "But I don't think they'll be ignored forever. And"—I winced, thinking of Penny—"I think you're dealing with far too many of them to arrest and try for treason, and they're far less easy to ferret out than you might imagine."

"My father is not a fool, and neither is the king, but they can't accept that the will of the people may actually amount to something. They want to be benevolent leaders," he added, almost as an apology, "but it seems they've underestimated those they purport to lead."

"And they won't listen to you?" I asked. "I only mean that— you're not exactly a minor noble."

"Sometimes fathers have a difficult time accepting their sons as peers, and uncles see only their childish nephews," Theodor said with a slight smile, "even when the fathers and uncles are princes and kings, and the sons and nephews are grown men who have been in noble council chambers for near a decade. Besides, my voice is only one. Years of study, and outside the noble canon, at Viola's salon, might have something to do with the fact that I see this quite differently than they do."

"Viola assigns more radical reading than your tutors?" I laughed.

"Immensely so. But I think it's lent me a better-informed position than theirs." He sighed. "No matter, at least at the moment. There's a garden to assess."

"Your acquaintances are busy running a country, so you have to show your work to a bumpkin," I said.

"Hardly! I wanted to show it to an artist. I hope you're not offended that I consider you—well, a peer of sorts. Someone who designs and creates."

This surprised me, and I couldn't help a bashful smile. "I'm not offended in the slightest."

"Your points about contrast were perfectly made," he said, leading me farther inside. I noticed the changes immediately.

Trees had been incorporated into the flower displays, standing sentinel behind them, and there were thick carpets of moss in many of the beds of foliage. Fruit-bearing branches and flowering shrubs were moved side by side.

"I love it," I said.

"Good," Theodor said. "Now that work is over, something for lunch?"

The low table under a pair of blossoming orange trees was distinctly romantic, decorated with trailing vines and its shadows illumined by candles.

"What is your plan, anyway?" I demanded without thinking, all the frustration of the past days emerging in an angrier tone than I meant.

"Plan? I had figured we'd start with fruit and move on to a cold ham and some mustard." He raised an eyebrow. "That's not the plan you mean."

"I just—that's not precisely a friendly table setting. It looks like something the nicer cafés do for wedding parties."

Theodor flushed. "You know, noblewomen tend to just play along and pretend they can't see through our ruses."

Despite myself, I laughed. "We've established I'm not a noble."

"Does seeing past the ruse ruin the effect?" he asked quietly, leading me to one of the chairs and then sitting across from me. He didn't release my hand.

"Hardly," I breathed. His hand on mine, the flowering vines on the table, the flickering candlelight. "It's quite effective."

He smiled and poured the wine. "Good. I try for effect."

It was an enjoyable game, almost like a dance, to let Theodor pour my wine and joke with me and brush his hand against mine as though by accident. I couldn't lose myself completely in the nuances of it, as the romantic little cocoon of the greenhouse was punctured consistently by thoughts of my missing brother, but I found myself smiling, laughing, leaning toward Theodor's touch without meaning to at all.

I had to hurry back to the shop after the lunch, a fitting appointment with the merchant's daughter and her green ball gown demanding my attention. A messenger arrived mere hours later, not a hired boy like most of the city's messengers, but a liveried servant. His gray silk frock coat bore the emblem of Theodor's house, and he dipped a polite bow as he handed me thick cream paper, folded in thirds and sealed with sky-blue sealing wax. The letter inside was written in a well-practiced script, but its contents were merely perfunctory—Theodor had spoken, without revealing who my brother was, to the Lord of Keys. Kristos was not under arrest, nor did the city's soldiery have any record of where he might be. By the time I had considered that I should pen a brief reply, the servant had left, and the only person outside my shop was a bearded vagrant with patched breeches and a ragged hood.

I sent Penny on a round of deliveries, usually one of her favorite tasks. I didn't have the energy to make small talk while Kristos was still missing, and I thought the assignment might cheer her up.

Instead, she came back looking like she'd been crying, her eyes swollen and red. I'd had enough waiting. There were a few cafés that I knew Kristos frequented most often—the Hazel Dell, the Fair Isle, the Rose and Fir. Perhaps someone there had seen him.

"Do you want to help me find Kristos?" I asked Penny.

She stood up like a shot. "Yes, anything."

"Alice, mind the shop," I said. Alice muttered something about all the work to be done, but I didn't have time to salve her feelings.

We started with the Rose and Fir; it was the closest. I carried a miniature of Kristos—it wasn't the best rendering, but when I added, "tall, loud, wears a red cap, and talks too much about liberty," the barkeep knew just who I was talking about.

"Wasn't here this week, though. We get crowded this time of year—just tapped the winter lagers—and his crowd likes a place they can sit and yammer and not get bothered too much."

"Have you seen any of them in the last couple of days?" I hoped out loud.

"Nope. Well, one fellow three days ago. But he was rabble-rousing, and I don't tolerate those kinds of shenanigans in my establishment. Threw him out, right quick."

He didn't know a name, and it wouldn't have helped me much anyway.

The waitress at the Hazel Dell wasn't any more helpful. She recognized Kristos—her bright-eyed giggle when she saw the portrait made Penny flush scarlet and ball her fists up behind her back—but said he hadn't been in for days.

"And the others, his…friends?" I asked.

"Come back after nightfall, some might be here. But they don't frequent the place during the day much." She left us to attend to a few customers eating slabs of ham and coarse brown bread.

"This isn't helping," Penny exclaimed as soon as we left.

"Well, we know we can go back there later and probably find someone who knows him," I said. Penny didn't look encouraged.

I was both relieved and very, very nervous to see a cluster of red caps at a table at the Fair Isle. I skipped talking to the bartender and approached them instead.

"Who's this, new waitstaff?" a tall blond with an overgrown mustache asked with a wink.

"No," I replied, "my name is Sophie and I'm looking—"

"Whatever you're looking for, I'd say you've found it." A broad-shouldered oaf missing a pair of teeth guffawed at his own joke.

"No, really. I'm looking for my brother and—"

Penny yelped as the blond smacked her square on her false rump. He shook his fingers in mock pain. "There's a damn road-block under those skirts!"

I'd had enough. I slammed the rickety table with my hand, knocking over three mugs of beer in the ensuing tremor. "I am looking for my brother, Kristos," I announced in a commanding voice. "Have any of you seen him?"

"Your brother? Some lad she fools with, more likely. Make you forget him," the oaf said. He spit unintentionally through the spot where his teeth used to be. I backed away, disgusted.

"Sophie!" I whirled—Jack stood a few tables away. "Is everything all right?"

I glared at the table of idiots, the oaf with the missing teeth in particular. "Fine," I muttered.

"Leave her alone," Jack said to the blond, who was angling for a look under Penny's petticoat. "Hey! Do you want to discuss this outside?" I wouldn't have crossed Jack's barrel chest, but the blond was as big as he was. Still, he mumbled an apology and shrank back into his bench. I remembered what Penny had said—that Jack and Niko were well respected among the Red Caps.

"Why are you here?" he asked, ushering us toward the door.

"I'm looking for Kristos," I said. "Haven't you seen him?"

"Not since last week—I've been on a job hauling bricks for the new masonwork going up." His brow constricted. "He's missing?"

"Yes," I answered, short. "I—if you see him before I do,

I'll...I'll box his ears when he comes home!" My lip trembled, and I turned away so Jack wouldn't see.

"All right, now, all right." Jack tried to soothe me with a hand on my arm. I shook him off. His eyes narrowed. "Fine, Sophie, that's just fine."

"I'm sorry." I swallowed. "I'm just...worried."

Jack took off his cap and ran a hand through snarled hair. "A few of the boys have been taken up by the guards," he said, voice low. "I don't think the Stone Castle knows who's who in our leadership, but it's possible..."

"I already checked," I said, pulling back a little. There was risk, certainly, in leading this movement—I saw that all too clearly now. "And he wasn't hurt in the...unrest in Fountain Square."

"No," Jack said, returning the cap to his head and straightening his broad shoulders. "I know every lad who was. And I was there myself, giving orders."

The pride in his voice reminded me of the chestnut seller everyone called Old Bruno, who had served in the army in his youth and recalled the engagements he had seen—border scuffles with Kvys dragoons, which no one listening recalled from their history books or their own memory—with similar zeal. Except this wasn't long-past service to the Crown; it was open insurrection, and Jack was leading it.

"And I don't suppose you intended for it to end in bloodshed," I said.

Jack's ears reddened. "Of course not. That was the soldiers' fault—firing without due cause." I didn't care to argue. He returned to his bench and his ale, and I motioned to Penny that we should leave.

I tied the ribbons to close my cloak and waited while Penny untangled her glove from her pocket.

"You're Kristos's sister?"

I turned. A waitress, younger than me and with a pair of thin braids framing her freckled face, waited expectantly.

"Yes," I said. "You know my brother?"

"Kind of," she said. "I mean, he's here a lot. Sometimes he reads stuff he writes—I like listening to it. I get in trouble sometimes for listening instead of working."

I smiled wanly. Kristos would have appreciated the compliment. "Have you seen him in the past couple days?" I had to ask.

"Yes," she said. My heart flopped.

"When? Yesterday?"

"No, two days ago. At night. He was here with some friends—"

"Not those men?" I asked, gesturing to the table.

She squinted. Her face wrinkled like a paper sack. "I don't think so. I can't keep most of them straight. Anyway, he was here, and he read some stuff, and I got yelled at and sent to the back to wash dishes, and when I came back, pretty late, he was leaving."

"Alone, I suppose," I sighed. He'd left a bar, late at night, and hadn't been seen since.

"No," she said. "There was a man leaving with him. They were talking, really serious."

"Who was he?" I demanded.

"I don't know," she apologized. "He was older, and wore a black greatcoat. But everyone wears dark greatcoats, so...I don't know." My heart, still beating fast, constricted like a fist. So close, and another dead end.

"Would you know him if you saw him again?" Penny asked, piping up for the first time.

"I think so," she said. "I mean, he had a distinctive face, I guess I'd say? Yeah, distinctive. Different. You know?"

"Yes," Penny said, "exactly. You see him again, you send him to us." She handed the barmaid a card. I hadn't thought of that.

"Should we go to the Stone Castle and report him missing?" Penny asked, trotting to catch up with me as I strode as quickly as I could from the tavern. I was angry—angry at the men who were more interested in propositioning me than helping, angry at the poor stupid barmaid who didn't know the name of the man Kristos had left with, angry most of all with Kristos. And Penny's question made me even angrier.

"What good would that do?" I demanded. "He isn't there— I've checked. And we've done more than the Lord of Keys and his soldiers would bother to. We haven't much to go on to begin with, and he's known to run in these anti-monarchist circles."

"It's still their job—"

"To tell us they've made a note and if he turns up they'll come round for a how-do-you-do, yes, of course."

"I just meant..."

I slowed and looked at Penny. Tears filled her big blue doe eyes, and she bit her lower lip like a chastised child.

"I'm sorry, Penny. I know you're as upset as I am. But trust me—the soldiers won't help us. They'd laugh us off."

And within a few minutes of brisk walking, we were right back where we started—in front of my shop, Kristos still missing.

18

—ᴍ—

I DIDN'T TELL PENNY, BUT I KEPT LOOKING FOR KRISTOS ALL evening. I even wandered into the cathedral as an evening service was ending. The placard by the entrance noted that the service was dedicated to the Sacred Nature of the Galatine Sea, and sure enough, a dozen fishwives clustered near the front of the sanctuary. They bowed their heads in contemplation as a choir's harmonies pierced a thick cloud of incense.

My brother wouldn't be here, I chided myself, and not only because his particular trade and interest was not the sea. Galatines gathered publicly to worship the divinity of the land and people who formed the nation; Pellians maintained reverence for their own ancestors and the family spirit and kept their prayers private, at home. The concepts were not so different, interested in an innate sacredness of either a national or personal nature. Kristos had never considered either worth his time. Still, I stopped for a few moments, appreciating the intricate vocal harmonies and the way the last of the sunset filtered through the stained glass and splashed pools of color on the long flagstone aisles.

A small alcove opened on my left, and I slipped out of the main sanctuary as the fishwives joined the priest in the final prayer of the service. The walls in the alcove were mosaics, depicting all of the Sacred Natures of Galitha—the sea, the fields, the forests, the spirit of trade and commerce, the divinity of governance. Candles punctuated the images, inviting the penitent to illuminate the alcove with a visible representation of their prayers. Flames flickered below the faces and landscapes, casting strange shadows. I hesitated, as this was not truly my faith or my brother's, but I picked up a long taper and lit a votive beneath the mosaic depicting the sunburst-flocked Day's Coin, honoring the labor of the working class, as though any small prayer, even half-believed, could help me.

Then I went to the Fair Isle, intent on keeping vigil in what was far closer to my brother's house of worship than the cathedral.

Midway through my first glass of subpar wine, someone tapped my shoulder. I nearly flew into the rafters, but it was only Emmi.

"You're not here by yourself, are you?" I said when I recovered my breath.

"No, my brother and his friends are playing dice—what is the matter with you?" She sat next to me. "You look like you've seen a demon."

Only a Pellian would say that, I thought as I laughed quietly. "No, I'm looking for someone. I thought—it's no matter." I glanced at the group of men, mostly Pellian, tossing dice and passing dice cups at a long table by the window. "You don't play?"

She wrinkled her nose. "Only old grandmamas play dice," she said. "And boys, of course. I'm just—watching." She blushed, and I understood; she was sweet on one of her brother's friends.

I remembered that feeling, the excitement of joining your brother for a game of cards or dice, hoping that his whole set would show up. What had that boy's name been? Maro. I smiled into my wine, forcing another sip. The only Pellian boy I ever thought handsome, another dockworker like Kristos, who walked me home a few times but was warned by his mama and grandmama against charm-casting girls, who might just be tricking you into loving them with a spell, even though the ethics I'd inherited from my mother prohibited making charms for my own benefit, and most charm casters followed similar self-governing rules.

I wondered if Emmi had the same problem. For me, of course, it was probably for the best—I knew now that the complication of a family would be impossible to balance with the shop, and that coverture laws meant a husband or his family could take everything from me. But for a girl like Emmi, who brought in a few coins each market day with her charms but little else, marriage was a necessity.

"Do you—Sophie, are you listening?" I turned my attention back to Emmi. "You're not married, are you?"

It was as though she were reading my mind. "No, Emmi."

"Is it—is it because men like their charms at the racetrack but not in their own kitchens, like Mama says?"

I laughed. "No, I'm—it's too complicated, owning a business. You won't have the same trouble I do if you keep selling charms at your stall in the market, though."

"I know, but—I guess I don't understand the laws well enough. What kind of awful man would steal from his wife?"

"I thought the same, once." I sighed. "I knew a woman who had a millinery shop. It was—she made the loveliest things."

"Did you make charms for her?"

"No, she was my first assistantship." I remembered Mrs. Davies, a plump, happy woman with a halo of blond curls, always festooned with one of her elaborate creations of organdy and silk. I had been very fortunate, finding a shop owner who was not only masterful in her field but also willing to hire and train a novice Pellian orphan. "I just sewed caps—sewing caps is the best training for any kind of fine sewing," I added. "Her husband would never have hurt her. But he fell ill, and the doctor's bill came, and then another, and his brother took over managing his finances while Mr. Davies was sick."

Emmi's eyes widened. "Her brother-in-law stole from her?"

"It wasn't stealing, legally. He just sold the shop, to pay the bills."

"And what did she do?"

"What could she do?" I gulped some more sour wine. "She couldn't recover the money to buy another storefront, and the Lord of Coin had blacklisted her as a failed business owner anyway. She does mending and some sewing now, but only what she can sell from her house." Laws prohibited hiring assistants or taking apprentices unless a person had an established business. I had tried, when my shop first opened, to see if she needed extra work, but she cheerfully declined, saying that her eyes were failing for fine work but her son's butcher shop would keep the family comfortable. I wasn't sure I believed her on either count as I watched her whip gather a length of delicate organdy.

Emmi nodded, understanding a little more. A little more how unfair the world could be, how I tried to even the field for myself by avoiding a husband.

"I'm sorry, Emmi—that was a sad story on a nice evening."

"No, I'm glad you told me. I wondered why—I mean, you're very pretty, Sophie. And you're not—before we knew you, we thought you must be unkind, to have a successful shop and no husband." She pressed her lips together while I laughed. "I'm sorry...I didn't mean—"

"No, I understand." I caught my breath. A harpy, that's what they thought I must be. "You don't have to worry about any of this, Emmi," I added, softer. "And I want you to come by the shop sometime soon, if you're still interested in picking up work.

We're getting busier, and I could use a spare set of hands a few hours a week."

Emmi grinned. "Thank you! Do you think—if it's not too impertinent to even ask—I might learn a few new stitches? Maybe watch your assistants drape?"

I laughed. Emmi was as enterprising as I had been at her age. "I think that can be arranged." She gave a giddy little hop and returned to her table, sitting a little closer to one young man than the others. I thought again of what Mrs. Davies had done for me, her patient, plump hands demonstrating stroke gathers or a rolled hem, the faint scent of rose hair powder wafting over her shop, and felt a faint twinge of guilt. I had been very lucky, I conceded—worked hard, of course, but without a benefactor I might never have learned the skills of my trade. Plenty of shop owners would avoid hiring a Pellian or even a provincial girl, worried that she would seem unrefined or bring bad habits with her, blemishing the shop's image. It was past time that I consider providing that kind of benefactorship with my own shop.

The freckled waitress I had spoken with about Kristos passed by me, and at first I thought she was only going to ask if I wanted more wine. Then, her thin hand gripped my elbow like the fire tongs I used to move logs in our fat stove at home, and I knew she had news. My throat tightened.

"Over there," she whispered.

"What?" I asked, shaking her conspiratorial pinch from my arm.

"That man's back," she answered, pointing. I swatted her hand down. Drawing attention to ourselves wouldn't help.

But I followed the line her finger had made across the room and saw him. Distinctive, like she had said; his shadowed profile was not handsome, precisely, but somehow authoritative. He turned his face so that the firelight illuminated him more fully—it was Pyord Venko. I inhaled the smoky air, and it burned my throat.

"How long has he been here?" I asked, trying not to stare.

"Most of the evening," she answered, rubbing her swatted hand. "It's like he's waiting for someone."

"Kristos," I whispered. What now? Did I hide here at the bar and pretend to drink while I watched him? Probably best, I thought. I didn't know what he was planning, or if it was even safe to talk to him. There was a dark edge to his regal looks, an arrogance that hinted at danger. I hadn't liked it when I was safe with my brother at the university or surrounded by my charm-casting friends at the coffee shop. I certainly didn't like it now, alone and vulnerable. I untied my cloak and began to slide onto a bench.

He looked up at just that moment and met my eyes. I felt cold, but knew immediately—there was no hiding from him.

"You recall that I am Sophie Balstrade," I said, my voice squeaking ever so slightly. "I am looking for my brother."

"Indeed." The word crackled like the logs in the fire behind him.

"Yes. And the barmaid said she had seen you with him."

"Nosy little wench," he said. Not angrily, but amused.

"You looked like you were waiting for someone. And I thought—"

"It might be him? No, I'm not meeting Kristos here." His smile turned up the corners of his mouth, but it didn't change his stern eyes. That was it, then. I felt empty defeat as my eyes prickled with hot tears.

"No," he repeated, "I'm not waiting for Kristos. I'm waiting for you."

19

—⚬—

"ME?" I CHOKED.

"You." He smiled as though this were a polite pleasantry, and motioned to the freckled barmaid. She scurried over, giving my shocked face one short glance before turning back to Pyord.

"Sir?"

"A bottle of red and two glasses."

"What kind of wine—"

"It doesn't matter." He stared at me as though the girl wasn't even there.

"I'm not thirsty," I said in a low breath.

"I didn't think you were." He folded his gloves on the table, neatly, like Alice folding fabric remnants. "I thought you might need a glass of wine."

I didn't reply, but my insides were growing cold.

"I imagine you want to know where your brother is."

"Yes!" I nearly shouted. The men at the next table shot me a look and sniggered. "Yes, very much so. You know where he is? You've seen him?"

"Of course." The wine arrived and the waitress fumbled with the corkscrew. I was nearly bursting by the time she finally left. "I'm afraid I can't tell you, however," he replied as he steadily poured two dingy glasses full of bloodred liquid.

"You...what?" My hands clenched around my skirt in my lap. What was this, some kind of game? "You'll tell me," I said, trying for authoritative.

"In due time, certainly. But I have a few requests you'll need to agree to first."

"I have very important friends," I said, changing tactics.

"Yes, I know," he said, laughing. He took a sip of the wine. "Rather one of the reasons I've had to arrange this meeting. But if you tell anyone what we are about to discuss, including your friend the esteemed Lady Viola Snowmont, I'll kill your brother."

The threat hung between us, finally verbalized. I was hollow, and it echoed within me. Kill Kristos. That threat would make me do anything.

"What do you want?"

"There we are." The wine swirled in his glass. I wasn't sure if he was talking about my question or the legs of the wine snaking down the glass. "You have certain skills. I would like you to use them for us."

"Charms?" I said. "I'll do whatever work you want, at a discount. No need to hold my brother hostage."

Venko cocked his head and took another sip of wine. His deliberateness was maddening, as was his calm demeanor—as though proving, always, that he was in control of our exchange. "I don't need charms. I need curses."

"I don't do curses."

"Hence the hostage. I had to find some way to convince you."

"No," I argued. "Even if I wanted to make curses, I don't know how."

He laughed. The wine was staining his teeth. For some reason, this put a chink in his impenetrable façade and made me feel less threatened. "You only think you don't know how. If you know how to make charms, you can make curses. It won't take long for you to learn the differences in the method."

"It's not that simple," I pressed. "It can't be." My mother had always indicated that the methods were fundamentally different, that curses were complicated, that even learning about curses was dangerous. That curses would corrupt the caster. Could she have been hiding the truth about the dark side of our gift to protect me? Perhaps even she didn't know.

Why would I assume that this man knew anything about charms, anyway? What he learned in books didn't mean anything in practice. If he was pressing me to work for him, clearly he couldn't do the work himself. He didn't have the gift.

"We'll discuss the theory and practice of curses in depth, at length, and soon," he said. He looked almost excited at the prospect, as though he were embarking on a new experiment, a new tangent of research. "For now, your role in what I hope you realize is a historic turning point."

"I had hoped, Professor, to keep my role in the current situation as removed as possible," I reminded him.

"Which is now an impossibility. I'm sorry it had to come to this—I had hoped, after meeting you, that you would agree to assist us of your own volition. Now I've had to take measures I would not otherwise have chosen." He sighed, exhaling something that was perhaps real remorse, or perhaps a very good imitation of it. "I've been forced to put your brother's life up as collateral, in exchange for one simple curse from you."

"Why would you kidnap one of your own?" I retorted. Kristos was a known leader in the League, a writer whose work had certainly persuaded many to put on a red cap.

Venko shook his head, his brow furrowed. "There are those of us who believe in action. A true...revolution, shall we say.

Not an exchange of words any longer, but of blows. Most of the Laborers' League has been convinced of this necessity. More are joining each day. Even workers from the countryside, some even traveling from the port cities in the southern provinces, and the mill towns in the west. We have the numbers we need now. I tell you this because I have to, because you must understand the seriousness of this endeavor."

I swallowed, hard. This man was openly admitting treason to me—not just anti-monarchist sentiments, but intentions of real, active treason. He even sounded as though there was a plan in place already, work under way.

And he wanted me to help him with it.

"I will not be a part of that. Kristos would never—"

"Exactly. Kristos was reticent to agree to take this movement to its natural conclusion. And clearly his gifted sister is even less inclined. Sadly, to do what we need, we must force a crack in the protections the royal family encases themselves with—their guards and spies and advisors. A curse will do that."

"You want to hurt the royal family," I summarized, stunned.

"Kill them, to be precise. The king, at least. But you know as well as I that any scheme will have but one chance at working, and will be a long shot at that. To get someone inside the palace, to overcome the guards, to avoid detection by the spies?"

"You're right, near impossible. You should probably give up," I said.

He wasn't amused. "We can do all these things, but our plan requires that a darkness already surround the family—at least one of them. That they attract disaster, not exist in a natural equilibrium in which self-preservation will aid them."

"I'm not making a cursed garment for a member of the king's family," I said, shoving the wineglass in front of me away, as though this alone rejected his deal. "Find someone else."

"There isn't anyone else," he replied. "Someone who can craft something the royal family would commission? Something they would welcome into the palace, something they would wear, something they would keep on their royal persons?" He shook his head, gazing into the wine in his glass. "I honestly don't know of anyone who does quite what you do. Two trades meshed into one. It's impressive." There was a hint of admiration in his tone—I didn't want any of it. "You know as well as me. You showed me as much with your—shall we call it a guild?—at the coffeehouse."

I thought of the ballad seller, inadvertently charm casting, of Namira practicing on coffee foam and Emmi blending herbs. If Pyord Venko's plan hinged on a piece making its way into the royal palace, worn by the king or one of the royal family, then none of them would suffice. "Yes, but those are charms. I can't do curses, I don't have any members of the family as clients, and even if I could and did—"

"None of that matters." He smiled, coolly distant. "What matters is that your brother's life hangs by a thread in my hands. You will do what I want, or—" His hands mimicked the motion of a pair of scissors.

I recoiled, sickened. "Who else knows?" I couldn't imagine Jack or even Niko agreeing to kidnap their friend and coerce his sister, and they were the loudest voices at the top of the League.

"No one. I am arranging this particular facet of our plan. Kristos's disappearance will be a mystery to everyone save you and me."

"How do I know you're telling the truth?"

He threw a red cap on the table between us. I picked it up with tentative fingers, turning the lip under, and saw—the initials I'd stitched into place. So Kristos would be safe. So he would wear the cap, so he wouldn't lose it. I bit my lip, guilt flooding me. If the charm had been stronger, if I had done more.

I shook my head. I couldn't blame myself for everything—charms and, I warranted, curses only influenced a person's fate. They didn't dictate it.

"He promised me he wouldn't give this away or lose it," I confirmed to Pyord, waiting with a patient smile. "What happens next?"

"Then you're agreeing?"

"I don't seem to have a choice." I traced the edges of the red wool cap, feeling my charmed stitches through the cloth. "But I want some kind of guarantee."

"You have it. If you do what I want, Kristos goes free."

"If I try? I've never done curses—I don't even know how. If I try and fail? If the royal family never commissions my work? What then?"

"I would advise against failure," he said with another maddening smile. "Meet me at the Public Archive tomorrow evening. I've arranged a private meeting with the curator, so you can read the same ancient Pellian texts I have and confirm to yourself the precise method of channeling your gift in this new direction."

"Very well." I stared at this man, this intelligent and educated man who could be more brutal and cruel than the Red Caps in their riots or the soldiers firing on them.

"Someday Kristos will appreciate this," Venko said, softening slightly. "He was the one who first approached me about linking the interests of the League with my own personal political interests."

"Your interests."

"Is it impossible to believe that only the dockworkers and bricklayers have some grievance against the nobility's hold on commerce, on governance? You would be surprised, I think, to know how many business proprietors like yourself, how many merchants and shipping magnates, agree with the Laborers' League."

"And a Kvys university lecturer?"

"Are you Pellian?" he retorted. "Of course you are by heritage, but would you know your parents' country? Would it know you if you returned to it?" He shook his head. "I have not returned to Kvyset in over ten years. In the League, we are all Galatine, regardless of our natal origin." He looked down his thin nose at me, as though judging me for being a shop owner, a sister, or a charm caster before being a Galatine. "I happen to be connected enough to have secured some funds for us from old family acquaintances, from patrician houses who believe in our cause, yes, because Galatines are not the only ones who would like to see a more equitable Galitha."

"I don't care about what Kvys want Galitha to look like," I snapped. "If I take you at your word, you treated my brother as a peer, as a fellow Galatine liberator, and then betrayed him when it suited your interests. Who can trust you?"

"Alliances are made of common interests. If revolt is not your brother's interest, he is no longer my ally." If Pyord held any fondness for my brother, even any consideration of him as a human life, it was entombed in icy pragmatism.

I burned with anger against his cold machinations. "If you hurt my brother, I won't do a thing for you. You clearly need me. So if you hurt him—"

Several customers glanced at us, curiosity piqued by my outburst. Pyord laughed, his wineglass held aloft as though he were making a merry toast at a party. "If I hurt your brother, you'll have only yourself to blame." He leaned toward me. "And remember—tell no one."

20

I walked home in a steady drizzle, the gray sky darkening at the edges of town, the clouds held aloft by street lamps freshly lit along my path. It wasn't that I would be breaking any laws, precisely—no laws in Galitha governed charms and curses. I made sure of that before I opened my shop. The gift was too rare to warrant specific laws, it seemed. Instead, one could be held accountable for using curses for whatever crime they resulted in. If a curse led to death, one could be held for murder. I would be complicit in murder—no, regicide—if Pyord's plans succeeded, and, worse, I was breaking my own rules. I had them for a reason. Mother warned, constantly, of charm casters who "went bad" by dabbling in dark curses. They were eventually caught and tried as murderers, or drove themselves mad, or died in back-alley stabbings at the hands of vengeful victims. Of course, her stories had the folktale quality of having been told a hundred times, with no real specifics—I had hardly believed them. Now I did.

I shivered, droplets of rainwater worming their way down my back. I wasn't going to make a life out of curse casting. I was being coerced, and I had to save my brother. My choice was a simple one.

Was it? Was I supposed to let Kristos be killed in order to uphold my principles? In order to keep the dark magic that fueled curses locked up? I couldn't go back now, I thought. Maybe someone else would have chosen some vague moral right over her brother, but not me. I couldn't choose anything over Kristos.

What was I going to tell everyone else? I realized with a start. Pyord had been clear: Tell no one. Yet I couldn't keep up the ruse of searching for him without taking time I didn't have away from the shop, and I couldn't very well just give it up without rousing suspicion. Pyord, it seemed, had failed to consider one vital aspect of his plan—maybe some people could fall off the streets of Galitha City with no one noticing, but not Kristos. Too many people knew him. I gazed out into the harbor, the grim clouds tangled in the tallest masts of the ships. Their white sails, hoisted and stowed like clipped birds' wings, shone like a replacement for moonlight.

Sails. Of course—Kristos was impetuous and always looking for work. He could have joined a ship and sailed off. Why he hadn't told anyone—I'd have to work that out later. And why he would leave in the midst of a burgeoning movement he was leading—another flaw. Pyord had left me with a frayed edge I couldn't neatly stitch up. But a ship, out in the ocean, unable to communicate—that would explain his absence, and I could plead ignorance to the rest.

And would break Penny's heart. I sighed. Tomorrow was not going to be an easy day.

I concocted and rehearsed the story until my candle burned out that night, and the next morning my splitting headache proved I hadn't gotten enough sleep. I hurried to work early, finished a love-charmed cap, and cut the silk for another commission. Real work felt gratifying and let me ignore the pending appointment with Pyord that evening. The silk, a russet taffeta, was crisp beneath my hands, and I could already see the tailored jacket taking shape as I pinned and basted, working with the lining I had already fitted on the client.

Alice trotted into the workroom, shaking rain from the hem of her skirts. "Penny's not coming in," she said succinctly. "She was crying all afternoon after you left, and said she was taking today to search for Kristos. She said you can dock her pay."

"Thank you," I said. I was relieved, and ashamed to be—I hadn't looked forward to breaking my fabricated bad news about Kristos. And, even as I reallocated the day's work to accommodate for her absence, I knew I wouldn't be docking her pay despite any strain on our shop's finances.

Alice and I worked in affable silence all morning, cutting, pinning, sewing, and completing most of the to-do list that had accumulated over the past few days. I turned my attention to Lady Viola's pink gown, drafting a pattern and cutting the lining fabric. I would baste it and do a fitting, then begin work with the pink silk itself. I pulled some creamy ivory silk from a remnant bin—it was perfect for the underlayer I'd envisioned.

"There's someone here to see you," Alice said, plodding into the studio from the front of the shop. My stomach clenched— if it was Pyord, I didn't want to see him, and I emerged from behind the curtain we'd rigged to separate the front and back of the shop with what must have been a terrified expression on my face.

Instead, Emmi waited, raindrops from a cold early winter rain clinging to her wool cloak. "Is this a bad time?" she asked, clearly reacting to my grimace.

"No, of course not," I said, forcing a welcoming smile. "I want this arrangement to be of the best benefit to both of us, Emmi," I said, taking her wet cloak. "So I do want to know—are you most concerned about earning some money, or do you want to learn some of the trade?"

Emmi paused. I realized I had been, by Pellian standards, almost brusque. Galatines were direct in their conversations about business, and even though Emmi was more acclimated to Galatine culture than most of my Pellian acquaintances, I had forgotten that business standards were probably quite new to her. She recovered quickly, before I could apologize.

"I would be lying if I didn't admit we need the money." She lifted her chin, displaying one of the common factors of both Galatine and Pellian cultures—pride in self-sufficiency. "But I also want to work on skills that I can keep using. I—I don't want to just sweep the floors," she asserted in a rush, her voice pitching a bit higher and the color rising in her cheeks.

I appreciated how hard it had been for her to ask. "In that case, I propose a dual system. I can't afford to pay someone for training time right now." I had worked my numbers already. "But I will pay for the more menial labor around the shop, as I would a low-level assistant, and for each half day you work for me, Alice or Penny or I will spend an hour on instruction." This was a more generous offer than most—apprentices often worked for free in exchange for instruction, and Emmi knew it.

She grinned. "I'll gladly accept. I mean—how many days? And what rate of pay?"

I laughed—I had already set a schedule that would allow for both the work I needed and the time set aside for instruction. I let Alice show her around the workshop, and set her to sorting remnants and sweeping the back. I allowed myself a small, contented smile.

21

━〜〜━

THE SHADOWS WERE LENGTHENING, AND THE DREARY GRAY OF an early winter evening was settling over the city by the time Emmi and Alice left and I tidied up the atelier, shelving bolts of fabric and putting away my threads. I had to face Pyord and the Public Archive.

The massive building, deep gray and ornately decorated with viciously toothed gargoyles, had never held much appeal for me. I read the humorous articles and poems in the gossip papers and, of course, the *Magazine of Style* that arrived quarterly at the shop. The thought of dusty tomes, thickly lined with rambling scrollwork text, made my head hurt—there was nothing written in those books for me.

I stepped inside, the heavy outer door of iron filigree giving way with a throaty creak. Three stories of balconies, each lined with shelves, rose around me on three sides. The cavernous vestibule in the center of the building echoed with the sounds of dozens of deliberately quiet people—coughing, sighs, scuffing shoes, hobnails on the stone floors, pages turning with aged crackles.

Tall windows sufficiently illuminated the building in the daylight, but now that the sun was slipping beneath the waves of the harbor outside, the room was filled with shadows. They stretched across long, polished wood tables and raked their fingers on the books that a few studious people were trying to read. I was the only person entering the building; everyone else was leaving.

I shivered. This place, so dark and gray and shadowed, felt cold, even if roaring fires and the steaming water pumped through pipes in the floor and walls kept it warm.

"You're earlier than I anticipated." Pyord's voice snaked around me, reminding me that I couldn't escape what I was here to do.

"Where to?"

"My, you're in a hurry," Pyord said. "We've a private room in the back."

The thought of tucking myself away in a private room with Pyord made my skin crawl. "Don't you prefer the ambience out here?"

"Doesn't everyone?" He smiled. His teeth were ordered in perfect rows and very white. "But I've asked the curator to set aside a few very particular books, and he has even granted us use of an oil lamp in the private reading space."

The room he led me to was surprisingly cozy, lacking the grandiose architecture of the rest of the archive and painted a pleasant blue like a robin's egg. Framed horticultural prints decorated the walls. A cheerful fire crackled in the fireplace, and lamps already sent golden light arcing around the room. The stark table and chair I had expected were replaced with a beautifully carved, if chipped, plush settee.

"Where is the curator?" I asked. I had counted on the benefit of a third person present.

"He isn't needed," Pyord replied. "He pulled these volumes for me personally, but did not feel it was necessary to stay."

I glanced at the leather-bound book already open on the table. It was clearly written in some ancient script. "It's not?"

"Of course not. I read Pellian better than the curator. And, frankly, given the pointed nature of our study, I didn't feel it prudent to invite additional parties into the room."

I swallowed. The cozy room felt suddenly colder. "Professor Venko, why, exactly, am I here? What purpose does this serve?" Our relationship was a contractual one. I would learn to cast curses, do as he asked, and he would set my brother free. I didn't need the trappings of private Pellian study sessions and special treatment from archive curators. I wanted to get in and get out of our deal, as quickly as possible.

"We aren't in lecture," he said, not looking up from the book. "We can dispense with the titles if you prefer to simply use given names." His tone was friendly, as was the gesture— Galatines liked reminding others of rank using titles—but I didn't want to be friendly with this man. "I want to show you the origins of charms and curses, and how they are quite linked, using ancient Pellian texts," he said, leafing through a few pages of the book. I expected to see dust swirling in the lamplight, but it was clean and the pages turned easily.

He beckoned me closer, but I didn't move. I crossed my arms, skeptical. Pellia was a backwater and had nothing to do with my life in Galitha—I had never needed to learn anything about my home country. If I remembered my ancient history, they controlled much of what was now West Serafe and had out-posts in southern Galitha once. That was long ago; now they didn't even have any thriving trade aside from fish.

"The ancient Pellians were the first to discover that some of their own had the gift of casting. In my limited study of the subject, it seems that descendants of Pellians are still dispropor-tionately gifted. Most other ethnic subgroups, excepting the

Serafans, have no interest in magical arts to begin with, so it is difficult to assess. Of course I knew already that you and your brother are Pellian—even if I didn't, the dark hair, the gold in your complexions. Galatines are much fairer skinned, even the southerners."

His tone was not unkind, but removed and sterile, and I didn't appreciate being examined like some anthropological specimen. "Yes, my parents came from Pellia. I was born in Galitha. This doesn't get us any closer to freeing my brother." No more information for him—who knew what he could use against me?

Pyord tapped the book in front of him. "That is precisely why we are here. Look at this. See?"

He pointed to an illustration, surrounded by text I couldn't read. The first image was a lump of clay, the next a flattened disk, and the third showed the same disk covered with designs I wasn't familiar with, though they looked vaguely like the tablets Emmi and Venia and the others made.

"This is a curse tablet," Pyord explained. "This one is a charm." He pointed to an inset picture of a flat engraved disk that looked, to me, identical to the first. "The caster made a disk of clay and then wrote the curse or charm on it."

"They look the same," I said.

"They are the same. The process is, as you can see, exactly the same. The only difference is the words on the tablets themselves."

"But I don't write charms into anything. There aren't words or even symbols."

"That's because what you do is refined beyond this rudimentary version of casting. You know that already—compare yourself to your casting friends in the coffee shop." I regretted that he knew them, that I had exposed them to him. He flipped a few pages. "See these?"

The images of flat disks looked identical to the others. "They look the same."

"They aren't. The first had words written into them. These are just symbols."

"Fine. That's still not what I do."

He sighed. "Don't be obdurate, Sophie. It doesn't suit you." He paged further into the book, like delving deeper into a cave. "The first casters thought it was the words themselves, and then believed it was the symbols. But tell me, if only the words matter, or getting the right symbols, then anyone could charm cast, couldn't they?"

"I suppose so," I said. I had never considered the theory behind charm casting. As soon as I had seen glimmers of light in my mother's charms, she had taught me the craft. Slowly, at first, and later I had developed the skill with the needle and thread. I had known that other modes of casting could work—sculpting, chanting, singing like the ballad seller's inadvertent charm—but my mother had never discussed why the process worked. I realized now that she didn't know. That no one in our chain of casters, perhaps, had known anything more than the pragmatism of pulling a charm into clay or fabric.

That this revolution-bent academic knew more about my gift—my livelihood, my identity—grated me. I breathed anger out through my nose, composing myself. I had to attempt to cooperate for my brother's sake. Only for his sake.

Pyord turned a page, his attention almost reverent. The book was filled with dense text. I felt lost without even a confusing picture to anchor me. "Incredible, really, how little of this philosophy is explored or understood even by its own practitioners.

Scholars in ancient Pellia realized that it wasn't the words or symbols. It was the process of casting the charm or curse itself. The process of connecting the great external forces of the world with the internal desire."

I almost laughed at his grandiose words. They weren't at all how I would have explained charm casting. But as I considered them, they were somewhat accurate. I thought of what I wanted the charm to be, and drew the positive, the light, into the work as I sewed. I could see strands of otherwise invisible light in each finished garment.

"Curse casting is exactly like charm casting," he said. "Listen: *The light forces in the Great External coexist with the dark. Though the dark was discovered first, the light is no harder to attain than the dark.*"

"Curse casting was done first?" I interrupted.

Pyord smiled, the expression somehow wise and cynical at once. "Humans' dark desires emerged far earlier than their more altruistic ones in this particular field. Antiquarians in the field uncover a dozen buried Pellian curse disks wishing their neighbors' crops to fail for every one we find blessing their own crops."

"But why?" I asked, brow furrowing. I didn't think people were that horrible, on the whole. Pyord was the exception, not the rule.

"I've studied this extensively, but there aren't any claims made by the ancient Pellians themselves. My working theory is that curses are not only more powerful magic; they are also able to be wielded in more precise and therefore more effective ways." I thought of Mr. Bursin and his mother-in-law. I could have cursed her to die, and that would have solved his problem directly. Instead, I could send only vague goodwill toward his wife through a charm.

"Perhaps true," I admitted. "But that doesn't answer for me how I'm supposed to turn charm casting into curse casting."

"Ah, but it does. *When a caster elicits positive desires from the external forces, he draws a kind of tangible light into the tablet itself, invisible to most eyes but of visible substance to the caster,*" he read. "Is that accurate?"

I swallowed. Having my process explained academically made me uncomfortable, as though Pyord had some kind of power over me. Nothing I did was a secret to him. "Fairly accurate."

"Then you need only refocus your requests of the external forces. *In contrast,*" he continued reading, "*the caster who creates a curse draws a dark substance into the tablet.*"

"That's it. I just change what I think about, and suddenly I can cast curses?"

"So simple, isn't it?"

"Why should I believe you?" I shoved my chair back and stood, arms crossed. "You know as well as I do that I can't read that. You could be making the whole thing up and I wouldn't know any difference."

"That's true. I didn't show you this to prove anything to you but that I understand, intimately, your art. That I know it better than you do."

"You've proven that you can make up a nice story based on Pellian texts," I said, but his words shook me.

"You can test my theory easily." Pyord's lips narrowed. "And I expect you to."

I began to argue, but he was right. When I found I couldn't draw darkness into a garment, he might not believe me, but at least I would have done all I could.

"Fine. I'll try. But don't say I didn't warn you."

"You had best avoid any attempts at tricking me." Pyord's

eyes narrowed. "I know this can be done. So if you 'try' and then claim failure, I will know you didn't truly make an attempt. I expect results."

My hands met the rough stone wall behind me, and I realized I'd backed away from him. "I have every intention of holding true to our bargain for Kristos's sake," I said in a low, angry whisper. "But I can't be held responsible for doing things I'm unable to."

Pyord cocked his head, his gaze nearly paternal and entirely unwelcome. "You're capable of so much more than you know, Sophie. So much more."

I seethed under his patronizing smile.

"Your next step, of course, alongside learning your new skill, is to obtain a commission from the royal family. You spend enough time playing at Lady Viola Snowmont's house. I am confident you will come into the acquaintance of the queen or princess soon." His brows rose as though he'd just remembered something, but I assumed it might as well have been an act.

"I can't guarantee that. I have many clients among the nobility, but—"

"I have no doubts a commission can be arranged. You seem on exceptionally friendly terms with certain highly influential members of the nobility. You have not only called on the Lady Snowmont's personal residence to do business—quite familiar behavior, I must say—you and the First Duke are on quite friendly terms, it seems."

I tried for words, but none came.

Pyord shrugged. "Yes, I had you followed. Insurance, you know. My man saw the duke's servant, in his full livery, at your shop." I recalled the man hovering outside my door in patched breeches, whom I had assumed to be a common gawker, and felt ill with the violation of my privacy. "You don't tailor men's clothing, so I assume the visit was personal."

"That seems to be more than insurance," I managed to say through clenched teeth.

"It's almost amusing, really, that a seamstress can worm her way into circles that a learned man cannot." Pyord's smile was cold.

Was Pyord jealous? I considered my words carefully. Angering him wouldn't benefit me now. "I suppose there is always a line between those of noble and non-noble families, even at the university."

"Despite my reputation and publications, despite everything I have achieved in my field." He flared, then reconsidered. His cool demeanor returned. "Yes. I have professional acquaintances, of course, of noble birth, but one does not socialize outside of one's station at the university. And given my birth, I will never be anything more than a subordinate lecturer."

I could appreciate his motivations—snubbed by the nobility, never elevated to equality with them in spite of working alongside them. And he was learned—he knew the downsides of our particular system, had studied the potential for others. The ancient Pellians, I remembered Kristos saying, were more democratic in their form of governance. Perhaps the modern revolution Pyord wanted had been born out of reading ancient texts. I considered, again, his demands of me, and his intentions to assassinate the king. A learned man, a seemingly ethical man, yet willing to incorporate dark magic and murder into his plans—it was paradoxical. Or, I considered as evenly as I could, perhaps it wasn't. I couldn't fathom believing in the seedlings of a cause so intensely that I was willing to do anything—truly anything—to see it blossom. Pyord did, and would water the seeds of revolt with whatever blood they required.

And he had Kristos. I imagined what he could have done to him already, what sort of horrid cellar or drafty attic he might have him imprisoned in. The taunts and intimidation he surely threw at him to keep him as compliant as possible, as he did with me.

"I want proof."

"What?" Pyord's forehead wrinkled with surprise.

"Proof my brother is alive, proof he's well. I want him to write me a letter. I want him to seal it and to sign over the seal."

"I could force him to write whatever I wanted," he said with a lilting smile, but the amusement was forced.

"You could. But you know as well as I that Kristos has his own voice in his writing."

Pyord ceded the point with a nod. "He's gifted enough that I could not copy him—and you know him better than I."

I hoped, fervently, that Kristos could slip details or warnings to me into his writing. Maybe he could give me some hint of where he was being held, or even what the plot against the king entailed. If nothing else, I would have some assurance of his safety. "So you will provide me with a letter from him. Soon."

"All right. I'll acquiesce, if only to prove to you that I do have him and that he will be punished if you do not do precisely what I ask." There was a cruel glint in his smile. I hoped I hadn't put Kristos in more danger.

"Thank you." There was no gratitude in my voice.

"I will contact you soon, and I expect a report on your progress with curse casting. And I shall have your letter for you." Then he put out the lamp and closed the book.

22

~~~

I arrived at the shop before Penny and Alice, determined to lay to rest Pyord's theories once and for all. He would know if I was lying, I was quite willing to bet, so I had to try as honestly as I could.

I settled myself into my chair behind the screen, where I did all of my charm casting. I picked up a scrap of purple-sprigged cotton and a needle threaded with stark white thread. What kind of curse could I even cast? I racked my thoughts—I could wish that Pyord would break his neck.

The mere thought chilled me. I couldn't wish that. I mustered my courage and instead thought about simple bad luck. Picking the wrong horse at the track, catching every cold all winter long. Stepping in horseshit on the street and tripping over loose cobblestones. I thought of Pyord suffering each of these mild misfortunes, ignoring an instinctive warning that made my stomach clench, and then reached outside myself as I did when I cast charms.

There was nothing. No light surrounded my needle as it did when I charm casted, but nothing else, either. What I worked into the cloth were plain backstitches.

Maybe, I thought as I tugged on the thread, I needed some sort of crutch. I had sometimes mumbled words to myself as a child, makeshift incantations to keep my focus on the charm and off outside distractions. I had long since outgrown this, but, blushing even though no one could see, I tried it again now. The words were an embarrassed jumble, and I felt even further from crafting a curse than before.

The stitches stayed plain. I sewed a few more absent inches, trying to feel only the linen thread under my fingers, the eye of the needle, situating myself solely in the present and the work itself. I inhaled and tried to exhale the habits and assumptions that surrounded charm casting for me. If I could expunge myself of charms, perhaps I could channel a curse.

I tried again, imagining misfortune, naming dark wishes in my mind.

Nothing.

The shop door banged open, and Alice called a greeting from the front room. Any experiment would have to wait until after my assistants left for the day. Not only could I not concentrate on something so difficult and foreign to me with them close by, but our full slate of orders demanded my attention. As pressing, and far less cheering: as soon as Penny arrived, I had to deploy my lie so that she could stop looking for Kristos.

Alice and Penny both waited for me in the front room. They held a market basket between them, a yeasty, sugared smell wafting from it. "We thought you could use some cheering up," Alice explained, lifting the cloth covering a beautiful array of scones and pastries. "My cousin works at the bakery down by the harbor and snuck these out for me. They're defective," she added, matter-of-fact.

I eyed something golden brown and glazed with cinnamon. Faint guilt surfaced that they were taking care of me, when as their employer I shouldn't have needed it, but the scones looked delicious. I hadn't eaten anything before attempting to work the curse, and even fighting unsuccessfully with it had left me ravenous. "Thank you, both," I said, then shored up my resolve—I had to deliver my lie to Penny.

I snagged the cinnamon scone from the basket and beckoned Penny to come outside with me. The morning sun wasn't doing much to warm the air outside, but I wanted some modicum of privacy.

"Penny," I began, chewing my lip, unsure what to say. "I heard from Kristos."

"He's all right! Where is he? Is he coming home?" She paused. "I'm going to box his ears."

"You're going to want to do more than that," I added, stopping myself as though I hadn't meant to say anything out loud. "He wrote to me once he was safely out of town—he decided to take a job as a sailor."

"Of all the—now? Why? The League, the movement—why would he run away from his work here?"

I shook my head as though just as bewildered as Penny. "I don't know." I thought of the explanations I could add—maybe there was a falling-out, maybe he had run afoul of the law, maybe he was afraid of the repercussions—but any of them could be investigated, exposed. "I don't understand," I added weakly.

Penny bit her lip, fighting with the words. "Why didn't he tell me?"

"Probably the same reason he didn't tell me," I lied. "He didn't want us talking him out of it."

"Well, why didn't he at least write to me?"

The question hung like ripe fruit between us. Of course—any real lovesick boy would have written to his girl. The potential flaw in my lie.

"I don't know," I said again.

"I thought I was actually special to him," she said in a low whisper. A tear coursed down her cheek. I felt like I'd been kicked in the gut. I remembered falling for a boy who worked at the butcher shop when I was fourteen—how I was convinced his confident grin when I bought soup bones meant he liked me, too, how I was overjoyed when he took me for a walk in Fountain Square on market day. And how I was devastated when I saw him promenading with another girl the next week. There was no way to protect Kristos except by lying, but making Penny question his feelings for her was cruel.

Cruel, but unavoidable.

"I'm sorry, Penny. You can...take the morning off if you want. Or the day. With pay. It's all right, whatever you need." Feigning ignorance was necessary to protect Kristos, but it also meant that I could find no good way to offer Penny any comfort. My financial loss in Penny's unproductive wages was worth any comfort I could offer.

"No, I'd rather work. I feel so stupid—but I should have known better."

I couldn't find any way to disagree with her without betraying the truth. Instead, we went back inside and finished a pair of mitts and a muff and a cloak. I imagined Kristos reuniting with a very angry Penny. Perhaps he could dream up a reason for ditching his sweetheart that I couldn't think of. Of course, that hinged on getting Kristos away from Pyord alive, which wouldn't happen before I had fulfilled my part in Pyord's scheme. Inside the workshop, it felt almost too much like a normal day, silk and cotton and linen transformed by needle and thread into gowns and jackets, that familiar magic never failing to please my sensibilities. The russet jacket I had begun was taking shape under Alice's careful construction, and I began the pinked and pleated trim while Penny hemmed a pomegranate-pink dressing gown, its main seams well-charmed for good health. I could almost fall into our shop's comfortable rhythms and forget about the task I had to return to, but as evening fell, shadows crept into the atelier, and Penny and Alice began tidying up for the day, I knew it was unavoidable. As soon as both had left, I returned to my corner and took up my needle and thread again.

I began at the same place as before, imagining misfortunes and trying to force them into the cloth with my stitches. Nothing happened except a row of jagged and uneven backstitches that revealed the frustration building in my chest, pinching my breath. There was something missing, something Pyord didn't understand because he knew only books and theories, not practice. I didn't want to discover it for myself, and I hated him for forcing me. It was an ugly feeling, a bitter, dark pit like the heart of a plum knitting itself into my thoughts.

In that moment, I realized the difference between my charm casting and how I had attempted to cast a curse. I didn't imagine good fortune for my charms—that is, I didn't envision good things happening as much as I accessed some form of vibrant, dynamic joy that existed outside my imaginings. This was the light around my needle. I didn't create it, as I was trying to do with the curse, with my thoughts—I simply harnessed it. I had grown so used to seeing it, to accessing it and gripping it with my needle—or, likely more accurately, my mind—that I had stopped looking for it, and in not looking for it, I had forgotten that I felt it, too.

I would have to actively look for the darkness—and I would have to find my way to it by feeling it first, through an invisible internal map like the one I had created, slowly and over time, for the light. I started with the angry, bitter pit of hate.

At first I merely circled it, tracing it with my thoughts, becoming more mired in it, and in myself. I forced myself outward, trying to tie what I felt to something outside myself, something as alive and independent as the light was. I began to feel a strange confidence that it was there, that what I felt, black and cold, in me, had a counterpart outside myself, inhabiting the ether as the light did. I pulled at it, pushed myself, and felt a final, strong resistance. I didn't want to see it, I understood—I not only didn't want to see it by training and disposition, but by some primal instinct, the same instinct that made rabbits run from foxes and hawks and made humans shy away from dark alleys and deep caverns.

I pushed past that resistance, trying to forget what I was doing, and it was as though a tiny yet fundamental door swung open in my awareness. I saw it—I could trace my own understanding of darkness into something outside myself and see it, black and glittering and repulsive and enticing.

Without thinking any further about the implications, I reached out and caught a strand of it with my thoughts, the way I did with the charm-bound light. I pulled it toward me, binding it to my needle, pulling it into the next stitch I took.

A thin black line twined around my needle, entered the cloth, and held.

I gasped, almost losing it back into the ether. Instead, I held it, taking a few small backstitches. The thread embedded the hard, dark sparkle just as it did the faint light I was used to. I kept sewing, pulling the darkness into the cloth.

I finished a seam, then looked up. My eyes felt hot, and a viselike pressure wrapped around my head. I set the needle down, blinked, and was promptly overtaken by nausea. I made it to the scrap bin before my stomach overturned, and my eyes flooded with tears as I coughed and retched.

I could do it, I realized with lead settling into my now-empty stomach. I could cast curses. And unlike the refreshed lightness that finishing a session of charm casting gave me, casting a curse was going to tax me in a way I had never encountered.

23

THERE WAS NOTHING TO DO WITH MY NEWFOUND UNDERSTANDING of curses except wait for the commission Pyord was sure would come, and in the meantime I had to keep the shop running as though nothing was amiss. Within a week, I was ready to fit Lady Viola's gown and decided that, instead of sending a messenger to request an appointment, I would go myself to see if she was home. I winced—Pyord was right that I had acquired a certain familiarity with Lady Snowmont if I was comfortable marching up to her door and knocking, and I checked for hooded figures outside my shop before leaving. I walked to her house, trying to put distance between myself and the guilt I felt for lying to Penny. It didn't work.

As I turned the corner onto the avenue that bordered the river, something tugged at my peripheral vision. I glanced sideways at the figure walking just behind me, a few paces off to my left. There was a flash of red where the cap he had stuffed in his waistband peeked out from under his jacket.

I picked up my pace, and he stayed alongside me, as though in step for some complicated military maneuver. My sewing kit, with needles and thread and wax and a single pair of very sharp scissors, knocked against my thigh, buried in my pocket.

I wrapped my hand around it, finding the scissors and gripping them.

The man, nondescript aside from the red cap he carried, was still there as I continued toward Viola's, turning off the crowded avenue and onto a narrow street. *Don't let a thief or a rake force you out of a crowded area,* Kristos had always said. And, *It's better to fight than let someone take what isn't theirs to have.*

My fingers constricted around the scissors, my only weapon. But if the man was Pyord's hired hound, what could I do? If I fought him, Pyord might retaliate by hurting my brother. In any case, this man was only one of the men Pyord must have at his disposal. He wasn't my problem; Pyord was. I let the scissors drop back into my pocket. If he wanted to follow me, I was powerless to stop it.

He peeled off as I reached Viola's gate, and I tried not to watch him stalk across the street and hover under an ornamental tree. The maid let me in and announced me to Viola, then invited me to wait in her private sitting room. A painting stood on an easel in the corner, unfinished. A woman, draped in a dressing gown and reclining in a chair, laughed at me from the canvas. The rich colors of the center of the painting bled into plain white at the edges, and the setting was unclear. I squinted, recognizing the upholstery on the chair the woman lounged in. It faced me across the room.

Of course Viola would paint here, I reasoned, but the picture possessed a faintly private quality—the intimate space of her boudoir, the casual dressing gown, the natural, laughing face. I felt as though I was intruding. This wasn't a formal portrait, but something I had never encountered before. Like a sketch composed in a moment, capturing a scene, but crafted into a painting.

"I suppose you want the gown off," Viola called as she swept into the room, her voice ringing ahead of her like a bell. She caught me looking at the painting and stopped.

"It's very nicely done," I stammered, convinced that I shouldn't have seen this half-finished work. "The painting, I mean."

"Thank you," Viola said, fumbling with the pins that held her gown closed. "It also should have been put away before you came."

"I don't see—that is, I wouldn't say anything . . . even if there were something to say."

Viola laughed. "Of course! The only one of my friends who wouldn't recognize, instantly, Princess Annette."

"Oh." I looked back at the woman in the picture. "But you paint the royal family practically all the time."

"Not like this, I don't. They wouldn't be pleased, I'm sure. Not with the wardrobe or the location or what both, combined, could be read to mean." She cocked her pert chin and gazed at the painted Annette, who almost seemed to look back at her. "Of course, they don't know her as well as they'd like to believe."

"You're friends?"

Viola's eyes widened, as though she were taking in the whole painting, all of Annette, at once. "She means more to me than anyone in the world." Then she shook her head. "And she's getting married in the spring and leaving."

"I had no idea," I replied.

Viola laughed. "You're dreadfully behind on your court gossip. Yes, the royal house is in the midst of final negotiations with the royal house of East Serafe. A marriage with East Serafe would confirm an alliance with them. Prince Oban couldn't inherit the throne without some kind of miracle—he's a second son by a second wife—but is still elevated enough that the match is considered viable. He's also, by all accounts, half a head shorter than Annette and quite dull at parties." Viola shrugged. "The perils of the nobility—you marry whom your parents want."

"You haven't married anyone," I said carefully, unpacking my pins and my tape measure and my notebook. I laid them in a neat row.

Viola smiled at my fastidious arrangement. "I have an indulgent father and my mother died years ago. It's mothers who force these things, you know. They're the great diplomats of the marital world."

I wasn't sure what to say—for common folk like me, no one orchestrated anything. People blundered into one another and fell in love, as far as I could tell, like Kristos and Penny. I had avoided that particular blunder, and Viola had sidestepped the political machinations that would have forced her to marry. We were alike in that regard—both consciously avoiding marriage and making the very deliberate choices doing so entailed.

"I am also not in line for the throne," Viola added. "Annette has to hurry up and produce an heir to take the throne if her father keels over, since her mother only managed three daughters." A sour taste reminded me that Pyord was going to force the issue of inheritance sooner rather than later. "Silly rule, I think, that daughters can't inherit—look at the Allied States. Princesses have the same rights of inheritance as princes there. But here, either Annette produces an heir, or the throne passes to the king's brother's house. Not that anyone minds the Prince of Westland, but succession is so much simpler father to son. Even better if we can avoid the mess of a regent if Annette's son were a minor." Her tone suggested that, in the long history of Galitha, simplicity in succession had proven an issue.

I decided not to display my ignorance of Galatine history, and instead picked up the muslin gown bodice. "Shall we see if it fits?" I said. Viola glanced at the half-finished portrait with a forlorn look and sighed loudly again.

I was pleased—the back fit perfectly, and I only needed to adjust the armscyes slightly, taking them in to more snugly fit Viola's narrow shoulders. Viola turned in the mirror, giving me an approving nod.

"The shape is beautiful. I can see already this is going to be perfect—the lines are so elegant."

"Thank you," I said, sinking a couple more pins into the refitted section.

"You should stay," she said impulsively. "For the evening. Some of my closest friends are coming for a card party." She handed the mock-up gown back to me. "Including Theodor."

At the mention of Theodor, my breath forestalled a touch and an unfamiliar lightness crept into my chest. I had avoided marriage so long that I had forgotten the benefits of courtship. I tried to read Viola's face, but she turned and fiddled with her hair in a small mirror. "I'm hardly dressed for the evening," I protested, half-hearted.

"Then go home and come back. Or borrow something of mine!" She caught my hand and dragged me to her wardrobe.

"I won't fit in anything," I warned, silently comparing Viola's narrow back and petite frame to my broad shoulders and ample bust.

"Nonsense. You would fit this...or, no, this." She shoved aside a purple wrapper and produced something delicate and sky blue. A chemise-style gown—with its gathered bust, waist, and sleeves, it would fit anyone in a fairly wide range.

"I can't ask to borrow your clothes." Still, I fingered the openwork edge of the sleeve. It was masterfully done.

Viola hung the gown on the door of her wardrobe. "Stop

acting like a charity case." She raised a dainty eyebrow. "It's not becoming."

"I am a bit of a charity case." I laughed. "I have to borrow clothes."

"I've seen your clothes; they're better than most of my friends'."

"I own," I said, shucking my jacket and accepting the gown, "exactly one gown appropriate for a somewhat formal evening." I slipped the pale blue silk on and fastened the minute hooks and eyes.

Viola pursed her lips as she considered this. "So, after you're done sewing and working all day, you just...go home? And...sit?"

"Pretty much, most days." I fluffed the skirts of the gown. It was beautiful, I had to admit as I caught my reflection in the mirror. "My brother goes to taverns and cafés. Sometimes I go along, but..." I stopped myself from finishing. Even before Kristos had disappeared, the talk of revolution over ale had driven me away. It didn't behoove me to mention that here.

"Not exactly eveningwear locations," Viola agreed. "We need to get you out more. Artists like us need inspiration."

I didn't argue, even though I wondered what Viola thought common people like us did for fun. We could afford oil for the lamp and a few candles a month—not exactly the kind of illumination one needed for entertaining. There was a perhaps insurmountable distance between the nobility and the common people, if such practical concerns didn't even cross Viola's mind.

"I admit to mercenary reasons for keeping you tonight, of course," Viola added. "Theodor asked and, well, I can't refuse one of my oldest friends." She fished an elaborate necklace of citrine stones from a paper-covered box on her dressing table. "This would look perfect with that gown and your complexion."

I wavered; she insisted. "I don't know what you've been doing to him, but he's in a much better mood than he has been the past few months. Ever since his father started making arrangements for him to marry one of the Allied States princesses—see, I told you that necklace would be superb, just look!"

I swallowed past the words that echoed in my ears. Of course I knew that anything romantic with Theodor was destined to be exceptionally temporary. Brevity was, I reminded myself, a benefit for someone in my position when it came to romance. Still, I felt a distinct pang of loss. I shook my head, the light dancing on the necklace. It was better if he avoided me now, anyway. Pyord was having me watched, and Theodor could become a target. I smiled at my reflection in Viola's dressing table mirror. I could enjoy his company, and then let it go—just that easily.

24

By the time the first knock landed on the door, Viola's salon was transformed into a miniature casino. Viola arranged her skirts on the settee, making me sit beside her, and welcomed the first guests with a broad smile and a wave to the maid to fetch a bottle of port. I tried to sit languidly on a plush chair like Viola did, but another worry had crept into my mind. Most card games involved placing bets and wagering money—of which I had a pitifully small amount with me. I might have been able to play a hand of kings at a local tavern, but I was sure the bets Viola and her friends laid were much richer.

I didn't belong here, I thought despite my forced smile. I was going to be humiliated.

I recognized Nia and Pauline from the daytime salon gatherings, and Theodor arrived soon after. He caught my hand and pulled me, subtly and so that the others wouldn't take notice, into an alcove.

"I'm sorry, but I haven't heard anything about your brother. No one has. I was going to send you a letter, but that seemed horribly impersonal," he said, low so the others couldn't hear.

It was time to employ the lie, whether I wanted to or not. "I think I know why. Fact is, I've found the rogue."

"What? Where?"

"Not exactly found—he signed up for a tar and sailed off. Merchant ship bound for East Serafe."

"And didn't tell you?"

"He...he sent a letter. From the last port they were in before beginning the crossing."

"That devilish—and made you worry like that? What an awful—"

"Please, don't. He's still my brother," I said, wounded. My story did make Kristos out to be a rake, but I didn't want to hear any more epithets. "He knew I'd object, so he left and notified me afterward." It wasn't a great story, but it was serviceable.

Theodor wasn't pacified. "If I had him in front of me, I'd deal him a square blow between the eyes for making you worry like that."

Unexpectedly, I found myself almost crying. Theodor noticed and softened. "I didn't mean to—"

"No, it's all right," I replied. "It's been..."

"I can imagine," he said, catching my hand in his as our eyes met. He pulled me into the hall. The final, thin rays of a pale winter sunset spread over the carpet, too stingy to impart any warmth.

Then he caught me completely off guard and kissed my hand. Not in formal greeting, but pressing his warm lips against my palm. "You're beautiful when you cry, but I don't want you to cry any longer, either. It's a terrible conundrum for me."

I laughed past my surprise, and then we joined the others in the parlor. Theodor claimed the chair next to mine and politely quizzed Pauline on a party she had held the previous week.

Then a dark-haired woman I hadn't met before, but whom I recognized immediately from the half-finished portrait, swept through the door. Princess Annette. Viola caught her hand and pulled her into a happy embrace.

I had always considered the nobles' world to be an easy one, but I didn't have to think about saying farewell to anyone I loved on account of arranged marriages. And had I wished to marry, I had my choice. I wondered if Kristos had ever considered the human side of the nobility he railed against.

As if on cue, Nia steered the conversation in a decisively uncomfortable direction. "Have you heard the latest on the Red Caps?" she asked, her brown eyes huge in the candlelight.

"They say they've called in the soldiers to dissipate riots three times this week," Princess Annette said, shaking her head as though this grieved her. It probably did, I realized with a start—wouldn't the king and queen and their children feel a particular responsibility to the country and its capital city? "At least no one else has been shot."

"I think the point to truly appreciate," Viola said, pouring fresh glasses of wine for Annette and Theodor, "is that the involvement of the soldiers hasn't dissuaded the protesters."

"In fact, I'd say it's encouraged them," Pauline said. She fished a fan out of her pocket and opened it, fluttering it as though mimicking a nervous heartbeat. "They say the Stone Castle is nearly full, but they aren't coming any closer to rooting out the source of the rebellion."

Annette frowned, her carmine-painted lips turning downward. She was remarkably pretty, I thought, with dark hair and snowy skin. I had wondered if Viola had perhaps enhanced her looks for the portrait, but I saw that she merely captured them. My respect for Viola's artistry grew. "The arrests have been— oh, astronomical."

Viola nodded. "It oughtn't leave my confidence, but—the jail is nearly full. They've questioned them—hundreds of them— about their leadership, and no one has given them anything."

"Nothing?" I said, surprised, then sank back into the chair, embarrassed.

"The names my father has gotten have been less than useful. Dockworkers and bricklayers who pass a message here and there, the occasional writer." I didn't move a muscle—Kristos. "No one he believes could truly be orchestrating the whole thing." Was this accurate, I wondered, or was the Lord of Keys severely underestimating the dockworkers and bricklayers who were fomenting revolution? Had someone given him Niko or Jack's name, and had he dismissed their abilities?

"Have they figured out who is printing this stuff? I'd think putting a stop to that would be useful," Pauline said.

Theodor's discomfort with this suggestion was clear. "It's never been our way to censor books and pamphlets," he said. "Even when that cartoon artist—what was his name?—made those hideously unflattering engravings of the king during the flour shortages ten years ago."

"Barnard," Annette said. "His name was Barnard. And yes, it's not our tradition to shut down printers, no matter how offensive their material is." The way she pressed her lips closed made me think she believed it might be time to break with tradition. "At any rate, it's not a licensed shop—someone has a press in a shed or a cellar somewhere."

Pauline sighed. "No reason to assume the worst. The workers are dissatisfied with their pay, and winter's coming early. It's just as likely as not to be street protests and nothing more, isn't it?"

"We all know it's more than that." Annette traced the rim of her wineglass. "The palace has already increased its security measures and transferred soldiers from the provinces to bases closer to the city." She turned the stem of the glass in her hand, slowly, methodically.

"I wonder if that's wise," Pauline said, "from a military perspective."

Viola took Annette's glass and set it down. "The ports are still fully garrisoned, so we needn't worry about anything interfering with trade. I don't know that we anticipate any particular international aggression, do you?" she asked with a teasing smile.

Theodor shrugged. "There is intelligence that Kvyset—or at least, some Kvys houses—are sympathetic to the Red Caps. Sympathetic enough that they've sent money. Maybe more."

"More?" Pauline's oversize pearl earrings bobbed as she leaned forward.

He lowered his eyes, staring at the delicately wrought silver buckles on his shoes. "It's possible that some of the patrician houses of Kvyset are supplying arms. It will be common knowledge among the nobles soon enough," he said. "Once we can confirm our intelligence, the council will have to decide what to do, if anything. So far the intercepted communications have been so heavily coded we're not sure if they're talking rifles or rutabagas."

Viola pursed her lips as though she'd tasted something sour. "It's hardly new for the patrician houses to meddle in Galatine affairs if they think it will benefit them in terms of trade or investments. Religious houses, as well. You know well enough that they have more in assets than most of the patricians. Still. That's not the same as the entire country colluding against Galitha."

"If it benefits them, Kvyset will ignore what their borderland patricians do," Theodor countered. "The council could decide to insist that the Kvys rein in their own."

"The Kvys have always prodded and pushed us when they could," Annette acknowledged. "Anything to reopen discussions

of the border agreements. Ignoring them is usually the best tactic." I had no idea what she referred to, but the others nodded in
agreement.

"Still—soliciting arms and funds from Kvys patricians suggests that this revolt is...escalating," Viola said, giving voice to
what we were all thinking. I had thought the same when Jack
had told me Pyord's plans, weeks ago. "How do they even have
the connections to pursue Kvys patronage?"

Theodor glanced at me, gauging my reaction, but I stayed
silent, averting my eyes toward the toes of my shoes, noticing for
the first time that they had gained some new scuffs.

"It's past time we admit that they are more organized and
likely more connected than the rabble of rioters the council
would like them to be," Theodor said. "At least the rest of our
international relationships haven't been affected."

"Not yet," Nia said, faint warning in her voice.

"You know something we don't, madam?" Theodor
asked. His tone was light, but I noticed that his hand rested on
his sword, as though foreign marauders might come bursting
through the door any moment.

"Of course not. You all know quite well that neighbors
become vultures when they suspect a nation's strength to govern
has been compromised."

No one countered this, and I took a shaky sip of wine. Had
Pyord considered the effects of coup on trade, border security,
and even the survival of the Galatine nation if some foreign
nation took the opportunity to slice into it by invasion while
Galitha tore itself apart from within?

"In any case," Nia added with a smile, "back in the Allied
States, my prince will not be eager to marry one of his cousins
to the Duke of Nothing at All."

Theodor laughed. "I don't have even the draft of a marriage

contract, and Nia threatens to revoke it." It was a joke, but I didn't find any part of it funny—the thought of Theodor marrying was almost as unsettling as the thought of civil war.

"What?" She laughed. "It's true. And of Serafe as well," she added pointedly.

Annette tried not to react, but her lip twitched. "You're quite right. Arrangements with Prince Oban of East Serafe are still precarious. This does come at an unfortunate time." The words were rehearsed, and I noticed Viola's hand slide toward Annette's under the table.

"What a mess," Pauline said with a sigh. "And with the Five-Year Summit approaching in the summer, too."

I listened, unsure what Pauline meant. Nia laughed. "I assume your father is still the delegate?" she asked Theodor.

"Yes," he said with some chagrin. "Poor man." This time everyone else laughed, and I knew I was on the outside of a longstanding joke.

Annette saw my confused expression. "Every five years delegates from Fen, Kvyset, the Allied States, East and West Serafe, and of course Galitha come together for a summit. After the Saltwater War thirty years ago, when we were all at one another's throats—"

"The Allied States maintained neutrality," Nia interrupted with a teasing smile.

"After we all nearly destroyed one another's shipping and naval capabilities except for the ever wise and benevolent Allied States, the summit is supposed to be an assurance of continued cooperation and negotiation or some such," Annette said.

"And it's of course quite important," Viola added, "but it's always tedious and involved. And this year the poor Prince of Westland will have to spend half his time making apologies for the black eyes that the Red Caps are currently giving Galitha, convincing the other delegates that we are still fully capable of running a nation without ruining it."

Theodor shrugged. "I don't envy him. But the summit is months away, and I didn't come here tonight to debate international politics," he said with a lopsided grin. "I came to lose some money to Viola."

Viola must have seen my panicked face—I had no money to lose—because she swiftly said, "No money tonight, Theodor. We're playing for pralines." She called to the maid hovering by the door, "Sacha, bring them in!" Perhaps Viola was more conscious of the less than wealthy than I'd given her credit for. Perhaps most nobles were. Yet the taverns and streets were full of Red Caps hungry for revolt, bearing real grievances against an unjust system, and the nobility had done very little to ameliorate the situation—aside from recalling troops for protection. Ostensibly to protect everyone, of course, but themselves most of all.

Whose side was I on? I chided myself. I was forced to cater to Pyord only until I had finished the curse, if I ever obtained a commission at all. I had never believed in violent revolt, let alone regicide. Yet I didn't hold the nobility blameless. Perhaps, I conceded, I didn't hold myself blameless for my silent consent to the policies I didn't agree with.

Thoughts swirled like dust in a beam of sunlight—fleeting and without concrete meaning. I set the wineglass down. Clearly I'd had enough.

We moved to the gaming table, and Theodor held my chair for me and then took the chair next to me.

At least, I thought as Viola dealt the first hand, Kristos had taken the time to teach me how to play whist. I had enjoyed a hand or two at the tavern, in a time not so long ago before Kristos's attention turned completely toward revolution, and together, my brother and I made a formidable team in the partner game. With anyone else, I wasn't very good at it and wished Viola hadn't dealt me into the first hand so I could watch and remember, exactly, how to strategize.

The first few rounds went quickly, with me losing most of my pralines and sitting out as Nia took my place. Annette was sitting out as well, eyeing Theodor's dwindling supply of candy.

"Viola showed me your work," Annette said, refilling my wineglass despite my protest. "It's lovely." I felt my hands grow cold and tremble slightly. I should have been elated—a princess was pouring me a glass of expensive wine while complimenting me on my sewing.

But I knew what was coming next—I had to wheedle a commission out of her. A commission that I could curse. I stared at the deep red liquid in my glass. The way the candle-light refracted through it, it looked as though I had blood on my hands.

"Thank you," I stammered. "That means she showed you—" I blushed. Underwear. Annette had seen Viola's underwear.

Annette laughed. "Yes, I know all about Viola's under-clothes. And I learned all about your particular brand of sewing. It's fascinating." She leaned forward. "Is it something you learned to do, or does it just happen?"

I was startled—people didn't usually ask such brazen questions. But after all, she was a princess. Maybe she was used to saying whatever came to mind, to the ease of setting the percep-tion of what was correct in any situation rather than fitting into a set of rules as I found myself, nearly constantly, analyzing and correcting my course.

"It's a little bit of both," I said. "I learned to let it happen, and to control it. To force it into the thread as I sew, to be precise with the charm. My mother taught me." I floundered—I hadn't expected to be talking about my mother with Princess Annette.

And strangely, though I usually didn't feel the deep ache of grief I had endured at her passing, my eyes filled with tears. Annette made a small noise, understanding immediately.

"She was a very adept charm caster." I recovered.

Annette smiled sympathetically, but loss nagged me. My mother was gone, my father gone before her. Was I going to lose Kristos, too? What I might have to sacrifice to keep him safe was quite literally sitting in front of me. Would I risk Annette's life with a cursed garment? Risk her mother, or her father? Let her live the tragedy of loss I had lived?

I had to, I reminded myself, resolute. Kristos was all I had.

Theodor lost his last praline and tagged Annette into his place. "Better luck than I had," he said.

"That's not hard," Annette said. "Have Sophie make you some kind of charmed hankie to stuff in your pocket before you tag back in."

"Could you?" he asked with a wink.

"Yes, but that seems...immoral," I replied with a wry grin. Theodor met my laughing gaze and held it, then caught my hand. I held my breath—for a brief moment, as his fingers brushed mine, the revolt, Pyord, even my brother felt like dust motes swirling, far away, not quite real.

"Play a few hands without us," he called, leading me to the stairs. My heartbeat accelerated. He held tightly to my hand as we ascended.

I checked myself. It was contemptible that I could let my role in Pyord's plan fade for a moment to fulfill something I wanted. That I could forget my brother in favor of a meaningless tryst with a duke.

That's all it could be, meaningless—even before I knew that Theodor was slated for an alliance marriage with a foreign princess, I knew that I was dabbling with the trivial. I had been happy with that—a frivolous dalliance was welcome relief from unwanted marriage proposals. It had been a diversion, nothing more.

But now diversions were selfish. I couldn't enjoy myself with my brother in constant danger, and I hated myself for nearly forgetting that.

I was ready to extract my hand, run back down the stairs, fetch my cloak, and be on my way, when I saw where Theodor had led me. Lady Viola's ballroom, encased in its walls of windows. Each was like a panel of stars.

"Oh," I breathed, scarcely able to take in the entire view at once. The city around us, dark except for flickering candlelight, the swaths of stars, the huge orb of the moon.

"This may be my favorite place in the whole city," Theodor said, his hand resting on my waist. "Even the palace doesn't have a view like this."

He guided me to an alcove of windows on the opposite wall, overlooking the river. It looked like a wide ribbon of silver. Just beyond it was the garden, and Theodor's greenhouse.

"I thought the moonlight would be hitting it just right about now," he said. I didn't have words. The glass and metal, so industrial-looking under daylight, reflected the moon. The steel ribs looked like polished platinum, the glass like mother-of-pearl.

"It's like a piece of jewelry," I said. "Like the city is wearing a new brooch tonight."

Theodor smiled and pulled me closer. "It's yours," he said. "The city thinks it owns it, but it's yours."

"That would hardly be fair," I said, his eyes difficult to avoid. "I don't think I deserve it, all to myself." I certainly didn't deserve it—I was effectively Pyord's lackey; I was supposed to curse the royal family; I was carrying on with a duke while my brother was held prisoner. "I don't deserve anything," I whispered.

"You do," he whispered back, and before I could react, his mouth pressed against mine, warm and electric and somehow comfortable. Before I meant to, I sank into the embrace, searching for something whole, something real in the brokenness Pyord had forced on me. I tasted the sweetness of the pralines on his breath, and something constricted in me, a wall between what was outside and what was here, between us. The taste of pralines and Theodor's mouth on mine, those were real. Nothing else could be. Nothing else could reach me.

His hands wrapped around my waist, drawing me closer. Velvet desire enfolded us. My hands traced his neck, his hair, buried themselves in his queue. I should have pulled away; logic demanded that I drop my hands, but I didn't. I couldn't.

Then a sharp shattering noise, like rocks cracking the ice in the fountains, interrupted us, followed quickly by a pointed scream from downstairs. Theodor released me and immediately had his hand on the sword he wore.

"Stay here," he said, feet already pounding the stairs. I felt as though I were floating, unmoored, and found myself hovering at the top of the steps craning my neck over the banister to get a better look. I stole downstairs, clutching the railing as though it would protect me.

The others crowded into the small drawing room opposite the salon. A maid hurried past with a broom and dustpan. The front door stood open, and Theodor brandished his sword on the portico at unseen assailants.

I glanced into the salon. A fat rock lay in the middle of a rug, surrounded by thick shards of glass. A single pane of the large window facing the street gaped with jagged edges.

Pauline was crying, Nia was cowering behind a chair, and

Annette was plastered motionless against the wall, but Viola stood in the doorway, hands clenched into fists.

"Miss?" The maid presented Viola with the rock and, ludicrously, a rote curtsy. Viola took the rock as though it were something distasteful—a piece of rotten fruit or a dead mouse the cat had hauled in. She turned it over in her hand, revealing a painted missive on its flattest side. I couldn't read it.

The maid resumed sweeping, Theodor came inside, and then Annette, Nia, and Pauline quietly settled onto the sofa, holding hands. Viola clutched the rock and lifted it as though she were going to throw it back into the street it had come from, but she stopped herself.

"Not that it will make much difference, but it is evidence." She deposited it on a polished demilune table, next to a porcelain shepherdess and an ornate mahogany box. Another bit of bric-a-brac in her collection.

"You're all right?" I asked.

She met my eyes. "It sailed right past my head. Inches, Sophie." Her hands trembled and she clutched them together.

I shivered. The protection charm glowed underneath Viola's gown, buried in her shift and drawers, visible only to me.

"We should get the ladies home," Theodor said, voice low. He checked the lock on the door and drew the curtain in the salon, covering the broken pane of glass. The draft sucked the curtain fabric into the hole and billowed it out again, making the drapery look like a silk ghost.

"Suzette, tell Marco to call for the carriages." Viola stopped the maid as she turned to leave. "Do not go outdoors yourself, you understand? Send a footman or the butler."

She swallowed, looking truly flustered for the first time since I came downstairs.

"You shouldn't stay here by yourself," Annette said, rising

from the sofa and clattering across the floor. She grabbed Viola's hand, and the fist unfurled.

"I won't allow them to chase me out of my own house," she retorted, but her hands stayed relaxed, held in Annette's.

"At least come to the palace tonight. You can have your favorite room," Annette said with a prodding smile.

"Absolutely not." Viola turned to the maid Suzette, who hovered in the hallway. "The carriages are here?" she asked. Suzette nodded. "Then you should all leave. Before anything worse comes through my window."

"I'll stay here with you," Annette pleaded, but Viola shook her off.

"You'll go home or your parents will have my head."

Annette finally agreed, reluctantly, and let Suzette fetch her cloak and muff. Pauline and Nia said low farewells and disappeared into the night, escorted by footmen who suddenly looked more like bodyguards.

I gathered my satchel, planning to leave quietly, but the shimmering silk of Viola's voluminous gown skirts stopped me. "Viola," I said in a low voice, hoping the others wouldn't hear, "I need to return your gown and..."

"Don't worry over it now," she replied with a terse smile. "Send it back by messenger tomorrow—I presume I can send your things to your shop?"

I nodded, and tied my cloak, then slipped quietly toward the door, feeling ashamed I had to borrow clothes and even more ashamed that I was selfishly worrying about what the others might think of me now.

"Where do you think you're going?" Theodor asked.

"Home," I said.

"Not alone, you're not. Not on foot."

"Theodor," I began, "it's truly not necessary. I'm not—I'll

be fine." My conviction was fragile and my voice brittle. I wasn't a noble, but would that protect me if I was fraternizing with nobles, a collaborator?

"That's not an experiment I'm willing to witness," Theodor answered, and waved to Viola as he pulled his greatcoat around his shoulders.

"Shouldn't you stay with her?" I whispered as he ushered me through the front door.

"She has a house full of loyal servants." As though to prove his point, Miss Vochant hovered at the top of the stairs, watching our movements below. "She's not alone. If she didn't want Annette there, she surely doesn't want me hanging around."

I thought of several good arguments—Theodor wasn't a princess with protective parents; he was a man who could provide some semblance of defense, and it was, as far as I could tell, his duty to protect a noblewoman—but I didn't voice them. In truth, I was grateful for Theodor's company in the uncertain night.

25

━⟋⟍━

WE PULLED AWAY FROM LADY VIOLA'S HOUSE, SILENT EXCEPT FOR the rattle of the wheels and the horse's shoes on the cobblestones. I glanced up and down the street, searching the dark for the shadow who had followed me to Viola's. I saw no one, but that didn't mean one of Pyord's men wasn't there, lurking, stalking me. Just because I wasn't a target didn't mean I couldn't be followed, I thought with a shiver. Theodor watched out the window intently, mouth pressed into a firm, determined line. As though he were on sentry duty, protecting us.

We turned onto a broad avenue and he finally leaned back in his seat.

"What did the rock say?" I said.

"What?" Theodor sat up straighter. "Oh, the one that came through the window. It said, *As glass shatters under the weight of one rock, so does a weak government under the people's will.*"

"How poetic," I said. "Where did they read that, some—oh no." It was probably from one of Kristos's pieces, I thought with sinking guilt I didn't deserve.

"I think you may be right," Theodor said softly. "Though I am sure he did not intend this particular use, or the violence I fear is building if the Red Caps are funding and arming themselves." He glanced out the window, a cursory scan. He seemed to confirm we were still safe. "Too bad he's out to sea or he could discourage his comrades from misusing his words."

I stopped the confused look that spread over my face—my lie. That Kristos was on board a ship. Not held captive by some revolution-prone professor who was likely connected, somehow, to the deviants who threw the rock. I realized I hadn't finalized a commission with Princess Annette before leaving—if Pyord wanted to chastise me for that, I'd be able to tell him it was, in a way, his own fault.

I leaned my head against the cool glass of the window, but my face still felt like it was burning. I sighed. "This is why you didn't need to take me home. I'm not the target."

"You're still a lady and a friend, and I feel, therefore, an obligation to protect you. Whether by taking you home or warning you that armed insurrection might be coming."

"I'm not a lady!" I almost shouted, surprising even myself. "I'm a common woman, a shop owner, a tradesperson. I'm not a lady. I'm not noble," I repeated, as though we both needed to be reminded.

"I know that. I know you're not noble—don't think I've forgotten, even if I can't seem to behave as though I remember. If it doesn't matter to me, who else might decide they don't care?" He clamped his mouth shut. He'd already said too much—that he didn't care if I was common. He'd thought about the impossibility of continuing an affair into something more. He didn't want to give it up.

And I laughed. Once I started, I couldn't stop. Almost hysterical, fueled by fear and guilt, I filled the carriage with peal after peal of desperate, joyless laughter.

"What's so funny?" Theodor asked, eyes wide with confusion. *He must think me mad*, I thought, clutching the velvet cushion under me as I forced myself to stop.

"It's just—we're just—if you did want to marry me—"

"I can't and we both know that," he snapped.

I waved my hands, trying not to laugh again. "If you did, the only way you could is if the Red Caps succeed in staging a full coup and you're stripped of your nobility. You'd get exactly what you want. Precious, no?" I stopped a cynical laugh from bubbling to the surface and averted my eyes from him, aware how inappropriate what I'd said was. Seditious, even.

A smile tugged at Theodor's mouth, threatening to break into a full grin. "How romantic." He lost the battle and laughed. "Now, given, I'd probably be dead if it came down to that, but otherwise, it's a delightful fairy tale."

It was macabre, but I laughed anyway, until my sides strained against my stays and my lungs burned.

Theodor chewed his lip as he watched me, then cracked open the carriage door and shouted something to the driver. His words were whipped away in the wind. I took a deep breath. Momentary madness had passed, and I calmed myself.

I watched Fountain Square pass by, deadly quiet this time of night, and then we turned toward the river. Not, I saw, toward my shop or my house. The carriage clattered on the bridge over the river, echoing over the cold waves below.

"Theodor," I said softly. "Please just take me home."

"I will," he said. "But let me show you one thing first."

I shook my head but didn't argue. In truth, the kindest thing I could do for Theodor would be to distance myself from him, to keep him safe from Pyord. We turned up the narrow road toward the gardens. The greenhouse had been magic once, why not again, I imagined Theodor thinking.

We didn't, however, stop by the greenhouse. Instead, we stopped by a pond circled by huge willow trees. Theodor led me from the carriage.

"Well?" I asked, more rudely than I had intended.

"I thought so," he said. He took my hand gently. His eyes were striking in the moonlight, flecked with the same gold as the autumn-hued willow fronds around us. The moonlight settled in hollows of his high cheekbones and he looked impossibly beautiful. I hated him for it.

"You thought what?" I wanted to retract my hand, but I didn't.

Inside the shelter of the willows, there were a dozen small ponds, cascading one into the other in miniature waterfalls, and finally one large fall sending the running water to the river below. Or, it would have been cascades and running water, save that it was frozen. Silent and beautiful, like a winter enchantment.

"I thought you would like this," he said simply, leading me to an island in the middle of the ponds, stepping deftly across a narrow footbridge.

I shook with anger and desire and utter sadness. He knew I would want to drink the beauty I saw here; he wanted to share that with me. But why?

"Sophie," he said, watching my eyes glisten with unshed tears. "What's wrong?"

"What's right?" I demanded. "You're a duke; I'm no one. You're noble, and I'm linked whether I want to be or not to people who want to destroy you. My brother is—" I stopped myself. "This is impossible."

Theodor did not, as I had expected, drop my hand. Instead he drew me closer to him. His body felt warm under his cloak. "You're correct that we are on opposing sides, by birth, of what I foresee will not be a short conflict restricted to riots and pamphlets."

I almost stopped breathing.

"I am quite sure my parents wouldn't approve of you, and your brother wouldn't approve of me."

I considered the fact that, for all I'd worried about Kristos, I hadn't thought about how much he would hate finding out a duke had kissed me.

"And I will likely have to marry someone I don't choose, and not in the far future. But this is still real. And it's here, now." He gestured around us, the ice reflecting broken starlight and the golden ribbons of the willow leaves fluttering in the cold wind. "And this." He held up our hands, still clasped. "This is real, too."

"But you just said—your parents, my brother, who we are."

"I didn't say a thing about that. I just said, this." He held my hand tighter. "And this." He leaned close and brushed my lips with his. "We have time. Common or noble, we're all allotted the same amount of that, and wasting it would be criminal."

I hesitated. "I'm not sure." There was so much he didn't know, so much danger he couldn't be aware of.

"Nothing is sure. Especially not now. Except this." His hands cupped my face, and he kissed me, fiercely, and I replied with the certainty my words could never have admitted.

We held each other, on that island of frost surrounded by ice, warm in our embrace until dawn began to crest the sky.

26

"THERE'S A MESSAGE FOR YOU." ALICE SHUFFLED THROUGH A FEW receipts and handed me a paper with a formal address, wax seal and all. I stumbled into the shop barely awake—I had gotten a scant few hours of sleep after Theodor finally brought me home. Even though I was late, I was still bleary-eyed and slow.

I took the paper, startled at the seal. I knew it—everyone did. It was the royal crest.

"When did this come?" I asked.

"The messenger was waiting when I got here," Alice said. "Not a hired messenger," she added. "A royal footman. In livery and everything." I could have sworn there was a slight smirk to her smile—*Aren't you sorry you missed that?* it seemed to say. Poor Alice. While Penny had been heartsick and I'd been distracted, she was doing extra work and holding the place together.

"It's from Princess Annette," I said. "She wants a commission." I kept reading. "Oh! Her mother does, too." I forced an elated smile onto my face, even though guilt nauseated me as I reread the message. This was happening; I had to go through with Pyord's curse.

Alice sighed and went back to sorting receipts. I'd given Penny the plum assignments lately because I knew she was sad about Kristos, but Alice was working so much harder. Even though I wanted nothing to do with creating a cursed commission for the royal family, for Alice, this was the most exciting thing ever to come through our shop.

"Alice, will you come with me to do measurements?" Her eyes shot wide-open. "At the palace?"

"But I assumed it was a...you know...special commission. You don't let others listen in on those." Trust Alice to remember my rules even when I didn't.

"Yes, but there are two ladies in question at this consultation. I will speak to one while you get the necessary measurements from the other."

Alice broke into a broad grin. "Yes! Thank you!" She paused. "When?"

"We've been invited at two o'clock this afternoon," I said. The incident at Viola's must have shaken Annette, if she was rushing to get this order so quickly. "I'm going to need some strong coffee before then. Do you want some?"

Alice grinned. "If you're buying, of course!"

I let the door swing shut behind me as I dashed down the street, breathing steadying drafts of icy-cold air. This was my dream—to accept commissions from the palace. This was the chance to establish myself in the higher echelons of Galatine shopkeepers, to engage a new level of clientele, and to expand the business. To become known for my draping and my work, to move the atelier into the most fashionable districts. To hire more Pennys and Alices and even Emmis, to give them the chance I had been given. But now I'd have to soil my dreams, my goals—one of these commissions would have to be cursed or Kristos would probably die. I sighed. It would be the queen's. She was closer to the king—it was what Pyord would demand that I do, given the choice. Besides, I had met Annette. She was kind. I couldn't wish harm on her.

I shivered. In fact, I could. I could cast charms for people I didn't like; surely I could cast curses on people I did care for. The cold objectivity of my gift left me feeling frost-cold.

"Good morning, Miss Balstrade."

I nearly fell over with surprise, and dropped several coins before I collected myself. Pyord had fallen in step beside me. He watched my copper coins jounce down the street with amusement, and bent to pick up the ones nearest to him.

I snatched them from him, and he laughed. "Very sorry for startling you. I've been waiting for you to come out of your shop. I couldn't wait for our appointed meeting, what with the latest developments in our project. It seems you had an exciting evening."

I recalled the frost garden, the sculptures created by the frozen waterfalls, Theodor's kiss flooding warmth into me. I stiffened. How much did Pyord know? Had I put Theodor in some danger? Or was he referring only to the card party? It had to be the latter, I calmed myself. It had to be.

"Why"—I forced a whisper—"are you here?"

"Because you have a commission from the palace," he replied easily. I gaped, but he didn't wait for me to ask the question. "I'm aware of what occurred at Lady Viola's last night— and that Princess Annette was there."

"Aware meaning you did it," I said. "You threw the rock?"

"I didn't throw it. What do I look like, some street thug? No, but I planned it. That's what I do, Sophie. I plan things, and other people do them. I write the blueprint and someone else lays the stonework." I didn't say what I was thinking—that this sounded like the kind of hierarchy that the Red Caps were trying to topple in favor of egalitarianism. "But yes, I was counting on a little vandalism forcing our princess and her mother to come to you. The messenger from the palace to your shop this morning confirmed that."

"He reports to you?" I asked, shocked.

"Of course not—that would make this much easier, though. No, my man saw him arrive—they're not very subtle in that livery—and reported to me."

"Yes," I said, "I have a commission from the palace." Pyord stayed in step beside me. "Is there something else?" I demanded, voice pitching with nerves.

He sighed. "Sophie, I don't have to impress upon you what an important meeting this will be, do I? This may be the only chance we're given to secure getting your work into the palace."

"I'm aware of the lengths you've gone to orchestrate it thus," I replied.

"There is one more requisite to your work." He pressed his thin lips together so that they nearly disappeared. "It is quite important that the commission be something that will be worn for Midwinter festivities. The ball, the concerts at the cathedral. It's likely that will be the request in any case. You will attempt to ensure this."

"There is only so much I can do," I said, measured. I couldn't dictate what anyone requested of my shop, let alone a queen.

"I expect that you will do everything that you can. One more thing," he said, stopping and turning to face me. "You will not try anything with this. You will not make her a charmed garment instead." He thought for a moment, and added, "Or in addition to. I will find out, and you know what I will do if you cheat me. Just because you're the only person in this city who can make a charmed garment doesn't mean you're the only one who can see it."

"If someone else can see a charm," I argued, "then they can cast. That's how it works. And it's the same with curses—I couldn't see the markers until I could cast a curse." I hated myself for allowing Pyord even this much insight into the practice. "As far as I'm aware, no one is selling curses in Galitha City."

"I am always surprised by your lack of knowledge," he said, not unkindly. "There are a couple of penny-ante Pellian curse casters in this city. That doesn't mean they can do what you do, that they can produce what I need. They craft curses from lumpy clay, not fine silk—the royals would never hire them for anything, down to sweeping the floors. But they'll happily let me pay exorbitantly to tell me if there's a curse or charm hidden in your work."

I swallowed—if I had harbored any latent hopes of sending the queen a piece devoid of a curse or replaced with a charm, they sputtered out like the last flames of a near-spent candle. "I will make what our contract requires," I confirmed.

Pyord resumed walking. "Good, as I needn't keep reminding you of your brother's precarious situation. Such redundancy is tedious and, frankly, beneath both of us."

I managed to control myself, well aware of the current of people flooding around us, separating and coalescing as though we were an island in their stream. Part of safeguarding my brother was keeping myself inconspicuous, but I wanted nothing more than to scream every obscenity I could think of at Pyord.

Instead, I folded my gloved hands neatly over my cloak. "I believe I was promised a letter from my brother. Shall I collect it soon?"

"Ah, of course." He slipped a hand into the chest pocket of his coat and produced a folded sheet of paper.

He was gone before I opened it, but I didn't care. I tore the glob of sealing wax aside—there was no device imprinted in it—and opened the letter.

Dear Sophie, it read. I almost choked on the tears of relief that flooded my eyes—it was his handwriting. Kristos's cramped, looping handwriting. *I hope you've been busy with your silks and not worried over me. Still, if the good professor has given you terms, don't fight him—he drives a harder bargain than a fishwife in the quarter, and is far less likely to compromise.* The writing was his, and the words, like something he would say over breakfast. *Please keep Penny from trying to find me—I'm afraid she might be a greater threat than Venko if she thinks I've spurned her, and I value the continued integrity of my kneecaps.* Yes, that was Kristos.

Be well.

And the letter was over. I searched the page—there must be something more here. A hidden message, a secret code. I scrutinized each letter, looking for differences. Nothing. I even held the paper to the light, trying to decipher hidden marks on the page. None.

Kristos had written me nothing save that he was alive and to do what Pyord wanted.

I should have expected no more—surely Pyord had watched him write the letter, perhaps even dictated what he was allowed to say. But I had hoped Kristos would give me something else, a sign as to where he was hidden, a clue to Pyord's weaknesses, some hint that would help me stop him.

I folded the letter, slipped it into my pocket, and turned back toward the coffee shop.

I brought back one of the shop's portable tins, noticing that Pyord had disappeared from the street. Alice and I drank our coffee, left plans for Penny, who seemed understanding but disappointed to be left behind, and finished our morning's work.

Short hours later we were standing at the iron fence encircling the palace grounds, presenting the letter from Annette to the uniformed soldier at the guardhouse.

I had seen the palace hundreds of times. It sat at the top of the highest hill in the city, surrounded first by the tall fence, like a fortress, and then wide plains of green lawn and manicured orchards and groves, like a park. Now I was closer than I had ever been, and was struck with the sheer size of the house and the ornate details everywhere—the lines of trees, the finials on each bar of the iron gate, the gilded buttons on the soldiers' uniforms.

"You'll be given an escort to the servants' entrance," he explained as another soldier joined him. "He will leave you with the housekeeper, who will keep you until you are needed. Do not go anywhere unattended. Do not speak to anyone without the express permission of the housekeeper. If you leave anything behind, it is forfeit. And if you take anything, you will be prosecuted," he rattled off as though reciting a long-memorized list.

"I'll only take measurements," I joked weakly. When he looked alarmed, I added, "I'm a seamstress. I'm supposed to take measurements."

He nodded crisply, and the second soldier took us to the entrance at the back of the palace. The building was white limestone, full of huge windows flanked with columns and crested with carved birds, stags, and lions. I felt dwarfed standing next to it and was secretly grateful we were entering at the subdued service entrance instead of the lion-flanked front.

The housekeeper, a ruddy-faced woman with wiry silver hair escaping from an absurdly large cap, seated us in the servants' sitting room, a low-eaved chamber lined with what looked like cast-off chairs and settees. A single maid sat in the corner by a window, darning a sock. Alice folded her hands neatly in her lap and appeared to be soaking in the admittedly lacking atmosphere.

I, however, felt sick to my stomach. I was in the palace—the home of the royal family, the seat of national culture, the acme of the country's couture. This should have been either the highlight of my career or—the thought was impossibly bitter now—the start of a grand new chapter in which sewing for royalty was an everyday occurrence. Instead, I was a traitor to my country and an accomplice to murder, armed with just a needle and thread.

The housekeeper returned and bustled us toward the door. "You're to go to the queen's salon," she said simply. The maid didn't look up from darning her sock. We ascended a dark stairway and emerged into the balconied, frescoed, gilded main entrance of the palace. Wide swaths of sunlight from enormous windows striped the floor. Beside me, Alice whispered, "Mercy."

We passed through a large atrium with a grand staircase leading to a wide balcony and huge double doors inlaid with colored glass. I gazed up at the staircase—a whole platoon of soldiers could have lined them for parade with room to spare. Then we turned down a wide hallway. Most of the doors were closed, but I glimpsed a study upholstered in red velvet and a formal reception room in gilt and cream.

We were led to a cheerful room where a screen and a large mirror had been set up. The curtains were drawn back to allow ample sunlight into the room. Everything was set precisely as I would have asked, had I the gumption to send requests to the palace.

Princess Annette waited on the settee next to a woman who looked so much like her I could only presume she was the queen.

There was no escaping this now.

"Sophie!" Annette jumped up from the settee and embraced me in the nobility's overly friendly, strangely formal hug and cheek kisses that I wasn't quite accustomed to. Alice's eyebrows shot up in surprise—of course, I hadn't mentioned that the princess and I had met the previous night.

"This is my mother, Her Royal Majesty the Queen, Emilia of Westmere." Annette laughed. "Mostly we call her Mimi."

"Your Royal Majesty, I—"

"You needn't call me Mimi," the queen answered, shooting

Annette a tolerant smile, "but Your Royal Majesty is a bit much. Madame Westmere, please."

I sighed with some relief. Between *madame*, the sort of address I used with all my married patrons, and the name of her ancestral noble estate, *Westmere*, the title was far less intimidating, and so was the queen. "Yes, Madame Westmere. I am very honored to be invited here today."

"Annette tells me you have particular talents that are as impressive as your draping," she said, with a subtle nod toward the pea-green gown I wore. I flushed, happy to be complimented on my sewing, and then remembered the talents I'd come here to employ. My stomach clenched into a knot, but I smiled.

"Yes. You have been correctly informed."

"And Viola, the Lady Snowmont, has already hired you for this specific kind of work?"

I hesitated. One misstep and I'd be thrown out—my chances at saving Kristos ruined. Still, I had my rules to adhere to. "Madame Westmere, I must confess—I do not disclose the nature or patrons of my commissions. Even to a queen."

She clapped her hands with a delighted smile. "Splendid! Annette was right—you are indeed the very image of professionalism. Which I confess I had not expected from a conjurer."

I didn't argue her terminology.

"If you would like to discuss your particular commission, madame, I will ask that we do so privately. I will dismiss my assistant."

"Annette and I wish to confer with you at the same time," the queen said.

I nodded. "Alice, please excuse us. I'll have you return to take measurements when we are ready."

Alice nodded dumbly and let the maidservant hovering in the corner escort her from the room.

"Viola told me what you made for her," Annette said in a rush. I thought I saw the queen tighten her lips slightly, as if in disapproval. Was she lukewarm on the idea altogether, or was it Viola she didn't like? The princess and the lady were very close; perhaps the queen didn't approve of Viola's influence.

"And you would like something similar?" I asked. I hoped so—if I couldn't protect her mother, I wanted to make something special, something with a charm that would cling to Annette at all times.

"We would," said the queen. "Annette will have the same as Viola. For my younger girls, too. And I would like a shawl—something I can wear anytime. Rather poetic, isn't it? Wrapping oneself in luck?"

"Yes, indeed," I said, forcing a smile past the bile that the queen's inadvertent irony brought to the back of my throat. "Quite poetic."

"I have a new gown for Midwinter Ball—if you can coordinate the wrap with that, it would be ideal. I don't mind clashing in private, but for a formal occasion, well, I ought to look like I meant to wear the thing—don't you think?"

"Yes, of course." I let out a shaky breath—precisely what Pyord had wanted.

"Perfect. Can the shawl be embroidered? The gown is in the eastern style and we have ambassadors from East Serafe in attendance—I have to do something as a gesture for them." Of course—delegates negotiating the marriage contract between Annette and their own prince. I nodded, encouraging the queen to continue. "Embroidery could tie all the elements together, yes? And you can charm the embroidered designs?"

Or curse, I thought silently. How perfect—all the stitches in embroidery, each infused with dark curses. "Yes," I said, my mouth dry.

"And you can produce these as soon as possible?" When I hesitated, the queen added, "You must understand, we would not demand such short notice if we did not feel it was imperative."

My chest tightened and I couldn't hold my calm smile.

"Despicable, I know," Annette said, misreading my shock. "But we hardly feel safe."

"I will deliver everything before the ball," I promised. "As soon as I can."

Annette smiled. "Viola also told me about the pink gown you're making for her."

"She did?" I said, startled out of my guilt for a moment.

"You're a genius," Annette gushed. "If there's time—Mimi said I could have a new gown made for Midwinter Ball."

I swallowed. On top of our regular orders, another formal court gown was almost too much. Almost. "We can manage that," I said.

"Perfect! Well, get your girl back in to measure Annette. You shan't need anything for me, will you?"

I stared, dumb, at her for a long moment before recovering myself. I was really going to do it, really going to create a cursed shawl for the queen. "Yes, the colors, please," I finally stammered. "The colors of your gown so I can coordinate with it."

The maid returned with Alice and was then sent for the queen's gown. While Annette stripped off the pert striped jacket and quilted petticoat she wore, she told me all about the gown she wanted me to make for her.

"I was thinking, first, of yellow," she said. Her jacket came sailing over the screen, catching on the corner. "But I'm not sure—Mimi is wearing pink and I thought we'd look too...I don't know. Like matching pastel springtime bunnies." I examined the gown the maid presented to me—it was, in fact, very pink. Draped in the "eastern" style that I knew was an affectation rather than a reproduction of foreign clothing, it had full sleeves, a wrap front, and skirts that looked haphazard but were, in fact, precisely pleated. The seamstress who had made this knew her trade—and knew that the queen would look particularly lovely in the borderline-obnoxious bright pomegranate color.

Despite myself, I laughed. They would look as though they were trying to coordinate if the princess wore bright yellow—and though that would have been sweet for small children, the princess wanted to stand out on her own. "Perhaps blue," I suggested. The petticoat flopped over the top of the screen.

"Blue is so...commonplace," Annette said. Her head poked around the corner, beckoning Alice to hurry with the measurements. She scurried to her work with her notebook and measuring tape clutched in hand.

"Blue doesn't have to be dull," I said. "Perhaps an icy blue with silver embroidery? For winter?" I heard the snap of Alice's tape.

"I don't really care for silver," Annette said. "I think I look better in gold."

Of course she thought so—even though her dark hair and white skin made her look like an ice maiden. A winter-blue gown would have been perfect. Alice's pencil scratched the notepad.

"In that case, perhaps dark midnight blue with gold?" I was less than convinced—it would be difficult to avoid the result looking garish with gold bullion and sequins.

"Maybe." The petticoat disappeared as Alice reappeared, signaling that the measuring session had ended. "I was thinking about green—a pale sage, maybe?"

I winced. Though pale green was one of my favorite colors, it wouldn't flatter Annette. I worried it would make her look pallid or even jaundiced, especially under the chandeliers and candlelight of an evening ball. But how to argue with a princess?

"Annette, listen to the seamstress," the queen said from behind me. I started. "She surely knows her craft better than you do."

I balked, but Annette just laughed. "All right, Mimi. You win. Sophie, you make whatever you want, and I'll wear it and look prettier than anyone else there."

27

ALICE COULD TALK OF NOTHING BUT THE PALACE THE NEXT DAY, but though I dutifully worked on their orders, I wanted to forget the exchange. They may have been princess and queen, but Annette and Mimi—I couldn't help but remember her as Mimi—were kind, normal people. I didn't want to curse them. If Mimi had been awful, would it have made things easier?

I admitted to myself that, yes, it would have. As terrible as it was, compromising my principles would have been less horrid if I had felt that the victims were deserving. Pyord certainly did—solely because they were royalty and stood in the way of his goals. Weren't there more people like me, like Alice and everyone else doing business on our street? I fumed quietly. People who perhaps wanted change but didn't want to tear the world apart to get it? Why did Pyord and the Red Caps speak for the rest of us?

Not that it mattered—to keep him from hurting my brother, I had to do what he said. So I cut a length of yellow silk and began sketching out designs for embroidery. I couldn't cover the shawl—not and have time for Annette's commission—so I mapped out a twining design of vines and buds and leaves, culminating in explosions of blooms at the corners.

I couldn't work on the cursed garment while Alice and Penny were in the studio—not with the violent side effects I was left with from curse casting. So I started on Annette's instead, unrolling a length of ice-blue silk taffeta and placing silver trims next to it to test the colors.

"There's someone here to talk to you," Penny said. "In the front. Oh, I like that one," she added, pointing to a silver braid that I also fancied.

"Cut a few swatches of the combinations I have laid out," I directed her. "And have them sent to the palace." Penny grinned.

To my surprise, Lieta was waiting for me in my front room. She had never visited me at work, and the lines of worry on her face concerned me. "Oh, Miss Sophie. I didn't mean to interrupt," she said.

I wished she hadn't been so deferent—I knew from observation if not from direct proximity that Pellian custom respected age, not status. But Lieta was meeting me here, a Galatine milieu, and seemed ill at ease doing so. "Grandmama," I said, hoping that I was using the respectful familiar term correctly, "what's the matter?"

"I need help," she nearly whispered. "The new taxes—I wasn't expecting them, and I owe the surgeon money, he pulled my tooth last week, and—"

"Wait—new taxes?"

"You don't know?" She sank onto the bench by the door. Lieta looked frailer than usual, her gray hair working its way out from under her kerchief. "They've levied a new tax, to pay for the new soldiers and patrols in the city. On the markets."

"They're taxing the markets? But not us—" And then I understood. The vendors at the markets were mostly poorer farmers, tradespeople who could neither afford nor negotiate for a permit to open a full business, and immigrants, especially

Pellians. The disenfranchised. The people who bred revolutions. This tax would punish them. I seethed—it was not only unfair, it was stupid. Lieta had never fomented revolution with her little stall selling teas and tinctures and charms, but those who did would only be fueled by this decision.

"How much do you need?" I asked quietly.

"I couldn't ask for money—I came to ask for work. I can sew a little, or run packages."

I shook my head. "Take this. No—it's right. You're my elder." In Pellia, a woman Lieta's age would never have been expected to work. Her family would have supported her through her last years. Galitha City was a harder place. I poured a dozen silver coins into her hand.

"No, this is too much—I only owe the surgeon two—"

"I have a feeling times may be harder before they're softer," I said. "Keep the rest in trust, and help the others if they need it."

She nodded in thanks, and I thought of something else. "Lieta, don't take this the wrong way, but—you've been casting charms far longer than I. Do you know of anyone who... who casts curses?"

Her eyes grew wide. "It's best not to speak of curses. To even speak of curses is to smell a demon's breath."

"I know, but I—an acquaintance is studying the ancient practice, and—" I stopped. Not too much, I cautioned myself. "I wondered if you knew of anyone who had. Of what might have... happened to them."

"Once. In Pellia. In the next village. There was a woman they said could cast a curse. I don't know how she did it. But after her lover left her for my aunt's daughter, things happened. Goats that died, for no reason we could find. And my sister lost her baby. And hailstorms on the wheat fields—but we never knew, of course, if it was the woman's curses."

"What happened? To her?"

"Probably dragged away by demons if she was cursing us." Lieta shrugged. "No, I remember. She married a man from the port city, Hyta? No, you wouldn't know it," she reminded herself—I had never lived in Pellia and was as ignorant of its geography as I was of Serafe's or Kvyset's. "Never heard from her."

I had almost expected another of my mother's dark tales of stabbings or suicide, but Lieta's story was comforting. A curse caster could, maybe, start over again.

Lieta felt the weight of the silver in her hand, and hesitated. "I can't repay you right away."

"When you can," I said, too aware of her pride to tell her to forget the debt. She slipped outside, and I wasn't surprised to hear shouting at the next corner from a crowd of Red Caps, railing against the new taxes.

Already feeling heavy, I almost cried when a message arrived from Pyord, demanding a meeting at the archive. Sunset. I sighed.

I folded the silk for the queen's wrap even though I wanted to throw it in the fire, and set out toward the archive as the sun melted into the horizon. It was a clear evening, with a clear night ahead, and it was developing into a bitterly cold one. He couldn't be asking anything more of me, could he?

I stepped into the echoing building's atrium, and though I didn't see Pyord, I knew where I should look. The cozy little room at the back of the building.

I picked my way past carts stacked with books and patrons making frantic last-minute notes before the library closed, and nearly ran into Nia.

"Sophie!" She caught my hand and dipped quickly in for

the awkward double-kiss embrace. "I didn't realize you were a regular patron here."

"I'm not," I answered too quickly, then covered. "I just had some...professional research to do."

"Antique and foreign sewing techniques?" Nia brightened. "Of course! There must be old manuals or sketchbooks here."

I had never considered that those kinds of books might be buried here. I might spend time reading if there were treasures like that hiding on the shelves. "Exactly. I'm, ah, meeting with the curator to inquire."

"You're heading in the right direction—he was talking to my tutor in the back. Once they get going, it's too technical even for me."

I considered something I hadn't before—Pyord wasn't the only person in the city who could read Pellian. Who knew what modifications to the curse magic he'd described might be present in those books I couldn't read? Could there be a way to lift a curse, or divert it? Could I finish the shawl, let Pyord confirm with whatever back-alley caster he paid to ascertain my work, and then rescind the curse?

Pyord wouldn't tell me, but perhaps someone else could. "You—you must be exceptionally knowledgeable in Pellian," I said.

Nia feigned modesty. "I am quite proficient, yes. Aside from my tutor and some of the academics at the university, I am likely closest to fluent in the entire city."

"I had hoped that perhaps—perhaps you could help me."

"Learn Pellian?" She raised an eyebrow. "Whyever do you want to do that?"

"Not learn, precisely. But the only written work on...my particular gift is in Pellian. I had wanted to learn more about it."

"You must understand, I am far more interested in the art and culture of ancient Pellia than I am in magic."

"Of course—I just need the words translated. Nothing in depth, I'm sure." I wasn't so sure.

"I thought you were quite skilled already," Nia said. "What else is there to learn?"

I didn't want to reveal specifics—that I wanted to see if charms or curses could be undone. Not yet. "There must be more theory than I learned," I said instead. "I was just taught by my mother, and only the practical application. Not how it works."

"Hmm," she said, considering this. "I suppose I could translate for you if the curator can find the right books for us."

I smiled as though surprised, as though happy. I still wasn't sure—she seemed oddly reticent, but that could be for any reason, including not wanting to spend time in the archive reading work that didn't really interest her. "Let's meet tomorrow afternoon," I said, eagerness bleeding into my voice. Pressing anyone, let alone an important diplomat's daughter like Nia, for her time felt uncomfortable, but I worried that any delay and it would be too late.

"All right, I'll see you tomorrow," Nia said, her saffron gown illuminating the dark halls of the archive like a candle.

I slipped past the last row of shelves and saw Pyord, deep in conversation with a man in a sharply tailored black suit of clothes. Even the cuffs of his shirt and neckcloth were black. Either he was in deep mourning or he was supremely eccentric.

"Ah, Sophie," Pyord said as he saw me, even though I was trying to shrink into a shadow. "Please allow me to introduce the curator of the Public Archive, Maurice Autland."

The man had a face like a barely fleshed-out skull, but his smile was kind and his greeting warm. "Miss, so lovely to meet another of Pyord's students. Two in one day—I am quite a lucky man!"

I stopped myself from emitting an audible gasp. Nia had left her tutor with the curator—her tutor was Pyord? Of course. I could have smacked myself, if Pyord hadn't been watching my every move with perceptive eyes. Nia studied Pellian. Pyord was, by his own boasting, a premier expert in the language. I forced a smile.

"It's very nice to meet you, as well," I choked out.

"I hate to cut short such a scintillating conversation, but Sophie and I must get to work," Pyord said, and the curator bowed and took his leave.

As soon as the door closed behind us, Pyord smiled. "This is all coming together better than I had hoped," he said. "Your visit to the palace was a long one."

I swallowed anger. "Stop having me followed. I will not be tracked like an animal. I will not stand—"

"You'll do as I say." Pyord's voice was like ice, and the room took on a chill despite the roaring fire in the hearth.

"I can't work if I'm frightened," I lied through clenched teeth, "and men following me frightens me."

Pyord just laughed. "Should I get a woman to do it? Or perhaps a little boy. Are you scared of little boys?"

"No," I said.

"Then you're just afraid of who my spies report to." He folded his hands. "Well, then. You've begun work on the queen's garment?"

He didn't know what the garment was—that was good, I thought. Maybe he didn't know that I was making Annette and the other princesses charmed clothing.

"I have," I replied. "Not the sewing. Not the...curse." I hated saying the word. "But it's begun."

"Very good." He ran a hand over the stack of books next to him with what I could swear was a reverent sigh. "Sophie, truly, it's a shame you don't know more about your own craft. From what I have read in the ancient texts and studied in modern practitioners, you are particularly talented, with remarkable control over the casting."

I must have looked surprised, because Pyord laughed. "It's such a pity no one ever bothered to educate you further on your gifts. You might have made more of yourself than a novelty seamstress." I bristled, but Pyord didn't react. "In the new government—no, the new Galitha—that we will create, I foresee a much greater use for those with your skills, nurtured correctly. Such power as could be developed, joined with democratic ideals…" He shook his head as though in wonder at his own imaginings. What he hinted at left me cold—if casting could be developed beyond simple charms and curses, if that capability could be harnessed by a government, it felt wrong, rotten at the core of the idea. It wasn't how I had been trained, and it went against the ethics of helping individuals that my mother—that every charm-casting mother I'd ever heard of—had instilled in her charge.

"At any rate—we have a project at hand already. Which of the Midwinter events is the piece intended for?"

I swallowed guilt. This was vital information, information he would undoubtedly use to plan. I could lie, tell him it was for the concert at the cathedral or the Winter Hunt. As he waited with inscrutable patience for my answer, I realized I couldn't. My brother's life was tied directly to my cooperation, and I knew the consequences of a lie.

"Specifically, the Midwinter Ball. It could be worn at other events, but it's intended to match her gown for the ball."

He nodded with a faint smile. "That will be best. And I am assured it will be finished in time?"

I had never in my life been late on a commission, but I couldn't resist testing how deeply tied my thread was to the rest of the scheme Pyord had woven. "I—that is my plan. It's a very complicated piece. It may take time. She'll wear it at some point regardless, I'm sure."

"Unacceptable." Pyord paced toward me, towering over me. "It must be finished before the ball, and she must wear it to the ball."

"I can only guarantee one of those."

"Good." Pyord smiled. "And you will guarantee it."

I swallowed. "Fine. It will be done by the ball. And I hope she decides not to wear it."

Pyord ignored the jab and searched my face. "I find it a little odd you didn't speak of the princess. Did she give you a commission as well?"

"You only need one curse. I'm giving you one. That was the agreement." I heaved a sigh. "The queen's garment makes the most sense. She is with the king most frequently, yes? The others don't need to be cursed if she is. Princess Annette requested a court gown. Not even charmed."

"Simply asking," he replied. "Our bargain is for the queen's cursed shawl, and no charms to counteract it." He paused, fingers tapping one another as though ticking off a to-do list. "As to your friend, the First Duke."

I exhaled, exasperated. "What could he possibly have to do with the queen's shawl?"

"For pity's sake, there's no need to get worked up—I merely wanted to know if he had contacted you for some kind of charm. I know your work is typically women's in nature, but—"

"No," I said hastily. I wouldn't be coerced into making a cursed garment for Theodor. "I don't make men's clothing. He knows that well enough."

Pyord searched my face as I spoke, surprised by my strong reaction, but he didn't argue. "Very well. Though you did create a cap for your brother."

I could have listed all the things that were different—it wasn't proper tailoring, it was a simple piece, my brother asked me. My brother.

"I could never deny Kristos anything he asked for," I whispered, and left Pyord standing by himself in the archive.

28

I WORKED GREEN SILK VINES INTO THE SHAWL, IMBUING EACH stitch with the dark sparkle I pulled from the air, until just before Alice arrived the next morning. I ran outdoors, was sick, and had cleaned myself up and stopped sweating before she walked in the door. I promptly sent her out for tea.

"It's looking very pretty," Penny said about the shawl when she came in.

I nodded weakly. I hated looking at it already.

I directed Penny in cutting out a muslin for Annette's gown, and planned the next steps in Madame Pliny's court gown with Alice. I tasked her with placing the boning in the bodice, and indicated to Emmi that she was allowed to watch Alice finish the innards of the structured bodice as long as she finished sorting all the scrap bins in time. She agreed eagerly.

And I worked on Viola's day gown, the pink confection I had designed when my only concern was my business and my creations. It was a beautiful piece, but the clean lines and perfect pleating that would have made me happy in the past didn't affect me now.

Instead, I started working a protection charm into the seams on the bodice and the curved hem of the skirt.

I made quick progress, even with the extra work of charm weaving, and was exhausted and famished by the time our lunch hour arrived. Working curses before the others arrived and then charm casting all morning taxed me more than I had guessed. I practically stumbled into the front room, scrounging for a scrap of croissant from breakfast.

I nearly ran into Theodor.

"I've been waiting for you. You need a bell on the door or something."

I sat down, hard, on the bench in the corner, breathing harder than I should have from surprise alone.

"Are you all right?" Theodor dropped to one knee next to me. "You're pale—are you ill?"

"No, I'm just—I need to eat," I stammered. "Casting charms, it takes a physical toll." I blinked—now I was sweating. How undignified.

"Perfect. I have a picnic in the carriage. I'll bring something in, and then we can go."

I pressed my lips together to hold my annoyance in. Theodor couldn't interrupt our daily schedule whenever he wanted to. It was easy to forget, when we were talking or, I flushed thinking of it, kissing, that he was noble. But this particular entitlement, that I'd drop everything whenever he asked, struck a sour chord in me. "Go? Theodor, I can't just go off with you—I have work to attend to. All afternoon."

"Not looking like that, you don't." Alice stood in the doorway of the studio, hands on her hips. Any more maternal and she would have started clucking. She shouldn't have had to watch over me, I reminded myself. She was younger than me, and my employee. But I let her bring me a cup of water anyway.

"Listen to Mama Hen," Penny added in a shout from the studio. "I've never seen you work like this. You can't keep up."

"Maybe you should hire a third person," Alice said, a little too pointedly. "I mean, in addition to Emmi. She's a help, but—" She cut herself off before she said anything that could hurt feelings or, more likely, call into question my wisdom in hiring an untrained Pellian girl. I wanted to argue, and to chastise her for talking about business in front of a guest, but she was probably right.

"I'll consider it," I answered.

"No badgering her now," Theodor said. I softened a little—he was spoiled, certainly, but he was also sympathetic. "She's taking a long lunch. Right?"

Penny and Alice agreed amiably enough, and Emmi was staring, mouth open, at Theodor's house crest and ceremonial sword that marked him as a noble. I groaned. "Make sure you finish the projects written up on the board first," I reminded them. "Wrap the finished orders. And cut more shifts." I had to stitch together the princesses' underthings. I would complete the commission as though it was unrelated to my contract with Pyord—indeed, he had as much as said that the queen's commission was our bargain and no more. Annette was kind, and the princesses were children. They didn't deserve to be swept up in Pyord's schemes, and I could offer a small amount of protection.

"We know," Alice said, rolling her eyes. "Now scat."

Practically shoved out the door by my employees and wrapped in my cloak by Theodor, I found myself in the carriage, still faint and sweating and embarrassed, but at least with a pastry in one hand. I glanced outside—no hooded figures or strange men loitering around my door today. Pyord must have given his man the day off.

"You can't keep doing this," I protested weakly between bites. What was this pastry made of—the angelic stuff butter became when it died and went to heaven? It melted on my tongue. And the lemon curd filling—I was nearly blinded with citrusy bliss.

"It's so convincing when you're almost purring eating that pastry."

"You know what I mean," I said, licking my fingers. "Or maybe you don't. Do you?"

He bit a lip, thinking. "I do interrupt your workday," he said. "Perhaps I shouldn't do that?"

His surprise was in earnest, and I bit back some annoyance. Though I was sure he didn't mean it maliciously, there was an ugly expectation that I was available at his bidding, waiting for him between his obligations. I didn't have council meetings and formal events on my calendar, but my work was constant, and persistently pressing. "Yes, it is a bit problematic," I said. "I know you're very important and assisting in running a country," I added, burying any bitterness at his assumptions behind a veil of humor, "but I'm quite tied up running a shop and earning enough to eat."

Theodor's ears reddened as he realized his mistake. He would not have expected his fellow dukes and counts, or even ladies like Viola, to be free at any hour of the day. Nobles arranged their schedules in advance and sent invitations and messages via their liveried servants. Though I lacked the servants, I still had obligations. "I suppose I owe you an apology."

I accepted with a gracious nod. "It's nothing we can't remedy. Perhaps you could send a note first. If we plan ahead, I can rearrange my work and assign Penny and Alice their tasks, and make sure Emmi has enough to do, and I shan't get behind."

"So you're saying you want to keep seeing me," Theodor said with a rakish grin. "Brilliant, my persistence is paying off."

I realized what I'd said—that I wanted to make seeing Theodor a priority. I blushed—very well, then, I did. "Yes, your charisma is quite effective," I said. I hoped Pyord didn't have a way to twist my connection with Theodor into his plan, too.

We arrived at the greenhouse, just as I had expected, and Theodor helped me from the carriage. I couldn't help but enjoy the feel of his hand under my glove, supporting me. Inside, in the center of the garden, a table and two chairs had been placed by the little fountain.

He held the chair for me, and I smoothed a freshly ironed napkin on my lap. Theodor poured two glasses of pink wine, and lifted his glass. I raised my glass to his. The crystal made a satisfying clink. "What's the celebration? The Red Caps have surrendered all their pamphlets and pitchforks?"

"Hardly," Theodor said. "If this threat were coming from a foreign nation, we would have at least attempted negotiations long ago. But with our people? The council is apparently at a loss."

I stared at the bubbles rising in my glass. The pink beverage looked far more optimistic than I felt. "Maybe they don't want to seem weak."

"They're going to seem much weaker when they can't put down a rebellion," Theodor replied.

"You—you don't think they can subdue the Red Caps?"

"I don't mean it to sound so dramatic. They will, even if it's allowed to continue on the course it's set on now. And that course will likely be bloody and undermine our authority with the people even as we try to shore it up. Certainly, it will hurt the trust other nations have in us. The delegation from East Serafe will leave, with no marriage contract for Annette, if the revolutionaries gain too much ground."

I smiled. "Annette might not mind."

"Perhaps not," Theodor answered, "but we need the Serafan trade routes to stay open to us."

"Most of my best silks are Serafan," I agreed. The Galatine mills didn't produce fabric half as fine, and the dye colors weren't as brilliant. In fact, I rarely worked with domestic silks at all. Or wools—the sheep of Kvys were legendary for their wool. Or cotton, which was grown in the Equatorial States and milled most finely in Fen. I considered the wide web of agriculture, production, and trade that existed in each of my garments. A disruption to international trade would create a disruption even in my little shop.

"And the Allied Equatorial States—they are our closest military allies. Yet they wouldn't hesitate to cease supporting us if they thought our kingdom was a dying one."

"I'm not entirely sure that the Red Caps have considered foreign policy in their plans."

"If their pamphlets are any indication, they have no interest in the potential side effects their chaos could sow. They do seem quite aware of the potential alliances they could broker, however. At least, their leadership does."

"Alliances?" With trade goods, I had a passable enough understanding to add to the conversation. With political intrigue, I was entirely unschooled. I was glad Viola and the others from the salon weren't here to witness my confusion. "It's only—who would want to ally themselves with an illegitimate government?"

The question seemed to impress Theodor; he nodded thoughtfully. "No legitimate government would, at least not openly. But Kvyset in particular has been…obdurate about our border agreements for decades. Not to mention, they've been squabbling with the Allied States about certain holdings in the Orian Sea. If it came to open war, we would almost certainly support the States."

"Because they're our closest military allies," I supplied, as though in a schoolroom recitation.

"Precisely. Kvys don't see our current regime as favorable to their needs. If they provide tacit support to an uprising, and that uprising in turn becomes the new government—"

"I see." My fingers traced the fine linen hem of the table-cloth, as though counting stitches could help me understand the depths the Red Caps and, I was sure, Pyord had plumbed in planning their revolt. Kristos had said that Pyord was integral to their organization; I was beginning to see how Pyord was the difference between riot and revolution.

"What kind of support?" I asked.

"Nothing proven yet. There has been some suspicious activity at the border, which General Drake reported as potential arms shipments, and some troop movement." Theodor hesitated. "Not from the Kvys government itself—the patrician families control units, mostly cavalry, raised from their lands, and professional soldiers for hire are legal in Kvyset. Still, it could indicate plans by some patrician families or even independent mercenaries to provide actual military support in case of a successful coup. That, in turn, indicates a view for a full-fledged revolution—a civil war."

"They've organized all of this," I sighed. "All in such a short amount of time."

Theodor raised an eyebrow. "Short?"

"They weren't this organized six months ago. Believe me—I would know." I recalled with a bitter nostalgia the late nights at the taverns, the first pamphlets passed from League household to League household. When words alone were the currency of the movement, potent in possibility but powerless to inflict destruction on their own.

"Interesting," Theodor said. "I had always wondered—it seemed as though we must have been missing something, some undercurrent building that we hadn't seen. Perhaps we hadn't missed anything but the turning point."

I nodded, knowing I could say more, could give a name. Pyord Venko. It hung from my fingertips like a man on the gallows, but I couldn't say it. If word reached him before he was arrested, if he knew I had betrayed him, he'd surely kill my brother. The more I considered it, the more likely it seemed that he would have mechanisms in place for others to carry out such retributions in his absence. I shivered.

"I'm sorry—this is unpleasant talk," Theodor said, clearly mistaking the source of my revulsion. I wasn't an innocent girl being given an upsetting primer lesson; I knew more about the ugly storm that was coming than Theodor did.

Still, I mustered a smile and agreed. "And this all looks delightful," I added, gesturing to the untouched lunch in front of us.

He speared a withered mushroom and devoured it. "My cook may actually be a sorceress—dried fungus never tasted so good."

I laughed. "I never did care for them," I admitted.

"Well, this might change your mind." He shoveled a few onto my plate. "Delectable."

"Better fresh?" I asked as I tasted one, holding back a grimace.

"No idea. Those are imported from Kvyset."

I almost choked—dried mushrooms, imported across the mountains or through the fjords? "Don't we have mushrooms here?"

"Well, yes, but not speckled brown caps—oh." He set his fork down. "I suppose it all seems a bit extravagant?"

"A bit," I said. I stared at the mushrooms, wondering if I should leave such luxury alone or force them down so as not to be wasteful.

Theodor sighed, a furrow forming between his eyes. "I think I understand my country, and then a moment later I'm proven a fool."

"Not a fool," I answered, too quickly.

"Yes, a fool." He pushed his plate away. "But if I'm a fool, at least I know it."

"You've been raised in one world, I in another, and we are both blind to what it didn't show us," I answered, thinking of Kristos. How often his impassioned speeches turned toward lambasting the nobility, never considering the particular hardships their station forced on them. Never considering, certainly, the delicate balance of international politics and trade. We were all half-blind, yet so sure we saw the truth.

"You show me," he said softly. "You do—don't argue with me; it's true. The common people were just—this sounds terrible, but it's true—faceless before I met you. That they existed but they weren't"—he winced—"really people."

I was about to snap off an indignant retort, but I realized I was no better. The nobility were names on my account book, their affiliation was a goal to achieve, but I hadn't ever known one personally. Even my business affiliation kept me from desiring open butchery like Pyord, but it took the past weeks in Viola's salon and Theodor's greenhouse to have any sympathy for them.

Instead, I clasped his hand in mine. "I understand."

He squeezed my fingers until they hurt. "My father wants me to go to the Allied States around Midwinter."

I knew what that meant, and my chest felt hollow. Still, I forced a smile. "Perfect timing. The dead of winter here, but still summer there, no?"

"You reminded me that winter has its benefits."

I drew my hand back. "You're not considering refusing your father, are you?"

He straightened his shoulders. "Yes, I am. I don't have to arrange this contract now. The country is in the midst of unrest—perhaps it should wait."

I swallowed. "Perhaps you have to go now, before the Allied States grow concerned that we are a weak country," I said. "Perhaps you need to secure a marriage contract before the Red Caps do anything more drastic than printing pamphlets and protesting." My voice sounded flat and dead, and the reality of what I was saying washed over me. It felt like grief.

"Quick learner." He traced the edge of his wineglass. "I'll have to have you appointed to my advisory cabinet when I'm Prince of Westland."

When he was prince. Someday in the future, he would be Prince of Westland, and I would still be Sophie Balstrade, the seamstress. He would be married and have little duke and duchess children by his wife. Why did that make me cold with anger?

"Don't," I said.

"You're right, the ones I have to keep on the cabinet all starch their neckerchiefs too much, they're quite unbearable—"

"Don't!" I stood in a rush, knocking my rickety chair over with my skirts. "Don't joke about it. It isn't funny, and it won't ever be funny." Blood rushed into my cheeks and tears stung my eyes. "I should never have agreed—should never have come—" The words choked me.

Theodor stood and reached a hand out toward me, but I recoiled. "I have to leave," I finally said. I rushed out of the greenhouse before he could answer.

29

I CLATTERED THROUGH THE STREETS, MOVING AS QUICKLY AS I could without looking like a common thief, running from the only thing I wanted. I returned to the shop, barely looked at Alice or Penny, and gathered the shifts Alice had cut for the princesses. I would stay up tonight sewing them, I resolved. I had a feeling I wasn't going to be able to sleep anyway.

I didn't want to see anyone, but I had planned to meet Nia at the archive, and I forced myself to remember that understanding curses was more important to the state of the entire nation than my petty heartbreak over a duke. Nia waited in the vestibule of the archive, as still as a statue with her ostrich-plume hat balanced on her lap.

"I had the curator pull some books," she said without any further greeting. "It appears my tutor already requested some of them, so they were easy to find." I didn't reply—Pyord had used those books to convince me of my ability to cast curses. If she didn't know any more about their content, I didn't want to tip her off to what I'd learned from them. I hoped I could trust that she wouldn't tell Pyord—that she wasn't, in fact, allied with him to begin with. But no—there was no way she knew what he truly was.

The curator had set a few tomes aside, not in the private room I'd used with Pyord, but in an alcove flanked by windows and equipped with a long table and a pair of chairs. "What can I do?" I asked.

"You can tell me exactly what you want to find," Nia said, slipping a pair of crisp white gloves over her dark hands.

Apparently my vague request wasn't going to suffice with Nia. "I think there might be a way to undo charms," I said, forcing some neutrality into my voice to hide my nerves. "I'm concerned it could compromise my business."

"A way to undo charms," Nia repeated, leafing through the first book. "This won't help us—nothing about charms, it's all about various curses." She raised a black eyebrow at me. "Which doesn't concern you."

I hesitated. "The process is very likely the same. If that book has anything about undoing curses it would be...maybe helpful?"

"It doesn't. There's no theory here, just directions for writing curses into tablets." She shrugged. "This is how research goes—you hit a lot of dead ends and read a lot of material that's not useful." She was already reaching for another book, and she squinted with interest at the page. There was something exciting for Nia about the hunt—even if it was through a stack of old books.

"There aren't many books here," I said, surveying the table. "What if none of them have what we need?"

"If none of them have what you want," Nia said pointedly, "we can ask the curator to do another search." She grinned. "That's what makes research such fun."

"Fun, of course."

"Yes, well, everyone's definition of fun is a little different.

How, exactly," she said, looking up at me, "would knowing how charms are undone help you?"

"If someone undid my charms, I'd know," I replied weakly.

"I'm not even sure I should help you with this," she sighed. My heart skipped. "A charm caster who can undo her work? That seems like a conflict of interest. You could extort people to put charms back in. Not that you would," she added hastily, "but it's an ethical conundrum, isn't it?"

"I wouldn't do that," I said.

"Maybe not, but theoretically, it would be possible. Plausible, even."

I tried to match Nia's detached logic. "But if someone else undid a charm, it would be unprofessional of me to not realize it, to not know how to redo it effectively. And besides," I added as I realized it, "if I knew how it was done, perhaps I could build in prevention."

"Perhaps," Nia said. "Here's something. It's a counter-curse—does that help?"

"What does that mean?"

"It reverts whatever was charmed or cursed in an item to the creator of the charm or curse."

I clamped my mouth shut—that was the last thing I wanted to do, but if it was my only option, perhaps I could take it. I wasn't being targeted; bad luck might not end in my death like it would for the royal family.

"It might be of interest," I said. "Maybe I could figure out more about the theory from it?"

"Maybe. I'll mark the page number and translate it later." She kept paging, and I felt more and more nervous. Nia's interest seemed to increase as she read, as though she had found some kernel of academic fascination in this topic after all.

She stopped, and wrinkled her brow as she read. "I think this is what you're looking for," she said. "It's how a caster can remove a charm and replace it with a curse," she explained as she read, "but it's in two steps. The first is just removing the charm."

"That's exactly it," I said, overly excited. "I mean, the part about removing. That's what I was worried could be done."

"All right. Let me see if I can figure this out," she began. "The text talks about the light matter tied into the charmed object. Does that make sense?"

"Yes, perfect sense."

"Sounds like gibberish to me, but I'll trust you," she said. "It's a long passage. I'll have to translate the whole thing. Pellian grammatical structures are different from ours—it makes translating quickly difficult." She pulled her gaze from the ink and parchment. "It's easier to translate into modern Pellian than Galatine. Should I do that instead? I'd be able to manage that far more."

I blushed. "I don't speak Pellian," I replied.

"I'm sorry. I had assumed." She bowed her head in apology for her imagined slight.

"It's a fair assumption. But I—I was born in Galitha." I recalled the earliest years in my household, rarely hearing Pellian except when my parents wanted to say something outside of my brother's and my hearing. Pellian was their secret language, and I never learned more than a few phrases useful in a marketplace or, I thought with a smile, the catchall Pellian profanity my father expelled on a fairly regular basis. "My parents—we only spoke Galatine together." They thought it was best, to acclimate us, and perhaps to appear more Galatine themselves.

"Then I'll have to do it piecemeal and then put it all together again." It sounded like a lot of work, but Nia looked excited at the prospect.

"That would be very helpful, if you don't mind," I said. I hoped she didn't mind.

"Not at all! It's excellent practice. I can have the translation to you—well, I have to leave in just a few minutes tonight, and then tomorrow is the charades party at Pauline's—I hate charades but it's her birthday so I think I'm stuck..." She ticked days off on her fingers. "I'll have time before Viola's music evening. I'll bring it then. You're going, aren't you? I assumed you must be coming," she said.

A social gathering while my brother remained prisoner and I had a curse to cast. "Oh, I have been so busy lately, so I don't suppose—"

"Busy! Take an evening off, Thimble Thumb!" Nia said with a smile. "You really should come. Marguerite is going to unveil one of her new harp compositions, and Viola talked Theodor into bringing his violin. He's quite modest about it, but he's very accomplished."

I stared into my hands at the mention of his name. "Of course he is." I sighed. "Very well, Nia, I—thank you."

She raised an eyebrow and laughed. "It's really not an imposition at all. You're thanking me as though I deserve the National Medal."

If only she knew.

"In all honesty, this was interesting—added another dimension to my studies. I'll have to tell Pyord about the prevalence of curses over charms in these books."

I smiled, unsettled. I didn't want Pyord knowing I'd been learning more about Pellian curse theory—and certainly didn't want him to know I was trying to undo the curse I'd cast. Not to mention that it could put Nia in danger.

"How well do you know your tutor?" I asked as innocently as I could.

"Not well," Nia replied. "He's a very secretive man." Her deep brown eyes developed a strange, dreamy look. "I'd like to know him better."

I almost burst out laughing. Nia had feelings for Pyord! I controlled myself. "He is a lecturer at the university, no?"

"That's right. I started attending lectures there when my father first brought me to Galitha. I was bored here; I hadn't yet met Viola and the others at the salon. He was...so interesting." Nia stared off into the dust motes, smiling vaguely.

I wondered, briefly, if he had hoped to recruit Nia. From the daydreams crisscrossing Nia's face, it was clear to me that he hadn't tried.

"I had studied Pellian at home, but my tutors were all limited in their knowledge. When I asked if he would consider taking a woman on as a private student, he agreed. My father, at first—" She bit her lip. "He doesn't trust Galatine morals overmuch. But he agreed. Pyord has proven the perfect gentleman," she added, faint disappointment coloring her voice.

I groped for something to say, something that didn't indicate I knew him better than Nia did. "He is unmarried?"

"Yes, he said once that he was married to his work. He left Kvyset for his research like a man leaves his childhood home for his wife, he said." She smiled. "And I had the impression he didn't socialize much. I would assume he was a homebody, but I invited him to the salon once, and he seemed...perturbed by the idea of being around nobles. I wondered if there was some old but deep slight, or some history, with the nobility. Perhaps a particular noble, I couldn't say."

I imagined Nia, scientific in her precision as she parsed the limited phrases Pyord gave her, forming keen conclusions about a man who revealed little. Pyord clearly maintained no fondness for Kvyset, and his frustration with the nobility's hold on the university and his inability to advance his career was clear. That could be the extent of it; Pyord wanted more importance than either his home country or his adopted nation would grant him. I wondered, however, if Nia was right, that some more personal grievance danced behind his stony façade as well.

In either case, their acquaintance was a liability. "I'd actually appreciate it if you didn't mention my research to him," I said. "In fact, I'd like to keep this quiet altogether."

"Why?" Nia asked, snapping back to attention. The faraway look was gone.

"I make my business based on indelible charms. It's not false advertising—I didn't realize they could be broken until now. But if word got out that people could undo them..."

"I see," Nia said, measured. "I'll keep mum."

30

—ᴍ—

I HOPED, DESPERATELY, THAT NIA'S FINDINGS WOULD GIVE ME a loophole to build into the cursed shawl, but I was acutely aware that I couldn't wait or stop working and still keep my brother safe. I stitched charmed seams on the princesses' shifts late into very cold nights. On less than adequate sleep, I dove into the shawl each morning at full speed at the workshop, making rapid stitches and quick progress. A week of repeating this cycle, and I had nearly fainted from the roaring headache that split my vision when I finally stopped working cursed stitches. I stumbled outside and retched into the gutter, and collapsed with my back against the rough stone, allowing ugly sobs to overtake me.

When I finally stood on shaking legs and went back inside, Penny was hemming a jacket and Alice was stitching the pleats into the back of a gown. I had set Emmi to washing the front windows, which, though not tied to learning our trade, had become necessary after the dust of a dry autumn had settled thick on the panes. I sank into my chair behind the screen with a cup of tea and a bit of stale bread, trying to compose myself, the pile of half-finished shifts next to me.

Someone knocked on the screen.

"I'll be out in a moment."

"Stay there." Alice's head appeared around the corner. "I sent Penny out for scones and told Emmi to wash outside while the sun is on this side of the shop. I want to talk to you."

I sighed. Overworking Alice had finally caught up to me—she was unhappy here. She was going to demand a raise I couldn't give, or give me her notice, or—

"Are you in trouble?" she asked frankly.

"What?" I stammered. "I—I don't know what—"

"In trouble. In the...feminine way." Alice blushed.

"Alice, are you asking if I'm pregnant?" I gasped and tried not to choke on the laughter that threatened to overtake me.

"I've caught you being sick outside three times this week," Alice answered, raising her eyebrow like a schoolteacher who's caught a student in a lie. Apparently I hadn't been as discreet as I thought. "My sister was sick every morning for months with her first baby. Plenty of women are."

"That's not—I just—"

"And the other day," Alice continued, now faltering a bit, "I followed you when you went out for coffee. You met a man on the street."

"Oh, Alice," I said, dismayed. "You shouldn't have done that."

"I know. But I was worried. There's something going on and you're not telling me. And without Kristos here—I thought maybe you needed some help."

I blinked back tears. Sweet, honest Alice. "You are too kind, Alice—I've overworked you horribly the past weeks and you're only worried about me."

"So you are in trouble."

"No! Not that kind of trouble," I muttered before I could stop myself. "I'm not pregnant, Alice. Please believe me. I'm just overwhelmed. There's...too much work."

"That's for certain." Alice pursed her lips. "It's not my place, but perhaps we need another seamstress. Emmi is very helpful but she can't help with most of the work we're behind on."

"I think you're right," I said, measured. Anything to move Alice away from the subject of why being overworked would make me meet strange men at the Public Archive, or why I was getting sick every morning. "First, teach Emmi proper hemming. It's moving her more quickly than I would have normally, but if she's proficient at it, we can task her with that for every piece in the shop if you want. And then, I want you to take the lead in finding someone else. Partial time only, a day laborer, not a contract hire. Place the advertisement and interview candidates."

"Me?" Alice squeaked.

"I know it's more work in the short term," I said quickly.

"No, it's not that—I've just—I've never done it before! And I'm just a seamstress, too."

"You'll make a wise choice, I know. You know the skills we need here, and how to measure those skills in another. And you may be my seamstress now, but I'd be lying if I said I thought you'd work for me forever. Someday you'll want to open your own atelier, and you'll need experience in hiring."

Alice gaped at me. "Really? You think I could have my own business?"

"Someday," I said, cautious. It wouldn't be easy, and it would take the perseverance to withstand refusals of permits, but if anyone had the pragmatism and dogged determination to do so, it was Alice. "I opened this place, didn't I?"

"Well, yes, but you—"

"Have a certain extra skill. I do, and it allowed me to open with less experience than most seamstresses. Someday you'll have that experience, and I've no doubt you'll be an excellent business manager, too. You'll either find a niche like I did or you'll fill a void when shops close." I didn't mention it, but Alice would have the benefit of her comfortably Galatine appearance and the fact that any association she had with Pellian superstition was a short assistantship early in her career. Though my talents were a unique niche, and had ultimately gained me my business, I could easily have been denied on distrust of Pellian charms or the assumption that a Pellian couldn't navigate the difficulties of Galatine business ownership.

Alice beamed. "Thank you. I'll place the advertisement right away."

I nodded, waving her off to get back to work, and took a deep breath. I would have to be more careful.

A messenger arrived after noon with one of Pyord's characteristic cryptic notes—looping handwriting in blackest ink that read, simply, *Sunset at the archive.*

I spent the rest of the day distracted, working too slowly and making poor decisions on what to delegate to whom. Princess Annette's gown was half-finished, and all that remained on Viola's pink day gown was the trim. Yet even though Alice was better at interior seams and Penny quite able at trims, I asked Alice to work on Viola's trim, leaving Penny struggling to attach a sleeve correctly. The day ended with Penny picking out stitches, Alice frustrated with Penny, Emmi avoiding both of them, and me dismayed at how little progress I had made on cutting out orders.

And the knot in my stomach refused to untie itself. Pyord, the shawl, Alice's suspicion, the way I'd left things with Theodor—I couldn't carry this all much longer.

I dismissed Alice and Penny, wrapped myself in my cloak, and set off toward the archive with a hollow sigh. I caught the flicker of a hooded figure behind me several times, and tried to ignore that someone was following me. One of Pyord's men again, I was sure.

The hollowness filled with trepidation as I approached the archive. Pyord already waited in front of the building.

"Come inside." His voice was as heavy as I felt, lead swirling in my feet as I followed him up a set of stairs to a niche on the west side of the building set on all sides by windows. It overlooked the square. People bustled from one building to another, trying to escape the bitter wind.

"You continue," Pyord said, "to spend time with your noble friends, one duke in particular."

"I—yes," I answered, my throat constricting my voice into strange tones. "I doubt I will see much more of him."

"How so?"

"He is most likely going to leave the country sometime around Midwinter." There was triumph in my voice—*You can't touch him*, I wanted to boast.

Pyord laughed, a cruel little hiccup of sound. "The duke is finally tired of you? I remember young love. It's a painful thing."

Rage welled in me, but I bit it back. "Who is to say I didn't tire of him?"

Pyord shook his head. "You didn't. An honest tradeswoman like you—no, the nobility tire of their playthings far sooner than the rest of us." He swallowed, and I could have sworn I saw tears brighten his eyes.

I remembered what Nia had said, about his distance from the nobility. "You—did you get involved with a noble?"

His laugh was bitter. "Hardly. I could never. But my sister—" He stopped.

"Go on," I pressed, my voice as quiet as I could make it.

"Why should I, when the story is an old one, repeated many times with many women, and always has the same ending? My father was a delegate from the Kvys trade guild. We lived here in the capital city. There were few enough Kvys to associate with— only diplomats and a handful of merchants with seasonal apartments in the city. Most didn't even bother to move their families here, and so my sister ran with Galatine circles that exceeded her status. She met a young count. He courted her. He promised her things he couldn't give, never wanted to give, all to convince her to give herself up to him." He snorted. "Their practices are different from ours, my girl—be glad your dalliance with the duke went no further. He'd have ruined you."

I bristled despite a strangely genuine concern in Pyord's voice. I wasn't a length of fabric to be ruined with the stain of a few kisses. Still, I kept my voice level. "Then this count ruined your sister?"

"Yes. And after the child was born, she slit her own wrists." The words were without emotion, but pain creased Pyord's face. I almost felt sorry for him. "We couldn't find a wet nurse who would work for a Kvys family, so we tried to raise the child by hand, goat's milk and the like. I'm sure I needn't tell a woman how difficult that is. He died a week later.

"We never heard from that count again."

"I—I'm sorry." The words felt strange, spoken to him, but I was sincere.

"Do not mistake my motives," he replied, sounding tired. "This is not some overcomplicated revenge plot. Had I wanted revenge on that count, I would have had it. But the way he used and discarded my sister, it began to reveal to me the depths of the corruption of this system of governance. If a nation's leaders are immoral, interested in serving themselves at the expense of others? That nation is corrupt. And it must change. This is my adopted nation, as it is yours, and whether you believe me or not, I am fighting for Galitha, not against it."

I watched him. He had never, for all his posturing and mystery, struck me as openly dishonest. He didn't now. He truly believed in what he was doing. Yet I recalled what I had thought while talking with Theodor—that we were all half-blind. Pyord didn't know the weight of responsibility Theodor felt for his role, that unlike Pyord he could not pursue his studies to their fullest extent. He didn't see that Viola tried to promote an educated and open-minded elite with her salon.

He paced toward the window. For a short moment a dark expression crossed his face, like the shadow of a cloud over the cobbles of Fountain Square on an otherwise sunny day. Then he turned back to me. "You are quite sure you would not lie to me?"

My fist found the rough stone beside me. "How many times must I say the same things to you?"

He pointed out the window. I followed the line his finger made. A stout figure in a blue cloak hovered by a corner of the building. "I think you've told someone."

"I haven't told anyone," I said, squinting. I knew that cloak—it was Alice. "I haven't breathed a word since I first took this forsaken commission."

"Then why did you have your employee follow you?"

"I didn't," I said, panic beginning to rise in my throat as I noticed two men standing near Alice. They watched the window, watched as Pyord raised a hand, still and rigid, in front of the glass. A signal. The men began to move. It made my words come faster, jumbled and shrill. "I swear I didn't tell her to—she's been worried about me; she knows something is wrong—she followed me on her own. I swear it."

The men were standing on either side of Alice now, and she'd noticed them. One gripped her arm and she struggled. "Tell them to leave her alone," I said, absurdly.

"You need a lesson in just how serious I am," Pyord said. One of the men yanked Alice's arm straight out from her cloak and ripped the white leather glove from it. He threw it into an icy puddle. Alice was screaming, but there was no one in the square to hear, and I couldn't make out her words. Thick panes of glass and stone walls separated her from anyone who could help.

The man restrained Alice while the other stepped very deliberately to her hand. He grasped her long, thin index finger—so perfect for the fine stitching she did. I choked on the understanding of what they meant to do to her.

"She's innocent!" I cried. "You'd rob her of her livelihood just to make a point? When you claim to champion the cause of the commoners?"

"You will keep your voice down, or everything that those men do to her will be done to your brother, as well," Pyord hissed. "She's made her own choices, and this is the consequence of meddling. Now watch."

"No," I whispered. "Don't do it," I begged to the one person who could hear, and he wouldn't bend for my tears.

With a single movement the man outside snapped Alice's finger, cleanly breaking it. I could see the anguish in Alice's face, but it didn't stop him from breaking two more of her fingers before he walked away and the other man released her. She collapsed on the cold stone, clutching her hand.

"You monster," I said, facing Pyord. "She had nothing to do with this." No pain in his past, no great plan for the future justified what I had just seen.

He swallowed, as though perhaps he did feel remorse at what he had just orchestrated, then quickly recovered. "I don't like hurting young women any more than you liked watching it. But she was meddling. This, I think, will convince you to keep her from meddling any further. And," he added, "it will convince you that I'm not making idle threats."

"She should go to the soldiers," I said. "I think we will."

"You did well not to scream here. For that, your brother's fingers stay intact. But if you go to the soldiers, his arms, his legs...perhaps even his neck will not be so lucky." He looked back out over the square, at Alice. I thought I saw a glimmer of conscience, but then his face hardened with stony resolve. "Our purpose moves us forward. Always forward."

"Let me go," I begged quietly, watching Alice writhe in pain on the street. Fortunately, a pair of women had come out of the butcher's shop across the square and spotted her.

"Don't go to her. Don't let her confirm that you were here. My men took all the money she carried—if she goes to the soldiers, it will look like a common street theft."

"Thieves break fingers?"

"Thieves break all sorts of things. Now you wait until she's gone before you leave. And make sure no one follows you again. I hope this proves that I am quite serious about that."

I sank into the corner, pressing the heels of my hands into my eyes to keep from sobbing.

31

—〰—

I FELT NUMB THE NEXT MORNING AS PENNY TOLD ME WHAT HAD happened to Alice, and of course I had to pretend I didn't know. Alice's sister had sent for Penny, who had stayed up half the night with her. The doctor had, Penny said, set her fingers, but the pain was too great for her to sleep at all.

I retreated behind my screen, shaking. Everyone around me was in danger from what I had agreed to. Anyone could stumble into the wrong information and end up hurt, like Alice. Or worse. I regretted involving Nia at all, and I hoped fervently that she would keep our discussion quiet. Theodor hadn't called on me or sent any word—the further from me he kept himself, the better, I reasoned.

I couldn't do anything to stop what had already happened. And I was forced to finish the cursed shawl. But I could also finish the charmed shifts. Not enough to counter all the darkness I'd allowed Pyord to spread over my world already, but some light was better than none.

I finished the shifts by noon and deposited them on the counter next to Penny. I scrawled a quick note. I knew I couldn't send them to the palace—not with Pyord's spies likely lurking right outside my door. So I sent them to Viola instead, with a note that she should give them to Annette. An additional insurance on my clients' anonymity, I claimed. "Send these by messenger to the Lady Snowmont. Immediately. Pay extra so he doesn't dawdle."

She nodded, and I bit back my guilt and worked my way through the narrow streets of the working-class homes to the brick row house that Alice shared with two of her sisters.

"She's upstairs," a woman nearly identical to Alice said. She pursed her lips in the same expression Alice had when she was worried.

I made sure each footfall on the stairs was as quiet as it could be, but it didn't matter. Alice was awake, sitting propped up in a bed by the window.

"I came as soon as—as soon as Penny told me," I said.

"I'm so sorry," Alice whispered. "I can't sew—for at least a month, the doctor said, until the casts are off." Her hand was thick with thick bandages and stiff with splints.

"You're sorry? Alice, this isn't your fault." I hesitated. "Can you—would you tell me what happened?"

"I know you told me not to," she said, "but I followed you again. You went to the archive and met the same man you talked to before."

"Yes, I did," I said, not committing to anything more than that. I had failed to keep Alice safe once, and letting her know the truth would not help her now.

"I waited for you to come out. I was going to confront you—to say that I understood you could feel ill from overwork, but I didn't know why you were meeting this man. That he seemed untrustworthy to me. But before you came out..."

"Yes?"

"I was attacked. A pair of thieves grabbed me and took all

the money I had in my pockets, and my rings. They broke my fingers when they went for the rings."

"By accident?" I asked, trying to sound ignorant. I felt sick.

"I don't think so," Alice said, misery tinting her voice dark. "I think they just wanted to hurt me."

"That's awful," I said. "Well, you don't worry about anything but feeling better. I'll come visit as often as I can—"

"I want to come back to the shop as soon as the pain subsides a bit," Alice interrupted.

"What? Alice, I won't let you hurt yourself further trying to work with injured fingers."

"I won't, I promise. But there are things I could do, aren't there? Ciphering and record keeping and directing the new person we'll hire."

I considered this. I could use the help, but more important, I sensed that Alice needed the work. "Yes, I suppose so. I shan't make you. And, Alice, I'm paying you for full days until you're well regardless. Don't argue." I stopped her. My shop's finances, and my hopes of setting aside money for a larger atelier, seemed suddenly pale and thin in comparison with the depth of the storm gathering around the city. Taking care of my own, making sure Alice and Penny and Emmi weren't harmed on my account, took priority. "It's already budgeted and I won't hear of you struggling for money on account of this horrible accident." *Accident*—that wasn't the right word at all.

"Thank you, Sophie. I can't afford not to accept even though I shouldn't. But I do want to work, too. I can't bear the thought of staying cooped up here for weeks or months."

"Very well. You can come back when you're ready. Not before." I forced a smile. It faded before I'd left Alice's room. I couldn't cross Pyord, not and keep the people around me safe.

I had only thought of Kristos. Now I saw that Pyord threatened the safety of everyone around me if they came too close to discovering my part in his plan. I thought of Nia, how she helped me, and shivered. I shouldn't have let her come so close. And I was even grateful that Theodor was leaving, to some jungle so steeped in summer that even Pyord's cold threats couldn't touch him.

I would finish Pyord's commission, I determined silently as I strode back to the shop. I would do it quickly, I would make sure my brother was freed, and I would walk away from this whole mess without allowing anyone else to be hurt. I turned onto the broad avenue by the river, catching the scent of the water carried in from the sea by a cold wind.

Except, I chided myself, the queen and her king. My king. Even if I didn't think the nobility was entirely right, even if I thought that the time for some changes had come, I couldn't reconcile regicide. There was no escaping what I was doing. Even if the law let me go free, guilt would shackle me. Very well, I thought, squaring my shoulders before walking up the steps to my shop. That guilt was a burden I would have to carry alone. All I could hope was that Pyord wouldn't hurt anyone else I cared about. My part in this was almost over, but who knew what violence and upheaval Pyord might spark in the city. When Pyord released Kristos, I resolved, maybe we could start again. Maybe it meant ushering my shop and my employees forward, or maybe it meant providing as best I could for those I cared about in the city and then abandoning my shop and my plans. Threads of a future I couldn't quite see twisted and tangled in my thoughts, but I knew one thing—I would distance myself as quickly as I could from the violence I had been forced to participate in.

32

—⁓—

With Alice not coming in early in the morning, and Penny tending to come in later and work late into the evening, I had plenty of time to finish the cursed shawl. Less than a week after Alice was attacked, it was finished. I wrapped it in a triple layer of paper and sent it by messenger to the palace. Guilt stabbed me as I thought of the queen—Mimi, the woman who seemed so kind and like any of the ladies I might meet here in my shop—opening the package of poisoned wishes.

I then sent a message to Pyord to tell him that the commission was done, sending it to the university and trusting it would find him. *It is finished*, I wrote. Nothing more. Nothing less. I had done the sewing he required and I had caused Alice's horrible injuries—I hoped desperately he would not, that he could not, extort anything more out of me. One cursed garment had woven a dark web that pulled into its snares too many people I cared about already.

I tried to pull our shop into as regular a rhythm as I could. Penny's stitching improved fivefold under the pressure of deadlines that should have had several seamstresses attending to them. Emmi picked up tasks quickly, and sometimes I found she had sorted a scrap bin or swept a floor before I had even thought to ask. I discovered that I stitched charms more quickly and deftly as well, having honed an unrealized part of my ability with the curse. Without the oppressive darkness of the curse hanging around me while I worked, weaving the brightness of charms into cloth seemed far easier than it had before. Still, on occasion, a darkness hovered at the edge of my mind as I worked, a black glimmer that threatened to infuse itself in my stitches without my bidding. I drove it away, but it concerned me—had I opened a door I couldn't close?

I spent the morning finishing Viola's pink gown. The cheerful blushing color defied the grim gray winter sky on the other side of the window, and I couldn't help resenting its optimism. The gown represented something I'd already lost, plans for a future for my shop that seemed, with each passing day, further from reality. I was relieved to wrap it in brown paper, and was tying the package's strings into a neat bow when Alice walked in the door.

I was surprised by the force in my own embrace as I nearly bowled her over.

"Don't break anything else!" she cried, stumbling into the wall.

"I'm so sorry," I said with a big, real smile, "but I'm so glad you're well enough to be up and about."

"It still hurts once in a while, but it's not so bad," Alice said. "And heavens! But I got bored." Her gaze darted around the shop, landing on one mess after another. "What should I start on? The advertisement for hiring another girl or the ciphering?"

I could have kissed her. "Either one. It's good to have you back, Alice. Don't overextend yourself," I added.

"No fear. I've been so bored I could work for four days straight. It looks like that's exactly what you all have been doing," she said with a laugh.

"You and Penny take it easy this afternoon—I'm going to run this to Viola." Alice smiled, and Penny clapped her hands, delighted to have her friend back.

I finished wrapping Viola's gown, and left Penny and Alice catching up on gossip as I slipped out to deliver it. Miss Vochant answered Viola's door, and Viola met me in the hall. "I saw you coming," she said, leading me to her boudoir. The salon was empty today. The quiet felt strange.

"Is everything all right?" I asked.

"Perhaps not." She pulled me onto a chair next to hers. My quilted silk petticoat wadded into the corners and bunched uncomfortably, but I didn't stop to smooth it out. Viola's voice had an urgency I hadn't heard before. "My father is investigating the murder of a messenger boy. About thirteen. Stabbed and thrown in the river. They found his body yesterday night, caught on an—it doesn't matter, never mind." Whatever gruesome detail Viola was envisioning, she was kind enough to want to shield me from it. "He'd been dead several days."

"That's awful," I replied, brows knitting. And it was—a young boy's murder was a horrible thing. But I didn't understand why Viola looked so disturbed.

"He was on his way here. From your shop. They found the delivery order in his pocket. What was he bringing here, Sophie? I thought at first it might have been my gown, but you have that here."

The shifts. My mouth went dry. Somehow, Pyord had discovered that I was sending the shifts to Viola and had killed to keep them out of the princesses' hands.

I took a shaky breath. "It was Annette's commission. Part of it. I sent it here to protect—for greater anonymity. I thought it would be—" I couldn't finish.

"The shifts? Then perhaps he was just killed for money, or

some personal grudge. I can't imagine," Viola said with raised eyebrows, "that anyone would kill for a few shifts."

"Perhaps," I said vaguely.

"You would be so kind as to write a short statement for my father? He'll want to know. But I see no reason for you to sit through questioning at the Stone Castle just to tell him you were sending the princesses' underclothes to my house." She produced a sheet of linen paper and a glass pen and ink, and I wrote a short note.

"Ongoing investigation and all that, so keep that between us," Viola said. "Not that I peg you for a gossip."

I nodded weakly. Not a gossip. Just someone who got other people hurt and killed.

"All right, something more cheerful. I want to try on this gown," Viola said, unlacing the front of her jacket. She hadn't even bothered to step behind the screen. Her agitated fingers tore at the silk cord, and it snagged on each lacing hole. "I am glad you made me those charmed shifts, by the way. There's a new pamphlet out. They're even clearer about their goals now, if there was still any question—open revolt, the need to erase the nobility."

A new pamphlet—did Kristos write it? Viola watched my strange expression, and I had to say something. "They might as well call it civil war."

"Perhaps they should." She gestured to the side table, where a crinkled pamphlet lay open.

I picked it up. "I hope your shifts are enough," I said, turning to the cover. "I added a charm to the gown, too—it's not much. But it's a protection charm." There were my brother's initials—K. B., written in large type right under the title. I bit my lip, eyes widening.

"Thank you for that. I know charm casting is an imperfect art, Sophie. I know it's not insurance against a deliberate assassination attempt." She threw her jacket on the nearest chair. The boning stood starkly upright, and the rest of the silk crumpled into a sad heap.

"You're worried about that?" I opened the pamphlet and skimmed the first page, and saw why—the language was starker, brasher, more openly violent than I had ever known Kristos to write. But it was his voice in the words. Was Pyord forcing him to write this? To call for *an uprising of righteous indignation to spark a fire of revolution* and for *the scythe and the rifle to work together to undo oppression*? I shuddered.

"Of course I'm worried. If this truly comes to violence, my father is going to be targeted early, mark me. The Lord of Keys? How many of them has he imprisoned?"

My stomach knotted—of course. And Pyord's cold eyes flashed in my memory—he wouldn't hesitate to target the family of high-ranking nobles. "If there's anything I can do—"

"I don't even know why I'm telling you this," she said, taking the gown from me, "save that I only feel it fair to warn you."

"Warn me?"

"You're becoming tied to us now. A part of my little circle," she said with a secret smile. "If the revolutionaries are truly determined, they may not stop with the nobles most in the way of their plans. The bloodshed might extend to those they feel are sympathetic to the nobility."

I shivered as Viola pinned her new gown into place. I could scarcely consider it. Kristos could never be complicit in widespread violence. He cared about the people he was goading into revolution—truly wanted the best for the common people of the country.

Kristos had never wanted open war, or violence against the common people. But his idealism had blinded him to the stark truth that, in order to effect his proposed change, war was inevitable. Pyord Venko realized it, knew before we did, and orchestrated a disheveled League into a means for revolt. Cold seeped from that understanding until it covered all of me, chilling me to the bone. I couldn't keep Pyord from harming anyone, could I? He had injured Alice and killed an innocent messenger. I had thought that, once the curse was finished, once the dark magic was out of my shop, I could be free of Pyord's schemes. No—the whole country couldn't be free of them, let alone me.

And Viola thought to warn me. I wanted to smack her for her kindness—*Don't warn me, don't worry about me. I'm partially responsible. This is my fault*, I wanted to scream.

"It fits perfectly," she said, turning in front of her mirror. "And it's beautiful." It was—clean lines and perfect rows of stitching. The front was strikingly geometric—a triangular inset of cream silk interrupted the pink, which joined into the fullness of the skirt's back. I had added a pair of loops and strings under the skirt so that it could be tied up into a full drape, a feminine contrast to the masculine tailoring of the front. There was nothing like it in the whole city.

"It hardly seems to matter now," I whispered.

"It never did," Viola said with a shrug. She smoothed a lock of her hair back into place in the elaborate pouf she had dressed it into. "And now we'll go on as though our lives are not about to be overturned. You will be at the music evening later this week, yes?"

"Yes, I was planning to." I had agreed to meet Nia then, with my translations, or I would have refused. I didn't want to see Theodor. I thought of the confusion on his face when I had run out of the greenhouse, and winced. At the same time, he hadn't contacted me, and that gouged at me. I could be easily set aside after all.

"Good. Revolution hasn't come yet, and I can still make the best punch in Galitha."

33

—◊—

OUR ROUTINE WAS A BUSY ONE OVER THE FOLLOWING DAYS. Our usual orders were backed up, and Annette's gown was coming slowly. Madame Pliny's court gown was nearly finished, but I put it off the priority list in order to accommodate Annette's. Madame Pliny didn't need the gown until spring, and Penny and Alice were both far more excited about the princess than a middle-aged countess, anyway. I let them dive into Annette's sky blue silk with abandon, Penny doing the actual stitching and Alice helping her by heating irons and pinning and pleating trim.

Emmi hovered in the background, quietly absorbing everything we did. She had proven adept at hemming, which made me hopeful that she would be a quick study on other elements of our trade, as well. With the flurry of activity, however, I hadn't had as much time to work with her as I would like.

"Is it going well enough?" I asked as Penny joined two lengths of silk for the skirts of Annette's gown.

"Oh yes!" Emmi beamed. "I'm learning so much, and I'm trying hard not to be any trouble."

"Trouble?"

"Getting in the way, you know, hovering too much. Staying out of the front when there are customers there."

I started. "Who said you aren't allowed in the front?"

"Alice...Alice said it would be best if I..." Emmi's smile faded. "That I didn't have the right appearance to be seen by customers."

"I see," I said, as neutrally as I could. I knew without asking what Alice had meant. In the rules of Galatine shops, image was everything, and Emmi projected the perfect portrait of a not-quite-acclimated Pellian girl. She wore a kerchief over her cap, and her clothes, though not traditional Pellian in cut, were made of the mismatched printed cottons many Pellians favored and were practical, not fashionable, in their draping.

In my preoccupation, I hadn't noticed or considered this. Pellian or not, Emmi was not a walking advertisement for well-made clothing like Alice and Penny were. "I'll tell you what," I said, thinking. "It will be time for you to learn how to cut and drape clothing soon enough. We'll start by making you a simple pleated caraco jacket. You can wear that here."

Emmi's eyes widened. "Oh, thank you! I—I was going to stop wearing my kerchief anyway." She blushed.

I considered this, hesitating. It wasn't fair of me to tell her it didn't matter—the printed cotton tied under her chin marked her quickly as Pellian, and being marked as Pellian in a fashionable shop meant something in the Galatine language of commerce. Fair or not, customers would ascertain a kind of cultural incompetency from even a Pellian kerchief, from overly bright cotton prints, from hair dressed in braids instead of dressed high on rollers and pinned into curls. I was accepted not because I looked less Pellian than Emmi in my physical appearance, but because I behaved as a Galatine, even in how I wore my hair.

"I won't tell you not to wear it, Emmi—that isn't my place. But I can tell you that most shops will insist on a certain appearance."

She nodded, thoughtful. The lines between the Pellian quarter and the Galatine merchant district seemed, in that moment, very starkly drawn. How long would those lines matter, I wondered, in the face of revolt?

I received a note from the palace confirming the arrival of the shifts, and a sour feeling settled into the pit of my stomach. Pyord had replaced them with plain, uncharmed shifts and sent them instead. How had he known? He said he could find someone to verify my work, someone who could see charms and curses, and I knew it was true—any of the charm casters in the Pellian quarter of the city could do it. Had it been someone I knew? They wouldn't have known—for a few coins, who wouldn't glance at a length of cloth to see if it sparkled magic between the fibers? Especially now, with the taxes on the markets levied higher than they could afford and winter bearing down on the city.

"Have you heard anything from Kristos?" Penny asked as we worked box-pleated trim onto a gown's neckline together.

"No," I replied, momentarily taken aback. I was lucky Penny hadn't asked more often. At least I had an honest answer ready. "No, he hasn't even had the decency to write," I added. Which was upsetting—I had sent the message for Pyord nearly a week earlier. I had expected Kristos home by now. Nothing.

"Is he—was he—I mean, with other girls, it's not like he's dead—like this?" Penny flushed deep magenta.

I hesitated. "Yes, to some extent. He's never run off on a ship before. But that's not about how he is with girls," I explained. "It's how he is about himself." I sighed, pinching the fabric between my fingers as though it were Kristos and he could feel my frustration. "He's impetuous—he gets an idea in his head and he can't let it go. It makes him passionate, but he's entirely illogical."

I realized I wasn't talking about sailing off on a ship any longer, and I stopped.

"It's why I liked him," Penny said with a disappointed little puff of breath. I hesitated—talking about my brother with my employee felt mildly unprofessional. Penny's big eyes won me over—she needed someone to talk to. Someone older, someone who would reassure her.

"It's not that he's bad," I apologized quickly. "He just—he jumps in with both feet, and he doesn't look before he leaps." I winced at the pair of metaphors. "He thinks with his heart instead of his head." So why hadn't he come home yet? Why hadn't he written? I didn't think anything could keep him from assuring me he was safe. Maybe he wasn't safe. Or, maybe—I took a deep breath—Pyord simply hadn't picked up the message yet, or was waiting to confirm something with me.

A perfectly round water stain appeared on the silk trim between Penny's fingers. "I'm sorry. I—I'll fix it," she said, hurriedly dabbing the tiny drop.

"It's all right," I said. "Take a few minutes; step outside."

Penny didn't return, but the day was drawing to a close, winter's pale afternoon light filtering through the windows. Perhaps, I reasoned, she had misunderstood me and gone home for the day. I finished the trim by myself and resolved to speak to her about it the next day.

When I arrived at the shop the next day, however, there was a weighty iron chain and padlock looped through the door handle and a thick sheet of paper nailed just above it with the seal of the Lord of Coin.

I smoothed the flapping paper with trembling hands. Behind me on the street, the tread of shoes on the cobblestone streets slowed and stopped. I seethed with humiliation, my cheeks reddening in the cold wind, as my neighbors and passersby watched me, unable to enter my shop.

"Closed by order of the Lord of Coin," it read in thick type at the top, wide margins making the words visible from the street. "Investigation under way. Proprietor accused of harboring enemies of the Crown."

My angry breath framed the words in a cloud. Accused—by whom? Did one of my neighbors turn me in, knowing who Kristos was? Or had someone discovered something much more incriminating—who Pyord Venko was and what I had done under his direction? I wanted to tear the paper down, but, as it reminded me in thin letters at the bottom of the page, doing so would violate several statutes.

I thought first of going to the offices of the Lord of Coin, even though that meant standing in line only to speak to one clerk after another, none of whom would be able to help me. The thought of what they might ask—what I might have to reveal—if I was given leave to speak to someone in authority, however, stopped me. What defense did I have? If they accused me of meeting secretly with Pyord Venko, witnesses could confirm it easily. If they accused me of having a revolutionary brother, I couldn't deny being Kristos's sister.

No, I resigned myself, I would have to wait for them. The thought touched my mind, briefly, of asking one of the nobles for help, but it faded as soon as it appeared. I was friendly with Viola, but I could never confide in her the depths of fear I faced here. Nia, though as clever as anyone I had ever met, was an outsider when it came to the tangle of Galatine bureaucracy that I was up against. I wanted, with some quiet desperation, to go to Theodor, but I knew that was unwise. He was marrying a princess of the Equatorial States; I wasn't going to beg his help or cry on his elite shoulder.

Instead, I returned home and sat quietly, sewing on the only thing I had in my house instead of the shop, a simple white organdy cap for myself. I felt Kristos's absence even more keenly than usual, fear building that Pyord might be holding him to keep his leverage over me. When a knock came at the door, I shot up, heartbeat flying, ready to face the guards or the clerks or whoever the Lord of Coin might throw at me, but hoping fervently that I would lift the latch and see Kristos.

It was only Emmi and Venia.

"Emmi told us about your shop," Venia said, shoving her way inside past my stunned frame.

Emmi pressed in after Venia. "Is there anything we can do? When can you reopen? Why in the world are they—"

"Emmi, not all at once," Venia cautioned. She took me by the arm, and sat me down at my kitchen table. Then she stoked the fire in my stove and put the kettle on.

"You—you all know?"

"Gossip travels faster than plague and is harder to contain," Venia answered in a Pellian proverb that I was fairly sure rhymed in its untranslated iteration. "Even before Emmi went to work and saw the sign."

I slumped in my seat. The whole city knew if the Pellian quarter knew, surely—my business could be ruined by a rumor like this, not to mention the hit I was going to take not fulfilling orders on time.

"It's not the disaster you think it is," Venia added. "You will be open again soon, and no one will care what happened."

"I wouldn't care," Emmi said. "The Red Caps are probably more popular with the people than the Lord of Coin, anyway. So maybe your business will get a boost!"

I smiled at Emmi's optimism, but it was misplaced. My clients were upper-class merchants, nobles, and people who were, by and large, in the favor of the Lord of Coin and likely wanted to keep it that way. For all I knew, I was as good as blacklisted. Though the Lord of Coin had certainly never been anyone's favorite in the working-class sections of the city, Pellian quarter included, I was taken aback by Emmi's assessment. "The Red Caps are that popular, are they?"

"Maybe not everywhere," Venia said. "I don't know about the merchant districts, or the Galatines that you know, Sophie." The Galatines I knew—the wealthy ones. "On my street, they are more welcome than the City Guard." She gauged my reaction with a laugh. "You're surprised."

"Only that the Pellian quarter has always kept to itself, for the most part. It's never seemed interested in the politics of the rest of the city."

Emmi wrinkled her brow, and Venia looked down at her careworn hands, folded unobtrusively on the table. "You've never lived in the quarter. The rest of the city has never had an interest in us. The politics of the rest of the city—of Galitha— have not concerned themselves with us."

"And the Red Caps have?"

"For my part, I don't trust it," Venia said. "That they have any particular interest in us. But a movement like theirs needs numbers, and there are voices and bodies aplenty in the quarter. And they're as dissatisfied as anyone."

I watched Venia's sun-browned fingers trace, lightly, the edge of the table. They brushed against the wood; her words brushed against her real meaning. "They're easy marks. Dissatisfied, at the bottom of the city's pecking order, and ignored until now."

Emmi shrugged. "Maybe the Red Caps are in earnest when they say the changes will benefit all the working folk, that all workers are united by their labor before they're split by other divisions."

"Did you get that from a pamphlet?" I asked, more sharply than I meant. It sounded like something Kristos could have written, something read from a makeshift platform in the square. Emmi nodded.

"It doesn't matter if they're in earnest or not, for the rest of us," Venia said as she poured the steaming water from the kettle into my chipped teapot. "The cause of the fire won't undo the ashes."

"Ashes that might include my livelihood now," I said, attempting a joke and failing.

"The same thing happened last week to the tea merchant and the tinsmith down the street from me," Venia said. "Three days later, both were open again. They got a summons to the offices of the Lord of Coin, and came back to open stores. You'll see."

If she meant to be reassuring, she only planted another worry. "Two businesses on your street alone, Venia? How many altogether?"

Venia shrugged. "I know of maybe ten."

"In the whole city?"

"In the Pellian quarter. I don't know much about anything outside of that," she apologized.

"There are as many everywhere, or at least close. I noticed on the walk to work," Emmi said. "More in the Pellian quarter and on Brinkwater and Broad Streets than Fountain Square," she added.

Brinkwater and Broad Streets—both lower-class shopping districts. It was, of course, entirely possible that any legitimate search would find its quarry in the discontented lower-class and immigrant districts. It was also impossible to deny that concentrating business closures there meant striking at people with little means to fight back, and prevented disrupting the city's elite in their shopping, even sparing nobles the indignity of sending their servants to a new greengrocer or butcher. How had I missed this? I was too busy crying over a duke and sewing ball gowns for princesses, I chided myself. I had been so engrossed in a world far above mine that I had missed what was happening in my own streets and alleyways. The nobility was certainly lost on how to quell the revolt, and in their attempts to uproot it were only driving it deeper.

"I'm sure this will boil down to nothing," Venia said. She poured me a cup of tea, brewed strong in the Pellian fashion.

I couldn't be so sure, and there was nothing to say aside from speculation. I had seen the influence of the Red Caps as the primary threat to my shop, their intended revolution destroying my clientele and affecting the international trade I thrived on. I hadn't anticipated the misdirected reaction of the governing bodies affecting me, personally, or hurting the rest of the city as they had. I couldn't change any of it, not now, and felt a pang of the sort of helplessness that motivated the Red Caps. I didn't even want to talk about it any longer. Instead, I took a sip of tea and a deep breath. "You're right, Venia," I said, not believing myself. "Forget my shop. Tell me how your sister's wedding was."

34

—m—

WITH MY SHOP STILL CLOSED, I DIDN'T HAVE THE DISTRACTION OF work from Kristos's continued absence. I had heard nothing from him, nothing from Pyord, nothing from anyone indicating my brother's safety or that my part in the plan had been fulfilled. Deep fear gnawed at me, that perhaps Pyord had never intended to release Kristos at all. That he could already be dead, with no more ceremony than the messenger boy found in the river. After all, I had no assurances since the letter I had requested weeks ago.

There was danger in confronting Pyord, from any continued association with him if his role in the Red Caps was discovered, from his calculated determination itself if he decided I was too much trouble. There had been no remorse in the eyes that coolly watched Alice's fingers snapped; I doubted there would be hesitation in dispatching me if I proved a hindrance to his plans. Still, I had to know where my brother was.

As I crossed the city, a light snowfall peppered the streets and statues with light powder. People pulled up hoods and pulled hats lower against the snowfall, but I let the faint flakes settle in my hair and melt down my neck. By the time I reached the university, the streets were nearly white and the wind had picked up whorls of snow and kicked them into small drifts along the curbs.

I found my way to Pyord's building easily enough, even as the white fronts of the structures blended with the blowing snow. I didn't know which office was his, but, undeterred, I pushed open the heavy door, inlaid with ironwork and scraping painfully on the stone floor. Fortunately, a handwritten list hung from a nail near the window with names and offices. Venko and Ipling shared an office on the third floor. I nodded to no one in particular and began to climb the stairs, putting off concerns of how to carry on a conversation in front of Venko's likely oblivious officemate.

When I found the office, its door open and the gabled roof sloping into the corner, I was right in my assumption that Pyord was not alone. The man sitting opposite him, however, was not a stranger, but Niko. I hadn't seen him in weeks, but I also hadn't frequented the League haunts since Kristos's disappearance. I realized in a flash that, to Niko, I had no good reason to be here, and hoped Pyord could concoct a lie more quickly than I could if he had not disclosed our arrangement to the League's leaders.

"Miss Balstrade," Pyord said, rising as a gentleman would to welcome a lady, ducking a bit to avoid hitting his head on the steep slope of the roof. "Please sit."

Niko watched, eyes narrowing slightly. He didn't make any move to stand, but I didn't expect that. Of all my brother's friends, I had never cared overmuch for Niko. His dark eyes always took in everyone and everything, and he seemed to distill what he observed into scalding jokes and biting retorts. Kristos had found Niko clever, but he didn't seem to care if he made a girl cry or provoked a fight between his friends.

"I have been providing Miss Balstrade some assistance in locating her brother," Pyord said smoothly to Niko.

"I thought he sailed for Serafe or some such thing," Niko answered, almost mocking in his tone. Did he believe this lie? Or did he think, perhaps, that I did?

"With my wide and diverse contacts, I have attempted to assist Miss Balstrade in returning him home. I've orchestrated some connections, we could say." He gave me a joyless smile.

"Despite that, Mr. Venko, I have not yet heard from him." My tersely controlled voice hardly sounded like mine. "I had hoped you might have some news for me."

"I'm afraid not," he said, folding his hands. Niko watched the exchange with some amusement. I felt like the butt of a joke and wasn't quite sure why. No one else knew where my brother was. "You do know Niko Otni, don't you?"

"Of course," I replied. I looked at him, leveling my eyes with his. "He's a close friend of my brother." Niko met my eyes only briefly before turning away.

"Something else of concern," I said quickly. "My shop has been closed."

Niko leaned back in his chair. "I'm sure that concerns you, but I can't say a milliner fresh out of doodads concerns us."

I didn't acknowledge him, and merely continued. "By the Lord of Coin. Suspicion of ties to the Red Caps."

Pyord's attention snapped to me, though he then attempted to control his reaction. "Perhaps they finally figured out who K. B. is," he replied, the barest hint of concern drawing his face a bit tauter than usual.

"Perhaps," I said. "I couldn't imagine what else it could be. I don't converse frequently with Red Cap leadership," I added with an innocent smile. "I don't participate in distributing broadsides—why, I don't even attend meetings."

Niko saw Pyord's hardened look and bit back the retort he seemed ready to fling at me. "We would not want to encourage the fiction that you have sympathies with us, would we?"

"It would be unlikely, certainly; their mistake could lead them to you anyway, I suppose," I said as though this suggestion had just come to me. "And when my reasons for visiting are so remotely related to the Red Caps—just trying to find my brother. Just hoping you have some shred of news to reassure a distraught sister."

"Let's hope he turns up soon. I'll send more inquiries," Pyord said, and I couldn't help but feel the barest warm triumph glowing behind the smile I pasted on in pantomime gratitude.

Niko screwed his mouth into a knot, annoyance at my intrusion becoming clearer. "I hate to dispense with the pleasantries, but we do have some ... details to arrange, and I'm expected back at—" He glanced at me and stopped talking. "I can't stay long."

I moved toward the door, knowing I had done everything I could. Despite any threat our continued contact might have carried with it, he was still in control of this exchange, and I could do nothing more to effect my brother's release. "I am sure one of us will hear from Kristos soon," I said.

Pyord smiled. "Of course, dear." He reached to take my hand, but I pulled away and retreated to the streets, which were filling swiftly with snow.

35

———✠———

I RECEIVED A SUMMONS THE NEXT DAY, BUT NOT TO THE LORD of Coin. Instead, a formal invitation to Viola's music evening arrived, letters adorned with curls and swoops on thick paper as white as snow. The custom of sending a final invitation the same day or the day before formal parties was the height of sophistication for Galatines, a suggestion that the guests might be so busy that they would forget engagements in their social calendars and require a reminder. In fact, I had almost forgotten my promise to attend, and wanted to avoid the press and gaggle of nobles, and especially seeing Theodor. If Nia hadn't promised me the translation at the party, I would have declined, sending a scrabbled note on cheap paper in reply to the beautiful invitation.

I left early in the evening for the party, hoping to see Nia right away and leave before I had to discuss my shop closure or see Theodor. I saw someone out of the corner of my eye—a threadbare gray frock coat and a red cap loitering behind a low wall. As I moved, he followed. I sighed—my bargain with Pyord was over. Why follow me now? I swallowed and walked on. Nothing to be done, even if he followed me all the way to Viola's. I had to get the translation from Nia tonight.

I paused for a moment beside the huge central fountain in Fountain Square. The water was turned off now, and the carved lions and stags at the base were up to their knees in snow. The eagles and doves at the top were dusted with frosty white, as well.

The red cap peeled off before I turned onto Viola's street. Surely he knew where I was going. It was almost becoming rote for the maid to open the door and take my cloak, and then escort me to the salon. Almost. Because I couldn't quite get used to being treated as a lady, not as a seamstress who worked for her living. An eye for fabric, ability to predict the newest fashion before it was commonplace, and hours sculpting elaborate trim allowed me to pass among them even if my gown was plain taffeta to their brocades and painted silks, but the calluses on my fingertips reminded me what I was—not a noble, but a hardworking woman who wielded her hands for her trade.

Viola's salon was beautiful in the candlelight, and on another night I would have been delighted by the enchanted forest she had created inside with greenery and branches. The tables and the mantel were festooned with evergreen sprays and waxy holly leaves, interspersed with bittersweet and the ruby-red stalks of dogwood trees. The broken pane of glass was fixed, and Viola looked as sanguine as if nothing had happened at all. She wore the pink gown, looked like a goddess in it, and everyone fawned over it. I should have been supremely happy, but it all felt hollow.

I saw Theodor across the room and flushed pink, avoiding his eyes. I spoke to Pauline and several of her friends, accepting their compliments on Viola's gown and their promises that they would be making arrangements for commissions with me soon. If they had heard about the Lord of Coin shutting my shop, they were polite enough not to mention it, and I was heartened somewhat that either the gossip hadn't reached them or they didn't care. Maybe Venia and Emmi were right—all would be well, soon enough.

"Very pretty gown—not that I expected anything less," Viola said, pulling me aside as Pauline changed the subject to the winter theater season. "I heard about the disturbance at your shop," she confided.

I flushed.

"Don't fret," she said in a conspiratorial tone. "The trouble has been cleared up. Your shop will be open tomorrow."

"But—" I clamped down on the argument. I should be grateful that the shop would reopen, shouldn't argue the good graces of a noblewoman who wanted to help me. There was something supremely unjust in it—how many businesses would remain closed because a noble wasn't advocating for them? More, there was an unresolved question at the heart of the matter. "Why was it closed to begin with?"

"I thought you knew—that you would have guessed," Viola said. "But perhaps you really didn't know anything—all the better, I can tell the Lord of Coin our trust was not misguided. Your assistant, Penny."

My shock was, at least, unfeigned. Of all the rebels I was associated with, Penny was the one whom they had closed my shop over?

And what would happen to her?

"I'm afraid I don't—I don't understand," I said, composing myself. "Was she arrested?"

"Yes, a couple of days ago. She's been distributing inflammatory pamphlets. They thought—well, it was assumed she might be tied to the author of those pamphlets, and it appears she may have been tied to one writer for the movement, but she insisted, thus far, that she hasn't done anything but attend meetings and deliver packages of pamphlets."

"I didn't think," I said, choosing my words carefully, "that distributing printed materials was illegal."

"It isn't," replied Viola. "If she's telling the truth, I'm sure she'll be released." She waved her lithe hand. "She was only arrested, and your shop closed, on suspicion of ties to the leadership of the Red Caps. That's where their attention is focused now—forget putting down street riots, though that still keeps the soldiers busy."

They had arrested Penny, closed my shop, arrested countless others, closed their shops, all on suspicion? Anger turned my hands into fists, which I dug into the sides of my skirts. "Excuse me," I finally forced myself to say, and retreated to a holly-bedecked window. I had to wait for Nia, or I would have run to the Stone Castle immediately—hopefully Penny had been released already, but if she hadn't, my heart broke for her, alone in a cold cell.

I felt almost complicit for understanding the tactic the nobility was taking. Eliminating the threat, as they understood it, meant eliminating a leader who would dare call for revolt. And that meant rooting him out, probably from the homes or shops of the citizens who supported him. It went too far, I thought, choking a little on even my own sympathy for the nobles. Too far to throw Penny in a cell in the Stone Castle, too far to close poor, overtaxed people's shops. Still, I knew Pyord Venko and what the movement he had guided was capable of—regicide, revolt, murder.

"Delighted you came," Theodor whispered in my ear. I jumped, rattling the holly against the windowpane. It was unavoidable now—I turned to face him. He was dressed in a suit of deep blue, embroidered with blossoming trumpet vine on the waistcoat. Each button depicted a pretty orange bloom.

"New suit?" I asked, aiming for neutral discussion, hoping to slip away from it quickly.

"Trust the seamstress to notice the clothes." He laughed. "Or are you miffed I didn't give you my business?"

I held up my hands. "I'm a seamstress, not a tailor. I don't know how to fit men's clothes, and I don't want to learn, thank you." I tried to read his face, but he was as charming and polite as the first time I'd met him. Was that the game we were playing at, then? Pretend that nothing had transpired between us? The thought strained my breath.

"Still, what do you think? Up to your professional standards?"

"Well, there's no good luck charm stitched into it."

He shook his head in mock dismay. "I knew there was something missing."

"Viola's done a lovely job decorating," I said, steering the conversation away from charms and their cousins, curses. I'd had enough of those.

"Yes, she deigned to use some greenery I brought from the public gardens. They were trimming back the trees along the river walk, and I snagged a few." He grazed his fingers along the bright red dogwood stem nearest him. The tenderness of his touch, his minute attention to the plant, sparked a deep ache as I watched him.

I broke my gaze from him and looked around the room for Nia, but she wasn't there. The guests were still milling about, tasting cheeses and sugared fruits laid out on platters. She wasn't late, I told myself calmly. I just hoped we would be able to steal a moment in private to discuss her translation.

Pauline spotted me across the room instead, and trotted over. Her teal gown was trimmed with gathered sheer organza, and she looked like ocean waves when she moved. "Marguerite is debuting a new piece tonight," she said by way of greeting before she dove in for the double-cheek kiss.

"Another?" Theodor asked. "She is quite talented. Any hints about it?"

"Just that she's saying it's inspired by winter." Pauline rubbed her hands together as though she were cold. "Though what's inspiring about winter I couldn't say. All it inspires me to do is bundle up and huddle by the fire."

"Sophie says winter is an excellent business model," Theodor said. I laughed politely, but the recollection of the conversation was bitter.

"Did you bring your violin?"

"I did, but I doubt anyone wants me to interrupt Marguerite's music with the caterwauling I call playing."

"I'd very much like it," the tiny dark-haired woman I recognized as Marguerite the harpist answered. "We had a grand time playing folk songs last time, didn't we?"

"*We* had fun. Let's not be too quick to assume those listening were pleased with me," Theodor said, but I could tell he was flattered. The role of learned, cultured gentleman fit him well, and he basked in it. I slipped back, conscious that this was his milieu, not mine. Perhaps, I thought, scanning the room, this could be my opening to slip away to some quiet corner to wait for Nia.

"You just rosin up your bow when I tell you to," Marguerite said, laughter in her pale green eyes. "But for now I think I had better get started." She dipped a little curtsy and took her position on the dais Viola had set up, seated next to her harp. I moved toward the back of the room, but Theodor caught my arm.

"I'd like it very much if you would sit with me," he said.

"I'm not sure that's such a wise idea," I replied. Marguerite tuned the harp; I disentangled my hand from Theodor's.

"I'm not sure what I said before, but I realize I must have hurt you. I am sorry, and I want very much for you to sit with me."

"You didn't say anything, and me being hurt is not your fault," I whispered back. Viola glanced at us with a raised eyebrow. "Now, we should sit down before we provide the first act to this performance."

"Quite right. Please." He gestured to the settee beside us— the only seats left in the room. I nodded crisply and sat. Theodor looped an arm behind my shoulders. I leaned away.

Marguerite's white silk gown and pale blue overdress didn't do much to encourage an impression of stature, but the moment she put her fingers to the strings she was the only person in the room. Even Theodor beside me melted away, and I was transfixed by the sounds undulating from the harp.

The notes were slow at first, long, delicate chords that lingered and faded before another set was introduced. Then the notes began to cascade and chase one another, like wind in the trees or snow swirling between branches. The piece crescendoed like a blizzard and dipped back into graceful quiet like a frosty night. It made me think of the frozen waterfalls Theodor had shown me, of the cold peace under those willow trees.

A final note hovered in the air as though suspended, and then Marguerite cut it off. She was a small woman next to a harp again, and the room erupted in honest applause.

I realized that I was not only leaning forward but also clutching Theodor's hand. I released it, blushing.

"I take it you liked it?" he said, pretending to rub life back into his fingers.

"Yes. I—it was as though I saw precisely what Marguerite wanted me to, felt what she wanted me to feel."

"She's a genius," Theodor agreed with an amiable smile.

"Well, are you going to join me?" Marguerite called from the dais, gesturing to Theodor and two others, a lady and a gentleman seated together across the room from us.

"I was promised punch first," Theodor retorted, and everyone laughed.

"Then you're in luck," said Viola, and opened the door to the hallway to let in a pair of maids carrying the largest punch bowl I'd ever seen. Punches were common enough in the cafés and taverns, served in simple earthenware bowls. But this—Viola's giant tureen was a sculpture adorned with stags and lions and a huge eagle—

"Oh!" I gasped in surprise as the maids backed away from the bowl and Viola adjusted a hidden dial on the side. It was an exact replica of the centerpiece fountain in the city square, and as she fiddled with the controls, it began to run like the fountain. Steaming red punch flowed from the open mouths of intricately scaled fish, and rivulets of punch washed down the flanks of the stags.

"The fountain in the square is frozen," Viola announced with a theatrical curtsy, "but mine is running nicely!"

I glanced around the room again. Nia was still missing. A dark fear crept out of the pit of my stomach. What if Pyord knew she was coming here? She hadn't told him about our meeting, had she? Had he found her translation? My teeth worried my lips.

No one else had noticed her absence, or at the very least no one had commented. "Theodor," I began, "Nia—wasn't she supposed to join us tonight?"

Theodor shrugged. "Must have gotten distracted by some old scroll in the archive," he said.

But the archive closed at sunset. It was black as coal outside, soft and pressing against the windows. I shook off the concern. She wasn't bound by oath to come to the music party, or to bring me my translation. I'd inquire about her address and call on her, or just visit the salon later in the week.

The maids filled cup after cup, and we passed them from person to person around the room. It smelled faintly of citrus and cinnamon, though I wasn't surprised when I tasted it that the base was strong red wine.

"The Snowmont family recipe," Theodor said between sips. "I have a feeling the secret is using good wine."

"Wrong," Viola said, popping up behind us. "I use cheap wine in the punch."

"Do you really?" I laughed.

"Certainly—for one, what a waste of good wine, throwing sugar and grapefruit and oranges and rum in it! But for another, the flavor isn't as mellow in cheap wine. It works better to balance everything else in the punch." She toasted us with her cup. "My father taught me that."

The thought of a lord fine-tuning his punch recipe with cheap swill made me laugh. But maybe there was something deeper to Viola's family punch recipe—something about ordinary wine forming the base of something extraordinary made me think of Kristos's impassioned speeches that the working class was the base of our nation.

Kristos—he could still be in danger. My visit had affected nothing, as I had heard nothing more from Pyord. Now Penny had been arrested, and who knew what the future held for my shop, even if the closure had been lifted. I set my glass down, not sharing the blindness that allowed the rest of those gathered to laugh over punch in the face of the dark reality pressing against the seams of everything they knew.

Theodor's gaze followed me as I crossed the room and pushed aside the heavy curtain of the window. Snow fell softly on the street outside. True to form, Theodor appeared beside me in a moment.

"There's something wrong." It was a statement, not a question. "More, I take it, than whatever I said in the greenhouse."

"I promise, it was nothing you said. I'm—" My voice caught. "I'm worried about my brother." It was true—but it was so much less than the truth.

"I know," Theodor said. "I was thinking how my sister cried when my father told us all about the plans for me to go to the States in a few weeks, and how really wretched it was of him not to tell you he was sailing off."

I forced a small nod of agreement, even though Theodor was empathizing with a lie.

"I don't have to play if you'd rather talk, or I could take you home." His hand rested lightly on mine.

I managed a smile. "No, I want to hear you play. And going home would just remind me that Kristos isn't there."

"Very well, I'll rosin the bow and pass out cotton wadding if anyone would like to plug their ears," he said.

Before he could begin, Miss Vochant hurried into the room and caught Viola's arm. "My lady," the maid whispered loudly. Viola rose, but before she could follow, a trio of uniformed city soldiers marched into the room. The oldest of them took Viola by the hand and pulled her into the hall.

Theodor's brow constricted. "That's the Lord of Keys," he said. "And I've never seen him look quite like that."

I gripped the windowsill behind me. They'd discovered me. That had to be it—someone had caught Pyord and he had ratted me out, someone had followed me and put together the pieces, Penny had told them something about me when she was questioned, Kristos had been discovered and everyone knew I was his sister... The possibilities churned like the river during a spring flood.

But Viola's scream of shock told me it had to be worse than that.

Theodor pulled me closer to him, instinctive and protective. I stood, rigid as a board, and with growing trepidation.

The Lord of Keys entered the room, Viola standing behind him in the hallway, trembling like a leaf.

"Lady Nia has been found dead in the river."

Pyord. It had to be—and it was my fault. My fingers hurt from their unrelenting pincer hold on the windowsill. I couldn't move. I had asked Nia for help and she had been killed. I knew he had me followed, and I'd been careless. I'd allowed Nia to be vulnerable.

I was so horrified I couldn't even cry, as most of the other ladies in the room were doing.

"She was dressed for an evening out," the Lord of Keys continued, "which indicates that she was coming here as she had intended." I saw Nia, dressed in one of her brightly colored orange or yellow gowns, the fabric twisting and rippling in the water like flames. Drowned flames. "If anyone knows her whereabouts before the incident, if she might have been meeting someone, alert us at once."

I shook. I knew. I knew everything. But there was no way to tell the Lord of Keys without endangering Kristos. A horrible thought passed through my mind, selfish but terrifying—after my visit to Pyord's office, it was even possible that murdering Nia was a message to me. *Don't force my hand. Keep quiet*, it seemed to whisper between the voices around me.

"This wasn't an accident?" Pauline asked, piping up like a timid mouse from the corner.

"No," Viola's father said simply. With Pyord, I knew, there were no accidents. Morbidly, I wanted to know how he did it.

Was she stabbed? Shot? Poisoned? Did Pyord have one of his men kill her, or had he done it himself?

It didn't matter. Even if Pyord killed her, she was dead because of me.

Theodor held me up even as I realized I was sinking against the window. "I'm taking you home," he said. I let him lead me from the salon.

36

—◈—

"You don't need to do this," I whispered as Theodor held my hand in the carriage.

"I think I do," he replied. He held up my hand, which was visibly shaking. "I saw Nia last week—I hardly know what to think."

I knew exactly what to think, but I shook my head. "I'm afraid," I said without meaning to. Theodor moved closer to me, but I still felt cold. The carriage wheels made a hollow echo as we crossed a bridge—over the river, I realized, looking down. The river was broad and choked with silt here near the sea. The brown eddies and whorls carried leaves and scraps of paper and one dead catfish past me. The river never stopped moving—it slowed here near its mouth, but it couldn't be halted. Pyord's plan felt that way now. I couldn't stop him from whatever he planned at the Midwinter Ball, or anything that followed it.

Pyord still held my brother. I had finished the shawl. I had no leverage. I could end up in the river just as Nia had. Theodor could be condemned to the same fate. I couldn't stop it.

"I'm not going until after Midwinter," Theodor said.

"What?"

"To the Allied Equatorial States. I'm not going until late winter. And now, after what happened to Nia, perhaps not at all." He glanced out of the window. A knot of Red Caps loitered by a tavern. I turned my face from them. "A diplomat's daughter killed here—it doesn't help us maintain our international allies."

"Is that what you're thinking about?" I demanded.

"No. I'm thinking about how she was always willing to go over my research with me, how she gave me seeds from her family's garden. I haven't even planted them yet." He pressed his mouth into a thin line. "I'm sorry, Sophie, but I can't—"

"It's all right," I said, finally gripping his hand in return. "Take me to the Stone Castle," I said, resolution building back in my voice after the shock of hearing about Nia. "I have business there."

"Business? Please, Sophie, don't make me leave you alone after this."

I searched his hazel eyes. Something in them made me agree. "If you want to come with me, you may."

The carriage drew to a halt in front of the imposing Stone Castle, once a fortress, when Galitha City was young, now a barracks and a jail.

"You don't have to come with me," I said, reticent even now to let Theodor see the business I had to attend to.

"Of course I don't have to," he replied, hopping out of the carriage as nimbly as a squirrel. "I want to."

Somehow, the thought of arguing with a clerk in front of Theodor made me more nervous than facing them by myself. I couldn't trust myself to stay calm, not to break down in tears or shouts of anger. I gathered my nerves and marched up to the counter blocking the rest of the Stone Castle from the vestibule. A thin-lipped, tired clerk of the guard drummed his fingers on the dark wooden surface.

"You are holding my employee here, and I ask for her release. I will pay her bond if need be."

Theodor, hovering behind me, coughed. I ignored him.

"Name," drawled the clerk.

"Mine or hers?"

He looked up at me. "Hers," he said after a confused pause. "Her name."

"Penny Lestrouse."

He flipped slowly through a stack of papers. The rustle of paper tracked like the second hand of a clock, methodical and impossible to hasten. I gripped the counter, frustration mounting. Theodor wisely kept his distance.

"She's being held in block B6," he announced, as though this meant anything to me.

"Yes?"

"Political block. I can't release her without confirmation paperwork from the Lord of Keys."

When Viola had argued for my shop to reopen, why hadn't she argued for the release of my employee? Why didn't she care more about Penny, cold and scared in a dark cell, than about my shop? I was important enough, elevated enough to help, but not a mere commoner like Penny?

She hadn't even thought about it, I realized. It wasn't cruelty. It was blindness.

"She is a girl. She works for me. She's—she's not dangerous."

The clerk just stared balefully. "I can't release anyone from B6 without paperwork."

"What about an order from the Duke of Westland?"

I didn't know until that moment that one could feel furious and relieved, grateful to someone while despising what they did. The clerk scrambled to his feet—he would stand for the Duke of

Westland, but not for a seamstress. He would shuffle his papers at breakneck speed and find the order for release for Theodor, but not for me.

"Let me see that," Theodor ordered. The clerk handed him the stack of papers—block B6 intake forms—with shaking hands. Theodor flipped through them, locating Penny's and setting aside several others. "These are all girls under eighteen years of age," he said, gesturing at the dates of birth entered at the top of each page on the pile. "Why are they being held?"

"They are political adversaries," the clerk replied weakly.

"I'll be speaking to the Lord of Keys about this," Theodor said sternly, as though he were in control of the situation. His wide eyes told me that even he was surprised. "These girls will be released under my order, tonight."

He watched the clerk fill out each order, and signed them himself. I wondered if there was any risk for him, what political capital he was expending to release these girls and Penny, if any. A guard led all of them from the dark hallway beyond the vestibule moments later, and Penny met my eyes with new understanding imbuing her surprise at being released.

"You?" she asked, standing a few leery feet from me.

"I tried," I answered. "It was Theodor, actually, who—"

"Of course it was," she said caustically. "I should have known it would take the influence of a noble." I wanted to argue with her, to implore her to be more gracious, but she was right. I had done nothing. I was purely ineffectual here, and the system only bent for the nobility.

"At any rate, I will come by to collect my pay by the end of the week," she added.

"What? Penny, I'm not firing you. I have no reason—"

"Of course you have no reason. I'm quitting. I can't work for you anymore, madame. Not with who you work for. Not after this."

My mouth went dry, but I couldn't find a good reason to compel her to come back. "I'm sorry to see you go, Penny."

She screwed her mouth into a tight line, and I realized she was trying not to cry. Swiftly, I excused Theodor and myself, and we escaped back to the carriage.

37

I LET THEODOR TAKE ME TO HIS HOUSE WITHOUT PROTESTING that he should take me home instead, arriving in silence at a tall gray stone building with narrow windows and an incongruous, peacock-blue door. I let him lead me from the carriage and through the front door, let him take my cloak and gloves. The servants didn't say anything, and I didn't care to speculate if that was merely because they were polite and well trained in their trade or because this was a regular occurrence.

"Build up the fire in the small parlor," Theodor said to a manservant. I followed him numbly through the beautifully furnished hallways, thick with expensive wool carpets and hung with botanical paintings. As the fire blazed in the hearth, Theodor pulled me onto the settee next to him.

"Thank you," I said. "For Penny. Even if she is...less than grateful."

"I don't blame her." He let the words fall quietly between us, more meaning in them than either of us knew how to express. He had seen the demands of the Red Caps, he had heard their shouts in the streets, and he had carefully read my brother's pamphlets, but I realized he had never seen himself as a despot until now. Until he had so obviously wielded power, even though it was intended to help, in front of others who didn't have it.

"There's no way out, is there." I sighed. "Even if your intentions are good and your actions benevolent, we still live by your leave."

"I think I see what has to change," he said quietly. "I don't know how, but the answer is neither revolt nor quashing it."

I shook my head. I couldn't solve any of these problems—I could sew and charm cast and run a business, but I found myself utterly helpless in the face of this standoff that was escalating into war, already claiming casualties like Nia.

"You know, I always imagined bringing you here," Theodor whispered into my hair. "I hoped you would like it here so much that you would refuse to leave. And that I could tell my parents there was a madwoman in my house so I couldn't get married after all."

Despite myself, I laughed. "That would do it."

"Why were you angry with me, before? At the greenhouse?"

I turned my face so that Theodor couldn't see it. "I wasn't angry with you."

"It rather seemed you were."

"I was angry with... myself, I suppose, for letting myself feel the way I did. I realized how impossible it was and..."

"I thought you had no interest in anything permanent," Theodor said. It wasn't an accusation, but I felt guilt.

"I know. I—I never thought I wanted anything permanent. The first time I do, and it's not possible." The fire burned bright, and I let Theodor pull me closer to him, feeling his heartbeat beneath my cheek.

He brushed my hair away from my face. "The world is changing. Who knows what might be different in the morning."

Even a month before, I would have brushed him off. Now

I felt a tiny hope that maybe he was right. Maybe in the barrage that was sure to assault us, we could at least find each other. I felt that, in him, I could gain something without giving everything else up. It was a foolish hope, barely worth being called a hope at all, but a nobleman's wife could have her own pursuits, her own vocation. Even without my shop, I could remain an artist of cloth and thread.

A frail hope, and I could hardly consider it now, with revolt brewing, Nia dead, Kristos still missing, and my own guilt clinging to me like the frost on the windowpanes.

"You know," I finally said, "I didn't get to hear you play your violin."

"That's right," he said softly, smiled, and turned back to the fire.

"Well?" I said, laughing. "I'd like very much to hear you play," I said with playful force.

"See, if I play, I can't lounge here on the settee with you. And I would need both hands." He tugged at his arms, wrapped around me, as though he couldn't be moved.

I swatted his chest. "Please."

"Very well." Theodor dipped a comical bow in consent, and then fetched his case from the back of the hallway where he had left it. He sat by the fireplace and began to tune the instrument.

As he concentrated on the tone of each string, I watched him. His face transformed from the joking laughter of before and was instead fully absorbed in the motions of his hands and the sound of his violin. A lock of hair slipped over his forehead and he ignored it, but a strange flutter rose in my chest, and a pang of something like loss gripped my stomach.

I loved him. I did—whether I wanted it or not, whether I would have asked for it or not. I loved Theodor, and I loved him more the more I saw in him.

He drew his bow softly across the strings, and I recognized

instantly a folk melody from the south. His version was more refined, and smoother, and of course lacked the words, but it still seemed to tell the story I remembered—a lover lost to the sea. Of course, nearly all Galatine folk songs were about lovers, and many of them involved someone either drowning in or choosing to sail off on their "true love" the sea. This was a particularly sad story about love lost to the inevitable tide, and I couldn't help but feel it could be about Theodor and me.

Then the bow sparked on the violin, like the flash of static when I stacked fabric on a dark, dry winter night.

I gasped, but Theodor kept playing, his attention turned fully to the music now, a soft rapture replacing the jokes of his performing face. As I watched, more bright sparks of light jounced off the strings, flashing briefly in the air before fading, like embers rising from a fire.

Theodor was charm casting.

As with the ballad seller, the music carried a charm, growing around him, and like the ballad seller, he seemed unaware of it. I gripped the arm of the sofa, digging my fingers into the fine brocade and not caring if my nails snagged the delicate fibers. Did he know? I considered how I saw the light woven into every charmed item I made—it was impossible to ignore. And if he knew he was a charm caster and hadn't told me, he had lied. To charm cast was an integral part of who we were.

Unless he didn't know. Was it possible to not know what I felt permeated every part of my identity? I watched him playing. The charm grew brighter, dimmer, flashed when the melody spiked. There was no indication he saw anything.

Then he finished with a flourish that sent a whorl of light spinning around his bow, and turned to me.

I stared back, dumbfounded.

"It was that bad?"

I gathered myself. "It was beautiful."

"You look like you've seen a spirit."

"You didn't?" I blurted out before I could compose a more eloquent question.

"What?" He laughed. "No one's ever compared my music to a haunting before—I suppose I'll take it as a compliment, but—"

"No one's ever noticed?"

"Noticed what?"

It wasn't impossible—those without the gift and the training to use it couldn't see the light, and whom had Theodor played for? Nobles, court guests? Unless there was a chance charm caster among them, no one would have noticed. I was again acutely aware of my ignorance even in this, so integral to my work and my world. I had never known a non-Pellian charm caster; I had assumed there was something in our blood that gave us the gift, or something in others' blood that made them immune to the ability. Perhaps I was wrong. There were rumors that Serafan sorcerers were charm casters of some kind; maybe they were. Perhaps the gift lay dormant in plenty of people outside Pellia who didn't have the benefit of a culture that welcomed it and mentors who taught it.

"Theodor, have the maid bring a needle and thread," I said, suddenly aware of how I could show him, how I could find out if he knew the capabilities he harbored.

"Do you end all of your romantic evenings this way?" he asked as he summoned a maid and requested a sewing kit. She dipped a curtsy but gave me a questioning look.

"Only with men I really like," I replied. The maid returned. I swiftly cut a length of white linen thread and pulled Theodor's cravat from his neck.

"Any idea how long that took me to tie properly?" he joked weakly.

I stitched a few whipstitches in, over the fine hem. I worked a charm quickly, for luck, for protection. He watched me, curious. His eyes, I noted, followed only my needle, not the swirls of light that I embedded into the fabric.

"Theodor," I finally said. "Take this end here, where I've already sewn." I handed him a length of linen, white on white thread glowing to my eyes with brilliant light.

"All right. Look at it."

"I am looking." Still polite, but brimming with frustration. I pressed on anyway.

"No, really look. Into it. Look into the stitches themselves."

"What does this have to do with anything?" he asked.

"Everything," I replied, impatient. "Now—if you look at the stitches, if you look at them with your instincts as well as your eyes, what do you see?"

"I see a line of stitches."

"Do you remember—" I smiled. "The night the Red Caps threw a rock through Viola's window. When we stopped in the gardens, by the frozen pools and the willows."

Theodor's face softened. "Of course."

"Just—think about how you looked at those frozen waterfalls. How you saw the stars that night. The way you—the way you looked at me."

He forced his gaze past me, into the dimly candlelit room, but I could see something loosening and opening within him.

"Now look at the stitches the way you look at me. Looking with more than your eyes."

He obeyed, squinting. Suddenly his eyes came alive and he dropped the fabric.

"There's light in it," he said, snatching the fabric up again. "I can see it now. It's woven into every stitch—you did this! This is what magic looks like, isn't it?" He turned the fine linen over in his hands.

The astonishment in his face convinced me, if I had held any doubts—he had never realized he had this gift before. Perhaps as a child he saw things, perhaps he even cast charms without meaning to. It was buried now. I wondered if it could even be developed this late in life. I certainly didn't know anyone who was trained in adulthood.

"When you played your violin," I said, "when you played your version of that folk tune, you were charm casting."

"That's impossible," he said. "I didn't mean to; I didn't even know I could."

"It wasn't very good casting," I said with an unintentional smile. "Just sparks now and then, not controlled. I see now that it was because you didn't know you were doing it." Like that ballad seller in the square, long weeks ago. I traced Theodor's hand, wondering how many others had the power to draw light from nothing hidden in their hands.

His mouth was still slightly agape.

"Could you teach me?" he asked. "Could I learn to control it?"

Pyord's cursed commission loomed over me, Nia's death, my brother's kidnapping. All due to my gift. Were I an ordinary seamstress, I would never have to face any of it.

I wasn't sure I wanted to make Theodor risk a similar burden.

But that wasn't my decision. With the threat of revolution hanging over the city, Theodor might need any help he could get. Charm casting might, someday, save him.

"I can try," I said. I returned his cravat to him, protection woven into the hem.

Were I an ordinary seamstress, I couldn't have given him this gift. I wouldn't have met him at all. I sighed and leaned into him, feeling his heartbeat and the golden light we shared all at once.

38

—⁓—

THE NEXT MORNING, THEODOR BROUGHT ME BACK TO MY SHOP. Responsibility reasserted itself. I had Alice and Emmi to consider, and it was up to me to take care of my shop and make sure they had work. And wait to hear that Kristos was safe. It was never far from my thoughts that what had happened to Nia was my fault. I had to be sure no one else was hurt because of me.

We worked diligently over the following days. Alice did what she could despite her hand, still thick with bandages, and I sewed as quickly as I could to make up for Penny's absence. Even with her best efforts, Alice could only do so much, but Emmi was a more adept learner than I had expected, and could soon work long seams to my satisfaction as well as rolled hems, and even effect some decent topstitching. Alice was apprehensive at first, both of the skills I allowed an untrained seamstress to practice on clients' commissions and of letting a Pellian work with clients in the front room, but her pragmatism couldn't argue with Emmi's nimble fingers. Once Emmi left her kerchief at home and finished a simple but fashionable jacket to wear at work, Alice lost any objection to her presence in the front room, either.

Emmi and Alice gossiped about the body in the river, but I didn't say anything. When Alice described the grotesque way she had been stabbed—expertly and precisely between the boning in her corset—I had to leave the atelier. It didn't appear that anyone else had connected her death to the messenger boy's, though both stabbed bodies had been found in the river. I should have known better. I should never have allowed her to put herself in danger.

The girls were gossiping again when I returned. "The Stone Castle!" Alice shook her head. "Nonsense. He told Sophie already—"

"Told me what?" I tapped my toe on the floorboard.

Emmi clammed up, but Alice plowed ahead. "Your brother wrote to you from port, yes? That he's at sea?"

"Of course," I answered quickly, flustered. I had heard nothing else from him, or from Pyord. I had done everything Pyord asked, so I had to cling to the belief that Kristos was safe and would be released soon. That perhaps he had been released and was hiding or escaping the city. That I would hear from him.

Alice folded her hands. "There's talk in some of the taverns that he's actually a prisoner in the Stone Castle."

"I'm sure that's not true," I answered.

Emmi, still uncertain around Alice, chose her words carefully and spoke more slowly than she usually did with me. "Some of the Red Caps in our market said he's being tortured for information about the leadership and their plans. That he's refusing to say anything." She hesitated, then added, "They said they even arrested Penny to make him talk."

"What nonsense," I said, a bit too quickly. "How would anyone in the taverns know what happens inside the Stone Castle?"

"They say they've heard from the other prisoners, ones who have been released," Emmi said. "They say he's been held ever since—ever since you said he disappeared, actually."

"Truly," I said with a shaky breath, "he's not a prisoner." I

prayed this new wrinkle couldn't reveal me and my own treachery. It was too late to stop what had already begun, in any case. I
retreated to the counter. An uprising was coming; violence was
coming—I could feel it like the first frosts, settling deep into my
bones. I couldn't stop it—no one could.

"These came while you were out," Alice said. Two
messages—one on the flimsy slips merchants and tradespeople
used, one a formal, heavy scroll. I opened the flimsy paper first.

Safe, hiding, more soon, was all it said. In Kristos's cramped
handwriting. No one could have mimicked it. I clutched the
paper in my hand and slipped it into my pocket, fighting tears of
relief. I couldn't let Alice see the emotion a scrap of paper inspired
without risking her discovering the truth. So I swallowed my
tears and my smile alike and picked up the other message.

I opened the heavy paper—Theodor's handwriting, an invitation to dinner at his home. The formality was half in jest, I was
sure, but perhaps not quite entirely—I traced the well-formed
calligraphy and knew that Theodor wanted to give me a fine
dinner like a gift, like all the other gifts he had given me—the
time in the greenhouse, the view from Viola's ballroom. Things
he knew I would enjoy.

I wanted, desperately, to see him. When I thought of the
revolution simmering in every alley and corner of the city, I
wondered if it was wise. I should, I reasoned, stay as far from
him as possible, as though the dark tendrils of Pyord's plan
could follow me wherever I went and poison Theodor. I imagined his hands writing out the note, the intensity I so admired
about him changing his features as he formed each perfect letter.
I had grown to accept that we were separated by class, probably
indelibly, but the only small moments of comfort I had experienced in the horrible past weeks had been from Theodor. And
he was leaving soon—for safety, but away from me. One happy

evening, I told myself. I would allow myself one bright memory in the swiftly approaching, unavoidable darkness that I knew could leave no one in Galitha City untouched.

I penned an acceptance to Theodor, my letters far less fine than his, and sent it off with a messenger.

When the early winter twilight darkened the shop, I hurried home to dress. I wore my best, a deep-blue silk with pinked and scalloped trim pleated along the sleeve and neck edges. Though I wasn't very skilled at it, I even dressed my hair with extra curls and a ribbon woven through the dark mess. His carriage pulled in front of my door—the first time I had let him see my ramshackle row house—and he took my arm to help me inside.

"What's the occasion?" I asked, my voice softer, more sensuous than I had intended. The perfume in my hair powder must have affected me more than I thought, I chided myself, flushing pink.

Theodor laughed and traced a callus on my finger, a spot where the needle had nicked the skin so often a permanent bandage had formed. "Can't I simply want to see the loveliest charm-casting seamstress in the capital city?"

"Try harder at your compliments next time," I replied, mock punching his arm. He feigned injury, then softened and leaned toward me. I let him sink into my skirts, his hands around my fitted bodice, his mouth finding mine. Then we hit a rock in the road and jounced out of our embrace.

"Serves me right," Theodor said, rubbing the shoulder that had collided with the carriage's paneling. A packet of paper shimmied from inside his jacket.

"What's that?"

"You mean you haven't read it?" he said, throwing one of Kristos's pamphlets on the seat between us. I avoided touching it. "Even my father read this one—for the better part of a year all the broadsides and pamphlets circulating this city were just words strung together to the council, and now they read them as though they hold the secret to ending this unrest."

"They do—or at least, perhaps they did."

"I don't know what concession now would stop it, and most of the council is still convinced that meeting any of their terms would only show ourselves to be weak." He breathed frustration through his nose. "They're sending my sister to my aunt's estate in the western lake region, my brothers to the naval stations and the Southern Fortress. To 'study martial topics.' To avoid them, more like, and spread the family out over a few hundred miles as insurance."

"Oh, Theodor," I said, catching his hand.

"And your brother apparently isn't at sea, is he?" He flicked the paper cover of the booklet. "He's here, rabble rousing."

The initials stared at me from the plain cover. "That's not possible," I answered flatly. "They—someone—must be using his name. Or perhaps he wrote it a long time ago, and they saved it." Kristos's note to me, in all of its painful brevity, flashed in my memory—*Safe*, it had said—but I didn't know anything else. Could he possibly be free of Pyord but avoiding returning to me? Or was Pyord holding him and forcing him to write?

"Smart move, actually." He leafed silently through the pages, and I peered over his shoulder. "He's really quite a good writer. This, for instance: *A single flake of snow means nothing, but no man would challenge a blizzard. A single crow worries no one, but a flock can strip a field.*"

"*Revolution must take wing under an entire flock, not one or two voices alone.*" I sighed. "Yes, he's ever so talented."

He clasped my hand. "At least he's not writing swill. It's good treasonous writing." I almost laughed, but Theodor grew sober again. "And my little voyage to the Allied Equatorial States is off."

Relief and disappointment fought one another for domi-nance in my reaction. I finally managed one word: "Nia?"

"Yes. The princes, I suppose, decided that if one of their diplomat's daughters isn't safe here, then one of their princesses certainly isn't." He stuffed Kristos's pamphlet back into his coat pocket. "I must admit—I am relieved."

My heart jumped, and then plummeted back to dark reality. "You'd be safer out of the city, just like your brothers and sister." And putting off one marriage didn't avoid them entirely, I left unsaid. To think—I hadn't wanted to marry at all in autumn, and now I begrudged someone's as-yet-unknown bride.

"I couldn't leave the city now. I might be a frivolous gar-dener and violinist, but I am the First Duke of Westland." He squared his shoulders. "I have some responsibilities, and I intend to see them through. Besides, I couldn't leave you right now." His hand rested on the hilt of his sword, unconsciously ready to defend me. I smiled.

I gazed out the window into the growing darkness. "But if you stay, you could be killed." Pyord's plan centered on killing the king, but perhaps also those in line for the throne. The Midwinter Ball was less than two weeks away. Tears blurred my vision, and the lights in the city washed together in the windowpane.

"Better that than find you had been hurt. I'd never forgive myself. All the princesses of all the Allied States couldn't make me forget."

"You're an idiot—you know that?" I sighed. "Your parents will arrange a marriage eventually, and it won't be with me."

"Perhaps not," he mused. "I have my own thoughts on that matter."

My brow knit and I opened my mouth to question him, but he waved me off. "It's just an egg of an idea, I shouldn't have even spoken of it. There will certainly be no weddings this winter. For now—please do me the honor?"

We drew up to the front of the most palatial house I had ever seen, aside from the palace itself. "This isn't your house," I stammered.

"No, it's the residence of the Prince of Westland. I've never brought you to my ancestral home before."

"Because you're hiding that you're having an illicit affair with a common seamstress from your parents? I figured."

"Yes, mostly. But they're away at a card party. And I paid off the servants not to tell on me. Though, frankly, I don't much care if they do."

"What's the worst they can do? Arrange a marriage for you?" Somehow, the specter of revolution and death that haunted the city made me feel cavalier, willing to accept danger and risk to be happy for a few days, for a night only. Theodor could be married to someone else in time—but tonight we could be happy together. Tonight was ours, and tomorrow alone was uncertain.

We pulled through the wrought iron gate and around the circular drive. As though we did this every evening, as though we were the Duke and Duchess of Westland and this was our house, Theodor helped me from the carriage and held my hand as we ascended the stairs. A servant opened the door and took my cloak with a secret smile, and another led me to the small private dining room built over the gardens at the back of the house. It was paneled with mirrors along half its height, carefully arranged to reflect light.

There were candles everywhere.

Dancing candle flames in chandeliers, votives in long lines down the tables, tapers burning in reflective sconces. The room was alive with candlelight.

"This is beautiful," I said, letting Theodor hold the chair at the head of the table for me. He sat next to me, at my right hand.

"And tonight it's yours. You're the lady of the house. Call for dinner when you're ready."

I laughed. "I don't even know how to do that," I confided.

He pointed to a miniature silver bell in front of me. "Just ring."

I lifted the bell and it pealed a single clear note. Our first course, a soup, was marched into the room by a servant, who gave me a not-so-subtle wink.

"Why are they being so nice to me?" I asked.

"They'd rather I marry a local girl than some foreign princess," Theodor said. "I don't blame them."

As we ate and talked and the candles burned lower around us, I was struck by how foreign yet familiar this scene was. It was opulent luxury I had only experienced in small doses with Theodor or Viola, of course, but I had never spoken so easily and comfortably with anyone.

"I never want to leave," I said as we shared a pear torte with burnt caramel drizzled on it.

"The cook is in top form tonight," Theodor agreed with a pert smile.

"Not that," I said, "and you know it."

"Someday," he said, the bold tone returning to his voice, "I will bring you here and you will never have to leave."

As much as Theodor may have wanted to make me his Lady of Westland, I knew another noble was probably waiting in his future. But that was for another day—another year, most likely. I shook my head. "Let's think about tonight only," I said. "It's all we truly have. All anyone ever really has."

He reached out and cupped my face in his hand, impulsive yet tender. "Now can feel like forever," he said, and he kissed me.

We rose from our seats, and the servant who had come to clear the plates shrank back against the wall with a broad smile, and then everyone and everything else in the room disappeared. I was swimming in a pool of candlelight with Theodor as my only anchor. His hands held me firm, and I buried my fingers in his hair, loosening it from its queue.

"We can't stay here much longer," he whispered in my ear, his words not bitter but an invitation. I acquiesced and we sank into each other before the fire. His arms encircled my waist with a fierceness I had never seen from him before. I returned it, my fingers working free the deftly embroidered buttons on his waistcoat, the fine linen neckcloth, the tiny thread button at his throat. I inhaled his scent—the gentlemanly pomade laden with clove oil, and underneath that, the baser smell of sweat.

My lips worked their way down his neck, to his collarbone, as his hand slipped beneath my silk petticoats. We were bathed in candlelight, both of us, reflected infinitely in the mirrored paneling of the walls. It was as though both of us, and the moment itself, went on forever. His fingers traced the clocked design of my stockings, my silk garters, my bare thighs. The room was silent save for the rustle of the taffeta. When he entered me, it was as though all the light I had pulled into every charm I had ever made collided with the light in him, mingled, joined together.

The tear that rolled swiftly from the corner of my eye into my hair was of pure joy, pure light—even if tonight was all we had, we were one.

39

—⚭—

THE NEXT MORNING WAS BRIGHT AND FRESH WITH NEWLY FALLEN snow. I had returned home in the small hours of the night, neither Theodor nor I wanting anyone aside from the sympathetic servants aware of our tryst. I threw open the window and breathed deep drafts of freezing air, clearing my head and filling my lungs with the new day. For the first time in weeks, I felt that there might be a future to look forward to. I had no word from Pyord, and the streets had been quiet. Though I had no more messages from Kristos, that word—*safe*—felt more like a promise this morning than it had yesterday. And I allowed myself the fragment of a dream that, perhaps, I would not lose Theodor. If anyone could work his way out of an arranged marriage, it was him. He said he had a wisp of an idea—and that was all I needed to stoke the hope I had allowed to spark within me.

I almost ran to the shop, finishing most of my day's work before Alice or Emmi even arrived. I set them to work finishing Annette's court gown—its perfect lines and silvery trim made me smile, the first time I had appreciated my own work in weeks. As I erased our work board and began to reassign tasks, the door banged open.

"Just a moment, I'll—"

"No rush," a familiar voice answered.

"Viola!" I dropped down from the stool I had to stand on to reach the board. "This is a surprise, I—" Blushing, I glanced around the shop at the mess the morning's work had already left in its wake.

"It's quaint. So bright and clean," she said honestly. "A true artist's atelier." Her voice dropped. "I came to talk privately—I hope that can be arranged?"

"Of course," I said, swiftly sending Alice and a gawking Emmi out the door to buy our lunch. "Is there something wrong?" I realized I was gripping my chalk, and let it drop to the countertop.

"No, not precisely. I have something for you," Viola said. "My father found a packet of papers addressed to you among Nia's letters."

He must have had her home searched looking for clues, I surmised. I was desperately curious to know if he had found anything that would tie the murder to Pyord, but of course I couldn't ask.

"It's a few pages of notes about curses and charms," Viola continued. She watched me for any reaction. "It looks like a first draft—there are notes in the margins and bits crossed out."

"Yes, I—she translated a few pages of Pellian for me," I replied. "Everything I learned was passed down from my mother, so I was curious what books on the subject might say. Nia was helping me."

"I see." Viola traced the pages with a light finger. "Curses, Sophie. You—you don't meddle in that, do you?"

"Of course not!" The force in my reply shocked even me. I flushed. "The only written work on charm casting is in Pellian, and ancient Pellians cast curses, too."

"My father—he didn't want to give these to you because of

how much the pages talked about curses." She smiled. "I convinced him to let me ask you about them."

"I was only interested in the theories," I assured her. Of course the Lord of Keys had a right to be concerned. Pellian immigrants importing an ability to cast curses had added to the legal code of Galitha, and though that self-important set of documents couldn't lower itself to specifically mention curses or charms, the Lord of Keys was certainly well aware of the laws dictating that any harm caused by "overt or covert maleficence, natural or supernatural" be prosecuted.

That counted for regicide, too. I tried to forget about that.

"Well, I hope this is helpful." Viola handed me the papers. "Poor Nia—still nothing on why she was killed or who killed her."

I shook my head. "I wish I could do something," I lied. I could have done something. But going to the Lord of Keys meant admitting everything and being hung for treason—if Pyord didn't find and kill me and my brother first. "Is there anything...new? In the case?"

"I'm afraid not. The palace wants to get some answers, and hopes that those answers don't make Galitha look like a festering cesspool of crime. Or worse, revolt. The Allied States are one of our strongest military allies—we can't look weak in their estimation. Unfortunately, they're reading Nia's death as linked to the revolutionary movement."

"And it isn't?" I said.

"Why would it be?" Viola watched me with a cocked eyebrow. "I should be leaving—Annette wanted me over for lunch. I think she's having a hard time with all of this, honestly," she added.

"Thank you," I said. "For Nia's papers."

"You're welcome," Viola replied.

The girls weren't back yet, so I opened the packet of papers with a deep breath.

The Pellians tended toward a warrior culture, Nia wrote by way of preface. I could hear her tone take on the erudite lecturer's cadence she had used in the archive. *They were highly competitive— most of their cultural pursuits were contests. Horse races, public boxing matches, and even arena fighting. It doesn't surprise me that they'd be more inclined toward cursing one another than casting charms, or that they would attempt to undo charms in an effort to displace them with curses.*

The text talks about the light matter tied into the charmed object. It says to untie the light from the object. (Literally—*the word is the same as untying a knot),* she added in the margin. *Though the process of creating the charm is falsely understood to be physical, it is in fact mental. As one could cast a charm without the physical tie, though difficult, so can one untie a charm from its object.*

Therefore, one may untie each strand of charm from the object and replace it with a curse of their choosing. Though it is easier to have an object in hand for focus and precision, it is not necessary, though it must be visible to extract the charm. It will be easier to learn non-tactile casting on a previously charmed or cursed object, as such items are more willing vessels than virgin objects.

I reread her final paragraph. It could be done—I could undo the curse in the shawl. I imagined Nia tracing each Pellian word with a gloved finger, reconstructing the sentences of long-unspoken words. She had given me the key, and she had died for it. All I had to do was figure out how to undo curses and then find a way to see the shawl again—in the next week.

I stitched a sloppy charm into a scrap of fabric. Easy as breathing—the charm was done in a couple of minutes, a glow-ing circle of backstitches on the plain linen.

Then I stared at it and tried to think about undoing those

sparkling stitches. Untie the sparkling line with my mind. I had never attempted to engage with charms without handling them, and so doing anything with my mind rather than my fingers was not only foreign but also confusing. Even when I tried moving my hands in the motions I would use to pick out stitches, it was like grabbing at air. I couldn't latch onto anything. I concentrated, but all I succeeded in doing was tightening my temples into the beginnings of a tension headache.

Perhaps, I thought, Nia had mistranslated or misunderstood the lack of physical contact with the charm. I picked up my needle and the charmed scrap and focused on unbinding the charm from the fabric as I snipped through the knot I'd worked in the end and plucked out each individual stitch.

What was left was a pile of dimly glowing thread scraps and a piece of fabric that looked smudged with light. The charm had stained it—though it would certainly be less effective now, it remained embedded in the cloth.

So part of what Nia had read was true—the charm wasn't merely attached to the stitches. It wasn't a purely physical tie. It was bound to the item with something deeper.

Maybe, I thought, a curse would be easier for me to undo. I'd want to pull the dark from the object I'd created more than I wanted to remove the light, by my own instincts. I whipped out a quick curse, an angry little wish for bad luck, in another scrap, ignoring the dull nausea that accompanied the task.

I set it against an unlit candlestick and thought about it. Instead of lifting my needle, I imagined the smooth metal sliding under a stitch and plucking it up, drawing it from the fabric. I imagined the stitch as a line of dark sparkle rather than thread. I wrinkled my brow and stared at the line of shadow stitches, willing them to loosen. Without meaning to, I pantomimed the actions with my hand, picking at a stitch and working it loose.

Before my eyes the dark line rose from the fabric, one piece at a time, and hovered over the table.

I gasped—I could do it. Learning this new skill had been easier than learning curse casting, as though I had strengthened some unseen muscle in developing the ability to curse as well as charm. I had felt, odd as it was to describe, more dexterous, more flexible in the invisible maneuverings that produced charms in recent weeks. But what now? The curse hung in a cloud instead of being tied to the fabric, but a floating curse wasn't much better than a bound one. I waved my hand. The cloud dissipated slightly. Could I just dissolve it back into the ether? After all, it had come from somewhere—it could go back to where it came from, couldn't it? More theory—and even if I'd had time to explore it, I couldn't read the ancient texts I would have needed to answer all the questions my experiment raised.

I swirled my hand, and then made a movement like erasing a chalkboard. The particles of darkness separated from one another and dispersed, growing smaller and fainter until I could no longer see them.

I repeated the experiment with the smudges of light left on the cloth, drawing them into a cloud above the table and then waving them away. So it could be done, and without touching the item itself.

Victory surged briefly in my mind before I considered the sheer expanse of the queen's shawl—thousands of stitches.

Emmi and Alice returned, mugs of street-vendor soup and thick brown bread in hand, laughing and gossiping about the upcoming Festival of Song. Behind them, a scrappy boy wearing a red cap rapped on the door. I handed the errand boy a coin for a tip as I took the folded paper from him, but I wanted to rip that cap from his head and box his ears for being foolish enough to wear the symbol of revolution.

The message was just an address, my brother's name, and an unwritten but unequivocal summons.

"I have to run out on an errand," I said, my voice strange even to me. Alice nodded, but Emmi tilted her head at my strained words, curious. I knew that both could read me well enough to know that this was no ordinary errand, but neither pressed me.

I found the address in Pyord's message and stood before an imposing charcoal-gray townhome in an older part of the river district. The entrance was flanked with carved dragons with stone flames protruding from their gaping mouths—the effect was more tacky than terrifying in broad daylight, but I wondered if they looked more sinister at night.

I rang the bell and a liveried servant, wearing clothes twenty years out of fashion, entered and led me to a dour study. The only cheerful thing in the room was a fire roaring on the hearth. Otherwise, it was filled with precisely shelved books and dark furniture and drapes that kept too much sunlight out.

Two tall wingback chairs faced the fire, and I saw that both were occupied. Pyord rose from one, gesturing for me to sit on an ottoman placed between the chairs.

But when the other person rose, there was no way I could have done anything but launch myself at him.

Kristos beamed as I hit him, full force, knocking him back into the chair.

"I was so worried," I cried, "that you'd be hurt!"

"I will be if you don't keep your elbows out of my rib cage," he said with a broad smile. "It's good to see you, too."

"You said—your note—that you were hiding," I said, brow knitting. "That you were safe."

"I was, Sophie. I was hiding here, and I was safe. I promise." He grinned and caught my shoulders in his large hands. I should have felt safe in his arms, but I didn't.

"It is done," Pyord said, nodding to me.

"Yes. It's done. I've done everything you asked me. Now you can let my brother go."

"Well, Kristos. You heard her—everything done according to plan."

They shared a smile.

I froze.

"Kristos," I said slowly. "You knew about what he was making me do? You're not angry?"

"Sophie, I know that this is going to seem difficult to imagine, but you casting a curse—that was my idea."

My legs buckled, and I finally sat on the ottoman. "Your idea? Then you—you weren't being held hostage?"

"No," he said, horribly gently. "Pyord supplied the details, but I knew you had an in with the nobility when you told me about Lady Snowmont. I knew you'd never use it to accomplish anything without a push. Believing I was in danger gave you that push."

My heart hammered against my corset, echoing into the void where my trust had been.

"I never had any intention of hurting Kristos," Pyord said. "He's one of the greatest natural leaders I've ever met—his disappearance inflamed the Laborers' League so much that I've had to request that they curb their rush for violence." He smiled. "They've even devised assault plans on the Stone Castle when we circulated the rumor he was held there—entirely their idea, entirely based upon their loyalty to Kristos. I of course recommended they not attempt such suicide."

"I don't care about that," I snapped. "But Kristos—you used me. For something awful. You made me help you try to . . . kill people." Saying the words out loud made them even more horrible. I almost gagged.

"Sophie, this has to be done. In order for a new, fair government to be enacted, we need a vacuum of power. Pyord taught me that. No change in regime has ever, historically, been enacted without unbalancing the power already in place." Pyord nodded as though observing a recitation. I seethed. "With the king gone, we'll have the opportunity we need. The king will fall, and we will strike quickly to assert a new government. Pyord has a brilliant plan, and Niko and the others have organized the Red Caps to carry it off, but it needed a stroke of luck. You're that stroke—you're the final words in the greatest plan ever written."

"I am not," I said. "I didn't want anything to do with this—I was only protecting you." I felt sick—I should have withheld sending the shawl until Kristos was freed. I was an idiot for not doing so, and an idiot for not seeing that Kristos had all the pieces except my motivation to get what he wanted.

I had just never believed that he could be so cruel to me. That he could betray my trust and lie to me and force me to be disloyal to my own principles. And I certainly never believed that Kristos was a killer. He was a writer, an idealist. Something had changed. I glanced at Pyord. He had changed my brother, corrupted him into something as single-minded as himself.

"And..." My voice nearly left me. "And Nia. You—you must have known about her, too."

Kristos looked, blessedly, confused, and Pyord sighed. "I handled that breach of confidence on my own." He looked almost sorry for it, but the detached words—*breach of confidence*—enraged me. Nia was a person, a brilliant woman, and Pyord had treated her as disposable.

That's all any of us were to Pyord—disposable. I clamped my arms around myself—would he dispose of me, too? Would Kristos even care enough to try to keep me safe?

"I thought—I thought I meant something to you. I chose you, Kristos—I chose saving you and compromising what I believed in. I became tied up in all this for you."

He shifted. "I know it was against your code of ethics, Sophie, but that code—it belongs to a different world. Not this place, not this time. Not when you were so needed."

"It belongs to me!" I shouted. "It wasn't yours to corrupt." If nothing else, the injustice of bending one's actions to fit someone else's beliefs ought to have resonated with him—but he would have never committed such a treasonous act of compromise, I thought bitterly, even to spare his own sister.

"You know that Penny was arrested," I said flatly. "Do you even care?"

He threw his hands in the air. "All of us knew the risks. She knew. She's safe now."

"And if I had been caught? If I had been arrested, if they had discovered what I did? What I created with my own hands?"

He rocked back on his heels, and then flat on his feet. He could never keep still when Mother lectured him, when he knew he'd done something wrong. As a child, he'd fidgeted as though he could wear an escape hatch into the floor.

His movements were more controlled now, but I knew why he couldn't keep his feet from worrying the thick carpet. He knew, from the outset, that I could be caught; he knew I could be killed, and he'd risked that anyway. In whatever calculation he used to justify himself, I'm sure that the chances I would end up on the gallows were slim. But he knew the chance existed. Silent, I turned to leave.

Kristos reached for my hand. "I'm sorry that you don't understand this now, Sophie, but I know that someday you'll see how vital this was. How important you were."

"I will not," I shot back at Kristos, jerking my arm away

from him. He cared more for ideals and words on a broadside than he did for me—for my business, for my ethics, even for my life. "I will only see this as the day I lost my brother."

"Once we get home, we'll straighten everything out," he said, begging me silently for another chance.

"You're not coming home with me. You can stay here if he'll let you, or go to one of your Red Cap friends' houses. But you're not welcome in the home I pay for any longer."

"Sophie—"

"No. You lied to me and used me. Alice was hurt because of you. Nia died for what you did. And some poor messenger boy, too—one of the people you would claim you want to help! Don't speak to me." I ran from the room, stumbling on the edge of the carpet.

Footfalls stalked me—Pyord, not Kristos. "I am quite disappointed in this turn, Sophie."

"What did you expect?"

"Reason. In truth, I had hoped that at some point you would come to understand what a great benefit someone with your skill could be to our new government, to the entirety of Galitha. I had imagined, to be honest, an elevated position for you."

Conscription was a more apt term. "I don't want any role in your revolution or anything that comes out of it."

"As it's too late for that, I'll have to resort to fear. Even though I have no intention of harming your brother, I still have leverage."

I already knew. "Don't tell or you'll kill me." I swallowed bitter rage that made me shake, down to my fingertips. "If you'd kill Nia, I know you wouldn't hesitate to dump me in the river."

"I wouldn't enjoy it, but yes, I would do it." He sighed. "It's not just me anymore, Sophie. Niko Otni, for instance—I have no doubt that he would intercede if he thought you were liable to compromise us."

I turned my face away, unwilling to hear what Pyord had to say about one of my brother's friends, but he continued anyway. "He suggested certain measures be taken when I discovered your little stunt with the shifts. Of course your brother would never agree, and hiding that from him would be...difficult. I insisted that the situation be addressed without dispatching you, but don't doubt that if you disrupt this revolution further, I can't continue to advocate for you, and in any case, someone might make decisions without my approval or your brother's input." His eyes seemed to swallow all of the light in the room. "The wheels have begun to turn, and the road is clear. I won't allow anything to obstruct it now."

"If you weren't threat enough, the gallows would be," I answered. Whether I liked it or not, I was bound to remain loyal to Pyord's secret, or my life was forfeit. Pyord smiled the prepared smile of a man who knew his hand would win the round of cards. He'd gotten his way.

I snatched my cloak from a peg on the wall and ran out the door, past the frozen dragons, and marched along the street as though I had some purpose, some mission. Pyord had won this battle, but he hadn't won the war. I couldn't change Nia's death or Alice's broken fingers. This wasn't like sewing—I couldn't unpick my stitches and start over. But I could decide what to do next.

40

⎯ɱ⎯

THERE WAS A PALL OVER THE CITY, TOO, A DULL, MALICIOUS QUIET.
Something waiting. Something biding its time. The protests
slowed, but the Red Caps gathered in knots in taverns, street
corners, no longer shouting but whispering. The whispers terrified me.

Alice and Emmi worked their normal days, did good work;
we took orders and delivered orders and restocked thread as
though the shop had never been closed, but they were quiet,
even Emmi. We all sensed something drawing tighter around
us, growing shakier beneath us. Only I had a date in mind—
Midwinter. Celebrated with parties in houses noble to common, marked with the Festival of Song during the shortest day
of the year, and, I was sure, the date Pyord had planned his
insurrection.

Masked by the quiet order of my shop's regular production
in the days leading up to Midwinter, I kept practicing pulling
curses and charms out of my own sewing. I was painfully slow,
and with mere days left to master the skill, increasingly frustrated. When Theodor asked if I could join him at his house
to practice his own charm casting, I agreed, grateful not only
for the break from my own dead-end work, but hoping that

teaching him would show me something I had missed. If nothing else, the past weeks had taught me that I had plenty to learn about charm casting. Maybe the same route that brought me to trouble could lead me out of it. The streets were as quiet as they had been all week, punctuated by quiet Red Caps of whom I couldn't help but feel vaguely, constantly suspicious.

No one followed me anymore, though, for which I was grateful, but I still moved quickly through the streets and arrived as inconspicuously as possible at Theodor's front door.

"I haven't been out in days. Father has the cabinet together writing a concordance to appease some of the Red Caps' demands," he confided. "It might be enough, if they can finish before the Red Caps make an attempt. Right now I doubt the cabinet's ability to finish debating before Midsummer. I've been compiling information—mostly from your brother's pamphlets—on their most frequent grievances."

"They didn't consider those demands until now?"

"Considered and promptly rejected dozens of times. Concession was seen as weak governance. They're more afraid of revolution, finally—that truly would make them look impotent." Theodor took my cloak and led me to his study. "Now. Enough talk about things we can't fix. Charms. I promise to be a good pupil," he said, folding his hands as though penitent.

"I'm sure you will be." I laughed. "I'm afraid it's my lacking as a teacher that we have to be concerned about. I've never taught anyone before. And, well...it may be too late."

"Why?"

"I learned when I was a child. So did my mother. Everyone I've ever heard of learned as a child." And, I added silently, for all I knew about the practice of casting, I knew little enough about how it actually worked, how the mind grasped the light and dark and drew it into obedience.

"Perhaps it's like music—it's easier to learn when you're young and can train yourself to think in a certain way more naturally. But I've known aged men who picked up the violin in their retirement." He shrugged. "They weren't virtuosos, but they were competent."

"It may work that way. It might not. Truly, I don't know." I held his hands. "But I know if anyone can learn, you could. So we'll try."

Theodor picked up his violin and tuned it. I watched him, thinking. How could one use a charm created by music? It couldn't, like my charms or the ancient Pellian tablets, be permanent, I guessed. I assumed it would accompany the music, fading away when the music did. At the same time, it might affect anyone who could hear, or even any space that the music filled, rather than my stable but localized charms. Could he infuse a whole military regiment with good luck, a whole hospital wing with good health? I wished ruefully that I knew more about the theory behind charm casting, for the first time actually agreeing with Pyord about something.

"What do I do first?" he asked. I stopped, stumped already. What did I do first, when I set about to charm cast? I sat quietly and gathered my equipment and my thoughts.

"Just...calm yourself."

"I thought I was calm," he said amiably.

"No, like clearing your mind. Or thinking only about what you're going to do next."

"Which is?"

"Good question," I said, unsure again. "When I sew, I start to stitch and kind of pull the light into what I'm doing."

"I do that by...what? Thinking happy thoughts?"

"Not really." I floundered. "It's more being aware that it's there. And..."

"Bending it to my will?" Theodor asked, laughing.

"Kind of," I admitted. "Look, just try playing something now that you're aware of what you can do. What you can see. Just notice when the sparks come through for you."

He picked up his bow and drew it deliberately across the strings. The sound was sweet and mellow, like a soft spring breeze instead of the winter wind raking ice across the window. He caught himself up in a melody, and as he drew out a particularly beautiful line of notes, a shroud of light appeared around his violin.

He was so shocked that he nearly dropped the instrument.

"Was there anything different about how you were playing then?" I asked hurriedly. "Anything you felt differently, anything you noticed?"

"Not particularly," he said, rubbing his thumb on the neck of the violin. "Just—this will sound stupid."

"No, it won't," I countered.

"It felt like I wasn't playing on my own anymore. That the melody had taken on a life of its own."

This surprised me. I always felt in control of my creations, like a dictator of needle, thread, and silk. But I was deliberate in how I worked—Theodor didn't know what he was doing.

"Try again," I insisted softly. "When you feel it, try to hold it, to keep it."

He nodded, determination overtaking his face, making his features look starker, older. The melody emerged again, and, sooner this time, light sparked around him. His brows constricted as he played, and the light grew. I felt warm and nearly weightless as the strains of music floated between us, comfortable and happy.

The light and the music faded together.

"I did it, didn't I?" Theodor smiled softly, and I felt the warmth of the music sloughing off me.

"You did," I said, surprised by the effects of his charms. "It's different from mine. I had no idea—"

"What did I do?"

"You tell me. What did you try to do?"

"I was just thinking about how happy I am...when I'm..." He blushed. "When I'm with you."

My lips parted. "That's what I felt," I said, "when you played. My charms are static—they just hang on a person in their clothes, surround them. But you made me feel what you intended."

"That hardly seems useful," he said, fiddling with his bow.

"Who cares about useful? It's fascinating!" I grinned. "And there may be more to it, who knows? Maybe it's a love spell of some kind, wrapped up in the music." I thought of the ballad seller—even if she didn't know what she was doing, surely her casting had the effect of a few extra coins in her pocket. Theodor's version of casting could be as useful as mine. "If only I knew more—but I think you might be able to charm a large space, or a whole group of people that way. Eventually. With practice," I teased.

"Today was a good start, though." He put the violin back into its case.

A porcelain clock on the mantel chimed. "It's that late? I have to get back to the shop—oh, Alice and Emmi will already be gone." Winter's early dusk pressed against the windows.

"I'll go with you," Theodor announced, mistaking my statement for worry about being alone rather than annoyance that there were tasks I knew my assistants hadn't known to finish.

"To a district of town full of Red Caps ready to hang a noble? Your father would box my ears. No, thank you."

"He'll only box mine," Theodor answered.

"Fine," I said, and let him call for the carriage. Ensconced in the privacy of the carriage, I leaned into him. It felt like stealing moments from the inevitable when I allowed myself to be happy with Theodor. The thick black of an early winter evening pressed against the windows. I sighed, content for a few short minutes.

"Wait," he said, his attention diverted to the street on his side of the carriage. We were on the same street as my shop—the same block, in fact.

"What is it?" I asked, watching the light from lanterns and torches bob past us. They coalesced in an undulating patch of light just ahead.

"I don't like to say 'mob,' but it seems to be a rather disorderly group of citizens," Theodor said.

He was right—as we approached the center of the well-lit mass, I could hear shouting and the strains of a song that I knew the revolutionaries had picked up as a makeshift anthem.

"We have to stop," I gasped when I saw where they were.

"Absolutely not," Theodor answered. "I've had fencing lessons and there's a pistol under the seat, but believe me, I'm no match for a mob."

"You just said 'mob,'" I said softly. "But Theodor—they're at my shop."

He pressed his face to the glass to confirm what I'd already seen—the mob was gathered around my stoop. Anger flared like wax poured on embers. They had made me compromise the most highly held of my values; they had stolen my brother from me—did they have to ruin my shop?

The carriage was forced to slow as we approached the group anyway, and I saw that the woman standing on my stoop and shouting was a stranger. There was something comforting in that—had Kristos been poised to ransack my store, it would have destroyed me. But the sight of this woman with a rock in her hand and pure hatred on her face just roused practical, pointed anger.

"Stop," I ordered Theodor.

"I'm not sure we have a choice." He watched the crowd with analytical intensity, then rapped on the roof of the carriage. We had already slowed to a crawl; now we halted.

Without giving myself time to think, I threw open the door and launched myself onto the cobblestones. The impact stung my feet, but I rushed to the front of my shop, throwing elbows when bulkish men didn't move.

I reached the base of the steps as the woman hurled the rock through the window. "This storefront is just one more way the nobles have infected even our common streets! We should tear it down, rock by rock!" I scrambled up the steps. If they knew that I was at the mercy of the nobility, too, that my shop had been closed because of my ties to the Red Caps, they had already forgotten or didn't care.

"Stop this!" I gasped.

"What for? This shop caters to the wealthy, to nobles and the elite who benefit from their rigged game. This shop is part of the rigged game," she added to shouts of acclamation from the crowd.

"This shop employs honest citizens." I caught her arm as she flung it back to throw another stone. "Would you take their livelihood from them?"

"And who are you to stop us?" she snarled at me and wrenched her hand from my grip.

Who was I? I was a seamstress. I was a charm caster. I worked for nobles, and the rabble assembled here could never have afforded my services. I choked.

I was also Kristos's sister.

I had to bank on the fact that they didn't know that I had renounced him and told him I never wanted to speak to him again.

"I'm Sophie Balstrade, and my brother is Kristos Balstrade. This is my shop. Please leave it alone." My voice rang out over the crowd, who had grown quiet while I'd scuffled with the woman.

She raised an eyebrow and laughed. "That so? If that's the truth, why aren't you on our side? Can't see the sister of the great Kristos Balstrade sitting idly by, sewing pretties for nobles. That is what you do here, isn't it? Sell yourself to them?" I heard several shouts of "whore" from the crowd. My shop was a tangible image of collaboration that they could burn like an effigy, and I was the symbol of everything wrong with the system they despised. "Raise yourself above the rest of us by clinging to *them*?"

"It's true," I said weakly. "I am Kristos's sister."

"I can vouch for that," a voice called from across the street. Theodor. He stood on the rail of the carriage, leaning out over the stones below.

"A noble!" someone cried.

"She was with him!" shouted another. I groaned— Theodor's presence was exactly what I didn't need. But still my heart swelled that he wanted to help me, protect me.

A rock, certainly intended for my store's windows, sailed instead toward Theodor. He ducked, and it collided with the paneling of the carriage, leaving a nasty gash across the wood. He retreated inside, and though the crowd shouted, black fear crept through me. I knew he'd reappear—and that he would have a pistol.

Foolish Theodor, I thought desperately. The single shot of that pistol might frighten a few of them, might distract them for a few moments, but it wouldn't dissipate the crowd. *Just drive*, I wished fervently. *Get away. Trust that they'll break more of my windows and ruin everything in my shop but leave me alone.* I was already banking on that hope.

On the fringes of the group, flickers of light caught my

attention. The torches were moving aside rapidly for a hooded man, his strides long and deliberate. My heart jumped.

Kristos.

He swung up beside me on the stoop of my shop, giving me one long look before throwing back his hood. His bold features caught the varying light of the torches in a dramatic pastiche of shadow and color, and his eyes rested on the carriage and Theodor emerging from the door only briefly before he began to speak.

"This is not the revolution we require!" he shouted. The crowd silenced themselves immediately, the hush so palpable that I thought I heard a hundred heartbeats, all at once. Then he continued. "Attacking our neighbors? Throwing rocks and hurling insults at those who make an honest living? Whether they sell to you or to nobles, their earning is honest—not like the nobility who live off our labor."

Shouts of affirmation followed Kristos's words, and I sank against the stone exterior of my shop. The woman who had thrown the rocks had slipped away as soon as Kristos appeared. I stared at my brother, seeing him for the first time as all of these people did. He was not my brother, not the child I had grown up with—he was a leader. Just like Pyord said, a natural leader. *What a great man he could have been*, I thought. In another place, another life—my breath caught. He was trying to create that place, that life, where he could be more than a dockworker, more than a day laborer. I had created it for myself with my skill and my shop—I was lucky. He wasn't—none of these people were. And so he carved the role of a leader for himself out of the bedrock of their need for change.

He was still speaking, and I looked out over the quiet crowd to Theodor. He had wisely tucked the pistol away, but he stayed firmly in the same spot. Unwilling to leave me.

I mouthed the word silently. "Go." He shook his head

slowly. I pressed my lips together, trying to dull the pounding of my beating heart in my ears.

"We should turn our attention where we can make an impact," Kristos was saying. "The nobility is our enemy, not one another."

My eyes widened. Kristos was looking straight across the street, practically daring Theodor to say something, to fight back, to run. I sank onto the cold stone, drawing my knees toward my chest like a frightened child.

The crowd sensed where my brother's eyes rested and turned to Theodor, too.

He didn't move. His thin jawline tilted upward, ever so slightly. My breath was ragged and audible, but Theodor inhaled and exhaled so calmly that he might have been sitting in Viola's salon or in his greenhouse.

Go, I begged silently. *Just go, get away now.*

Kristos glanced at me, eyes narrowing. He exhaled once, a huff of angry air, and raised his arm. I covered my face, terrified to see what he was about to order his people to do.

"Let's leave this place," he cried. "Tomorrow is the Midwinter Festival of Song. We've long planned to show our numbers at the cathedral when the nobles gather to sing away winter—they won't sing us away!"

Some in the crowd replied with shouts of affirmation, but most responded only with stony silence. "This is not how we earn the governance we deserve," Kristos continued. "Arson? Vandalism? We are not street criminals. We are revolutionaries, soldiers in an army of ideals. We will show our force tomorrow and convince the nobility to acquiesce to our demands, to call for truce before war begins. Blood need not stain these streets!" he shouted.

I looked up at him, and he gave me a long look that I couldn't quite read. Disappointment? Anger? Loss? All of these, or was it only that they were what I felt toward him? Then he swept away, pulling his cloak back over his features, obscuring himself even from me.

He strode up the street, toward the cafés and taverns, and the crowd followed him, dissipating so quickly that it was hard to tell what I'd been so terrified of until I saw the shattered pane of glass and imagined Theodor broken under their hands instead. I stumbled down the stairs, each step as unsure as a toddler's.

Theodor met me in the street and pulled me inside his carriage. He slumped against the corner.

"I'm sorry," he said. "I'm useless."

"No," I insisted. "You're not. That was a mob—there, I said it, too." Neither one of us was ready for humor.

"Do you think he meant it?" he asked after a long silence. "That we might still forestall open revolt?"

I hesitated. "Even if he did, just now…" I thought of Niko's determination and Pyord's careful calculations and knew, somehow, that the machine was already in motion, the gears wound too tightly to prevent them from springing forward.

"I'll never be the man your brother is," he finally replied.

"That," I said, my voice teeming with the anger I'd forced back until now, "is certainly true." Theodor's face met mine, shocked and hurt. I shook my head and explained, "He's an awful person. He *doesn't really care* about other people." I forced each syllable through clenched teeth. "He cares more about his ideals than his friends. Than his family."

"He saved you," Theodor said. "And, might I note, me."

"Yes. This time he did."

"When he speaks, others listen. He's made of something I'm not, crafted out of leadership when I'm merely born into it."

"But he's…" I wanted to tell Theodor everything—that

Kristos had forced me to betray myself, that he was complicit in a plot against the king. Instead, I choked my confession back and said only, "He's lied to me and hurt me."

"I know," Theodor said, even though he didn't know the depth of Kristos's betrayal. "Let me bring you to my home."

"It's not necessary. Just take me home."

"Not a chance—I'm not letting you stay alone tonight."

I agreed, defeated and exhausted.

41

THEODOR'S HOUSE WAS QUIET, THE CANDLES OUT, THE ONLY FIRE
still blazing the one in his bedchamber, so he took me there and
let me sit, shivering in front of the flames. "I—I'll wake the maid
and have her stoke a fire in the other bedroom," Theodor said. I
took his hand before he could open the door.

"Please—stay."

He sank beside me, sitting on the floor next to my chair. He
rested his head on my knee, and I found my fingers stroking his
honey-brown hair. "This will all be over soon," I whispered. It
was true—the Midwinter Ball was two nights away, and whatever plan Pyord had would begin. The waiting was worse, perhaps, than anything he had planned.

No, that wasn't true. Nothing would be worse than civil
war in the streets.

I pulled my hand back and closed my fist, letting my nails
dig into my palms. I should say something, tell Theodor. But
what could I say that didn't incriminate myself? What could I
say that wouldn't send my brother to the gallows? I couldn't do
that, even after what he'd done to me. I relaxed my hand.

Theodor took it in his. "I spoke to the king today," he said
quietly. "I didn't want to say anything earlier. I—I told him I

thought I had a better plan for my marriage than an alliance with another nation."

I looked down into his upturned face, the firelight playing games in the shadows it cast. "What plan is that?"

"An alliance with our own people."

I slid off the chair and knelt next to Theodor. "What do you mean?" I asked.

"I suggested that marrying a person without a title might assure our people that we truly do have the best interests of the entire country in mind. That we are not so insular. It's only one idea, of course—a wedding can't resolve a revolution. But he said he would consider it. It was part of a larger conversation— how to stop this insurrection before it escalates any further. That takes precedence, of course, over anything else."

I turned and looked into the hearth, at the coals radiating heat and the flames licking the logs. I knew from my charm casting that a little light could go a long way. It could even, perhaps, begin to mend the relationship between the nobility and the common people. "It's a lot to consider," I said. "For the king and for me." All of the fears I had held, for years, stitched tight to the idea of marriage itself, weren't resolved by marrying a noble instead of a commoner. Yet I was weary of being guided by fear—fear for my brother's life, fear for the coming revolt, fear for my own safety. Theodor was the only part of the patchwork of my life that seemed guided by hope instead of fear, light instead of dark.

Theodor gripped my hand. "I—I'm sorry. I should never have assumed."

"You had to assume a little," I said with a smile.

"I won't assume any longer," he said quietly, gathering me to him, wrapping my body in his arms. "I want you to tell me what you want."

I sank into him and traced his chin. Stubble had begun to soften the line of his jaw. His fingers—deft, deliberate fingers—waited expectantly at my waist. The hazel of his eyes brightened to green in the firelight, and I knew what I wanted. Desire bloomed thick and heady within me, and I took his face between my hands and kissed him.

"I want you," I whispered in his ear, kissing the soft space just behind it, delighting in the gasp it drew from Theodor. "I want you always."

He stood, pulling me up with him. "And I, the same." Carefully, methodically, he removed each of the pins that closed the front of my gown, lacing each sharp point back through the fabric, and then pulled the gown from my shoulders. I reached behind me to untie my petticoat, but he stayed my hand.

"I want to do it," he said, untying each skirt and gathering them in a bundle of silk and cotton. Then he found my staylace and slowly pulled it through each eyelet, his fingers tracing my back in the gap between the boned edges of my stays. The corset fell to the ground, still shaped like me. My shift drifted, translucent and unshaped, away from the curve of my body.

"I wanted to see all of you," he said. "Even though your clothes are so very much a part of you, I wanted you without them. With nothing between us, nothing brought in. Just two people," he said, dropping his ceremonial sword on the chair and shucking the coat with his family's device pinned to it.

"Everyone wears a shift and a shirt," I said, touched by the metaphor inherent in our clothes. "Noble and common alike."

"In that, we are all the same."

"Your linen is finer than mine," I whispered, taking his shirt ruffle between my fingers.

"Then let's take it off," he suggested, and pulled me into his bed.

42

—⁓—

AS IF IN DELIBERATE CONTRAST TO THE UPHEAVAL OF THE NIGHT before, the streets were quiet the next morning, as was the shop, giving me ample time to practice lifting curses. I had given my assistants the day off for the Festival of Song, as was customary for small shops like mine. Most of the city usually gathered in Fountain Square and on the broad avenues to "sing away winter," a custom so old no one remembered where it came from.

This year only a few carolers roamed the streets, their sparse numbers feeling all the shabbier given that no one was stopping to listen to them. Stubbornly, the nobles carried on with the liturgical service at the cathedral, despite the crowds of Red Caps I knew had gathered outside. No one interrupted me and my needle and thread as I worked and unworked curses past midday and into the afternoon. I grew more proficient, but it was still a slow task. I wasn't sure how long it would take, plucking the whole curse from the queen's shawl. Worse, I couldn't figure out a way to see the shawl. Midwinter Ball was the following night, and I would have wagered my shop that Pyord planned to attack the royal family there.

I had the key to removing the curse, but no way to fit it to the lock.

The door to the atelier banged open, and a gust of cold wind swept all the way into the back of the studio. I couldn't imagine what customer would visit any shop save a chocolate seller or confectioner while the Festival of Song was under way, but I was still surprised to see Jack Parry waiting for me in front of the doorway, his large frame ill at ease and his boots dripping icy water onto the floor.

"Jack," I said, edging against the counter. Why was he here? This couldn't be a mere social call, even if social calls were common at Midwinter. A dark thought crept into my mind like the cold draft snaking up my skirts—was he here on Pyord's orders, to silence me even as carolers passed by the window?

"I guess you're here alone?" he said.

My heart rising into my throat, I nodded. Lying could do me no favors now.

He relaxed slightly, and swept the red cap from his head. "Good. I wanted to talk to you without anyone overhearing. It's..." He strode toward me and threw his cap on the counter. I didn't move. "I wanted to warn you."

I sighed, my heartbeat slowing slightly. "I don't need the warning, Jack. I know what's coming. I know more than I want to. After all, you know what I did," I said, and he nodded, looking chagrined. "And I know about my brother," I continued, as calmly as I could. "What he did. Did you know?"

"Not at first. I know the whole mess now," he said, avoiding my searching look. "I guess that's part of why I'm here, too. I wanted to apologize. I wouldn't have gone along with that. Lying to you, making you use dark magic? I wouldn't have gone along with a few things, but they're past changing now." There was fear in Jack's voice, I realized. One of the leaders of the movement, afraid of what he'd done? "The revolt is under way. Not coming—it's started. Those Red Caps in the square—that's not a demonstration for anyone's benefit but our own, one last gathering before we strike."

"I thought that was what you wanted." I fought to keep my voice level. "I thought the idea was to strike quickly and force a compromise, to force your demands."

"It was, at first. But we disagreed, in the end. I was happy with compromise, with reforms, but Pyord convinced Niko and your brother that we need to start fresh. That reforming a broken system won't work, that the nobility can't be reasoned with. Pyord's lined up reinforcements because this won't end with what happens tomorrow. Midwinter will be the beginning, but it won't be the end."

"An extended revolt," I said.

"In the end, more like civil war. The Crown's soldiers against the people and the Kvys mercenaries we've hired. Might as well confirm that—your noble friends already assumed, didn't they?"

I nodded dumbly, finally finding words. "Troop movement at the border, yes—I don't know that they have any confirmation about what they're doing." I felt numb, and even the cold draft from the door, still ajar, didn't affect me. "And I thought a cursed shawl was frightening enough."

"Your part in the whole business is still true—that the curse and the attempt on the king's life go together, and that assassination will create chaos in the nobility. But Pyord's not talking about a coup made in one night. He's made sure that we'll have more troops at our disposal once more of the Crown soldiers show from the garrisons outside the city."

I could feel the warmth drain from the room and the blood from my face. "I suppose I should have guessed," I admitted. "That the idea of a coup alone was..."

"Idealistic?" Jack said with a snort. "If we're lucky, it will be over quickly, but I doubt we will be. It's too late to change anything about it, and maybe I wouldn't even if I could. Maybe Pyord and your brother are right—that there's only one real way to do this thing." There were dark circles under his eyes, I realized, creases in his forehead, a far cry from the confident man I'd argued with outside a tavern at the close of autumn. Short months separated the gentle arbitrator of tavern brawls I had known from a conflicted member of the revolt's leadership, someone who counted stockpiled weapons and ran some sort of rudimentary arithmetic pitting untrained dockworkers against the king's soldiers.

"Why are you telling me this, Jack?"

He squared his broad shoulders. "Like I said, I wanted to apologize. If I had known where Kristos was, that he was in on it with Pyord the whole time, I wouldn't have gone along with it."

My breath was shaky. "I'm glad you didn't know. You might not be alive if you'd argued."

Jack considered this. "I never cared much for Venko. He talked over my head, seemed to think he was better than us. But we needed him. Now he seems like maybe he doesn't need us."

"You may be right," I said. "I know it's too late to tell you to be careful, Jack. But take care of yourself as best you can."

"You, too, Sophie. There's still time to get out of the city. I thought maybe you should."

"As a general precaution or because I'm in some particular danger?"

He stared out the window, his eyes fixed on some far-off point. "It's pretty likely that the nobility, down to the most minor, will be targeted. I don't like it," he said quickly, as though pleading with the light snowfall outside the window. "That's . . .

that's more Niko's side of things, he's more of a strategist about the fighting itself and I'm just..." Jack brought his attention back inside, back to me. "And along with the nobles, anyone who sympathizes with them. Niko insists that once the dogs are out of the cage, they're going to bite anyone they think has beaten them."

"His words?"

"His words," Jack sighed. "I know you've got noble friends. If I was you...I would call in a favor and get outside the city, somewhere protected."

I wondered what it cost Jack, in pride, in lost hope, in sleepless nights, to come to me. "Thank you for warning me, Jack."

"It didn't seem right," he said. "The mob that showed up here—that wasn't right, either, and I had nothing to do with that. Niko's right that we can only do so much to control people once they've got a taste for revolt."

"I suppose that's true at this point," I said softly. It was too late to change the course that the Red Caps had chosen, but I couldn't help but wonder if, somewhere, sometime early in the germinating revolt, another path was available and ignored. Who was culpable if I traced back that far—those members of the Red Caps who steered toward violence, or the blithely ignorant nobility? Both, I acknowledged. And, I considered, those like me, too, who tried to force a changing world into a mold that it had overfilled already.

Jack cleared his throat and continued. "You might not be with us, but you've never been against us. If the Red Caps hold the city after tomorrow night, you'll be counted as an enemy because of your work, because of who you have lunch with. No one knows what you did for us."

I looked away. "Under duress, Jack. What I did under duress. Because it turns out no one can stay neutral in this, can they?"

"Just stay safe, then," he said. He reddened even more, bent down, and kissed my cheek. I let him.

"You too, Jack." He let in another bitterly cold gust of wind as he left.

A knot tightened in my stomach. I could leave the city. If keeping myself safe was the only thing that mattered, I could be on board the next ship out of the harbor, or hire a coach. Keeping myself safe, I admitted, had been my goal ever since discovering that Kristos was not only safe but never in danger to begin with. Now that I had stopped protecting him, what was I protecting? No longer any ideals or ethics, but myself.

Despite my efforts to learn how to undo a curse, I had no way to effect any real change in Pyord's plans. After all, how could I get into the palace, see the shawl, and undo my part in the plan without admitting my guilt? I had neither invitation nor entry to the Midwinter Ball or anything else in the palace. The knot grew larger, pulling more of me into its grip. If I confessed, I could be tried for treason and hanged. My shop, my trade, my craft—everything I had built, everything I staked my pride on—all gone in a moment.

Theodor claimed he loved me, but would he love me after he knew what I'd done?

If I didn't confess, the king and queen would very likely die, and perhaps others with them. And that was only the start—the revolution Pyord and Kristos imagined wouldn't stop at regicide, but would spread to the streets, to the citizens. What they called revolution would result in civil war, and not merely of common people against nobles and Crown soldiers as Jack had described. The split had been evident even in my shop—Penny supporting the advancement of new government at any cost, Alice resisting the violence and lawlessness that would surely accompany any coup.

And I believed I could stay neutral, I thought, sinking into the knot, letting it tie me up and force me to see the truth. I thought the worst was over, that I would have to carry the guilt over what I did, but that I could untie myself from the forces that were moving through the streets, the city, through all of Galitha. That I could survive unscathed. I couldn't. I had to decide now.

I wiped a tear off my cheek. I already knew what I had to do. It was a risk—there was no way to mitigate that any longer.

The door opened, softly, with a plaintive creak.

"Alice," I said, voice hollow.

"That was the worst Festival of Song I've ever been to," she said mildly. There was more, I knew. She was searching my face. "What's wrong?"

"Plenty," I answered. "Did you go to the square?"

"For a little while," she said, and hesitated. "It was overrun with Red Caps. More than I've ever seen—I mean, I didn't even know there were that many."

"They're growing an army," I said. Alice's eyes widened, but she didn't disagree.

"Sophie," Alice began, and then stopped.

"You saw Kristos?" I guessed.

She started. "Yes. So you knew—"

"I saw him, too. Twice."

"So it's true, that they held him in the Stone Castle? Did they make him write a false letter to you? How did—"

"No, none of it is true," I said. "It was a ruse the Red Caps created."

"Penny is with him."

I nodded. It didn't surprise me. "Alice," I said slowly, "I have to...there is business I have to attend to. If I am not back in a timely manner, I want you to...handle things here."

Alice's lips pursed as she considered this. "Why wouldn't you be back? Where are you going?"

"Not far," I said with a wan smile. "But if I am delayed or...Take care of the shop." I tossed Alice the key. Her cheeks blanched as she realized what I meant.

I plucked my cloak from the peg and left before she could decipher my meaning.

Then I went to Theodor and told him everything.

43

I GRIPPED MY HANDS TOGETHER IN MY LAP, WORRYING THE calluses worn into my fingers by the needle and scissors, willing Theodor to speak. To forgive me, to condemn me, to yell at me, to say anything.

"You should have come to me sooner," he finally said.

"I know," I said carefully. "But I—I was afraid."

"You should be," he snapped. I cringed but didn't allow myself to turn away. I deserved this.

"I was afraid for myself. I still am. But I was afraid for you, too."

Theodor paced to the other side of the room, a parlor in masculine deep gray as somber as our conversation. He leaned against the windowsill and stared through the glass as though he could see some answer on the street below.

Maybe I shouldn't have come, I thought with a shiver. *Maybe it's too late.*

No, I told myself forcefully, fighting the darkness rising in my thoughts, whorls like the dark sparkle I had seen in the curse. At this point pessimism was just as deadly as a curse, I reminded myself.

"I'm not here to confess for my own good, Theodor. I'm here to try to stop this." I hesitated before I spoke again, but what I was about to say was true. "I could have kept quiet. I could have slipped away and allowed all this to happen. But I'm not doing that. I'm here. So you have to listen to me."

"I listened!" Theodor turned back toward me with fire blooming in his hazel eyes. "But what are we supposed to do now? If I go to the Lord of Keys, you'll be arrested. And probably killed."

I realized what I'd asked Theodor to do, and tears sprang hot into my eyes. "Then do it. Or I will."

"No," he whispered, pacing back across the room. "No, don't ask me to do that. I..." He stopped in front of me, and my breath stilled when he looked at me. "I love you, Sophie. What I said last night—*I* should be furious that I said those things to you, that you were keeping this from me then, but I'm not." He pursed his lips. "I wouldn't ask you to condemn your own brother."

I wiped the tears from my cheek with the back of my hand. "And a lot of good that did."

"What now, then?"

"If the only way to stop this is to tell the Lord of Keys... well." I waited, watching hurt curl in his face, then pressed on. "We don't matter compared with the whole country, do we? I don't matter."

"Every person matters." His voice was flat. "Every person deserves a fair shot. I thought that was a central tenet of the revolutionaries."

I sighed. "I'm not with them. I never wanted to be."

Theodor softened. "I know. But we have to figure this out together, no involvement from anyone else." I began to argue, but Theodor shook his head. "It's the only way I'll even entertain this. So what do we do?"

I started with what we knew. "There's something planned for the ball," I reminded him. "An attempt on the king's life."

"What's planned?" Theodor asked. Understandable question.

"I don't know," I answered. For as closely tied as I was to the plot, there was plenty I had never been told. Plenty, I assumed, that most of the Red Caps hadn't even been told. "All I know is that Pyord was insistent that the queen wear the curse at the Midwinter Ball."

"So it could be an outright attack or he could be poisoning the soup," Theodor said, eyebrow raised. "There's no way to cancel the event without having you arrested by the Lord of Keys and on the gallows before you can say 'pass the salt.'"

I ignored the nausea that rose in my belly at this. "If I told the queen not to wear the shawl—"

"And then she'd know something was wrong with it, wouldn't she?"

I sighed. "Yes."

"And there would be an inquest, and like as not you're arrested, gallows, the whole bit. I can't let that happen," he said, pulling my hand into his and gripping it fiercely. "Is there anything else we could do?"

We—there was so much comfort in that word. I had felt so alone for weeks, forced into silence and secrecy. There was hope in having someone beside me. "I can undo curses. Remember, I said Nia had been killed because..." I couldn't finish. "But I learned from what she translated. If I can undo the curse on the shawl, the king and the royal family will have a much better chance," I said. "I can do it. If I am there."

Theodor nodded. "I can take you to the ball with me. That will help, won't it? If the curse is gone?"

"Yes," I said. I now had access to the lock with the key Nia had given me. "But it's more than that. If they're fomenting an entire revolt, how will we stand against that?"

"We rely on the soldiers. If it were only revolt, there would be no need to curse the king. An assassination removes the legitimate head of power."

"Creating a vacuum," I remembered. "The plan has to be twofold—an uprising and a direct attack on the king."

"And what do we do about the revolt?" Removing the curse could prevent, or at least diminish the chances of, regicide, but in the face of a Red Cap uprising I was completely powerless.

"No one has yet been able to ascertain the timing of any planned coup or uprising. That alone helps."

"And how do you explain how you came by that information?" I asked. "An informant happened to walk into your parlor and hand over the information, and no one asks you who?" I managed a wan smile.

"The Lord of Keys can be reasonable. You could come by that information far more innocently than planting a curse on the royal family." He pressed his lips together. "Though, in that case, how do we keep you safe? If Pyord has any hint that you've turned on him…"

I bit my lip. He was right—I was as good as dead if Pyord suspected treachery. Another body in the river, another victim of his revolution. A thought bloomed in my mind. "Arrest me."

"What?"

"Have me arrested. Publicly. If he thinks I'm in the Stone Castle, he won't be able to hurt me." I tried for a smile. "Being First Duke must have some privileges—I'm sure you can order the City Guard to arrest a simple seamstress for…well, make something up." I shrugged. "Maybe arson. Or counterfeiting coinage."

"Yes, that's almost believable," Theodor said with a soft smile. "Why can't we just arrest this Pyord and be done with it?"

"It's not only him. There's other leadership as well. I—" I stopped myself. Even now, I wouldn't give Jack's name. Or, even, Niko's. "The Red Cap network is so wide across the city—I think the plan may work even if he's not involved." The way Jack spoke, the trigger had already been pulled, and there was no unloading the rifle now.

Theodor nodded. "You're probably right. And the plot has to be attempted and fail, from a political perspective," he said. I watched him, curious what he'd say next. "The people want change, but I have a feeling many would be horrified by regicide and violent revolt. If it's attempted and does not succeed, many will turn against the rebels. Not to mention, our allies have to see us in a position of strength. Soundly defeating a revolt will do that. We have to be decisive and keep these…reinforcements from assisting the rebels. There's time to warn the fortresses just outside the city and that's about it."

He paused and toyed with the medal pinned to his coat, the family device etched in the gold under his thumbnail. "If we try this and fail—"

"I know." If we failed, either the rebels would succeed and Pyord would find and kill us both, or they would be defeated and I'd be tried for treason, likely with Theodor facing charges alongside me. "Last chance—you don't have to do this. You can go straight to the Lord of Keys with all of this."

"Even if I could live with myself knowing I'd had you hanged…" He shook his head. "No. This is better. If we can nip this revolt in the bud, it won't become the bloodbath it could be. And our best chance of doing that is to let Pyord believe he's succeeded and draw him out, defeat him soundly, and terrify the people enough with a taste of the violence he could have brought down on the country. Everything will be in place to do that."

"That almost sounds like it could work," I said.

"We can only hope," Theodor answered.

44

I HUDDLED IN THE CELL IN THE STONE CASTLE ON A THIN STRAW tick that smelled faintly of summer and strongly of mold. The guard, taking pity on a woman who didn't look like a hardened criminal, had clandestinely slipped me extra blankets. I wondered if they had been so kind to Penny, or if she, a political prisoner, had been treated less humanely. Even with the blankets, the cloying cool of the cell settled into my bones.

Hot humiliation countered the cold, however. For Pyord to believe I wasn't a threat, he had to know I'd been arrested. I was sure he had eyes all over the city, but I had to be sure the rumor would reach him quickly. So I had gone to the square, packed with Red Caps, and the City Guard had tracked me down, loudly. Once everyone in the square had managed to find a spot to gawk at my arrest, the soldiers dragged me off.

Possibly the most humiliating part of the whole affair was the false reason—an expired permit. I had always prided myself on my perfect record with paperwork, and had just stood in line for hours to renew all of my permits. Still, we had to select a reason for arrest that wouldn't alarm Pyord, and a bureaucratic blunder did the trick, and the arrest had to be loud and obvious. Moreover, the arrest of a common shop owner for a paperwork error, especially one who had already been maligned for ties to the rebellion, was sure to further inflame the Red Caps—they were more likely to use it as rhetoric than ask questions. And so Pyord was bound to hear, and soon, that Sophie Balstrade was held in the Stone Castle.

The squat stone building served as the city's guardhouse, barracks for the City Guard, and, carved into the bedrock below it, dungeons. I shivered—the cells beneath the ground were notoriously cold, hard places that no one escaped from. I wasn't trying to escape, but the thought of being locked up like a rat in a trap didn't sit well with me, either.

Only one day. *Nothing so bad I can't handle it for one day,* I thought to myself in a hollow attempt at reassurance. I could use the time to think through my plan and practice lifting curses.

Daylight had faded from the cell, however, and even I couldn't sew in the pitch black that descended into the room. I lay on the straw tick, bundling blankets around myself, fighting off dark thoughts, dangerous thoughts. That this was where I belonged, that I deserved nothing better than death for my involvement in Pyord's plans. My business was making charms, influencing fate. How much fate could one influence? I wondered. Could I have escaped this one? I doubted even one of my strongest charms could have changed this outcome.

As I lay there in the cold, listening to echoes in the stone halls, I remembered an old story my mother told Kristos and me when we were little. I remembered the scent of harbor drifting into the window of the flat our little family used to rent, and tried to ignore the musty air and foul wafts from other cells that assaulted me. She liked to tell stories, my mother—stories she said her mother had told her. This one was about three sisters, the most powerful charm casters who ever lived. They lived in a shack by the seaside, my mother said, and would cast a charm in spun wool for anyone who came to them, free of charge. But their charms were so strong that they angered the gods—this was a very old story, she always stopped to remind us, when the people believed in many gods—and one day the god of the sea sent a great tempest to sweep their shack out into the waves.

This seemed unjust to the goddess of spinning and weaving, however, and she caught them up, all three, and gave them a job to do in her own house. The eldest spun the wool of every man and woman's life into thread. The middle sister wove it together with others' lives, creating a web of connections, one person to another. And the youngest, when a person's life was done, cut the thread.

I always shuddered a little at that line of Mother's story—the part where she would bring her fingers together like scissors, snapping them shut in a decisive metaphor for death. But it was only a story, a version of the world in which Fate determined everything. There was a contradiction in the story itself, because the women were charm casters, influencing fate before they became Fate. Surely our destiny wasn't predetermined by three women spinning and weaving, or by anything else.

I fell asleep and dreamt of drop spindles making thread out of liquid light and sparkling dark, looms spread with charmed tapestries, half-finished, and a devilish Pyord sneaking beneath it, snipping threads with golden scissors.

With the first light that crept through the slits set high into the wall that served in place of windows, I took up my needle and began to work. I had my sewing kit in my pocket and no one had thought to take it from me. So I practiced. I stitched curses and charms into the scraps of fabric I had been given, and then undid them, over and over again. At first, dark smudges and stains of light remained on the fabric. As I practiced, I removed more and more of the curses, and charms were unbound from the fabric and disappeared.

My speed improved as well, but I hoped it would be quick enough to undo the thousands of stitches I had worked into the queen's shawl. When I considered the hours of work creating the curse had taken, and considered that I would be lucky to have ten minutes to work at the ball, I felt queasy.

Food arrived three times—a stale roll for breakfast, a thin soup and another stale roll at midday, and a stale roll with dried beef for supper. I wondered if the jailer had some kind of agreement to buy stale bread from a local baker.

The light had faded from my cell when Theodor opened my door. He wore a dark greatcoat, as though this would disguise his identity from anyone who intercepted us. This seemed unlikely, however; the corridor was empty, and all the other cell doors were firmly closed and bolted. I wanted, more than anything, to kiss him, to feel some warmth come back into me after the long darkness of the cold night alone. But there was no time, and Theodor couldn't be seen in these halls allowing me to escape after orchestrating my arrest the day before.

"This way," he said in a low voice.

He led me down the narrow hallway, lined with cells. They were full, mostly with more than one inmate in each iron-barred room. "All right. What I'm about to show you is a secret—most nobles don't even know about it. There are several tunnels and hidden passages in the Stone Castle that lead into the streets."

"To make jailbreaks easier?" I asked.

"To make assembling and forming outside easier for the soldiers quartered here." Of course—the top floors of the Stone Castle were soldiers' barracks, usually housing only City Guard but now filled with regulars, riflemen, and grenadiers, with even more encamped outside. Theodor opened a door and led me into a narrow hallway. "Privilege of being the son of the current heir to the throne—I get my own set of keys to this place."

He led me down a winding hall that ended with another door. This one was locked, and he fished a minute silver key from his ring. The lock clinked open.

"You'll come out of a small doorway at the edge of River Street," he said, and handed me the key. "You'll need this—the door is locked. Make sure no one sees you."

"Believe me—I will."

"I have to hurry—the Lord of Keys called several of us to meet with him before the ball. He's taking your suggestion that the clock strikes for the coup at Midwinter quite seriously." He grinned and gripped my arm. "This is going to work, Sophie. We'll get through this."

He hesitated and looked down the empty hallway, then ducked his head and brushed my lips with his. I caught his warm hand with my freezing fingers and pulled him closer. "Good luck," he whispered, and then he closed the door behind me.

I ran—or, rather, trotted, for the corridor was narrow and rutted—until I reached the door at the other end. I cracked it open, ascertained that the street was clear, and slipped out onto the cobblestones.

Now to get myself to a royal ball.

There was, of course, one problem. I didn't have a gown. I almost laughed at the dismal absurdity of it—a seamstress, unable to go to the ball because she didn't have a dress. I had a nice gown, of course, the one I had worn for dinner at Theodor's, the pretty blue silk I pulled out for weddings and parties. It was a nice dress. But it wasn't a court gown.

I was going to have to break one of my rules—never, ever using client commissions for personal use. Because Madame Pliny and I shared fairly close dimensions, and her court gown stood finished in a corner of the atelier, waiting on a mannequin for a few final sequins to be added.

No time for that. I slipped through back alleys to my shop, fished a key from my pocket, and dashed inside. I carefully pulled the gown from the form, its cream silk shimmering in the lamplight, the pale pink flowers I'd carefully embroidered with their gold sequin centers spreading under my hands like a bouquet. *Like rose balsam*, I thought with a faint smile. Thank heavens she didn't need it until spring—and that she was wintering in the south and wouldn't be at the Midwinter Ball to see me arrive in her gown.

"What are you doing?" I started and nearly knocked the mannequin over, but the voice was just Penny's. She watched me with saucer eyes. "I thought someone might be here even though it's Midwinter." Someone—not me, not while I was locked in the Stone Castle. She had hoped to catch Alice or Emmi and avoid speaking to me again. I didn't blame her.

"I just came for my pay," she continued. She could scarce afford not to collect the wages I owed her—with winter approaching, I wondered what she intended to do for work. Few shops were hiring anyone, save day laborers, and those wages would never come close to what she had earned with me. I thought for the briefest moment about offering her job back to her, but she stared at me with such frozen dismissal in her deep blue eyes that I refrained. "And I'll leave my key," she added, as if it were the final punctuation to any question I might have raised, any proposal I might have made.

I reached under the counter and found the silk bag I'd sewn for her, charmed with wealth and luck, to put her final wages in. I handed it to her, fully aware that her eyes were on the swish and drape of the court gown's silk rather than her pay. "I'm—it's too much to explain, Penny. Don't tell anyone I was here. Not even Kristos." Panic edged my voice—all our plans came down to Penny keeping her mouth shut.

"Why are you taking the gown?"

Please, Penny, I begged silently. *Please have enough leftover loyalty to me not to say anything to my brother. Please.*

"Because I need a court gown and I don't have one."

She eyed me warily. "You were arrested, and now you need a court gown?"

"Yes." That was the plain truth of it. I didn't have time to argue. "Please, Penny. Keep to yourself tonight. Keep off the streets. Stay here if you want to."

"You're going to the ball," she guessed.

"Yes. Please, Penny—just don't tell anyone."

She nodded. "All right." She understood. I hoped she understood.

"Thank you," I said. She tucked the bag with her pay under her cloak and left, the door banging a hollow farewell behind her.

I was breaking yet another of my personal rules by wearing a charm, as well, but I was faintly grateful. I could use the good luck imbued in the embroidered flowers. I set the gown gently on a worktable and then wrestled the cage worn under the skirts from the mannequin. I gathered the whole mess in my arms and bolted out the door.

I would have looked ridiculous, shoes clattering on cobblestones, wire skirt supports bobbing in the wind, and supple cream silk waving like a flag, but I kept to back alleys and side streets to avoid anyone seeing me. I couldn't afford to have Pyord hear that I was freed now. I careened into Theodor's courtyard, winded and my hair a mess, and after a moment's hesitation, pounded on the peacock-blue door.

I shouldn't have been surprised that he answered himself. "I made it in time, didn't I?"

"Indeed you did." Theodor found my hand in the pile of pale silk and squeezed it. "I suppose you need to change."

I nodded and pushed past him through the door, the skirt supports pinging faintly as they caught on the hinges and sprang loose again. Theodor backed away with an amused look, letting me wrestle myself into the front hallway.

"Are you all right? I can hardly forgive myself for making you stay in that place last night," he said, ushering me to a small parlor. I threw the skirt support on an ottoman and carefully laid the dress on the settee.

"It wasn't someplace I want to visit again soon," I said, still breathless. My ribs pressed against my corset. I was acutely aware for the first time how much sweat was dripping down my back. "But it's over."

"And you'd rather not discuss it," Theodor supplied.

"Precisely." I waited. "Theodor, I need to change. Without an audience." The underpinnings and lacings of the court gown were complex enough without attempting a conversation at the same time.

He glanced at the bloated pile of silk encroaching on his furniture. "Of course. Lend you a maid?"

"Fine."

Dressing for a royal ball, in a sumptuous silk gown, should have been an event unto itself, but I didn't have time for niceties. I had my jacket off and the wire support fastened before the flustered maid Theodor hustled into the room even arrived. Her apron was crisscrossed with gravy stains and she smelled, faintly, of onion. He had clearly pulled her from duty in the scullery. She helped me into the full skirt, then laced the back of the gown's bodice without speaking. I could feel her hands shaking as she threaded the bodkin through the eyelets. I willed her to work faster.

"Miss?" she whispered as I adjusted the sleeves. Madame Pliny was narrower in the shoulders than I—the fit wasn't perfect. Only a seamstress would notice or care so much, I chided myself. But the shoulders drooped lower than I would have liked.

"It will have to do," I said firmly.

"But, miss—it's quite disarrayed," the maid said. I was ready to argue, when she added, "Your hair. I can dress it quite quickly if—"

"Yes, quickly." My heart beat against the tight boned bodice. Quickly was important. But she was right. I couldn't very well march into a royal ball looking like I'd had my hair dressed with a rake.

She hurried out, a slim little blur of gray wool and white apron, and returned promptly with several wool rollers stuffed fat with batting and a large sheet. "Where did you find those?" I asked. I didn't imagine that Theodor dressed his hair in anything other than a simple queue.

"They're mine," she replied, threw the sheet over my shoulders to protect the gown, and set to work.

"I'll be sure they're returned," I said, then my mouth fell open while I watched her work in the small mirror hanging over the fireplace. She mercilessly combed the tangles from my hair, dosed my hair with sweet-scented pomade and powder, and then rolled sections onto the wool pieces, creating the towering hairstyle favored in court.

"I don't suppose you have anything to put in it," she said, pinning a curl into place. "Jewelry or a ribbon or—"

"How about flowers?" Theodor stood in the doorway, smiling softly. He held a bunch of rose balsam in his hand. "I saw that the gown had pink flowers, and these were in the dining room, doing nothing but dying."

"Perfect," I said.

"Flowers aren't really fashionable this time of year—"

the maid began, then flushed fuchsia and fetched them from Theodor.

"Are you a scullery maid or a hairstylist?" I asked with a small laugh. She was right—fresh flowers were considered a bit pastoral and simple for a winter formal ball.

"Just a scullery maid, but maybe someday, a hairstylist," she said. She knew her aspirational trade well. She pinned blossoms at precise spots to highlight the sculptural shapes my hair created. The rose balsam matched the embroidered flowers precisely, as though I had known when I stitched them to blend the colors and form the leaves just so.

"You're ready?" Theodor asked. I stood in front of the tiny mirror, craning my neck to see all the angles of the gown. I couldn't quite get a full picture.

"I think so," I said, adding, "and thank you," to the scullery maid who was already disappearing down the hall.

"You are," he confirmed, taking my hand in his and turning me slowly. "You look a vision." I could have brushed off his words, but his face, faintly stunned and smiling like an idiot, told me his compliments were not exaggerated.

"Then we should hurry," I said, leaving my gaol-stained clothes on the ottoman and wrapping myself in my cloak, which was still in the hall where I had dropped it.

Theodor's carriage was waiting, the horses dancing with excitement, their coats gleaming. I gulped—arranging a draped skirt like the one I was wearing on a mannequin was one thing, but avoiding rumpling it in a carriage's narrow seats? I sat as gracefully as possible, mindful of the silk, but the frame underneath pinched my thighs. I had made a fair number of court gowns over the years, but I had never worn one. I wondered if there was some trick to moving and sitting in them, or if the women who wore them simply got used to being uncomfortable.

"What next?" Theodor said, his singular focus homing in on the task ahead of us. I caught his hand in mine. Seeing the little wrinkle form between his eyes—it was as though he were scrutinizing a bed of flowers or playing his violin, not about to stop an assassination attempt. And I loved that about him.

"I have to undo the curse." I ticked off what we knew like items on a list. "If anything bad happens at the ball, it will affect her. And, by extension, her husband. Pyord's real target." Like the charmed caps I had made for my brother would offer some protection to those near the wearer, the cursed shawl would bleed onto the king seated next to the queen, drawing darkness toward him.

"As a mere point of clarification—anything? Like if there are bad prawns, she'll get sick?"

I hadn't thought of it this way before, but Theodor was right. "Yes. Anything—the assassination attempt or just chance."

"Whatever he's planning, it can't be precise enough that he felt comfortable without your curse as a safety net." Theodor stopped and thought for a moment. "So we need to be prepared for quite a few possibilities. Bad prawns notwithstanding."

"Exactly. I need to pull the curse off the shawl." I heaved a deep breath. "And that's where I need your help."

"Anything."

"First, when and where. I haven't ever been to a formal ball, you know. You're going to have to guide me—where I can sneak off to work the reversal, when it wouldn't be noticed."

"During the meal, most certainly. The king and queen will be presented, along with the entire royal family, just before the meal begins. The king and queen will sit on a dais in the center of the room for the duration of dinner."

"How long is dinner?" I chewed my lip. The longer the better.

"Probably four or six courses—not terribly long."

"That sounds like an eternity," I replied.

"Not compared to state dinners and wedding feasts. Twelve, fourteen courses—land sakes, you get sick of food." Theodor stopped himself. "Sometimes I can see why the revolutionaries want us dead," he added ruefully.

"But four to six courses—what, an hour? Two?"

"Perhaps two for us, less for the royal family. They'll be served first, while we wait."

"And when they're finished—"

"They might leave the dais."

"And I'll lose my work. So I need to finish during the dinner, while the queen is in full view of me. Where?"

"That we'll have to figure out when we get there."

45

---∿---

I WAS NEARLY SHAKING WITH ANTICIPATION BY THE TIME WE reached the palace. It was a strange experience being brought to the front entrance in a carriage instead of directed around back by the guards, and to ascend the wide stairs rather than be let in at the servants' entrance by the housekeeper. I wasn't here as a guest, I reminded myself—I was here to undo what I'd done and try to save the king. A man, I realized, I had never met, only seen from afar at public events. A figurehead in a golden crown presiding over festivals and New Year's celebrations at the cathedral. The profile on the coins I used to buy biscuits and bolts of cloth. A person so distant I hardly thought of him as a person— until I had met Annette and Mimi and understood him not only as king but also as a father and husband.

Still, the scene inside the courtyard within the palace walls nearly took my breath away. It trickled to a thin white stream in the air. Ice sculptures, some twice as tall as me, populated the interior courtyard. A trio of half-translucent ice women in ancient dress danced around frost-dusted flowers; a pair of frost-lions wrestled on the flagstones; a unicorn dipped its horn into a frozen pool. Anchoring the scene was a frozen fountain, the ice rivulets mimicking flowing water carved all over with flowers as though it were spring in the middle of winter.

White paper lanterns hung on crisscrossed lines across the courtyard, plain candles suspended in each, and the trees edging the grounds were draped in sheer white net with silver spangles, to catch and reflect the light.

"Is it like this every year?" I whispered.

Theodor took a tighter hold on my arm. "Yes, but it's never been so beautiful."

Inside, footmen took our cloaks and escorted us to our table. Quietly, hastily, they added a plate for me, apologizing for the inconvenience. I flushed red—I knew full well that the mistake was not theirs—there was no lost response indicating that the First Duke of Westland was bringing a guest.

Our table was toward the back of the ballroom, and I quickly spotted an entrance used by the servants and flanked, mercifully, by a large pair of statues. The corner behind one huge statue dipped away into an obsolete shadow. There was a clear line of sight from the hidden corner to the dais where the royal family would sit. I nudged Theodor and pointed toward it. "I can lift the curse from there," I whispered in his ear in answer to his questioning look. I smiled—this plan could work. I was finally confident that it would work. It had to.

I watched as Viola arrived, and others I knew from her salon. She saw me across the ballroom, and grinned as she recognized me. Others, perhaps, would not be so amenable to a common seamstress accompanying the second heir to the throne to a royal celebration, but I felt somewhat comforted that Viola was, at the least, amused rather than scandalized. Our table was populated with lesser nobility—first dukes and duchesses like Theodor, the sons and daughters of the dukes and duchesses who sat nearer the dais in the center of the room, and counts and countesses. I tried to listen and smile and attempt, fairly successfully, to dodge questions about myself.

Still, I heard some nasty comments. The nobility all knew one another, and we had failed to create a backstory explaining my presence. "One of the First Duke's playthings," someone whispered snidely at a nearby table. "Would think he'd know better than to bring such people here," another whispered in answer.

Normally, this would have stung, but tonight I didn't care. I wasn't here trying to horn in on the nobility, usurping a place for myself at their ball. I wasn't even concerned with Theodor's clearly controversial suggestion that a marriage to a common woman was possible and perhaps even favorable. I lifted my chin and let Theodor slip his hand through mine under the table. Probably a horrible breach of etiquette—I smiled to myself—but I was grateful for the reassurance of his touch.

Instead of talking to my tablemates, I looked around the room, especially at the dome above me. I probably looked like a poor country relation, gaping about the ballroom, but I wanted to see if I could spot any hint of Pyord's plans in action. The dome was enormous, white stone arching to a center point of windows where I could just glimpse the winking light of stars outside. The ballroom was beautiful—and looked completely safe. The single entrance to the ballroom—the grand staircase I had seen on my first visit to the palace—was guarded by dozens of soldiers, and I knew that more were stationed outside. Poison was still a possibility, but I wondered how possible it was to infiltrate the royal kitchens. I sighed. There was no way to guess what might happen. I had a single job to do, and that was pulling the curse off the queen.

A bright fanfare, and the king and queen arrived, ascending the wide steps of the dais to join the courtiers they had selected to sit with them. I could see the curse in the queen's shawl glinting like crystallized night. Princess Annette, in the icy blue court gown my atelier had crafted, herded two younger children—the Princesses Beatrix and Odessa—in front of her, both wearing sweet and completely impractical white silk gowns. I bit my lips—I had expected Annette to be here, but not the two children. I wished, fervently, that they were wearing the charmed shifts I had made. Likely they believed they were. Before I could panic at the thought of children being killed by Pyord's plan, a nursemaid appeared and hustled both girls off to bed.

I breathed relief, but it was short-lived. The black sparkle seemed to emanate off the queen, gathering her husband and daughter and the courtiers nearest to her in a dark cloud.

I couldn't attempt to draw the curse sitting at the table, and fortunately no one questioned my leaving. I slipped away to the corner behind the statue, the hiding place I'd picked earlier. The statues were bronze centaurs; they trained their metal eyes toward the ballroom as though guarding me from prying eyes. The light danced between molded flanks and immobilized tails.

I focused on the darkness in the queen's wrap, on one stitch. She moved, and I lost my mental hold on it. I blinked and found another stitch, picking it apart with my thoughts, plucking it from the moorings of fabric that held it to the queen. She laughed, oblivious to the danger she was shrouding herself in.

I took a steadying breath, trying to focus not on the entire mass of darkness woven into the shawl, but on one stitch—just one first. The weight of what I had done, and of all the plans Pyord could have in place, crowded my thoughts. I glanced back at Theodor, sitting stiffly at our table, trying to have a polite conversation with the gentleman to his left. If assassination succeeded tonight, who knew what danger Theodor was in? His position as an heir, so long a distant possibility with a young and healthy king whose daughter was ready to marry and have children in the king's line, would be suddenly not only very present but very dangerous. The gaping pit of worry in my stomach began to contract around that one thought.

No, I reminded myself. One thread at a time, one countermove to Pyord at a time. Pulling the curse from the shawl was my only concern right now. I finally tugged the first stitch loose, and a thread of dark hung in the air above her. I was already exhausted, and feared the process of picking the rest of the curse free, but I found that the next stitches came loose far more easily, and then the entire dark line unraveled at once and hung in the air above her. I exhaled, a short burst of triumph, and kept spooling the curse out from the fabric.

Then the queen stood up and clapped her hands. I almost reeled back in surprise. The dark line crept back toward the shawl. It wanted to stay embedded in the fabric. I recalled the stains of curse and charm I had left on my first practice removals. Panicking, I started to pull back on the charm, but it was like wrangling a living thing, a snake that writhed every inch of itself at once, worming itself back into the cloth.

In a rush, I thought of something I hadn't tried before. Imagining, as foolish as it seemed, a giant pair of scissors above the dark line, I drew the line taut and severed it. The darkness I had pulled recoiled back up into the air above the queen. I breathed, slowly, deliberately, and began again. One stitch. I tried to ignore the servants ferrying trays to the tables, the clearing of empty dishes that marked the swift passage of the time I had to work. I repeated the process with each string of black sparkle, each line of stitches I'd worked into the shawl. The loose cloud grew larger until all the darkness had been plucked and unraveled from the shawl.

Now what? The curse hovered above the dais, winking like

splinters of dark jewels. I had to dissipate it, but it was too far away. Even though I waved my hands wildly, it barely fluttered. I tugged the darkness, drawing it toward me. It slowly edged toward me, and I tugged more.

The darkness moved more quickly. It roiled like waves over-taking each other on the shore and crested toward me. I swirled my hand and the wave nearest to me faded slightly, its edges blurring. It was coming too fast. The dark began to roll toward me, plummeting quickly downward.

I coughed a ragged breath, still trying to diffuse the dark-ness, and in my other hand, gathered a tiny net of light, weaving it between my fingers. Maybe I could catch it or stall it. Maybe.

It collided with me, the net in my hand insufficient to hold it. The glittering dark ballooned around me, and with a dim awareness of roaring in my ears and utter blindness, I collapsed.

46

"SOPHIE!" THE ROARING IN MY EARS WAS DISPLACED BY A SINGLE voice, repeating my name over and over. I wallowed in blackness, groping for something familiar, something to hold on to. That voice was familiar. "Sophie!"

I forced my eyes open, leaving the darkness and seeing instead a face, very close to mine, hazel eyes wide with concerned fear. Theodor.

I remembered in a rush where I was—still hidden behind the centaur statue, his wide flank shielding us from the ballroom beyond. The shawl, the carefully unpicked curse, the cloud of darkness. I sat up through a wave of vertigo and scanned the room. No dark glitter remained—it had dissipated. I breathed relief.

"It's gone. It's done. I did it," I whispered.

"You're all right?" Theodor asked.

"What?" I glanced down at myself. I looked no worse for the wear, aside from a few fresh wrinkles in the cream silk gown. "I suppose so."

"Thank heaven—I saw it, Sophie. I saw that black thing— like the light from the violin in reverse. I thought for sure you must have been—"

"I wasn't." I gathered myself and stood, shakily. "I couldn't control it and it…" The room tipped and wobbled, and my legs felt like a pudding that hadn't set properly. "I feel a little woozy, though."

"No wonder." Theodor looked around. "What now? Just go back to our seats?"

"I hadn't thought that part out," I said. "Anything else would be suspicious, wouldn't it?"

"We'll give you another minute to recoup," Theodor said, and I couldn't argue.

I leaned against him, flexing my hands to take the numb buzzing sensation, blinking to regain my focus. I gazed up at the dome. I could see where it had been recently repaired, lighter colored new mortar bisecting huge chiseled rock. Square panes of stained glass created a ring of windows in the dome itself. The moon was pure and full outside, and I saw the stars winking through the glass, alongside fluttering wings. I squinted. There were birds outside, too—fluttering past the windows. Scrabbling claws licked the glass and wings silhouetted in black against the windows.

And a figure that looked very much like a man, crouched away from the crows.

"Theodor," I said, pointing with a shaking hand. He followed my outstretched finger.

"I see him," he said.

I looked again at the new masonry. Fine particles of dust hovered against the new mortar, and I thought I could see cracks forming. I wanted to believe it was just my light-headed eyes and brain seeing things that weren't there, but a dark thought seized me. "Are there any points of entry in the dome?"

"I don't think so. I mean, royal architecture can be eccentric, but I've never—" He glanced again at the dark figure on the other side of the stained glass. A few crows flew away, and I noticed another pair of dark figures.

My mouth was dry, and the words scratched it as I spoke. "Theodor, it was repaired recently." I pointed to the new mortar, recalling Viola's joke about the palace needing a construction permit with an empty satisfaction of finally piecing together the whole puzzle. "What if—what if they did something to the dome? A fault in the dome? Some entry point? It wouldn't be hard, for a Red Cap to be on the masonry crew."

Theodor's face whitened and he looked as ill as I felt. "You think that this could be it—invading the ballroom through the dome could be his plan?"

Suddenly I heard a distinct cracking noise, even over the noise of conversation and music. Some of the guests had heard it, too—they looked up from their plates of roasted pheasant and chestnuts, looking from the birds on their plates to the cacophony of live birds above.

The mortar around a pane of glass trembled, the garnet-red glass shivering for a moment in the starlight before it plummeted to the floor below, shattering into blood-colored shards on the stone.

Birds plummeted with the debris, saving themselves at the last moment by spreading their wings and swooping over the tables. Winter crows—they migrated to the city from fall until late spring, badgering each other all day in small flocks, gathering in the late evening in larger night roosts.

I stood as though rooted on the spot, watching as one of the figures leaned into light. He was dressed in a dark jacket and trousers, cut slim, a brace of pistols slung across his chest. Another pane of glass trembled. The mortar was faulty, I realized, strong enough to hold the glass until someone tested it, and then it would collapse. Amethyst glass plummeted and shattered on a table, sending splinters into plates, goblets, and shocked faces.

Panic flared in the ballroom as the assembled crowd of nobles realized that something was amiss. A tide of silks and velvets rushed toward double doors that blocked the staircase, the only exist, from view. I wondered what they thought—did they know this was a grand-scale assassination plot? Women stumbled on overturned chairs in their delicate slippers, and men tried in vain to shove tables out of the way to make room. Family crests winked through the dust as guests ran, and shouts and screams punctuated the chaos. I saw a group of women cluster underneath a table.

As the glass gave way, I assumed that the failures in the dome were focused on those brilliantly colored panes, that the open holes where the windows had been provided the entry point that the assassins needed. A crash of sapphire and gold glass, however, was accompanied by a deeper cracking, a grating that set my teeth on edge and made me shudder.

A section of the dome itself was disintegrating, the mortar that bound the stones together developing myriad spreading veins in mere seconds. The pale stone trembled and, in a rush, fell into the far end of the ballroom.

I choked on a scream as I saw, in the cloud of dust, silk and velvets and, nauseatingly, what I realized were limbs, tangled in the broken mass of stone.

The reason for the collapse was soon apparent. The occupants of the ballroom had been moving toward the sole exit point, the king among them. Now there was no way out.

The panic was palpable. The crowd nearest the stones clawed at them, heaving them out of the way in an effort to clear the exit. The King's Guard, positioned around the room, wavered. "Get to the king!" Theodor shouted at the nearest pair of guards. They bolted into action. My heart thudded in my throat as Theodor pressed me to the ground. "There's nothing you can do," he said. "Stay down and stay safe."

I spotted the abandoned musicians' corner, the music stands and instruments left behind. A violin sat ajar in its case. I pushed Theodor aside and ran toward it, shoving ladies in bejeweled gowns and men in richly embroidered suits as I ran. The fabrics, silk and velvet and brocade, were like a puddle of spilled paint to me, running together and blocking my way. I dodged a shower of mortar and pebbles that peppered my hair, but I reached the musicians' risers. The violin. I nabbed it and the bow and turned back toward Theodor.

I shook my hemline free from the corner of a music stand just as a pane of emerald glass fell inches from me. I traced the embroidered flowers on the gown, imbued with charms, feeling oddly euphoric and empty at the same time.

I dashed back to Theodor.

"Play," I said, forcing the violin into his hands.

"What?"

"Play a charm. A protection charm."

"I don't know if I can—"

"You don't have a choice," I answered.

He lifted the violin from the case with absurd care, given the circumstances, and began to tune it.

"Are you insane?" I handed him the bow. "Just play. The music is a vehicle for the charm—it doesn't have to be perfect."

"What do I do?"

I wished we had taken more time to practice, but at least he had managed to sustain one charm. "Think about safety, about life. Put those thoughts into the music. Just try," I begged.

The figures in black above us had shifted their positions,

clearing the glass and the remains of the windowpanes. They were repositioning to get a clear shot, I saw with dark understanding of the entire plot. The assassins couldn't be guaranteed a clear shot at the king, or that their pistols would fire true to aim, but with a curse sitting right next to the king, it would draw ill fortune to him, and with it, the assassin's bullets. The first drew his pistol.

Theodor began to play, a delicate melody like a cathedral hymn. It was a hymn, I realized—a hymn for New Year in spring. Familiar and gentle—it even felt like safety. The charm bloomed around the bow as he played.

The first pistol shot rang out, briefly silencing the room before fear took over again. Theodor faltered, and the white light flashed out. A trio of noblemen ran past, giving Theodor a strange look. He must look like a madman, drawing music from the violin while the roof collapsed around us. I pulled his arm and made him face me.

"Try again," I said. "It's working."

He resumed the melody and the charm.

A tenuous string of light expanded out into a soft wave. The undulating cloud hovered above Theodor's head, growing as the melody grew, and I reached out with my thoughts and captured a strand. I imagined one hand holding it firmly, and then caught another strand.

In my mind's eye, they tugged and pulled and danced beside one another, alive and unused to being constrained. I concentrated as hard as I could, and drew them together, tying them into a knot.

It held. I wove them quickly, pulling more strands into the web I created as Theodor played. I pushed the woven end away from us, casting the net over the staircase. As if testing my ability, another shot rang out. It ricocheted above the golden canopy, chipping stone and shattering glass high above us. I couldn't be sure—perhaps the charm net had prevented the shots from passing through, but more likely the charm for safety had countered the assassin's aim. I kept weaving. The king and queen stood surrounded by more guards—though what the guards expected to do against shots fired from above, I didn't know. I could protect them better than a guard, I thought grimly, casting the net Theodor and I made wider and wider. Swiftly, I covered the king and his family, and the guards around them.

Two more shots rang out. I risked a glance upward, even though my concentration was wavering as it was. One of the men had disappeared, and the second followed him. I heard a telltale scrabbling on the roof that told me they were descending quickly. A throng of nobles in court dress crowded the fringes of the room and pressed against the blocked doors. Several watched Theodor, the violin's high notes piercing even the shouts and clamor. I didn't have time to wonder what they might think of us. Some of the guards had begun to attack the rubble, too, clearing it more quickly. I covered more and more of the ballroom with the net Theodor and I wove together, edging the perimeter where most of the nobles stood.

I glanced up again as the final assassin readied his pistols. He took aim—directly at the king, I saw—but the report was so loud when he fired that I flinched. He fired his second pistol, and I thought I could hear the clattering din of servingware hitting the floor above the shouts and cries of the nobles. I looked to the king. They had missed. They had all missed.

"It's open!" An authoritative voice rang out through the dust and debris, and the sea of brightly colored silk and velvet moved from the edges of the ballroom toward the staircase, a path carved through the fallen stone. Theodor slowed his bow, but I shook my head.

"Until they're gone," I managed to say in a hoarse croak. The cleared section of staircase was narrow, and it would take time to move everyone out. Perhaps the assassins were reloading. I looked at the empty windows, the darkness outside pressing into the dome, but didn't see anyone outside.

Holding the net we had woven together was easier than the creation of it, and I looked around the room. I spotted Annette and Viola, hands clasped together, moving with the king and queen down the stairs. Pauline and a knot of sumptuously dressed women were close behind. There had been some hurt in the panic and by the falling mortar and glass. Those who couldn't walk unassisted were supported by others; I saw a serving boy in livery carried by a duke in black velvet, and several servants struggling to move a corpulent countess to the stairs. Those beneath the heaviest stones were, I knew, lost. They had been left where they lay. When the last of the guests and servants began to descend, I nodded to Theodor.

He stopped playing. I let the charm settle to the ground, where it swiftly pooled into a sea of gold over the bodies and the stones. Theodor gripped my hand in his and we ran for the staircase, running through a cloud of stale dust. I slipped and Theodor caught my arm, holding me up. We were safe—here I was, his arm in mine. His eyes met mine and he leaned toward me.

A scream from the atrium below stopped us before his lips found mine. Several nobles in front of us started as well, jostling each other to see what was happening below. I looked down, craning my neck to see around the nobleman in front of me. The nobles crowded into the atrium below, but they were still panicked. Swords drawn, screams, clattering shoes, and then I saw it—flashes of red. Red wool caps.

Before I understood what was happening, I watched as a

Red Cap ran a nobleman in a deep brown silk suit through with a scythe. He collapsed as lifeless as my dressmaker's mannequin.

The dome was only the first stage in Pyord's assault on the palace. I saw it in a flash, the brilliance of the plan—the nobles who survived the dome collapse would remain concentrated within the palace. The king would be, per his plan, dead, but there would be nobles who would, of course, contest any revolt Pyord put into action. There would be—I gripped Theodor's hand—heirs to the throne. The assassination, my part in casting a curse, was only part of the plan, and not even strictly necessary. If the king hadn't been killed in the ballroom, he could easily be killed here alongside his nobles. The plan counted on this—that the guests would all converge at the atrium, driven by fear from the ballroom. Gathered like cattle in a stockyard. It was a simple, brilliant, and horrible strategy. How the Red Caps had overrun the palace guardhouse, how they had gotten into the palace itself—questions swirled but had no time to find any purchase in my mind.

Before I could even think of what to do next, there were three of them mounting the stairs.

Theodor pressed me behind him, but there was nowhere to go. I scrambled up a few stairs, instinct fueling my motions. *Get away from them.* Away from the steel in their hands and the hate in their eyes.

Two of the three Red Caps were already fighting with nobles farther down the stairs. The third advanced on us. Theodor's hand was on his sword, but it stuck in the scabbard as he tried to draw it. I backed up another step, and fell, my dainty slipper finding no traction on the dust-covered stairs. I pressed myself backward, hands grappling to steady myself.

My hand curled around a large rock.

I brought it with me as I rose, wavering, to my feet. The

Red Cap, a stocky blond who looked like any of a dozen dock-workers Kristos had worked with, had nearly reached Theodor, sword still sheathed. He retreated until he was standing beside me, frustration and fear contorting his face.

I gripped my rock tighter.

The Red Cap was armed with only a large knife, but it looked deadly enough. Decisive anger surged through me. I couldn't let this man hurt Theodor. I wouldn't let him touch me. In the few seconds it took him to ascend the final steps separating us, I lunged forward and swung at the side of his head with the rock. His eyes locked with mine for the briefest moment before my makeshift weapon made contact, and my chest tightened. Then the rock cracked against his skull and he fell to the ground, a thin trickle of blood coursing down the side of his head and onto his white shirt.

I dropped the rock with a strangled cry, and Theodor grabbed my hand, pulling me toward him. The stairs were clear, but the fighting continued below, on one side of the atrium. Nobles with ceremonial swords fought Red Caps armed with scythes, knives, cudgels. The guards who remained inside the palace formed ranks with the nobles. The melee was already too cramped for them to use their rifles. Instead, they fought with their hangers and long knives.

My breath caught in my throat as Theodor finally wrenched his sword from the sheath and squared his shoulders. He squeezed my hand. "Stay behind us. You'll be safe." Then he ran down the stairs to join the fighting that concentrated on the far side of the atrium, near the servants' entrance. The guard and nobles combined held the Red Caps back, undulating in a line of fighting like waves pressing further up the shore. I watched Theodor join a line of palace guards, not taking my eyes off his honey-brown queue until the press of fighting forced me to retreat down the stairs.

I clattered the rest of the way down the staircase, veering away from the fight and toward the crowd of women pressed against the far side of the atrium. My hands shook, and I wished, absurdly, that I'd kept the rock. I nearly tripped over the foot of a Red Cap who lay sprawled over the landing, blood pooling beneath him. As I stumbled away from him, I saw his upturned face.

Jack.

I screamed, not in fear or grief but pure anger. He wore a red sash across his chest, like an army sergeant would—this was his role in the Midwinter night's attack. Leading the assault on the palace. I wondered if this was part of what he had disagreed with, or if he was proud to don the sash and lead a charge against the first wave of nobles to emerge from the ballroom.

I tore myself from looking at his glassy eyes. Jack was a good man—I had never known him to hurt anyone. Had my brother and his pamphlets turned him into this, first a fighter, now a corpse? I struggled down the remainder of the stairs, furious at the revolt that had set my friends to killing one another.

Viola met me at the bottom of the stairs and caught my arm. Her vibrant purple gown had a large gravy stain down the front, and she was missing one earring. "I couldn't have believed it of her," she said, and I followed her gaze past the fighting to the open servants' door.

It was held open by Miss Vochant, and a ring of keys hung from her hand.

"She knows the servants here. She must have gotten a set of servants' keys somehow. That little..." Viola's voice faded into anger. "That's how they got into the palace, all of them. Through the servants' entrances." I remembered the labyrinth of stairs and hallways connecting the servants' chambers by which I had entered the palace.

The ringing of metal on metal and shouts spread over the atrium, and the fight spread farther into the atrium. The noble-women wouldn't be safe for long. Soon Red Caps would break through, and they were here intent to massacre any nobles they encountered. I'd seen that in the face of the man I'd hit— probably, I thought with a sour feeling creeping into my gut, killed. They weren't here for a mere fight, but extermination of as many of the nobility as they could. "There are rooms all along this hallway, aren't there?" I said.

"Yes," Viola answered. "But what good does it—"

"Barricading themselves inside would give them some time," I answered, my voice wooden as I watched the bright tip of a rapier delve into the chest of a dark-haired Red Cap. Bile rose in my throat, but I clamped it back. "And time is what we need—eventually more soldiers will come back to the pal-ace, and these men can't stand against more soldiers." They had relied on two separate but simultaneous plans—assassinate the king in the ballroom and then bloody as many nobles as possi-ble in the atrium. Perhaps they intended for their fight to target other heirs, but I doubted it, watching the melee on the blood-slicked marble floor. My part in the plot felt suddenly small, and any sense of triumph still resonating from drawing the curse from the queen's shawl swiftly faded. Having failed in the ball-room didn't mean they couldn't still succeed overall.

Viola nodded and pushed her way through the crowd to Annette and Mimi, who were remarkably calm, reassuring the noblewomen around them. Viola whispered to Annette, who began herding the women toward the long corridor. The queen took the arm of an elderly gentleman who trembled with the indignity of being led away from the fight.

I pushed those nearest me toward the mass of silk and velvet moving down the hallway. Rooms filled, doors closed, and I heard the scrape of furniture on the floor as it was moved to block entrances.

The fight continued, the ranks of soldiers and nobles tightening to prevent any more Red Caps from breaking through. But their ranks were thinning, and though Red Caps had fallen as well, their numbers had been greater. I wondered if they were reinforced, more Red Caps spilling through the warren of servants' stairs and hallways into the atrium. The front doors remained closed, and I didn't see any Red Caps spilling into the atrium from other entry points. Miss Vochant had provided a single point of entry, but the servants' keys apparently only worked for the servants' quarters, and the rest of the palace remained locked. Though we were trapped, the Red Caps were bottlenecked. This was, at least, one mark in favor of surviving the night.

Most of the women were hidden in the rooms lining the hallway, Mimi and Annette ushering the last of the women into the first room on the left, a salon alive with peacock-feather-hued tapestries that winked absurdly bright and cheerful in the reflections of candlelight on flashing steel.

"You, too," Viola said, looking at me.

I followed her into the salon, cramped with bodies and smelling of sweat and sour spilled wine. One woman, in pink brocade, clamped part of her skirt to a slash wound in her leg. I looked away, to the diamond-clear windows overlooking a dark lawn. We were trapped on the first floor of the palace proper, but it rose twenty feet over the ground below, perched on an elevated foundation and the servants' quarters beneath. If the palace had been less grand, an ordinary house not built on an artificial rise and the servants' floor below, we could have escaped through the windows.

Maybe, I thought with trepidation, we could. Not all of us, I was sure; the wounded woman in pink and the frail elderly duchess whose dress seemed to weigh more than she did wouldn't be able to climb down, but perhaps, I thought, the idea crashing to the forefront of my mind wildly, I could. It was a gamble, but if the Red Caps had breached the fence instead of the guardhouse, it was possible that there were more soldiers there who didn't realize that the palace had turned into a battleground. Reinforcing the nobles could be the difference between being massacred in these grand parlors and salons, or escape.

"Viola," I said quietly, my voice surprisingly even, "do the windows open, or would I need to break one?"

"They open outward, to let in—you can't be serious." Her painter's gaze took in the dimensions, the height, the full scene at once. "It's twenty feet down."

"There's yards of curtains here," I suggested. "If I can get out, I could bring reinforcements."

Viola screwed her mouth into a knot, but agreed. "I hope you've a good luck charm as strong as mine," she said as she discreetly elbowed her way through the crowd. "And if you're caught?"

I shook my head. I didn't want to consider that possibility, or the horrible choice an open window would give the besieged noblewomen if the door was breached—jump or be killed inside. "Just help me with the curtain."

If the queen and the others guessed at what we were doing, they didn't say. They stood with attention fixed on the door, pressing their ears to the seams in the doorframe, trying to guess at what was happening outside. Viola and I tore a curtain down, and she helped me knot it to a heavy settee by the window. I tied the second curtain to the first.

"Do you have any idea how to climb down a rope?" Viola joked wanly.

"I'll find out. There may be more of them outside," I thought aloud. With some difficulty, I pulled the wire supports for my skirts from underneath my gown. I wouldn't fit them through the narrow window opening.

"Well, we shan't all follow you," Viola replied darkly, watching me kick aside my skirt supports with the realization that I was really going to do this drawn all over her face.

I tested the knots with a sharp tug, as I'd seen sailors do on the ships in the harbor. Viola helped me sling the curtains through the window, and we waited, inhaled breath choking us, for some reaction from the lawn below, for a Red Cap to run out and shoot at the window, for one to wait at the bottom with cutlass drawn. No one came.

I gripped the curtains, a thick silk velvet, and slid out the window. My arms protested immediately; I didn't have a dock-worker's corded muscles to help me, and I slid more than climbed down to the snow below. Swiftly, I ducked behind a topiary that barely concealed my skirt, the pale silk shining like a beacon in the moonlight. The snow-covered lawn beyond it was silent. An imposing fence ran the perimeter of the grounds, and I didn't see any activity along its metal length.

Just ahead, a man in palace guard uniform lay facedown on the cobblestone path. Probably a sentry, I thought, fear curdling my stomach. Probably someone who could have warned us or brought reinforcements.

No time for that. I shook myself.

The guardhouse interrupted the fence, and the only way to reach it was to cross the wide expanse of open lawn. If there were any Red Caps patrolling the palace grounds, I would be

402   *Rowenna Miller*

seen. And if the guardhouse had been overrun, there would be no escape. I ran a finger over the charmed pink flowers embroidered into my gown and exhaled. There was no other way. I took as large a breath as the tight bodice afforded me and took off at a sprint across the snow.

My breath came in great white clouds, and I barely felt the snow seeping through my impractical slippers. I slammed into the wall of the guardhouse—no point in subtlety now—and pounded against the windows, the doors, everything I could find.

A man in a soldier's uniform opened the door, and I almost started crying with the relief that rippled through my tightly coiled nerves.

He looked me up and down once, bewilderment clouding his craggy face. "What in the...?"

I choked on the words. "Palace attacked. Red. Caps. Came in servants' entrance."

He turned back to the interior while I swayed against the door. "Hey! Gear up. Problem at the palace. Get her inside."

He pulled me inside, and I let out a shuddering breath when I saw the full unit of men in the guardhouse. Two dozen, all armed better than the Red Caps. Someone had thought to station extra men here. I sank against the wall, letting the gown crumple beneath me.

"You stay here, miss. You'll be safe so long as—"

"Go!" I shouted at him. He followed the last of his men outside, toward the manicured lawn and the fight beyond.

47

THERE WAS NO POINT IN RETURNING TO THE PALACE. I COULDN'T fight, and with the reinforcements running to the atrium now, it would be over in minutes. I didn't need to see any more nobles or Red Caps killing one another. How had it come to this? I buried my face in my hands and let out a low moan. My people, my countrymen, killing each other.

I had used the last of my energy in the sprint across the palace grounds. Pulling the curse, dissipating it, and everything that followed had left me a hollow shell. I leaned against the wall, breathing as evenly as I could. In. Out. In. I stared at the lantern suspended from a hook on the wall, swaying slightly, the light casting variable shadows on the wall. In. Out. In.

Theodor found me swaying along with it.

"Sophie?" He dropped next to me, fear clouding his eyes. "Sophie, talk to me."

I realized how bad I must have looked. "I'm all right. Is it over?"

"The palace is cleared and guards are posted. The Red Caps didn't breach the rooms with the noblewomen and the queen, and the king still lives." He hesitated, and I saw the truth he wasn't telling me.

"Still lives?"

"Injured in the fight. I'm not sure yet—the cutlass slash he took might have been a surface wound, but maybe not." He apologized for having to tell me without saying a word. My chest felt like it was going to implode, to constrict my heart so severely that I would cease to be. What I had come to do—I might have failed. The king could still die. I gasped for air.

"Was this it? Are they—"

"There is still fighting in the streets. I've no doubt the soldiers stationed at the Stone Castle will put it down. It will all be over, whether the king lives or—this revolt won't succeed."

He was so sure of himself that I almost believed him.

"If we slip out through the servants' entrance, we can leave," he continued.

"Leave?" The headache pounded in my temples. I didn't want to move, let alone face the battle in the streets.

"They will put this rebellion down. But you're not safe. If someone reveals that you worked with Pyord? The king may demand a level of justice that will have your head along with your brother's and Pyord's."

I drew away from him. "That's my risk," I said.

"It's mine, now, too. I can hide you. If it comes to it, help you get out of the country. Fen or Pellia or Serafe. Somewhere you'll be safe."

He paused and pulled on my hand. I didn't budge. "We need to leave now."

It didn't matter how many times I saved the nobles, how many lives were beholden to me, if it was discovered that I was complicit in the plot. If Pyord was captured and gave them my name.

In that moment, it hardly seemed to matter. I would have let them arrest me if it meant I could sleep. But I couldn't do that to Theodor.

"All right," I said, forgetting as best I could, for the moment, that leaving meant leaving my shop—my livelihood, my successes and my goals, who I had styled myself to be. Tonight I didn't have the luxury of identity, only survival. Theodor arranged for his carriage to pick us up at the servants' entrance. I let him half carry me there, where several servants gathered, shocked and terrified, under the eaves. The housekeeper recognized me and caught my hand in her plump paw. "Safe travels for you, miss."

I thanked her and all but collapsed on Theodor once we were inside the carriage. A thousand questions swirled around me—how to stay safe in the streets? Where would we go? How in the world were the First Duke and a woman in a stained court gown going to avoid detection?

In the distance, torchlight bobbed in the square and in the avenues along the river. We drove past small knots of people who eyed the carriage suspiciously but let us pass.

"We'll head for the harbor," Theodor said as a particularly menacing group of young men wearing red hats stared us down as the carriage rattled past. "There's a ship in my father's employ. The captain will answer to me. We can hide you there until we know more."

I murmured something like an assent and leaned on his shoulder.

I was wrenched fully awake as the carriage skidded to a stop. A single voice shouted at the carriage from the empty street in front of us. Empty, except for one person blocking the carriage. I knew that voice.

Kristos.

"I want to see Sophie."

Theodor stiffened. His sword hand raised the blade, letting the light glint off its clean edges and show the shadow where blood still clung to it. "Not a chance. You're a traitor and I should turn you in to the soldiers immediately."

"I don't want to fight with you. But I will if you try to stop me." Kristos's words were heavy and resigned, but he unsheathed the sword he wore just enough to let the steel wink at us.

"Don't," I said, my voice weak. I laid a steady hand on Theodor's arm. "Kristos, I don't want to speak to you. I don't want Theodor to turn you in. I just want you to leave and never come back."

Kristos took off the red cap he was wearing—the charmed one I had made. He didn't deserve it. I wanted to tear it out of his hands and throw it in the river. "I didn't think you'd be at the palace. I'm sorry. I never would have—"

He never questioned risking my life in another way, tying me to their revolt, forcing my collusion in regicide. Even now, if found out, I would die by the gallows, and he had been willing to risk that. "That doesn't matter anymore." My voice was hollow with exhaustion.

He hesitated. "Maybe not. I can't—I can't ask you to forgive me for putting you in danger. But trust me now. There's been a...shift. In the plans for tonight."

Something in his tone made me colder than the icy wind whipping under the carriage and through my clothes, through my very bones. "Kristos, what do you mean?"

"Our intention was always a vacuum in governance—with the king gone and the nobility in disarray, we could assert an elected government. We decided, long ago, on a temporary council of the League's leadership—"

"You and Jack and Niko?" I said with a flagging, painful smile.

"And Pyord," he shot back, defensive. "Yes. We ran a revolt; we could run a government. Then open elections. Once things...calmed down.

"But Pyord never intended to turn the governance over to us. We disagreed on...oh, plenty, from frequency of elections to the process of writing a national charter. I thought we'd come to agreements," Kristos said, the words and his breath forming an angry cloud. "We hadn't. Pyord and Niko always pushed for a complete coup, before I agreed, before Jack went along with it. They pushed the people past where I would have, were I alone in this."

"Too late for that," I said. "They're already fighting in the streets." And he had never, I thought bitterly, had any qualms about regicide.

"Maybe not. I found a few letters. In his study. I was editing a few manuscripts in case...if I fell, I wanted more pamphlets and broadsides ready for printing." Of course—on the eve of war, Kristos was still sharpening his pen instead of a sword. "He should have burned them, but I suppose the academic in him was saving them for his memoirs. As the Savior of Galitha, the bringer of democracy." I could swear that in the dim light I saw his lip tremble, just slightly, before he clenched his jaw. "His letters indicate that any of us who didn't conform, he intended to dispatch. Including me."

I couldn't muster any surprise. Pyord had been willing to dispose of anyone in his path—a nameless messenger boy or his own pupil. "Kristos, you idiot."

"That's fair. I should have seen. But now you have to trust me."

"For what?" I flared. "You're the defunct leader of a revolution that's run away without you."

"The people are still loyal to a cause, and to the leaders who pulled them into that cause. For many of them, that's me and Jack. We're one of them—Pyord, well, I think he always wanted to be accepted as one of them but he's..."

"He's like me, Kristos," I said, the last of my restraint whittled hollow. "Just elevated enough to seem outside their world."

Kristos hesitated, but he agreed. "From what I can tell, Niko is still with him, and Pyord trusts him. But what they plan—it's not the cause I pulled people into the movement over. Pyord intends to take governance for himself, and it seems Niko supports him doing so. There's several squads of Kvys patrician-paid mercenary cavalry waiting on the other side of the border, under Pyord's orders. We thought they were reinforcing us. No. He's paid them to follow his orders alone. I knew we should have all been involved in the negotiations, but he understands Kvys customs better than we do and—" Kristos shook his head, enmeshed, certainly, in more regrets than that decision alone.

"It's already begun, Kristos." I thought of what Jack said, of the people being like beaten dogs set free from their cages. An ugly metaphor, but was it possible to cajole them into parley now? Or was it too late?

"I still have more clout in the League than Pyord or Niko. I'm going to try to stop the fighting tonight," Kristos said. "Even if Pyord's intentions are good, a dictatorship won't serve Galitha. Not long.

"Which is why you need to trust me now. In order to be sure that Galitha will be without leadership, they'll be trying to eliminate all the immediate heirs. The plan was for the king to be killed at the palace, but it was unlikely that the rest of the heirs would be eliminated in the fight there. Clearly they were unsuccessful," he said with a smile that mixed regret and gratitude, "and so there will be assassins looking for you, First Duke of Westland."

Theodor stiffened. "I should say something noble and aristocratic about having nothing to fear from this rabble, but I clearly do. What do you suggest we do?"

Kristos seemed, momentarily, taken aback, surprised by our lack of resistance. "The one place that the Red Caps have no plans to attempt to breach is the Stone Castle. They can't. Not without reinforcements."

"Then we'll make our way there," Theodor said, resolutely wrapping an arm around my waist, as though I were the one who needed protection.

"How did you know where to find me?" I asked.

"Penny said you were at the shop late this afternoon, and that you took a court gown. It was too late to stop you from getting to the palace." *Damn it, Penny,* I cursed silently. I should have counted on her inability to keep quiet—even if it did benefit me, unexpectedly.

"Kristos—the king isn't dead," I said in a rush. "The assault on the palace is over, and the Red Caps there are beaten. The soldiers know about the revolt now and they're fighting back. What are you going to do?"

"I'm going to find Jack and our sergeants, and then together—"

"Jack is dead, Kristos." My voice was cold, hanging in a cloud of frozen air.

Kristos's eyes closed, briefly, and then he recovered. "Our sergeants and those loyal to us, then. If we can call it off from underneath Pyord, we can stop this tonight. We were willing to fight and die for a government of the people, but only done the right way. Most of the laborers in this city feel the same." He glanced at Theodor. "No offense meant to present company."

"Sophie, we have to go," Theodor said, low, urgent.

"Don't worry about me," Kristos added. "Just get to the Stone Castle. Don't stop for anyone—promise me."

"I promise," I whispered. I wavered, then threw myself into

his surprised arms. "Please stay alive. Please. Run away from here." I broke away and turned back to Theodor.

I gathered the now-soiled skirts of the court gown in my hand and let Theodor help me back into the carriage. I felt as cold as the fine flakes of snow that fell on us from a bitter sky.

I looked back to the street, where Kristos stood alone, looking lost. "We should make haste," I said. "Forget the harbor. Get to the Stone Castle."

"I promised to keep you safe, and I will. We'll get you out of the country somehow."

"No, not now. I'm not safe if I'm killed by a rabble between here and the harbor or thrown off a ship by an assassin looking for you, am I?"

"I won't trade my life for yours."

"Hardly an even trade. The danger to you is here, now. Assassins hunting the heirs? That's a more immediate threat than the potential to be tried for treason later. Who knows what tomorrow morning brings?"

Theodor sighed. "If anything happened to you—it would be my fault."

"It's no more your fault than any of this is. We can outlast it together."

"Tomorrow I've no doubt this revolt will be put down," Theodor said. "But tonight is a no-man's-land."

When I looked back out into the street, Kristos was gone.

We had to pass near the center of town, near Fountain Square. As the torches grew denser in the streets and I began to see side roads barricaded and, to my horror, guarded, I wondered if we'd made a mistake in leaving the palace. But no— Kristos said the safest place would be the Stone Castle.

"This doesn't look promising," Theodor said, voice low. I looked outside.

The carriage was surrounded by people.

Lanterns and torches swarmed around us, a rising tide of angry voices. Some carried scythes and pitchforks—agrarian workers. Others had made clubs or carried kitchen knives. I saw the light glint off more than one gun barrel, probably supplied by Pyord's Kvys contacts.

"Let us pass," the carriage driver said, trying for authority. But we ground to a halt nonetheless.

"Nothing stands between us and the government buildings," a gravelly voice replied from deep within the crowd. "We're under orders."

"Whose orders?" The driver fought to keep control of the horses.

"Straight from the top."

Theodor tested the handle on the door. "No," I hissed, shaking my head. They would know him, far too quickly, by his sword and his family crest pinned to his coat.

He pressed his lips into a firm line, steeling himself to either hide in the carriage or open the door and face them. I wasn't sure which.

Then the carriage rocked precariously on its wheels.

"Hoy! Leave 'em be!" the driver called. I heard high whinnies, and then the crowd parted as the horses trotted away. They had been cut from their yokes. I was sure Kristos would have some eloquent metaphor comparing hacking through horses' leads to what the people were doing tonight. Breaking the reins of nobility.

He wasn't the one trapped in a carriage and surrounded by a crowd that wanted to kill him.

We both heard the shouts as the driver was pulled from his seat. "Just saving you a hard fall, brother," the gravelly voice insisted. "You're not one of them."

I was fairly sure I heard the driver protest, but his voice was drowned out by the shouts and cheers outside. The carriage rocked again.

"We can't just sit here," Theodor said, resting his hand on his sword hilt.

"No," I said, pulling his hand into mine. "You can't. You'll be killed."

"We'll both be killed." He yanked open a compartment in the wall of the carriage and produced a pistol. Already, I was sure, loaded. "We have a better chance if they don't know who I am, which they haven't figured out yet. They might be imprisoning nobles who don't fight, but if I'm slated to be killed..."

"We need to get out of here before they discover that you're an heir." I looked out over the people gathered. I didn't know any of them, but I could have. They were laborers like my brother, dockworkers and sailors and farmhands and bricklayers. I couldn't believe it of them, that they would hurt someone for the sole crime of being noble. But I couldn't believe it of my brother, either, and he had helped plan regicide.

My gaze caught something else, however. We were south of Fountain Square, pressed into a side street that spliced into River Street.

River Street. My hand flew to my pocket, burrowing into my skirts to find what I had hidden there before the ball.

The key to the secret tunnel into the Stone Castle.

"Theodor," I said carefully, forcing my words past the tremor in my voice. "Do you think, with a little luck and some swordplay, we could make it from here to River Street?" There were fewer people on the south side of the carriage—the street was narrow here and most people poured in from the north.

"A lot of luck," he said, holding the door closed as someone outside tried to jimmy it open. "Fat good it does us."

"I can get us somewhere safe," I said. "With this." I produced the key.

"Brilliant," Theodor said. "We can get back inside the Stone Castle."

"How do we—" I hiccuped as the carriage rocked again, this time violently.

"No time," Theodor said. "Look. I'm going to open the door and fire this." He checked the pistol's priming and cocked it. "That should give them a bit of pause—then I jump and you run."

"You run, too." There wasn't time for heroics like single-handedly fencing an entire crowd of armed revolutionaries.

"I run, too." He gripped my hand, pulled me roughly toward him, and kissed me full on the lips, then put his hand to his sword. "Now."

He flung open the door and fired the pistol into the crowd. I didn't have time to wonder if he'd hit anyone before his sword was drawn and he was on the rails of the carriage. I jumped past him and dashed through the rent the pistol shot had torn in the crowd.

I wanted to know if Theodor followed me, if someone else followed me, but it took all my strength to keep my feet pounding the cobblestones. I couldn't slow myself by turning. I reached River Street and swung wide, diving down the little side street with the door. My breath was ragged, and my dress felt like a hundred-pound weight.

As I slid the key into the keyhole, I finally turned. No one was there.

My hand shook and I nearly dropped the key. What was the point, I wanted to scream, if Theodor hadn't come with me? The strength of my reaction shocked me—if he wasn't there, I wasn't opening the door. I wasn't going to save myself without him.

Then his sky blue silk suit tore around the corner.

"Open it! For heaven's sake, Sophie, open it!" A half dozen large men followed him.

I fumbled briefly with the key—it stuck in the cold lock—but then I felt the sheer relief of the tumblers clicking into place. I flung the door open, all but fell inside, and Theodor clattered in behind me. I slammed the door shut and turned the key in the lock on our side.

Fists made contact with the door on the other side. We didn't wait to see if they would try to tear it down or if they'd move on to easier targets. Instead, we picked our way carefully down the pitch-dark tunnel together.

48

—⁓—

No one stopped us as we limped out of the tunnel and into the hallway I had been in mere hours earlier. The main floors of the Stone Castle were empty save a few guards who recognized Theodor and his family crest.

One of the captains stopped Theodor, and the two discussed the situation on the streets in quiet tones. I leaned against the wall, my legs wobbling like an undercooked pudding. As we had seen, the side streets were barricaded to force the path of the soldiers. But the League had not expected the full force of the soldiers to deploy all at once, and so quickly. The king's troops had secured the palace, the government buildings, and the perimeter of the city.

The streets were still chaos. There was no escape for me tonight. No escape at all. I took a shaky breath and resigned myself to the king's justice, and hoped for his mercy.

"No idea on losses yet," the captain said, "but I've had dozens of wounded roll in already. And it's been less than an hour since they left." He shook his head. "This isn't going to end without a fight."

Theodor listened attentively as I slid down the wall. The exhaustion that had throbbed in my bones since the ball was overtaking me swiftly. Cream silk ballooned around me as I sat down, hard, on the cold stone floor. The hem was filthy, and I had ripped a large hole in the bodice leaping from the carriage. Madame Pliny was not going to be happy when she returned from her winter home in the south. I almost laughed, but it hurt too much.

I leaned my head against the cold granite behind me. Crags in the rough stone caught my hair and I winced. Theodor told the captain, briefly, without names or sources, what Kristos had told us—that there was a rift in the revolutionaries themselves. His voice was low, hurried. Who was there to keep a secret from? No one, I thought, except that the truth of what was happening was so ugly that it was hard to declare it loudly.

Without meaning to, I fell asleep there on the floor. My dreams were confused and dark—roasted pheasants turned into winter crows and pecked out the king's eyes, and a dancing troupe of women in court gowns leapt and dodged a huge puppet made of rocks and stained glass, its strings held by Pyord high above in the palace dome.

I woke with a start, freezing and stiff, less than an hour later. Theodor sat beside me, staring absently at the opposite wall.

"The palace holds," he said before I could speak. "And most of the city is secure."

I found my voice. "But it's not over?"

"Not yet."

"The hired soldiers with the Red Caps?"

"Haven't arrived. Perhaps they weren't intending to come until later, perhaps they were stopped."

People moved past us—soldiers with dirt and blood staining their uniforms ferried wounded men into the building and boxes of ammunition out of it. I swallowed, watching those crates trot past, imagining the crates that must have already been spent on the streets tonight.

I still felt like I'd been run over by a team of oxen, but I couldn't bear to sleep while the city fought. I inched, slowly, up the wall until I was standing. If only I had my sewing kit with me—but, foolishly, it was sitting on Theodor's ottoman with my clothes.

"Do you have a penknife?" I asked a clerk with a blanched expression as a trio of soldiers hurried past, dragging a comrade whose leg was a torn mess of blood and flesh and brown wool. I gripped the edge of the clerk's desk, hard.

He stared at me as though I were speaking Pellian.

"Or scissors? Shears? Anything with a sharp edge?"

He shook himself and rummaged on the desk. "Penknife," he replied. His words stuck to his mouth.

I snatched it from his trembling hands and dodged a troop of soldiers marching a group of prisoners, arms crossed behind their heads, to the cells below us. Theodor waited in the little alcove I had fallen asleep in, the puzzled expression on his face fading as he saw how I used the knife.

Carefully, delicately, I sliced into the hem of the gown. Dozens of embroidered flowers grew there, spattered with mud but still vibrantly pink and still imbued with the good luck charm I'd stitched into them. The charm glowed past the mud, past the stains. I cut, pruning each flower from the embroidered vine trailing the edge of the skirt. And I dropped each square of silk bearing a flower into Theodor's hand.

"Give them out. To the soldiers. They're charmed. For luck."

"You should—"

"They'll take them from you. They'll know your sword, your family crest on your medal. They'll trust you."

And they did. Each man Theodor stopped accepted the flower, tucking it into a pocket or, more often, lopping it over a button or sliding it through a pin. Somewhere visible.

Watching Theodor, how he clasped the hands of the soldiers, offered them a few words of encouragement, of thanks, of sympathy—something stirred in me. He made a good duke, could be a good prince or king.

Soon all the flowers on my gown had been cut off. I wrapped myself in a blanket that one of the prison guards brought me and, despite myself, fell into a deep sleep.

49

I WOKE TO LIGHT STREAMING THROUGH CURTAINED WINDOWS and Theodor sitting on the floor beside the crude cot I was sleeping on.

"Where...what time...did they...how long?" I murmured through a sleep-tied mouth.

Theodor laughed. "Slow down. You're in the Lord of Keys' room in the Stone Castle. It's nine o'clock in the morning. And it's over outside. It seems a large number of Red Caps abandoned the fight midway through."

"Kristos managed to convince them," I said. "Kristos! Is he—did they find—"

"No word."

I closed my eyes. That was not the worst news I could have received.

Theodor wrapped his hand around mine. "My father arrived from the palace along with the Lord of Keys half an hour ago. There were two small detachments of Kvys hired cavalry stopped at outposts outside the city. They didn't put up much of a fight. It's possible Pyord had more hired than were due to arrive in the first wave, but they've dispersed if so."

"They aren't still on the way here?" I asked.

"No, not how they would operate. Pyord hired them, probably a limited contract reporting to him alone. They most certainly aren't under order from the Kvys government—tacitly permitted mercenaries hired through lesser oligarchs, likely. When it benefits Kvyset, they claim their victories, and when it doesn't, they pretend to know nothing about them. I have a feeling they'll dissipate quickly, now that their contract is void."

"Void?"

"They found Pyord last night, trying to escape the city. When it became clear he couldn't win, he ran."

"Coward."

"My thoughts exactly. He was killed trying to scale a wall—rather inglorious."

"It feels like there should be more," I said. "Like that can't be the end, somehow."

"I'm sure it's not," Theodor said, sounding weary. "Likely what my father wishes to discuss, before anything else—the possibility that they might mount another attempt."

"Your father is here," I said, then sat bolt upright. "Your father! And the Lord of Keys! Do they know that I—what did you tell him?"

"Well, my father had noticed that I brought a strange young woman to the Midwinter Ball. In fact, he asked me who the lovely young duchess or countess was." He choked back a laugh.

"And?"

"And my father thoroughly chastised me for trying to be a knight-errant last night, leaving the palace when we were supposed to stay under guard, but he was so wrapped up that he forgot to ask who you actually were." He shrugged. "I'll straighten him out later. But you should be safe remaining here."

"It feels as though—as though it can't be over." I picked at a loose thread in the blanket.

"You're probably right. We stemmed the tide last night, but there are still scores of unhappy people and a very real revolution in thought. The leadership of this particular attempt fell to bits, but it doesn't mean that the motivation of the participants in last night's attempt at a revolt wasn't real. They found ways to arm themselves once, secured funding once—they can certainly do so again." He hesitated. "And the king is not well."

I sat up straighter. "What are you saying?"

"He was badly injured last night. It's too soon to know much, but I'm rather forced for the first time to truly consider my role as an heir."

I swallowed and stared at my hands. An heir—and the words he didn't say: *to the throne*. The great chasm between us, between our stations, widened just a little more as he spoke.

"I suppose I'd never really thought I'd be in line for the throne," he said. "First I figured that the king would have a son, then that Annette would have a son before the king died. Now—maybe not. The line could pass to my house."

"And greenhouses and studying flowers have to be put on hold if you're the heir apparent." *And affairs with seamstresses, too*, I thought.

"It's not a bad thing, really," he said, toying with the fringe at the edge of a throw pillow. "I want to put botany aside if I can do more good in taking on my role as a noble. I mean, truly take it on. Your damn brother," he added with a rueful laugh.

"What?"

He tossed a pamphlet on the bed between us. "Before that movement went off the rails, before it turned to regicide and Pyord's dark schemes, this was all there was to it."

"Talk," I said. "Words and talk and idle hours in cafés."

"No, not idle," Theodor said. "Talk about making things better. And your brother, for all his faults, had some good ideas.

He took the theory and the economics and the philosophy and he applied it in such ingenious ways—some of this is actually possible, Sophie. Not only possible but plausible."

I remembered how he'd looked the night before, handing my charmed flowers as talismans to the soldiers. How he'd seemed to carry hope with him. How he didn't shy away from shaking the hand of a scarred man splattered with blood.

How he looked, in that moment, that he'd been made to lead men.

A knock on the door, and Viola's face appeared in the crack she opened. "Hate to interrupt," she said, "but my father wanted to speak to Sophie."

I started, my head feeling very heavy. Perhaps I wasn't so safe after all. Perhaps one of Pyord's men had given me away. To add more insult to the prospect of being arrested, I was still wearing the scraps of Madame Pliny's court gown.

Viola scanned the rags with a neutral expression. "Stay there."

She returned with spare clothes, plain linen petticoats and a loose bedgown with tattered ribbon ties. "Wear these. You look ridiculous."

"Are you all right?" I asked as I unlaced the bodice of the ruined gown.

"I'm fine. Plenty of others aren't—I'm sure in noble homes and common ones this morning. Now put on those clothes. I went to a lot of trouble to fish them out of the bin of goods confiscated from prostitutes and thieves." Her tone was even but her hands shook slightly, and there was a haunted look behind her eyes.

I threw the clothes on and followed Viola to her father's office. She opened the door and shoved me through with a gentle push, but waited outside. My head still throbbed faintly, and

I felt as weak as a kitten. But there was a vague relief that it was truly over now. No more hiding. No running.

The Lord of Keys waited in a sparse sitting room, his dark uniform and leather helmet blending in with the dark wood and stone of the castle. I sank onto the nearest chair, winded by the trip downstairs.

"It's over?" I asked.

"Yes," he said simply. Theodor and his father slipped quietly into the room. "For now," he amended. "We've been questioning participants all morning." My heart sank—he knew. I gathered what little courage I had left to face the charges I was sure were about to be read against me.

But the Lord of Keys continued. "There's some indication of a shift in leadership—a committee that crumbled, or a single leader and his sergeants who disagreed. We can't be sure." I was sure—Kristos wouldn't stand for a dictator after being fed on democracy, and it turned out that many of the Red Caps were loyal either to his ideals or simply to Kristos himself. Pyord, in his final calculation, had made an error. "But many of them say one of the members of the leadership is hiding in the city, biding his time until he can mount a second attempt. It's come to my attention that this man may be your brother."

I clamped my mouth shut. Even after everything we had been through, I couldn't betray Kristos. I wouldn't.

"I don't know where my brother is," I answered honestly. "I saw him last night, briefly. But I don't know where he went. I—" I hesitated, but continued. "I told him he should escape while there was still time."

To my surprise, the Prince of Westland smiled wanly. "I would have probably done the same for my brother. And he for me." Theodor's father looked very much like him, I thought as he spoke.

"I appreciate your honesty, Miss Balstrade," the Lord of Keys said. "The picture we have established from those held prisoner is fairly clear—this revolt failed and they're not able to produce another in short order. I have to investigate all potential elements."

I considered this. "The rebels offered all this information willingly?"

"They believe they're going to be killed. They were taunting me."

"Are they going to be killed?"

"I'd advise against it," Theodor said. He looked older, somehow, his face poised with the same concentration it wore when he played violin or discussed the finer points of botany. "Find and execute the leadership, yes, what remains of it." I thought not only of my brother, but of Niko, still unaccounted for. Of those just under them, their sergeants, who might be considered highly ranked enough to hang. "But let the common folk go."

"I agree," the Prince of Westland added. "Making martyrs will only further this divide and harden their resolve."

"What would you have me do?" The Lord of Keys paced toward the fireplace. "It's the king's decision, regardless."

"Indeed. Hold those arrested until the king recovers. Or until"—the prince's face constricted and his voice cracked—"until he does not recover." The possibility of the king's death spread through the room like the cold when a door swings open in a strong wind.

"How did they do it?" I asked after a long silence. "How did they get into the dome?"

"The masonry around the windows and the stones above the entryway was replaced with a weaker compound," the Lord of Keys said. "There was work done on the exterior just a week ago. I failed, I suppose, to thoroughly vet the masons who did the job because I am sure now that they must have been in alliance with the rebels. Slight pressure deteriorated the compound around the windows, allowing access to the dome itself."

"And the blocked stairs? The weakened compound was that precise?" Theodor asked.

"It was." He rubbed his temples. "It is, admittedly, an incredible plan."

I wondered—was the plan with the weakened masonry Pyord's work? Or simply an enterprising mason bent on destruction of the monarchy instead of building and repairing? The promises of the people the Lord of Keys had interrogated chilled me—they were capable, I knew, more than even the Lord of Keys did, to ply their trades and skills for a cause they believed in. Like my brother, they were willing to use or to spend their lives.

Viola burst into the room. "He's—the king—he's—"

"Oh, heaven," I murmured as I watched the tears stream from her face. The Prince and Duke of Westland followed, somber and shocked.

"The government buildings are secure. All appointed magistrates are in their place, and guarded by soldiers. It is a tragedy to lose the king, but not the chaos it could have been." The Lord of Keys stood straight and official. "All appointed magistrates except you, Your Highness." He inclined his head to the prince.

"I must get to the palace," he agreed. "I—I should have been there. I should have been with my brother." We all stood, dumb and rooted to the ground, until I saw a single tear course down Theodor's father's face.

I rose and crossed the room, taking the new king's hand in mine. "I'm so sorry for your loss," I whispered. Then I ran from the room.

50

—∞—

THE CORONATION WAS A SMALL AFFAIR, SHORT AND FORMAL IN the chapel of the cathedral, draped in black crepe and unearthly quiet save the droning of the Lord of the Scepter. He placed the crown on Theodor's father's head, and even from the back of the sanctuary, I could see the bright spots of tears in his eyes.

The queen—queen dowager now—and Princess Annette were seated on the risers with the rest of the royal house. Annette wasn't going away to be married. The delegation from Serafe had returned home as swiftly as possible after the Midwinter Revolt, as it was already called. Besides, I thought with a sour feeling, there was no reason to hurry her marriage now. No need to produce an heir.

In a short addendum to the ceremony, Theodor was named Prince of Westland and first heir to the throne, and I felt tears spike my eyes. I had always known that distances we couldn't erase with lunches in the greenhouse and trysts in the garden separated us, but the formal invocation took my vague understanding and forged immutable iron around it. Theodor accepted the signet ring of the Prince of Westland, but his eyes found me as he recited his oath as heir.

I unabashedly cried into my handkerchief.

A flood of black silk and velvet washed out of the chapel and into the white streets. The tenor in Fountain Square was changed—riots replaced with women selling black crepe mourning armbands and white silk roses, revolution displaced by grief. The malcontent of the people was still simmering below the surface, but it was clear that most of them had never wished death on anyone.

My brother was still missing.

Several Red Caps who had served as martial sergeants during the revolt and hid caches of weapons had been captured. Their trials were swift and their hangings swifter. Niko was never found. I recognized the names of a few of the sergeants, and Theodor reported that the woman who had led the mob at my shop was found guilty of storing and distributing weapons. My neighbor said she went to the gallows taunting the soldiers. I didn't attend the executions, but instead lit a candle in the alcove of the cathedral for Jack the day after they were carried out. Perhaps it was for her, too. Perhaps it was even for Pyord.

The Lord of Keys and the new king were in agreement not to hunt down the entire Red Cap army. I hoped against hope that Kristos had escaped. But there were many missing who were presumed dead.

I set off, back to my shop. Back to work, back to the life I had built for myself. Back to Alice, coaching her to leave me and begin her own career someday, back to Emmi, training her nimble fingers. Back to the flurry of commissions that had followed the Midwinter Ball. Back to begin again on Madame Pliny's court gown, as I had destroyed the first version beyond repair. Back, even though nothing would ever be the same.

"Wait!" The familiar voice echoed past the frozen fountain and caught me. Theodor. He trotted beside me, his gold-brown hair bobbing in its queue.

"I don't think running across Fountain Square is considered dignified behavior for a prince," I said as he caught up.

"Hang dignified," he said. "Come with me."

"Don't you have some formal dinner to attend?" I replied. "Some coronation feast?"

"Nope. Did away with that, in consideration of the state of deep mourning the whole nation's in. Mother's insisting on throwing a ball in the spring. I was hoping to convince her to hold it in the public gardens," Theodor answered with a soft smile. He took my hand.

"Please, Theodor," I begged without trying to find any more words. "Please." It was over. A common seamstress couldn't marry the prince, heir to the throne. Perhaps there had been a chance when he was First Duke, several steps removed, but now? It was impossible. We would always have the greenhouse and the dinner in the mirrored room and the night after the riot, preserved in memory. But if there was no way forward, I couldn't keep wallowing in the impossibility of it.

"Come with me," he insisted, and I relented.

The carriage was the same, even to the driver who had emerged from the scuffle after the ball unscathed, but the Royal Guard following it was new. They trotted on identical chestnut horses behind us into the public gardens, through the wrought iron gates, past the river walk, over the bridge, and to the doors of the greenhouse. They had the decency to leave us at the door.

"I have an even stronger affinity for this place," said Theodor. "Now that I am not going to study in the tropics, I am all the more attached to the tropics I've created here."

He opened the door and led me inside. A table was set with a simple lunch and three chairs. He sat next to me, never letting go of my hand.

"Theodor," I whispered, "I can't. This will never come to anything, between us. If it ever could, that's over now."

"I—we will have to discuss the peculiarities of our relationship at some point," he conceded. "I'm not giving up on my cockamamie scheme to manage to marry you. Not yet. I have the ear of the king now, you know. It might even be politically advantageous—solidarity with the people, marrying one of their own."

I found I had no voice, but I managed a slight nod of assent.

He smiled. "I promise not to get myself betrothed to some foreign princess if you promise not to marry some side-street butcher or barber."

Despite myself, I laughed. "Not right away, anyway."

"But it isn't why I brought you here."

The door at the back of the greenhouse opened, the one between a pair of orange trees laden with white blossoms, and a man walked out.

Kristos.

I leapt to my feet, but stopped myself from running to him. He strode quickly to me, however, and wrapped me in his arms before I could speak. Anger at him was, for the moment, overcome by relief. He wasn't dead.

"What are you doing here?" I finally said.

"I'm sorry, Sophie." He dropped onto the chair next to me.

"I—it's a little late for that," I said quietly, glancing at Theodor. He had lost his uncle, his father had lost his brother, our country had lost its king. And that was only the beginning—dozens of nobles and hundreds of common people had died in one night of failed insurrection. The repercussions had yet to be accounted for—businesses that would close, families whose income would be cut off. I had been outraged that he had put my life up for wager for the revolution he believed in, but he had risked far more lives than just mine. Kristos's apologies were inadequate now. "Why did you stay?"

"It wasn't entirely altruistic. The king's soldiers were everywhere, the roads out of the city blockaded, ships not permitted to leave the harbor. I could have tried to run overland, but I'm no woodsman. Figured staying and hiding here was preferable to starving in the woods in winter."

"And your comrades have kept you hidden?" There was a touch of gall in my tone, and I didn't rein it in. "Tell me, what do they see you as: a hero of the failed revolt or their enemy, who abandoned the cause?"

"Neither. I'm the embodiment of their disappointment, but I'm the only reason most of them are alive."

"You stopped them. When they were still fighting for a man that had betrayed them," Theodor said.

Kristos responded with almost automatic defense. "His ideals weren't entirely corrupt—he didn't want to be made a king or anything like that, from what I could get from the letters. He simply intended to be the sole executor of the transition into democratic governance. But he taught us too well—I know what consolidated power can do. It was never what we intended. We had a committee of leadership set from the beginning."

"And he paid Kvys mercenaries to ensure his plans went off as he intended?" I asked.

"We agreed to the mercenaries," Kristos said. "We didn't have the army on our side." Had they tried? I wondered. What a mess that would have been.

"At least it didn't come to that," Theodor said. "This insurrection could have escalated to international war."

"Pyord had planned on it," Kristos said. I gasped, and he laughed. "Not quite that dramatic—just that he said, if it came to international conflict, all the easier to position ourselves where we want to be. 'Let the big hounds fight themselves ragged,' he suggested once."

"Yes, he was very smart," I replied drily.

"At any rate," Kristos continued. "After I left you that night, I tried to find as many of the leaders of the League as I could, the sergeants who were leading our men in the streets. I could stop the fighting through them. And the things I saw…" He trailed off. I waited. "I saw my comrades fighting in the streets, bloodied and killed. But what gnawed at me, carved my soul like no sword could, was seeing them bloodying and killing the king's soldiers. Not that I have an overactive amount of sympathy for those who take the king's silver, but I saw my comrades turned into something ugly, something I didn't intend. I thought I knew what revolt was, what war was, but…" He swallowed hard, pushing past memories hidden from me to continue. "The brutality of my own comrades shocked me. Frightened me. They had so much rage, so much momentum flowing into a single goal—taking life. I didn't know men could become beasts so quickly. It was horrid, Sophie."

I saw the haunted look in his eyes and knew he was not lying. The anger I wanted very badly to hold on to threatened to recede, a wave pulling back on a defeated and tired shoreline. So much of my brother, so much of what I had loved even as it frustrated me, was his idealism, his belief in something greater than himself. I never understood how he could look beyond our gray workaday lives into some hazy, golden future; it was a gift I didn't share. Without it, he seemed a diminished version of himself, smaller and faded. "What had you expected?" I asked quietly. "That—men turned to beasts, butchering each other in the street—that was always what I saw when I looked into the future you wanted to make."

"I...I thought there would be something righteous in it, something heroic. Maybe there was, but I couldn't see it in their faces. Not then."

"You stopped it, Kristos. You kept it from going further. It could have gone much further," I added, overripe fears still spilling from me. There were those of the Red Caps who wouldn't have been content with new governance, or even with extermination of the nobility. Some would have come even for those like me who didn't support them, who they saw as colluding with the nobility. "You saved them from their own worst natures."

Kristos nodded, ready to hold this idea, to examine it, but not quite ready to swallow the antidote to his guilt. "I saw something else." He cocked his head and looked at me strangely. "I saw an emblem on the soldiers' coats—an embroidered flower. And I knew that design."

"My charm," I whispered. "You recognized my work?"

"It's one of your oldest ones—one of the ones Mother taught you," he said. "The members of the League still in the street were calling them the Rose Soldiers. They thought they must be some special unit, specially trained, the best of the garrison, because they fought with such purpose and intensity."

"They were mistaken," I said. "My charms don't work like that—I can't make a man a better soldier."

"Oh yes, you can. They had something they believed in, and though I didn't know how you had given them out or that the prince was involved, too, I knew that my little sister had inspired something in those men. Somehow. I had this strange sense—it doesn't end here. You were right. There is a way to change without death in the streets. There has to be. I have a lot of people out there who need to be convinced of that."

"You prize idiot," I said, ignoring the pair of tears that coursed down my cheeks. "You could have been captured and executed."

"I was willing to die for one cause, why not another?"

"Not funny," I said. "They won't pardon you."

"I wouldn't want to be pardoned," he said, raising his chin. "The ideals I believed in—I still believe them. I would still fight for them," he added, "with all respect, Prince. I've been writing again. The press will keep publishing what I write. But it doesn't advocate revolt this time."

"I've appeased him with assurances that there will be no restriction on the proliferation of his pamphlets in his absence," Theodor interrupted.

"Absence?" I looked from Kristos to Theodor, waiting for an explanation.

"He's leaving the country," Theodor said with a raised eyebrow. "I know a ship in need of a sailor. One-way signing contract only. If he were caught, I couldn't stop the process of justice for him. So he needs to leave if he wants assurances on his life."

"Where?" I asked, fumbling at how to feel. Kristos would be safe, but this could be the last time I saw my brother.

"Does it matter?" Kristos said with a lopsided smile.

"Yes, for some reason."

"Fen. For now," he added. "Pyord was right about something, and that was that knowing about other forms of governance can encourage one to see the weaknesses in one's own. In order to keep writing, I need to keep studying."

Fen was no country of scholars. Neither was Kvyset, or Pellia. I nodded, knowing what he was saying—the Allied Equatorial States, with the public libraries funded by their princes, or West Serafe, with its universities open to anyone with the tenacity and talent to find a sponsor. It was enough.

I turned to Theodor. "Why would you do this for him?" I wiped the tears from my cheeks with the back of my hand.

"To be completely frank, I'm really doing it more for you,"

Theodor said with a lopsided smile. "But he's right. We haven't extinguished this revolution, and without some changes, it will only wait for another opportunity to flare up and consume this country. We need some reforms. If we're to avoid another attempted revolt, more riots, we need the populace to consider those reforms as an alternative to violence. They may listen to appeals for prudence from the same writer who led them to revolt," he said, with a pointed look at Kristos. "I'll be presenting a bill to the council this month with some measures I believe will alleviate some of the concerns of the people. Some measures from your brother's pamphlets."

"At least someone was reading them," Kristos said, with a pointed look at me.

"Don't you have a boat to catch?"

"I missed you," Kristos said with a little sliver of his old grin. I hadn't forgiven him yet; perhaps I never would, completely. But I could agree with him on that point. I missed him when he was gone. I still missed him, even now as he sat two feet away from me.

"Stay safe, Kristos," I said quietly.

He nodded, turned to leave, then turned back toward me and enveloped me in his arms. Then he rumpled my hair and disappeared through the door behind the orange trees.

"Thank you," I whispered.

"He would have made a good Privy Councillor," Theodor said. "If he hadn't ruined himself with revolution, he could have built reform."

"What is this, the Greenhouse Summit?" I asked, unconvinced. *Reform* sounded too weak a word when compared with revolt. But that was where Kristos's writing had started, with reforms. With ideas.

"For now. But next week I take my seat as the head of the Council of Nobles. And despite the fact that I would rather dig in the dirt here than chair a meeting of panicked and squabbling noblemen, I'll do my duty to the country, which I think requires, at this point, changes."

My fingers inched along the simple white trim on my gown's black sleeves. "We can't go backward," I finally said, "so we might as well try to go forward."

"I want to go forward with you rather than without you." He put it so simply. Could it be as simple as that?

"But it's not so simple," I answered him and myself. "Kingdoms are united, treaties are sealed…"

"See, I think paper and pen should handle that just fine. I know I can't promise anything. I can't ask you to want to step into this hornet's nest with me. And even my best plans might still fail, but if I have to rule a country, I want you beside me."

I bit my lip. I didn't want to lose Theodor, but I wanted my life unchanged, with the daily rhythms of my shop and the comfort I could find in a needle and silks. I didn't want to be queen—but Theodor didn't want to be king, either. What a pair we'd make.

"What do you want, Sophie?" he asked again, and I saw him as I had seen him the night after the riot, in his bedroom, both of us wearing simple linen. Equals in this if not in title or blood.

I breathed the heavy air of the greenhouse, thick with flowers and fruit and, under it all, soil and moss and bark—I wanted to drink in everything here. I looked down at my hands, the familiar calluses on my fingertips from the needle—I wanted to keep sewing, keep charm casting. I watched a fresh shower of snow settle gently on the bare branches outside—I wanted to keep living in this city through whatever changes were coming.

I looked back at Theodor. I saw an uncertain future, and a role I never wanted for myself. But I also saw trust, and hope, and love.

"This." I took his hand and drew him to a bench by a bed of deep pink rose balsam. "I want this." For now, it was enough.

**The story continues in the next
Unraveled Kingdom novel,
coming in April 2019**

Acknowledgments

I am fortunate to have an incredible team surrounding this book, and admit freely that there's no way to express my gratitude adequately or completely.

Thanks to my agent, Jessica Sinsheimer—your enthusiasm and steadfast support are beyond measuring. You deserve all the macarons. Thanks as well to the whole team at Sarah Jane Freymann Literary Agency.

The team at Orbit is truly the most amazing group of talented, creative, and dedicated people I could have landed among to produce this book. As a writer, you hope that, when you're offered a book deal, it's with a group of people who get the narrative, the characters, and your vision, and I am so fortunate that this is exactly what happened—you have all made *Torn* better in so many ways. First and foremost, my editor, Sarah Guan, is a genius who saw straight to the heart of this story. Your insight and encouragement have challenged and developed this novel—and me as a writer. And the rest of the Orbit family—thank you to Tim Holman, Anne Clarke, Ashley Polikoff, Lauren Panepinto. Lisa Marie Pompilio, thank you for the beautiful cover. Thanks on the publicity and marketing side to Alex Lencicki; Ellen Wright, for the ingenious crafty tie-ins; Laura Fitzgerald; Paola Crespo; and Derrick Kennelty-Cohen.

Randy, you've been on this ride with me for years, and your support has been unwavering despite my frequent disappearances into my laptop and my latte-while-writing habit. Eleanor, your patience with "Mommy is working" is remarkable for your five years. Marjorie, thanks in advance—you don't know what you're in for, pumpkin.

Thanks to the extended family of voracious readers who inundated me with books, especially my parents. Dad, thanks for teaching me to explore and trespass (that's what writing is), and Mom, thanks for teaching me that a good cook cleans up her mess (that's what revision is).

Finally, all the sewists who have inspired and taught me, and whom I've been privileged to learn alongside, especially but certainly not limited to the seamstresses and tailors of the IRV, Dean's Co'y, and the NWTA.

extras

orbit

meet the author

Photo Credit: Heidi Hauck

Rowenna Miller grew up in a log cabin in Indiana and still lives in the Midwest with her husband and daughters, where she teaches English composition, trespasses while hiking, and spends too much time researching and re-creating historical textiles.

Author Interview

When did you first start writing?

I was obsessed with books from a young age, and I don't remember not wanting to create books of my own. I was so small I had to dictate stories to my (very patient) mother because I couldn't properly write yet. I never truly stopped, but I got more serious after college when academic writing wasn't a huge part of my life anymore. (I actually love writing research papers...)

Who are some of your most significant authorial influences?

It might sound weird, but reading nonfiction, first-person historical accounts developed my sense for voice and purpose in storytelling, and for how individual character and perspective shapes the story being told. The events don't change much, but different people see them very differently, and it changes the entire narrative. In fiction, I love the wonder in C. S. Lewis, the emotional complexity of Irène Némirovsky, the depth of place, imbued with history, that Tolkien creates...and I won't pretend I am able to even come close to any of their skill!

How did you come up with the idea for Torn?

I was actually researching eighteenth-century women's fashion, and particularly the (incredibly cool and innovative) women's jackets of the 1770s, 1780s, and into the 1790s. Some of the best resources for researching high fashion are plates from the

French *Magasin des modes*, so I was poring over a ton of those online and realized—wow. Some of these pieces were produced right in the face of the French Revolution; these beautiful, elaborate designs were created while the world was turning upside down. What did the seamstresses who made these garments think of the unrest and debates and changes occurring around them? If they could, how would they influence the outcomes?

What, if any, research did you do in preparation for writing this book?

Research was inspiration for the story, and historical garments, clothing norms, and sewing technique are a research hobby/passion/geek sphere of mine. So though very little research was done specifically for this book, lots of banked and new research crops up in various ways. Some of my favorite little snippets to write were descriptions of Sophie and her assistants' actual sewing, as I was able to translate the "experimental archaeology" I've done re-creating historical garments into words.

Sophie's sewing magic is such a unique ability. What made you choose this specific power for your heroine?

I liked the idea of playing with a magical system that wasn't the overriding power in the world it existed in. Giving a cottage industry the spotlight also let me focus my story on a female-focused, marginalized skill set. We often focus our attention on more visible, public skills—martial, political, and monetary spheres—so I wanted to play with something more traditionally part of the domestic, female-dominated sphere.

A major theme of Torn is difficult choices: the choice between familial and romantic love, between ambition and community, between different forms of government, etc. What compelled you to write about this?

I've always been fascinated by the neutral people in a conflict. For instance, there are some estimates that one-third of colonists during the American Revolution were (or attempted to be) neutral. We tend to brush this group aside or even think of them as cowards, but I've always been interested in what was motivating them—family, finances, fear? Were they more afraid of losing something they had than they were motivated by something exterior? The choice to attempt to stay out of a conflict can be as interesting as the choice to become involved, and I wanted to dig into the other factors that contribute to choices besides the (ever-important) ideals and ethics we often discuss in relation to this conversation.

Strong female characters are often portrayed as gun-wielding, ass-kicking heroines, but **Torn** *has a range of female characters, all of whom are strong in their own unique ways. What were your inspirations for these characters?*

You don't have to look very far to find quietly strong women—today, or historically. I think of my grandmothers, both living through the Depression, or the returning adult students and first-generation students I've worked with who all have overcome incredible challenges. What strikes me, often, is the motivation for these women—taking care of their loved ones, making sure their families are okay. It's a source of strength but also a demand on their tenacity.

Torn *has an amazing cast of characters. If you had to pick one—other than Sophie—who is your favorite? Who was the most difficult to write?*

I'm fond of Alice. She's probably the least fun person at a party, very unlikely to crack a good joke, and effortlessly predictable. But she's steadfast and pragmatic and compassionate, if awkwardly so, and those are such positive—but not often celebrated—characteristics.

All of the characters had their own challenges, but writing a calculating and intelligent antagonist like Pyord without turning him into a caricature was difficult—fun, but difficult. I didn't want the reader to doubt his capacity for doing really bad things, but also to trust that he believed in his ethics. People usually don't think they're being evil.

What's one thing about either the world or the characters of* Torn *that you loved but couldn't fit into the story?

Writing a story set in a city was strange! I'm kind of a hick, and I had all these images of rural Galitha—pastoral agricultural regions, salty harbor villages, rich river valleys—that weren't in Sophie's experience, let alone within the parameters of the story itself.

Torn *is the first book of the Unraveled Kingdom series. What's in store for us in future books?*

Savvy readers probably noticed that Sophie's idea of "happily ever after" is "I don't have to change and nothing else has to change, either," but her aversion to risk and her love of stasis are going to be challenged more. In *Torn*, she had to make decisions about how to respond to outside issues, but she'll have to address decisions in her personal life. I'm also looking forward to building the world out a bit more—to see more of Galitha and even surrounding nations through Sophie's eyes.

If you could spend a day with one of your characters, who would it be and what would you do?

While nerding out over sewing tips and creating a gorgeous piece in Sophie's atelier would be fun, I think I'd have to go with letting Viola plan an over-the-top social event. You know the food, wine, and company would all be excellent, and it's the best excuse to wear something fabulous.

Lastly, we have to ask: If you could have any magical power, what would you choose?

The ability to create portals to anywhere I want to go. I have both serious wanderlust for places I've never been and severe nostalgia for places I've loved, but not much time for travel (and planes with small children...not fun). Being able to pop across an ocean (or even across the state) for a day would be the best.

if you enjoyed
TORN

look out for

THE TETHERED MAGE

Swords and Fire: Book One

by

Melissa Caruso

In the Raverran Empire, magic is scarce and those born with
power are strictly controlled—taken as children and conscripted
into the Falcon army. Zaira has lived her life on the streets
to avoid this fate, hiding her mage mark and thieving to survive.
But hers is a rare and dangerous magic, one that
threatens the entire Empire.

Lady Amalia Cornaro was never meant to be a Falconer.
Heiress and scholar, she was born into a treacherous
world of political machinations.

But fate has bound the heir and the mage.
And as war looms on the horizon, a single spark
could turn their city into a pyre.

Chapter One

"Here, my lady? Are you sure?"

As the narrow prow of my boat nudged the stone steps at the canal's edge, I wished I'd walked, or at least hired a craft rather than using my own. The oarsman was bound to report to La Contessa that her daughter had disembarked at a grimy little quay in a dubious corner of the Tallows, the poorest district of the city of Raverra.

By the time my mother heard anything, however, I'd already have the book.

"Yes, thank you. Right here."

The oarsman made no comment as he steadied his craft, but his eyebrows conveyed deep skepticism.

I'd worn a country gentleman's coat and breeches, to avoid standing out from my seedy surroundings. I was glad not to risk skirts trailing in the murky water as I clambered out of the boat. Trash bobbed in the canal, and the tang in the air was not exclusively salt.

"Shall I wait for you here, my lady?"

"No, that's all right." The less my mother knew of my errand, the better.

She had not precisely forbidden me to visit the pawnbroker who claimed to have a copy of Muscati's *Principles of Artifice*,

452

but she'd made her opinion of such excursions clear. And no one casually disobeyed La Contessa Lissandra Cornaro. Her word resonated with power in every walled garden and forgotten plaza in Raverra.

Still, there was nothing casual about a Muscati. Only twelve known copies of his books existed. If this was real, it would be the thirteenth.

As I strolled alongside the canal, my mother's warnings seemed ridiculous. Sun-warmed facades flanked the green water, and workers unloaded produce from the mainland off boats moored at the canal's edge. A bright, peaceful afternoon like this surely could hold no dangers.

But when my route veered away from the canal, plunging into a shadowy tunnel that burrowed straight through a building, I hesitated. It was far easier to imagine assassins or kidnappers lurking beyond that dim archway. It wouldn't be the first time I'd faced either in my eighteen years as my mother's heir.

The book, I reminded myself. Think of the book.

I passed through the throat of the tunnel, emerging into a street too narrow to ever see direct sunlight. Broken shutters and scarred brickwork closed around me. The few people I passed gave me startled, assessing glances.

I found the pawnbroker's shop with relief, and hurried into a dim wilderness of dusty treasures. Jewelry and blown glass glittered on the shelves; furniture cluttered the floor, and paintings leaned against the walls. The proprietor bent over a conch shell wrapped with copper wire, a frown further creasing his already lined face. A few wisps of white over his ears were the last legacy of his hair.

I approached, glancing at the shell. "It's broken."

He scowled. "Is it? I should have known. He asked too little for a working one."

"Half the beads are missing." I pointed to a few orbs of colored glass still threaded on the wire. "You'd need an artificer to fix it if you wanted it to play music again."

The pawnbroker looked up at me, and his eyes widened. "Lady Amalia Cornaro." He bowed as best he could in the cramped shop.

I glanced around, but we were alone. "Please, no need for formality."

"Forgive me. I didn't recognize you in, ah, such attire." He peered dubiously at my breeches. "Though I suppose that's the fashion for young ladies these days."

Breeches weren't remotely in fashion for young ladies, but I didn't bother correcting him. I was just grateful they were acceptable enough in my generation that I didn't have to worry about causing a scandal or being mistaken for a courtesan.

"Do you have the book?" I reminded him. "Muscati's *Principles of Artifice*, your note said."

"Of course. I'd heard you were looking for it." A certain gleam entered his eye with which I was all too familiar: Cornaro gold reflected back at me. "Wait a moment, and I'll get it."

He shuffled through a doorway to the rear of the shop.

I examined the shell. I knew enough from my studies of artifice to trace the patterns of wire and understand the spell that had captured the sound of a musical performance inside the shell's rune-carved whorls. I could have fixed a broken wire, perhaps, but without the inborn talent of an artificer to infuse new beads with magical energy, the shell would stay silent.

The pawnbroker returned with a large leather-bound book. He laid it on the table beside the conch shell. "There you are, my lady."

I flipped through the pages until I came to a diagram. Muscati's combination of finicky precision in the wirework schematics and thick, blunt strokes for the runes was unmistakable. I let out a trembling breath. This was the real thing.

The pawnbroker's long, delicate fingers covered the page. "Is all in order, then?"

"Yes, quite. Thank you." I laid a gold ducat on the table. It vanished so quickly I almost doubted I'd put it there.

"Always a pleasure," he murmured.

I tucked the book into my satchel and hurried out of the musty shop, almost skipping with excitement. I couldn't wait to get home, retreat to my bedroom with a glass of wine, and dive into Muscati's timeworn pages. My friend Domenic from the University of Ardence said that to read Muscati was to open a window on a new view of the universe as a mathematical equation to be solved.

Of course, he'd only read excerpts. The university library didn't have an actual Muscati. I'd have to get Domenic here to visit so I could show him. Maybe I'd give the book to the university when I was done with it.

It was hard to make myself focus on picking turns in the mazelike streets rather than dreaming about runic alphabets, geometric diagrams, and coiling wirework. At least I was headed in the right general direction. One more bridge to cross, and then I'd be in polite, patrician territory, safe and sound; and no lecture of my mother's could change the fact that I'd completed my errand without incident.

But a tense group of figures stood in the tiny plaza before the bridge, frozen in a standoff, every line of their bodies promising each other violence.

Like so many things in Raverra, this had become complicated.

Three broad-shouldered men formed a menacing arc around a scrawny young woman with sprawling dark curls. The girl stood rigidly defiant, like a stick thrust in the mud. I slowed to a halt, clutching my satchel tight against my side, Muscati's edge digging into my ribs.

"One last chance." A burly man in shirtsleeves advanced on the girl, fists like cannonballs ready at his sides. "Come nice and quiet to your master, or we'll break your legs and drag you to him in a sack."

"I'm my own master," the girl retorted, her voice blunt as a boat hook. "And you can tell Orthys to take his indenture contract and stuff it up his bunghole."

They hadn't noticed me yet. I could work my way around to the next bridge, and get my book safely home. I took a step back, glancing around for someone to put a stop to this: an officer of the watch, a soldier, anyone but me.

There was no one. The street lay deserted. Everyone else in the Tallows knew enough to make themselves scarce.

"Have it your way," the man growled. The ruffians closed in on their prey.

This was exactly the sort of situation in which a young lady of the august and noble house of Cornaro should not involve herself, and in which a person of any moral fortitude must.

Maybe I could startle them, like stray dogs. "You there! Stop!"

They turned to face me, their stares cold and flat. The air went dry in my throat.

"This is none of your business," one in a scuffed leather doublet warned. A scar pulled at the corner of his mouth. I doubted it came from a cooking accident.

I had no protection besides the dagger in my belt. The name Cornaro might hold weight with these scoundrels, but they'd never believe I bore it. Not dressed like this.

My name meant nothing. The idea sent a wild thrill into my lungs, as if the air were alive.

The girl didn't wait to see what I would do. She tried to bolt between two of the men. A tree branch of an arm caught her at the waist, scooping her up as if she were a child. Her feet swung in the air.

My satchel pulled at my shoulder, but I couldn't run off and leave her now, Muscati or no Muscati. Drawing my dagger seemed a poor idea. The men were all armed, one with a flint-lock pistol.

"Help!" I called.

The brutes seemed unimpressed. They kept their attention on the struggling girl as they wrenched her arms behind her.

"That's it!" Rage swelled her voice. "This is your last warning!"

Last warning? What an odd thing to say. Unless...

Ice slid into my bone marrow.

The men laughed, but she glowered furiously at them. She wasn't afraid. I could think of only one reason she wouldn't be.

I flattened myself against a wall just before everything caught fire.

Her eyes kindled first, a hungry blue spark flaring in her pupils. Then flames ran down her arms in delicate lines, leaping into the pale, lovely petals of a deadly flower.

The men lurched back from her, swearing, but it was too late. Smoke already rose from their clothing. Before they finished sucking in their first terrified breaths, blue flames sprang up in sudden, bold glory over every inch of them, burying every scar and blemish in light. For one moment, they were beautiful.

Then they let out the screams they had gathered. I cringed, covering my own mouth. The pain in them was inhuman. The terrible, oily reek of burning human meat hit me, and I gagged.

The men staggered for the canal, writhing in the embrace of the flames. I threw up my arm to ward my face from the heat, blocking the sight. Heavy splashes swallowed their screams.

In the sudden silence, I lowered my arm.

Fire leaped up past the girl's shoulders now. A pure, cold anger graced her features. It wasn't the look of a woman who was done.

Oh, Hells.

She raised her arms exultantly, and flames sprang up from the canal itself, bitter and wicked. They spread across the water as if on a layer of oil, licking at the belly of the bridge. On the far side of the canal, bystanders drawn by the commotion cried out in alarm.

"Enough!" My voice tore out of my throat higher than usual. "You've won! For mercy's sake, put it out!"

But the girl's eyes were fire, and flames ran down her hair. If she understood me, she made no sign of it. The blue fire gnawed at the stones around her feet. Hunger unsatisfied, it expanded as if the flagstones were grass.

I recognized it at last: balefire. I'd read of it in Orsenne's *Fall of Celantis*.

Grace of Mercy preserve us all. That stuff would burn anything—water, metal, stone. It could light up the city like a dry corncrib. I hugged my book to my chest.

"You have to stop this!" I pleaded.

"She can't," a strained voice said. "She's lost control."

I turned to find a tall, lean young man at my shoulder, staring at the burning girl with understandable apprehension. His wavy black hair brushed the collar of the uniform I wanted to see most in the world at the moment: the scarlet-and-gold doublet of the Falconers. The very company that existed to control magic so things like this wouldn't happen.

"Thank the Graces you're here! Can you stop her?"

"No." He drew in a deep, unsteady breath. "But you can, if you have the courage."

"What?" It was more madness, piled on top of the horror of the balefire. "But I'm not a Falconer!"

"That's why you can do it." Something delicate gleamed in his offering hand. "Do you think you can slip this onto her wrist?"

It was a complex weave of gold wire and scarlet beads, designed to tighten with a tug. I recognized the pattern from a woodcut in one of my books: a Falconer's jess. Named after the tethers used in falconry, it could place a seal on magic.

"She's *on fire*," I objected.

"I know. I won't deny it's dangerous." His intent green eyes clouded. "I can't do it myself; I'm already linked to another. I wouldn't ask if it weren't an emergency. The more lives the balefire consumes, the more it spreads. It could swallow all of Raverra."

I hesitated. The jess sagged in his hand. "Never mind. I shouldn't have—"

"I'll do it." I snatched the bracelet from him before I could think twice.

"Thank you." He flashed me an oddly wistful smile. "I'll distract her while you get close. Wits and courage. You can do it."

The Falconer sprinted toward the spreading flames, leaving the jess dangling from my hand like an unanswered question.

He circled to the canal's edge, calling to get the girl's attention. "You! Warlock!"

She turned toward him. Flame trailed behind her like a queen's mantua. The spreading edges crawled up the brick walls of the nearest house in blazing tendrils.

The Falconer's voice rang out above the clamor of the growing crowd across the canal. "In the name of His Serenity the Doge, I claim you for the Falcons of Raverra!"

That certainly got her attention. The flames bent in his direction as if in a strong wind.

"I don't belong to *you*, either!" Her voice was wild as a hissing bonfire. "You can't claim me. I'll see you burn first!"

Now she was going to kill him, too. Unless I stopped her.

My heart fluttering like an anxious dowager's handkerchief, I struggled to calm down and think. Maybe she wouldn't attack if I didn't rush at her. I tucked my precious satchel under my coat and hustled toward the bridge as if I hoped to scurry past her and escape. It wasn't hard to pretend. Some in the crowd on the far side beckoned me to safety.

My legs trembled with the urge to heed them and dash across. I couldn't bear the thought of Muscati's pages withering to ashes.

I tightened my grip on the jess.

The Falconer extended his hand toward the girl to keep her attention. "By law, you belonged to Raverra the moment you were born with the mage mark. I don't know how you managed to hide for so long, but it's over now. Come with me."

The balefire roared at him in a blue-white wave.

"Plague take you!" The girl raised her fist in defiance. "If Raverra wants my fire, she can have it. Let the city burn!"

I lunged across the remaining distance between us, leaping over snaking lines of flame. Eyes squeezed half shut against the heat, I flung out an arm and looped the jess over her upraised fist.

The effect was immediate. The flames flickered out as if a cold blast of wind had snuffed them. The Falconer still recoiled, his arms upraised to protect his face, his fine uniform doublet smoking.

The girl swayed, the fire flickering out in her eyes. The golden jess settled around her bone-thin wrist.

She collapsed to the flagstones.

Pain seared my hand. I hissed through my teeth as I snatched it to my chest. That brief moment of contact had burned my skin and scorched my boots and coat. My satchel, thank the Graces, seemed fine.

Across the bridge, the gathering of onlookers cheered, then began to break up. The show was over, and nobody wanted to go near a fire warlock, even an unconscious one.

I couldn't blame them. No sign remained of ruffians in the canal, though the burned smell lingered horribly in the air. Charred black scars streaked the sides of the buildings flanking me.

The Falconer approached, grinning with relief. "Well done! I'm impressed. Are you all right?"

It hit me in a giddy rush that it was over. I had saved—if not all of Raverra, at least a block or two of it—by myself, with my own hands. Not with my mother's name, or with my mother's wealth, but on my own.

Too dangerous to go to a pawnbroker's shop? Ha! I'd taken out a fire warlock. I smiled at him, tucking my burned hand into my sleeve. "I'm fine. I'm glad I could help."

"Lieutenant Marcello Verdi, at your service." He bowed. "What is your name, brave young lady?"

"Amalia Cornaro."

"Well, welcome to the doge's Falconers, Miss..." He stopped. The smile fell off his face, and the color drained from his bronze skin. "Cornaro." He swallowed. "Not...you aren't related to La Contessa Lissandra Cornaro, surely?"

My elation curdled in my stomach. "She's my mother."

"Hells," the lieutenant whispered. "What have I done?"

if you enjoyed
TORN

look out for

THIEF'S MAGIC

Millennium's Rule: Book One

by

Trudi Canavan

In a world where an industrial revolution is powered by magic, Tyen, a student of archaeology, unearths a sentient book called Vella. Once a young sorcerer-bookbinder, Vella was transformed by a sorcerer, and she has a vital clue to the disaster Tyen's world faces.

Elsewhere, in a land ruled by the priests, Rielle the dyer's daughter has been taught that to use magic is to steal from the Angels. Yet she knows she has a talent for it, and that there is a corrupter in the city willing to teach her how to use it—should she dare to risk the Angels' wrath.

But not everything is as Tyen and Rielle have been raised to believe. Not the nature of magic, nor the laws of their lands... not even the people they trust.

CHAPTER 1

The corpse's shrivelled, unbending fingers surrendered the bundle reluctantly. Wrestling the object out of the dead man's grip seemed disrespectful so Tyen worked slowly, gently lifting a hand when a blackened fingernail snagged on the covering. He'd touched the ancient dead so often they didn't sicken or frighten him now. Their desiccated flesh had long ago stopped being a source of transferable sickness, and he did not believe in ghosts.

When the mysterious bundle came free Tyen straightened and smiled in triumph. He wasn't as ruthless at collecting ancient artefacts as his fellow students and his teacher, but bringing home nothing from these research trips would see him fail to graduate as a sorcerer-archaeologist. He willed his tiny magic-fuelled flame closer.

The object's covering, like the tomb's occupant, was dry and stiff having, by his estimate, lain undisturbed for six hundred years. Thick leather darkened with age, it had no markings – no adornment, no precious stones or metals. As he tried to open it the wrapping snapped apart and something inside began to slide out. His pulse quickened as he caught the object...

...and his heart sank a little. No treasure lay in his hands. Just a book. Not even a jewel-encrusted, gold-embellished book.

Not that a book didn't have potential historical value, but compared to the glittering treasures Professor Kilraker's other two students had unearthed for the Academy it was a disappointing find. After all the months of travel, research, digging and watching he had little to show for his own work. He had finally unearthed a tomb that hadn't already been ransacked by grave robbers and what did it contain? A plain stone coffin, an unadorned corpse and an old book.

Still, the old fossils at the Academy wouldn't regret sponsoring his journey if the book turned out to be significant. He examined it closely. Unlike the wrapping, the leather cover felt supple. The binding was in good condition. If he hadn't just broken apart the covering to get it out, he'd have guessed the book's age at no more than a hundred or so years. It had no title or text on the spine. Perhaps it had worn off. He opened it. No word marked the first page, so he turned it. The next was also blank and as he fanned through the rest of the pages he saw that they were as well.

He stared at it in disbelief. Why would anyone bury a blank book in a tomb, carefully wrapped and placed in the hands of the occupant? He looked at the corpse, but it offered no answer. Then something drew his eye back to the book, still open to one of the last pages. He looked closer.

A mark had appeared.

Next to it a dark patch formed, then dozens more. They spread and joined up.

Hello, they said. *My name is Vella.*

Tyen uttered a word his mother would have been shocked to hear if she had still been alive. Relief and wonder replaced disappointment. The book was magical. Though most sorcerous books used magic in minor and frivolous ways, they were so rare that the Academy would always take them for its collection. His trip hadn't been a waste.

So what did this book do? Why did text only appear when it was opened? Why did it have a name? More words formed on the page.

I've always had a name. I used to be a person. A living, breathing woman.

Tyen stared at the words. A chill ran down his spine, yet at the same time he felt a familiar thrill. Magic could sometimes be disturbing. It was often inexplicable. He liked that not everything about it was understood. It left room for new discoveries. Which was why he had chosen to study sorcery alongside history. In both fields there was an opportunity to make a name for himself.

He'd never heard of a person turning into a book before. *How is that possible?* he wondered.

I was made by a powerful sorcerer, replied the text. *He took my knowledge and flesh and transformed me.*

His skin tingled. The book had responded to the question he'd shaped in his mind. *Do you mean these pages are made of your flesh?* he asked.

Yes. My cover and pages are my skin. My binding is my hair, twisted together and sewn with needles fashioned from my bones and glue from tendons.

He shuddered. *And you're conscious?*

Yes.

You can hear my thoughts?

Yes, but only when you touch me. When not in contact with a living human, I am blind and deaf, trapped in the darkness with no sense of time passing. Not even sleeping. Not quite dead. The years of my life slipping past — wasted.

Tyen stared down at the book. The words remained, nearly filling a page now, dark against the creamy vellum. Which was her skin…

It was grotesque and yet…all vellum was made of skin. While these pages were human skin, they felt no different to that made of animals. They were soft and pleasant to touch. The book was not repulsive in the way an ancient, desiccated corpse was.

And it was so much more interesting. Conversing with it was akin to talking with the dead. If the book was as old as the tomb it knew about the time before it was laid there. Tyen smiled. He may not have found gold and jewels to help pay his way on this expedition, but the book could make up for that with historical information.

More text formed.

Contrary to appearances, I am not an "it".

Perhaps it was the effect of the light on the page, but the new words seemed a little larger and darker than the previous text. Tyen felt his face warm a little.

I'm sorry, Vella. It was bad mannered of me. I assure you, I meant no offence. It is not every day that a man addresses a talking book, and I am not entirely sure of the protocol.

She was a woman, he reminded himself. He ought to follow the etiquette he'd been raised to follow. Though talking to women could be fiendishly tricky, even when following all the rules about manners. It would be rude to begin their association by interrogating her about the past. Rules of conversation decreed he should ask after her wellbeing.

So…is it nice being a book?

When I am being held and read by someone nice, it is, she replied.

And when you are not, it is not? I can see that might be a disadvantage in your state, though one you must have anticipated before you became a book.

I would have, if I'd had foreknowledge of my fate.

So you did not choose to become a book. Why did your maker do that to you? Was it a punishment?

467

No, though perhaps it was natural justice for being too ambitious and vain. I sought his attention, and received more of it than I intended.

Why did you seek his attention?

He was famous. I wanted to impress him. I thought my friends would be envious.

And for that he turned you into a book. What manner of man could be so cruel?

He was the most powerful sorcerer of his time, Roporien the Clever.

Tyen caught his breath and a chill ran down his back. *Roporien! But he died over a thousand years ago!*

Indeed.

Then you are…

At least as old as that. Though in my time it wasn't polite to comment on a woman's age.

He smiled. *It still isn't – and I don't think it ever will be. I apologise again.*

You are a polite young man. I will enjoy being owned by you.

You want me to own *you?* Tyen suddenly felt uncomfortable. He realised he now thought of the book as a person, and owning a person was slavery – an immoral and uncivilised practice that had been illegal for over a hundred years.

Better that than spend my existence in oblivion. Books don't last for ever, not even magical ones. Keep me. Make use of me. I can give you a wealth of knowledge. All I ask is that you hold me as often as possible so that I can spend my lifespan awake and aware.

I don't know… The man who created you did many terrible things – as you experienced yourself. I don't want to follow in his shadow. Then something occurred to him that made his skin creep. *Forgive me for being blunt about it, but his book, or any of his tools, could be designed for evil purposes. Are you one such tool?*

I was not designed so, but that does not mean I could not be used so. A tool is only as evil as the hand that uses it.

The familiarity of the saying was startling and unexpectedly reassuring. It was one that Professor Weldan liked. The old historian had always been suspicious of magical things.

How do I know you're not lying about not being evil?

I cannot lie.

Really? But what if you're lying about not being able to lie?

You'll have to work that one out for yourself.

Tyen frowned as he considered how he might devise a test for her, then realised something was buzzing right beside his ear. He shied away from the sensation, then breathed a sigh of relief as he saw it was Beetle, his little mechanical creation. More than a toy, yet not quite what he'd describe as a pet, it had proven to be a useful companion on the expedition.

The palm-sized insectoid swooped down to land on his shoulder, folded its iridescent blue wings, then whistled three times. Which was a warning that...

"Tyen!"

...Miko, his friend and fellow archaeology student was approaching.

The voice echoed in the short passage leading from the outside world to the tomb. Tyen muttered a curse. He glanced down at the page. *Sorry, Vella. Have to go.* Footsteps neared the door of the tomb. With no time to slip her into his bag, he stuffed her down his shirt, where she settled against the waistband of his trousers. She was warm – which was a bit disturbing now that he knew she was a conscious thing created from human flesh – but he didn't have time to dwell on it. He turned to the door in time to see Miko stumble into view.

"Didn't think to bring a lamp?" he asked.

"No time," the other student gasped. "Kilraker sent me to get you. The others have gone back to the camp to pack up. We're leaving Mailand."

"Now?"

"Yes. *Now*," Miko replied.

Tyen looked back at the small tomb. Though Professor Kilraker liked to refer to these foreign trips as treasure hunts, his peers expected the students to bring back evidence that the journeys were also educational. Copying the faint decorations on the tomb walls would have given them something to mark. He thought wistfully of the new instant etchers that some of the richer professors and self-funded adventurers used to record their work. They were far beyond his meagre allowance. Even if they weren't, Kilraker wouldn't take them on expeditions because they were heavy and fragile.

Picking up his satchel, Tyen opened the flap. "Beetle. Inside." The insectoid scuttled down his arm into the bag. Tyen slung the strap over his head and shoulder and sent his flame into the passage.

"We have to hurry," Miko said, leading the way. "The locals heard about where you're digging. Must've been one of the boys Kilraker hired to deliver food who told them. A bunch are coming up the valley and they're sounding those battle horns they carry."

"They didn't want us digging here? Nobody told me that!"

"Kilraker said not to. He said you were bound to find something impressive, after all the research you did."

He reached the hole where Tyen had broken through into the passage and squeezed out. Tyen followed, letting the flame die as he climbed out into the bright afternoon sunlight. Dry heat enveloped him. Miko scrambled up the sides of the ditch. Following, Tyen looked back and surveyed his work. Nothing remained in the tomb that robbers would want, but he couldn't stand to leave it exposed to vermin and he felt guilty about unearthing a tomb the locals didn't wanted disturbed. Reaching out with his mind, he pulled magic to himself then moved the rocks and earth on either side back into the ditch.

"What are you *doing*?" Miko sounded exasperated.

"Filling it in."

"We don't have time!" Miko grabbed his arm and yanked him around so that they both looked down into the valley. He pointed. "See?"

The valley sides were near-vertical cliffs, and where the faces had crumbled over time piles of rubble had built up against the sides to form steep slopes. Tyen and Miko were standing atop of one of these.

At the bottom of the valley a long line of people was moving, faces tilted to search the scree above. One arm rose, pointing at Tyen and Miko. The rest stopped, then fists were raised.

Follow us:

f **/orbitbooksUS**

🐦 **/orbitbooks**

▶ **/orbitbooks**

Join our mailing list
to receive alerts on our
latest releases and deals.

orbitbooks.net

Enter our monthly
giveaway for the chance
to win some epic prizes.

orbitloot.com